CAGE'S
BEND

ALSO BY CARTER COLEMAN

THE VOLUNTEER

CAGE'S BEND

CARTER COLEMAN

WARNER BOOKS

NEW YORK   BOSTON

On pages 165, 166, and 232, the words of Jack Kerouac are from ON THE ROAD by Jack Kerouac, copyright © 1955, 1957 by Jack Kerouac; renewed © 1983 by Stella Kerouac, renewed © 1985 by Stella Kerouac and Jan Kerouac. Used by permission of Viking Penguin, a division of Penguin Group (USA) Inc.

Warner Books

Time Warner Book Group
1271 Avenue of the Americas, New York, NY 10020
Visit our Web site at www.twbookmark.com.

Printed in the United States of America

First printing: January 2005
10 9 8 7 6 5 4 3 2 1

Library of Congress Cataloging-in-Publication Data

Coleman, Carter.
    Cage's Bend : a novel / by Carter Coleman.
        p. cm.
    ISBN 0-446-57661-1
      1. Brothers—Fiction. 2. Brothers—Death—Fiction. 3. Manic-depressive persons—Fiction.
    4. Southern States—Fiction. I. Title.
    PS3553.O47376C65 2005
    813'.54—dc22   2004042007

Book design by Giorgetta Bell McRee

For
Mary Carter Hughes Coleman
8 December 1937 to 15 February 2004

Author's Note

This book is a work of fiction. All of the characters, incidents, and dialogue, except for incidental references to public figures, are imaginary and are not intended to refer to any persons, living or dead. Though Cage's Bend is a real road where my family has lived for seven generations, the Cage family of the book bears no resemblance to the settlers, long departed, who left their name upon the place.

CAGE'S
BEND

A man who has not passed through the inferno of his passions has never over-come them. They then dwell in the house next door, and at any moment a flame may dart out and set fire to his own house. Whenever we give up, leave behind and forget too much, there is always the danger that the things we have neglected will return with added force.

—C. G. JUNG,
Memories, Dreams and Reflections

Dad is sad
very, very sad.
He had a bad day.
What a day Dad had!

—DR. SEUSS,
Hop on Pop

Victory
1977

Eighty of us crowded behind a chalk line in the shade of huge evergreen oaks draped with a few dying wisps of Spanish moss. In a jumble of uniform colors—powder blue, puke yellow, rising-sun red, Orange Crush—all of us wore old-style basketball tops and bottoms, except for two runners from a New Orleans day school who looked girlish in green ultralight nylon minishorts. I overheard the starter tell the line judge, "Most of 'em white boys look like they come out of a concentration camp." The line judge laughed. A strong wind kept gusting off the lake and the damp air felt colder than the forty-four degrees on Father Callicot's key-chain thermometer. Short, balding, wearing a goatee, thin mustache, and a black suit with a clergy dog collar, Callicot stood on the line smiling like an evangelist at the six of us with *Episcopal Knights* in scroll across our gold jerseys. He put the thermometer in his pocket and placed his hand on my shoulder. "You're the next state champ. I don't need to tell you a thing."

"Gee, thanks." I rolled my eyes and stared down the fairway toward the lake.

"Circle up," Callicot said, and we formed a wheel, holding our right arms to the center and stacking our hands on top of the coach's. "Our Father, let us run like the wind ahead of this pack of heathens from across the state of Louisiana."

"Amen," the other Knights said automatically as I shouted, "Hallelujah! Running for the Lord!" Everyone laughed except for Father Callicot. We broke the circle and the team formed two lines behind me and my brother Nick.

I smiled at Nick. "Don't let that coon ass from Point Coupe outkick you today."

Nick hated these moments before a race. At home, sitting on the roof of our house, he'd prayed it would storm, but the afternoon sky was clear except for columns of smoke rising over the river from the Exxon refinery. Nick said without conviction, "He's going to eat my dust."

I just held my fists out in front of me at the edge of the line.

"Runners on your mark." The starter raised the gun over his head. A handful of students and parents yelled from the sidelines and then there was silence.

I'm going to win. I'm going to go faster than ever before. I'm going to push through the pain. I'm going to win.

Nick looked queasy. His hands trembled. I gave him a fierce look and whispered, "You can take him."

"Set."

Pikh! Lost in the wind: the firing of the blank, the muted cheers of the spectators. Barefoot, Ford led three other black runners from cane plantations to the head of the pack, which funneled from the chalk line into a narrow stream along the center of the fairway.

After the first quarter mile, on the rise of a tee, Ford and I were out front, running side by side.

I glanced back. Nick was twenty runners behind.

"Think you can beat me today, Ford?" I said his name like he did—*Fode.*

"Beat you here last year." Ford's head bobbed up and down, almost touching my shoulder.

"You're natur'ly more powerful than us. That's what I heard." I kept my voice from sounding too winded.

"Tell me sompin new."

"No way any white boy could run barefoot."

"Too much shag carpet."

"And you've got a big dick and an extra tendon in your leg."

Ford looked up and grinned. "Yo' mama knows about one of them things."

"The dick or the tendon?"

"The tendon." Ford laughed, breaking his smooth stride.

I accelerated a yard ahead before Ford realized I was pulling away.

Nick was back there watching me gradually shrink into the distance. Nick trained harder than anyone in the state, while I showed up hungover Saturday mornings and kicked his butt. Outclassed by big brother, who knew you so well, even what you were thinking.

At the half-mile mark Father Callicot squawked in his high voice, "Right on time!"

Rounding a corner coming out of magnolia trees, I looked over my shoulder and I was ten yards ahead of Ford and twenty ahead of the pack. Nick was idly picking off the competition, composing a poem for the school mag:

Hemmed by runners on every side,
Pain ingrained on every face,
I hurt more with every stride,
I must increase the pace.

Breaux, the tall Cajun from Point Coupe, was loping along behind Nick, using him to break the icy headwind off the lake. Nick had never beaten the Cajun, though the last three races he'd been within seconds. Nick lacked the killer instinct—he didn't believe he could beat him and therefore he didn't.

I led the first lap around the golf course with nobody pushing me. Ford was my only competition and I'd broken his spirit by beating him the last five races of the season. There was no one left but the clock.

By the third lap the pain had set in for even the strongest. This was the pain Nick dreaded from the night before. This was much worse than the pain of practice which Nick dreaded through every school day during fall cross-country and spring track season. Nick wanted to turn down the pain, slacken off just enough to secure fourth place, and ride out the last five minutes of agony. Nick distracted himself from the pain by reciting his poems. I burned it like gasoline, turned it into rage.

Father Callicot yelled my time at the two-and-a-half-mile mark. Dad was dressed just like Callicot. Mom wore a plaid wool coat. Little Harper had on my letter jacket, which hung to his knees and hid his hands in the sleeves. Dad cupped his hands, yelled, "You're breaking the record!" My girlfriend, Robin, was hopping up and down in her cheerleader getup.

Long rolling strides glided me along the fairway. A half minute back Nick and Breaux were crossing the creek. Ford had gained a yard, so I turned, fixed my eyes on the fluttering plastic ribbons of the chute, and switched into overdrive. The kick was the consummation of the pain, a purity beyond thought. I gave a rebel yell and leaned forward, my mind filled by an imaginary sheet of liquid flame racing before me across the grass. The tape broke across my chest, the judge shouted a new state record, and I raised my arm in the Black Power salute like the brothers who lost their medals in the '68 Mexico City Olympics, then careened through the chute, tripped, and almost knocked down one of the cane poles at the end. I picked myself up, turned around.

Ford was decelerating down the chute, hadn't even bothered to kick. Smiling as he reached me, I stuck out my palm for a soul slap but he looked away and jogged off toward a couple of black coaches from Ascension.

I limped along the edge of the fairway toward the long string of runners. Nick and Breaux were shoulder-to-shoulder coming down the homestretch. Nick was drowning in the pain of his lungs and arms and legs all shrieking, begging him to slow down. Breaux broke away, doubled the length of his stride, gained a yard.

"Kick, Nick! Kick! Kick! Kick!" I shouted, sprinting toward him, just out of bounds. "You can take him! Take him! Kick!"

Nick screamed a lame-ass version of my rebel yell and pulled even with Breaux, who was wavering, flapping his arms like broken wings, while Nick's were pumping smoothly like pistons. Both their faces were twisted, their tortured breathing audible across the fairway.

"You've got him, Nick." I was running flat out trying to stay with him.

Neck and neck, twenty yards from the chute with Breaux not slowing, Nick's pain fused into a sense of inevitable defeat. He just couldn't outkick Breaux. He never could. Black spots floated before him in the gray air. He felt faint. My voice was hoarse from shouting. "You can take him, dammit! Don't give up!"

"Go, Nick!" Mom yelled from the finish line.

"Come on, son!" Dad yelled.

"Go, dammit, go!" Little Harper squealed, and Mom did a shocked double take.

Nick heard the cheering as from a long distance and forced his knees higher. The black spots bloomed bigger, obscuring the mouth of the chute. We were all out of focus. He heard me yell, "Breaux's fading. Now, brother! Now!" Suddenly believing he could take him, clawing deeper than ever before into the primal instinct, Nick broke through the pain and edged past Breaux into the chute. His momentum carried him a few feet more, then he nearly tumbled but caught himself and moved along like a blind drunk. I grabbed him before he fell coming out of the chute.

"*I took him out!*" Nick gasped.

"Yeah. You dusted him." I slapped him on the back. "I been telling you all season you could beat him." I opened my hand wide the way Dad used to when we were tiny, and said, the way he used to, "Put 'er there, pal." Nick smiled and clasped my hand.

Coach Callicot scurried over to congratulate us, and Nick, copying me as usual, said, "Thanks be to Jesus."

Breaux passed us, heading for an underfed, bony-faced girl with puffed-up blonde hair, and I called out, "Hey, coon-ass boy, best you get used to staring at the back of Nick's jersey."

"Fuck you, rich boys. Wait for track season." Breaux's chest was all bowed up.

"Hell, we ain't rich," Nick, the diplomat, said. "Just go to a rich school's all."

"That's right, Breaux. We're all bros," I called out.

"Bonjour, Monsieur Breaux," Dad said, coming up from the side. He was as tall and slender as the muscular Cajun runner whom he patted on the back. In the twenty-five years since he was a quarter-miler at Sewanee, he had run five miles at first light while saying his daily prayers.

Breaux's chest fell and he humbly shook Dad's hand. "Bonjour, Père Rutledge."

"Coon-ass Catholics have an inbred respect for clergy," I whispered to Nick as Dad inquired after Breaux's family, and I suddenly felt bad about being mean.

"My boys." Mom, a foot shorter and ten years younger than Dad, bobbed up and down, beaming like a lighthouse. "My champions. Where are your warm-ups? You'll get pneumonia."

The other runners were crowding through the chute.

"Come on, Nick, let's go congratulate the losers. I'm going to miss Ford."

"Shouldn't you wait for your warm-ups?"

"Robin'll bring 'em, Mom," I said over my shoulder, placing my arm around Nick's back. "It's going to be just you and Breaux next year. You saw you can beat him today. Don't ever let him beat you again. Drive him down. That's what I did to Fode. Hell, his kick used to be twice as fast. I just beat the spirit out of him."

"The Machiavellian approach." Rubbing his arms, Nick shivered and looked around for Robin. "Where's your girlfriend? I'm freezing to death."

After a race I never felt the cold. "You're my wingman, Nick. Couldn't have a better wingman."

"I've got a better one." Nick looked straight at me. "I got the best wingman in Baton Rouge."

1989

Cage

I struggle not to see, not to hear, to hold on to the vision which melts away into red darkness. Then I open my eyes. Black water slowly swallows the sun. The beach is bathed in faint pink light and the ocean breeze combs the tall sea grass like invisible fingers through thick fur. I'm not sure how long I've been dreaming on this dune. Waves roll in endlessly, rushing back and rolling in again. Silently I pray, Where are you, Nick? Are you with me? Don't abandon me now out here on the edge of night. I'm not the boy I used to be. Can you forgive me? A falling star streaks across the paling sky. I tell him, "Little Harper's coming tomorrow, but he's all grown-up now. Bigger than you and me. He's the only one of us who's as big as Dad."

"Harper?" a soft voice whispers in the wind. "Who's Harper?"

I turn and watch as her hair darkens, the lines across her forehead disappear, and the flesh beneath her chin draws taut until she's the age when she brought me into this world.

"Cage, do you hear me?" the girl asks, smiling like she's about to burst out laughing.

I realize that she is the girl who gave me the acid and I cast around my head for her name. "Do you hear me?"

She laughs. "Where were you?"

"Tripping," I say.

"No shit, Sherlock. You were *gone.*"

"Time tripping." It's too difficult to explain. "Did I tell you you look like my mother? She's very beautiful."

"That's a line."

"That's the gospel truth. Same raven hair and angelic face. Just like my mama in the full bloom of youth."

"There is something very, very wrong with you."

"And you are very, very intuitive. Where are you in school again?"

"Sarah Lawrence."

"I forgot. I'm very, very impressed."

"Let's go." She lifts a half-empty bottle of Rolling Rock, stands up, and reaches her hand down to me. "We're out."

"I like your spirit." I rise and brush the sand from my pants, then brush off her small, flat ass. She laughs and pushes my hand away. I pick her up by the waist and she tilts forward, kicking her feet and giggling as I carry her over the dune. "Were you ever a cheerleader?"

"Hell, no." She twists free.

"I dated a cheerleader in high school. A homecoming queen. I was just thinking of those provocative uniforms. Imagine dressing up the prettiest girls in tight sweaters and tiny miniskirts and having them jump up and down, bouncing their boobs and flashing their crotches at all the middle-aged dads in the crowd. It's perverse."

"Are all southern boys as crazy as you?" she asks, smiling.

I stop walking. "What do you think?"

"I hope not."

Harper

In late May after my freshman year at Tulane, I leave the South for the first time. I'm worn-out from exams and partying but too excited to sleep, since I've never been so far north and never been to an East Coast resort island. I'm nervous about going someplace full of rich Yankees who might take me for a hick but I'm also thrilled to spend time with Cage. It's just like him to get me a cool summer job. He's ten years older and has always been the ideal big brother. On the long flight from New Orleans to Boston, I remember times he took me fishing and hunting and how when I was in high school he would come to Baton Rouge nine hours from Vanderbilt in his ancient Oldsmobile just to cheer me on during championship meets, the way he would run along the field beside me, urging me to run faster. And I did. Broke the freshman half-mile record when he was driving me on. Cage is a very cool brother.

Indirectly Cage was responsible for my first sexual experience. When I was fourteen, I met him over Mardi Gras in Pensacola, where we stayed in a house with some of his college friends. We were deep-sea fishing on his friend's boat. One night a girl named Katy took me to a bar and we shot tequila. She had long curly hair and huge breasts and a really sweet smile and I could hardly believe it when she started kissing me at the bar after last call. We got in her car and she stuck her hand down my pants, the first time a girl had touched me there. I gathered up courage and un-zipped her jeans and in a matter of seconds I was looking right at that object of long speculation. I'd only seen them in magazines. I didn't know what to do, so I started lapping it, my head bobbing up and down like a puppy. Suddenly she came to her senses and pushed me away. She hardly said a word to me for the rest of the week. Remembering Katy always makes me wince with humilia-tion and lust.

I was never close to my other brother, Nick, who was eleven months younger than Cage. He was always nice to me but we never did much together. He thought of me as his annoying little brother, a pest, not as a comrade. Nick was in grad school at Berkeley. He wanted to be an ecologist. In July it will be two years since his car crash on the Golden Gate Bridge late at night. A drunk nailed him head-on in the wrong lane. They both died. I wanted to sue the guy's insurance company but Mom and Dad said, We're not that kind of people. No one should profit from this tragedy. I had just turned seventeen. Mom and Dad were out of town on a spiritual retreat and Cage was the one who found out first. He went out and got Nick's ashes. He told me that the reports said Nick was over the limit, too, though it obviously wasn't his fault. Still, we never told Mom or Pop.

Nick crashed two months after my parents moved from Baton Rouge to Memphis, where Dad was consecrated the Episcopal bishop of Tennessee. It was the last move after six different cities. Dad's first church was a tiny one in Thebes, the farming town outside Nashville where Mom comes from. Cage was born there. Nick came along when Dad was a chaplain at Georgia Tech in Atlanta. Then the family moved back to Tennessee, Knoxville, and I was born in Bristol. We moved to Roanoke, Virginia, before I could walk and then to a big church in Baton Rouge a few years later. Mama told me that Nick, who'd been alienated in Roanoke, came out of his shell and became as popular as Cage. Nick surpassed him academically, though he never beat Cage running. They were competitive and they were as close as two brothers could be. Nick quietly looked up to fast-talking, quick-witted Cage. To Nick, Cage was a romantic hero.

Nick's death sent Mom into a tailspin. Except for attending the small early Sunday morning service, she dropped out of all the church activities. She dropped all her charitable work. She dropped the workshops she did in inner-city schools for the botanical garden, giving children their first opportunity to grow a plant. One by one, she dropped out of everything and spent more and more time in her own garden. I'd stayed on in Baton Rouge as planned to finish my senior year at Louisiana Episcopal, living at my best friend's home in our old neighborhood, so I didn't witness much of this, but Dad told me that for a time she was sleeping through the days and gardening at night. Then, after about a year and a half, she reentered society, took up where she left off, and was as active as ever.

When Nick died, Cage was at Vanderbilt two semesters short of an M.B.A. and a law degree, a tough year-round program. He was making mainly Bs and a few As. The next semester he logged all Cs and at Christmas he announced that he was taking some time off, going to Mexico for a couple of months and then up to Nantucket, where a friend from Sewanee was going to renovate his parents' house. By the end of the summer a dozen homeowners had asked him if he would shut up their houses and open them up in spring, repairing anything that had been damaged during the winter storms. In late August he was still promising Mom and Dad that he was going back to Vanderbilt for his last semester. Then, when school was about to start, with twelve grand in the bank from Nantucket, Cage flew to Memphis and announced he was on his way to Mexico for the winter to write a novel. Mom and Dad were furious that he would jeopardize his degrees and Mom demanded that he pay them back for some of the school costs instead of heading off to surf and smoke pot. The next day Cage caught the train to New Orleans and spent the night at a hotel in the Quarter, took me out to get drunk on hurricanes before he caught a plane for Cancún. That was the last time I saw him.

The single-engine prop plane from Boston flies through so much rain and fog that I don't glimpse the ocean until we're almost to the island. Cage isn't in the arrivals area. I check the restaurant and then wander outside and stare at the parking lot, which is empty except for an old, rusty Bronco.

"Are you lost?" says a deep bass voice from the doorway behind. Startled, I turn around expecting to see a big black guy.

Cage gives me that wide, winning smile that girls always fall for. I hardly recognize him. The last time, he still resembled the clones at Vanderbilt with their short hair and oxford cloth shirts and pleated khakis. Now he looks like Indiana Jones. He has a deep tan and long, sun-bleached hair. He's wearing an earring, a leather jacket, faded blue jeans, and suede cowboy boots. He hugs me and claps me on the back. "Welcome to Nantucket."

"Damn, Cage, you look . . . different."

"I am." He winks. "And it looks like you've been burning the candle at both ends."

"Well, I'm just glad school's out for the summer."

"School's out forever." Cage strums a couple of chords in the air, then picks up one of my duffel bags and starts for the Bronco. "A girl gave me some acid yesterday. We tripped on the beach. I had some kind of memory vision. You were in it. Just a punk in your St. James uniform standing along the edge of the LSU course with Mom and Dad at the cross-country championship senior year." Cage talks rapidly, crossing the parking lot with long strides. "I typed it out last night when I was coming down. You should check it out. It's not bad. I wasn't tripping any longer, I just had so much energy I couldn't sleep. I was like Jack Kerouac banging along on my old Royal. You know what Capote said about Kerouac? That's not writing. It's typing." Cage laughs and runs his hand through his hair.

"Remember the first time I did shrooms?" I say, trying to connect. "We were hiking in the Smokies. I was fifteen. Nick was worried I would trip first with the kid who'd transferred to Episcopal from L.A., Buzz Vanderpost, and freak out, so we decided to do them together. At the last moment you changed your mind. You didn't ever want me to trip. And you and Nick started fighting by the campfire. I was afraid one of you was going to get burned."

"In the end we gave you such a small dose you didn't get off." Cage snorts, lifting the rear door of the truck open. He throws the duffel in the back, walks around to the driver side. "That was back when we suffered from the romantic delusion that psychedelics could reveal inner truth. And we listened to rock lyrics like they were poetry. Imagine looking for truth from a drug-addled pop singer." Cage climbs in the car and rests his head on the steering wheel for a moment, then turns and looks at me, and he has tears sliding down his cheeks. "I miss him, Harper. Two years now and not a single fucking day goes by when I don't mourn him."

"Y'all were close." A miserable little laugh catches in my throat. "Like brothers."

"Irish twins." He starts the car. "That's what we were—two brothers born within a year."

The island is still cold in May. Driving from the airport toward town, we pass heath moors and cranberry bogs. The Algonquin Indians, Cage says, believed the island was made by Mashop, a mythical giant so large he could only sleep comfortably along the shore of Cape Cod. One night, restless and irritable from sand in his moccasins, he kicked one of them off. It landed not so far off-shore and became Martha's Vineyard. Later in the night he kicked the other moccasin harder and it formed Natockete, "the far-off place."

The town's deserted, so we park right in front of a seafood place on the edge of the harbor. A dark-haired hostess about my age recognizes Cage when we stroll in, her blue eyes lighting up like candles.

"Charlotte, I want you to meet my little brother, just arrived from Sin City, you know, the Big Easy, Nah Ahlens." Cage drapes his arm over my shoulder. "He was working as a stripper on Bourbon Street, pulling in more money than a Nantucket plumber. His name's Harper. He's kinda shy."

Charlotte laughs. My cheeks feel hot. I mumble, "Hi."

"You can call him Long Schlong John. That's his trade name."

"Shut up, Cage." I elbow him in the ribs.

"You in college down there?" Charlotte presses two menus to her chest and leads us to a booth. "What's your major?"

"I don't know."

"Whatcha going to do with that?" She sets the menus on the table.

"Strip, I guess," I say, sitting down.

"Bring him to our next party." She smiles at Cage, touching his arm for a second. The moment she's gone, another waitress, red-haired this time and with an Irish lilt, slams down two glasses of water, puts her hands on her hips, and says, "What happened to you, Cage? I waited three hours at the Chicken Shack."

Cage just sits there smiling at her until her tight-set mouth breaks into a grin.

"Molly, sweet Molly, my leprechaun Molly, I told you I might get hung up finishing off that job 'fore the owners arrived today. This, by the by, is my little brother, Harper."

"Fair family resemblance." She studies him, then me. "You a naughty lad like your brother?"

"He's not naughty," Cage answers for me. "He's nice."

"Won't be for long under your evil influence. So what's your fancy tonight?"

Cage tilts his head and narrows his eyes.

"From the menu."

As she walks toward the kitchen, Cage says, "You're in for an exciting summer. A southern accent breaks a lot of north Atlantic ice."

"Yeah, with you as my wingman, I might—"

For a moment Cage looks as if his eyes are tearing up. He takes a deep breath. His voice sounds far away: "What do you remember most about Nick?"

I stare at the small candle burning in an orange glass on the center of the table. "I try not to think about him but I did on the plane today. He wasn't outgoing like you. He was serious, quiet, and when he spoke, it made you pause. He was the star of the family. I struggled to make Bs and he was at the top of his class. I was always jealous. What do you remember?"

Molly sets down two mugs of beer, gives Cage a hard look, shaking her head, then walks off without a word.

"The way he used to quote poetry." Cage takes a big swallow.

"Yeah." I laugh. "He told me poetry was the best way to get in a girl's pants. He also said that there's a special place in hell for guys who use great poetry to seduce innocent girls."

"Then that's where you'll find Nick," Cage says.

"Remember that time outside Giamanco's in Baton Rouge? You said something about Claudia Parlange, remember her? Nick hit you in the face and the next moment y'all were rolling around on the parking lot. Dad whisked Mom and me into the car and drove off. We left you slugging it out. You had to walk home."

"Brothers will fight. Law of nature. But brothers ought to always back each other up, that's what Granddad used to tell us. Even over women." Cage sticks his hand across the table. His grip is strong, a carpenter's.

"I'll stick by you, Cage," I say finally.

"There was this French guy at Sewanee named Gilles du Chambure. He was a big, handsome rugby player who'd gone to a fancy school in England. He was the most dashing and sophisticated guy any of us southern boys had ever seen. I used to type papers for him." Cage is telling this to Robert Wirth, a Wall Street guy with a huge house on the beach where Cage is building a new deck. "Every girl fell for Gilles before he even opened his mouth. Then, when they heard the accent, they just about started taking off their clothes in the middle of the pub. I used to take him rock climbing and he was about the best friend I had. After college I'd get an occasional postcard from London and then Hong Kong. He was that kind of guy."

Smiling and nodding, Wirth opens another bottle of beer. Cage shoots his empty bottle across the deck into a trash can and takes the fresh one.

"So, summer after my second year in law school, Nick gets us both jobs with the forest service in Montana. We're out cutting trails and fire lines. There's one pretty girl at the headquarters named Caroline whom I'm flirting with every time we're in Missoula, and she's promising to catch a supply truck to our camp when she gets a week break toward the end of the summer. I'm marking off the days on a calendar like a prisoner." Cage shakes his head. "The idea of her arrival is the only thing that keeps me going through August. You know, it's a funny thing what deprivation will do. A girl who'd hardly turn your head on Nantucket starts to look like a goddess out in the mountains."

"I hear you." Wirth laughs.

"About two days before she's coming, I twist my ankle so badly I can't walk. I just sit in a camp chair and read and dream about Caroline." Cage stretches out on his back along a large wooden table. "The night before she's due I can't sleep, so the next day I'm napping when she calls out my name and I look up and she's standing there in the door of the tent, a vision of beauty." Cage lifts his neck and visors his forehead with one hand like he's peering through into glare. " 'Come here, Caroline, and give me a hug. I can't stand up.' " He props himself up on one elbow. " 'God, you're a sight for sore eyes.' She comes over and kneels by my cot and gives me a hug. I'm thinking, Hallelujah, praise the Lord, the two-backed beast will be sleeping in this tent tonight.

Then I look over her shoulder and who do I see standing in the doorway of the tent with a big, guilty smile on his face?"

Wirth guesses, "Nick?"

"Nah, it was someone I hadn't seen for years."

"It was Gilles." I laugh. "Fucking Gilles du Chambure."

"Under normal circumstances I would have been jumping off the cot to give Gilles a hug. But all I can manage, knowing that I'll be awake again, listening to the two-backed beast moaning from a spare tent, is, 'Oh, hey. Great to see you, um, guy.' "

I look at Cage with unabashed admiration. He's obviously Mr. Popularity on the island. From the lumber stores to the inner circles, everyone's charmed by him. And while Wirth spits out a mouthful of beer, laughing at another of Cage's stories, I think this guy—my big brother—really has it all wired.

The Green of the
Garden of Eden
1960

An hour before daylight on an April Sunday, Margaret Madeline Cage Rutledge screamed and jerked her hands against leather restraints. From the time she was too small to remember, the conversation among the women in her clan had led her to believe that this would be the most painful moment in her life, more agony than any man would ever experience. It was worse than she expected. And it was only beginning, though it had been going on for hours. A clock on the wall over the door showed 4:28. Each time she glanced over, the hands seemed to be moving backward. She wished that dawn would end the darkness. She wasn't sure which was worse, the contractions or Mrs. Hennessey sticking her hand inside her every ten minutes. Two hours and her womb had not dilated even a half inch. She pictured a melon, a tiny hole in the depression where the stem had been. Her womb, woven with bundles of powerful fibers, a perfect egg of muscle, was pulling itself open in infinitesimal fractions, drawing up along the floating plates of the fetus's soft skull.

"Where's the goddamn doctor?" Margaret yelled when the pain seemed about to kill her. It was the first time in her life that she had broken that commandment, and in her mind she was safe because she had deliberately thought it in a lowercase *g*. The door beneath the clock opened. Wearing nurse whites and hat, Mrs. Hennessey came inside, shut the door softly, crossed the room, took Margaret by the hand, looked at her sternly. "Dr. Trout will be here soon, honey. Now you just try to relax. You're going to be fine."

Suddenly Margaret's womb was still and her eyes flicked to the clock: 4:29. The nurse wiped the sweat off her brow. Breathlessly Margaret whispered, "Please undo these straps."

"They're for your own good." Mrs. Hennessey reminded Margaret of her mean-spirited fourth-grade math teacher.

"Beg your pardon?" Margaret panted, trying to catch her breath. "I feel strapped to a table in the Spanish Inquisition."

"You don't want to scratch yourself or the baby," Mrs. Hennessey said. "Why, they've used restraints at Thebes County General since before I started."

"Since Oedipus was king," Margaret muttered, watching the red second hand sweeping again at normal speed. Mrs. Hennessey put her thumb and two forefingers on Margaret's wrist.

At 4:31 Margaret bellowed. Her uterine muscles were like fingers clawing the edge of a door, straining to open it against an overwhelming force. She screamed from fury as well as pain—the tail of an eight-month-long comet of fury. Margaret had been cross from the moment the doctor confirmed her fear, which was a few weeks after she lost her virginity. A honeymoon baby. Possibly conceived even that first night of their marriage. Margaret was angry because she and Frank had taken precautions. Of course they wanted children. But not nine months after they were married. Margaret had goals. She had just graduated from the University of Tennessee, had done very well, particularly in English. She wanted at least a master's degree. She wanted to teach literature at a high school or college. Back in her hometown, Margaret was proud of her handsome husband from Memphis, proud to be the rector's wife. She wanted to become a leader of the women at the new mission church. She wanted to help Frank convert select Methodists and Baptists of Thebes into Episcopalians. She wanted to reach out to the poor and to the oppressed colored community. She wanted to help Frank climb from a congregation of two hundred in her farm town to a parish of thousands in Nashville or Louisville or Atlanta, climb all the way to the bishop of Tennessee. Through the year of their engagement, when it was difficult not to succumb to the great passion, the palpable temptation, Margaret planned the first three years of her coming marriage. She wanted to wait at least that long before devoting herself to raising babies. She shouted, "Where in Christ's name is Dr. Trout?"

Mrs. Hennessey snapped, "Save your breath, young lady."

Margaret's wailing carried fifty feet down a corridor through swinging doors to the waiting room. The Reverend Franklin Malone Rutledge tensed his mouth with each shriek. The loudest made his whole face wince. He sat alone, dressed for the eleven o'clock in a tan poplin suit, black shirt, and white clerical collar. For a heartbeat he did not believe Margaret had taken the Lord's name in vain. The second time he smiled. She never ceased to amaze him. Her spirit. That temper. He stood up and paced, remembering when he had asked her father for her hand. "Every girl needs a bit of bulldog in her," her father had said, smiling. "Margaret's blessed with quite a bit." As her screaming peaked, Franklin prayed aloud very softly, "Dear Lord, spare her pain, deliver them both safely into my arms. In Christ's name I pray." Her screaming stopped and Franklin stopped pacing. He squared his shoulders, stood up straight and tall, three inches over six feet, his posture perfected a decade before on a two-year tour at Fort Knox which had ended with an offer of a scholarship to West Point. He had possessed no hesitation declining, though it meant working his way through UT as a journalism major and then through seminary at Sewanee.

"Morning, Morgan, Mary Lee." Franklin's smile was strained as Margaret's parents arrived in the waiting room. "It's going very slowly but she's doing just fine. Mars has got true grit. That's what the nurse says. She looks like she ought to know."

"Mrs. Hennessey knows her business." His mother-in-law smiled and nodded.

"Where's Trout?" Morgan asked. "Looking for the hair of the dog that bit his hindquarters last night?"

Look who's talking, Franklin thought, though in all fairness Morgan Elijah Cage V had been dry for over a year. He turned his palms toward heaven. "The good doctor is AWOL."

"That old s.o.b. ought to be here by now." Morgan reached inside his seersucker jacket for a cigar, stuck it in the corner of his mouth.

"Now, Morgan," said his wife soothingly. Dressed for church, Mary Lee Drake Cage perched on the edge of a chair with her handbag on her lap. She smiled, thinking, Whatever You in Your wisdom grant us will be a blessing. Oh, but there is nothing sweeter than a little girl.

Out of the silence came Margaret's crescendo of screams as if she were being set on fire.

Mary Lee thought back to 1937, the year that Margaret was born. Soon after, she had come down with the fevers. She pictured the hospital room where she had wasted away for six months in Nashville. She remembered the day everyone thought she was dead. As her daughter screamed, Mary Lee recalled the scene vividly, how she looked down on a woman who was herself. She talked to Margaret silently: I never told anybody this because I didn't think that they would believe me. I had been through so much. That whole period is a blur but one day I remember. I was hovering high over the doctors and your daddy and grandmother, looking down at them, looking down at myself with the most wonderful feeling of comfort and joy, just this marvelous feeling, and I kept thinking, This is so good and I'll just go on, and I thought, No, I can't leave that baby for Mother and for Morgan to take care of. That just wouldn't be right. I can't go on. I've got to stay here. I've got to go back.

Wrenched over and over, her daughter wrestled the pain, tried to fight back at the pain. But the pain kept coming, relentless and vast as a thunderstorm.

In the waiting room Morgan was chewing his cigar and staring out the window at the first pink hues of dawn, occasionally cursing Dr. Trout under his breath. Several times Mary Lee took off her white gloves, then put them right back on. Franklin stood erect, chest high, breathing in slowly as if he could inhale his wife's agony.

Daylight filtered in through venetian blinds. Mrs. Hennessey looked down and thought the girl's eyes now resembled those of a doe dead on the highway. "Margaret."

With great effort Margaret nodded.

Mrs. Hennessey wiped her forehead with a warm cloth. "Your cervix is open now. The worst's over."

Margaret smiled weakly. She thought of a lecture on the suspension of disbelief in fiction and decided that this was somehow good advice for childbirth.

"Your labor's changin' now, honey. Listen. Mark my words. When you feel the contractions coming, *push*. Push the baby out." Mrs. Hennessey cupped Margaret's chin, helped her sip some water.

Margaret was bathed in sweat, dozy from Demerol, aware of the pain but no longer caring so much. She felt somehow remote from the sound of her own screams. For a few minutes she drifted pleasantly and without fear or anger in the eye of the storm, outside of time. She didn't notice a second nurse come in the room. She closed her eyes and coasted down the long tunnel of oaks that led to the house where she was born to images of firelight flickering on cave walls, crude paintings of stick men chasing hairy elephants, then blackness, balmy and serene, a waking dream in which she thought she was floating in her own mother and felt somehow every moment of her past in the present. She thought of the opening of her mother's womb, her grandmothers' and great-grandmothers' . . . and now her own. It was perhaps the only moment in her life when her womb would be wide open. She sank into herself and her deepest emotions, a sensation akin to those long, slow moments after making love to Franklin but deeper, dreamier.

At six o'clock the hurricane hit and furious winds wrenched her body in a hundred directions, tumbled her through space. The whole of her womb contracted downward, and she felt a heavy rushing from her center out to her legs and pushed with the motion. Suddenly Mrs. Hennessey was saying something and holding a baby, smeared in white waxy vernix, with a head of thick sandy hair. A nurse she had never seen before was unfastening the hand restraints. The baby wasn't crying. Its eyes were wide open, a vivid blue like Franklin's, darting around alertly. "Would you look at him. He looks like he already knows where he is," Mrs. Hennessey said. "Take him, Margaret." Enraptured, Margaret took the baby and held it to her soaked gown.

"Oh, he's gorgeous," the young nurse said. "He's the prettiest baby I think I've ever seen." The two women crowded in close.

"A boy," Margaret marveled. "A beautiful boy."

"What are you going to name him?" the young nurse asked.

Margaret's voice was strong and clear. "Call my husband."

"Not until we cut your cord," Mrs. Hennessey said firmly.

The baby seemed to look at the two nurses in turn.

Then he smiled.

"My Lord," Mrs. Hennessey said. "I've never seen that. They ain't supposed to smile for at least a month."

The baby looked at her, then back at his mother. He smiled again.

"He's something else," the young nurse said.

Striding down the corridor, Franklin felt hollow, remembering the first time he met his father. When Frank was eight, he came home from school and found a strange, glamorous man eating ice cream with his mother in their living room. The man offered him a bite off his cone. The wild son of a Memphis preacher, he had left Frank's mother while she was pregnant. The boy never grew close to his father, but he loved his grandfather Rutledge, who came back to Memphis after retiring as the bishop of Panama. He was sad that the old bishop had not lived long enough to meet his great-grandson, though he believed in some broad interpretation of heaven most of the time.

The sight of the baby bundled in a blanket in his wife's arms dispelled the gloomy thoughts and he rushed to her side, saying, "What a beautiful Madonna and child."

"Oh, Frank." She held out the baby and he took it awkwardly and said, "Aren't you something."

"My goodness, he is gorgeous," Mary Lee said, coming up to the bed. "Look at the way he studies everything. Surely he can't see very far."

The baby smiled at her.

"Why, I declare. I never."

"Where's Poppy?" Margaret asked.

"He went out for a stroll." Her mother laughed. "Toward the end he couldn't tolerate all your caterwauling."

Just then her father bustled into the room, stared at the baby, and pronounced, "He favors Frank."

"He does," her mother said. "The hair and the eyes."

Frank thought he smelled bourbon on Morgan's breath, and prayed silently, Dear Lord, help us keep his troubled soul sober.

Margaret gazed out the window at the lush St. Augustine grass, a preternatural green after the long, wet winter. "I never remember a spring so green."

"Like the garden of Eden," her mother said.

"That's it." Margaret laughed. "All the promise of creation."

"Green will be his favorite color," her mother said. "Have you settled on a name?"

Margaret looked at Frank, then said, "Cage Malone Rutledge."

"Wayooyayaoah." Cage moved one hand up and down, conducting an underwater symphony. "Oh . . . oooo."

"He's the brightest little baby I've ever seen," Mary Lee said.

"He knows he's got an audience." Morgan laughed. "He's trying to communicate. He's much older than a baby."

Cage

Twenty-nine years and two months old, and the clock is ticking. Every year, a year of our lives becomes a smaller fraction—one-twenty-ninth, one-thirtieth, one-thirty-first—and so time seems to accelerate as we grow older. We are racing toward oblivion. Or heaven. I watch the minute hand sweep forward on the cheap wristwatch that Grandfather Cage gave me as a joke on his deathbed. Poppy was a shell of himself, bald and thin, with sunken cheeks and the palest white skin. Pretending he was passing on a great heirloom, he said, I give this to you not so you will be ruled by time, but so you will not spend every moment trying to conquer it. The battle against time only reveals to man his folly and anguish, and victory is an illusion of fools.

Ten o'clock. The Folgers are expecting me across the island with the rest of the lumber. "Let it slide, slide, slide," I sing to myself. "Baby, let it slide." I turn off the sander and step back to stare at all thirty-six feet of my 1957 Angelus ketch on blocks in the yard and decide to spend the rest of the morning sanding the hull so that I can prime it this evening. Finishing her by the end of the season is my number one priority now. I'll have to rig up some lights so that I can work late at night. I've got three months to refit every inch. In mid-September I'll sail down south. I'll be a Caribbean charter skipper in the winter and a Nantucket boat-builder in the summer. On my fortieth birthday I'll single-hand around the world. One must have goals and the American dream is no longer a house and college education for your kids, a safe retirement. The new dream is freedom from drudgery, time to travel. I dream of sailing the seven seas. Rather than conquer time I will run with it. The name of my ketch will never let me forget who I am.

Harper

In mid-June, after I've been on the island about a month, I hear Cage is renting out rooms in the homes he's supposed to be care-taking to kids landing on the island looking for jobs. I haven't seen Cage for a week. I can never get him on the phone. I catch him only at night at the Chicken Shack. He's always too distracted by some girl, usually a different one, to talk for long. One day I check the post office and find a card from Mom, who is with Dad at a conference at Canterbury, and a dozen envelopes addressed to Cage from the First Nantucket Bank which appear to be bounced checks. I just leave everything in the box and walk over to the Blakes' house, where a bunch of guys from Amherst are smoking a joint and looking through the want ads. I tell 'em they ought to move out pronto before the owners arrive and throw them out, which could be any day now. Early the next morning before work I leave my attic room and ride fast through cold fog across the is-land to Cisco, where Cage is house-sitting a two-story clapboard Victorian with a wide front porch set in front of a grove of scrub oaks.

Reaching the picket fence, I get off the bike and stand staring in the mist for a long time. The front yard has been transformed into a nautical graveyard. A dozen wooden boats lie wrecked on their sides, stranded on the grass carpet. There are sloops, ketches, yawls. I can't remember the difference. A couple are al-most skeletons, like the rib cages of whales displayed in natural history museums. A few of the hulls are more or less intact, with only a hole or two staved in the rotting sides. Two, sitting up on blocks, appear to be seaworthy. The hull of one has been recently primed and the deck stripped of varnish. On the stern, painted crudely, as if they're being tried out, are the words *Cage's Bend*.

The front door swings open when I knock. The inside smells like a frat house, stale smoke and rancid beer, and the stereo is playing Bob Marley down low. Empty rum bottles, stained glasses, and ashtrays overloaded with cigarette butts clutter the tables. I walk over local newspapers, sandy footprints, boat magazines, granola bar wrappers, turn off the stereo, and open some windows to air out the room.

The silence is broken by a girl's cry from upstairs and I almost jump out of my skin. She moans on and on. After a minute I walk into the kitchen and fill the kettle and put it on a big gas stove and search for a clean coffee mug. The moans become wild shrieks of ecstasy. I hear Cage's voice but I can't make out what he's saying. I load up a ceramic funnel with a filter and coffee and place it on the mug. Suddenly she stops and it is dead quiet, then the whistle of the kettle startles me again. I pour milk in my coffee to cool it down so I can drink it quickly. A few minutes later, when I hit the bottom of the cup, I walk back to the living room and yell, "Brother!"

Cage appears at the top of the stairs, pulling on a sweatshirt; he has some kind of sarong tied around his waist. He grins. "Hey, youngblood. Want some coffee?"

"I just had some. I arrived in time for the, uh, yodeling contest."

"Always put her pleasure first," Cage says, laughing, bounding down the stairs. "That's the golden rule."

I spread my arms out wide, encompassing the mess, my jaw hanging open in total disbelief. "Hurricane Cage?"

"Just a party." Cage stares back with the same expression. "I'm going to clean it up. Chill out."

"What's with the boats?"

"I'm renovating them." He steps past me. "I'll have a whole flotilla."

"Only a couple look like they'll ever float. Where'd you get them?"

"Beached by a really high tide. Where do you think?"

"The dump?" I follow him into the kitchen, thinking of the girl he left behind upstairs.

CAGE'S BEND

"Bingo. The sloop and the ketch I bought for a song."

"Have you been tripping every day? I think you're starting to lose touch with reality."

"You don't have the vision to see that I'm building a business."

"Yeah, Commodore Rutledge and his flotilla of ghost ships."

"Just wait till we sail to the Vineyard." He puts the filter on the cup I used and pours in tepid water. "You won't be so negative then."

"Listen, Cage, you've got to get those Amherst assholes out of the Blakes' house."

"Why?" He sets the kettle on the stove and lights a roach on the gas burner. "I'm making a thousand a week between the Blakes' house and the Treadwells'. How do you think I bought the boats?"

"You rented out the Treadwells' house, too?"

"Yeah, some girls from Sarah Lawrence. One's upstairs right now." He holds out the joint.

I shake my head. "It's dishonest."

"What they don't know won't hurt them."

"That's not the point. They're going to trash the houses. The owners could show up anytime. And even if they don't see them, they're going to find out. It's a small island."

Cage smiles, putting his hand on my shoulder. "It's all under control, little bro."

I shrug his hand off. "When do the owners get here?"

"Not till next week." He exhales a lungful of smoke and smiles. "Plenty of time."

"I got to go to work. Let's have dinner tonight. You gotta get a grip, okay?"

"Sure, Harpo. I'll come pick you up in 'Sconset at seven." He sucks in a deep toke and raises his hand.

At the front door I hear someone and turn around. A pretty, dark-haired girl in a sweatshirt and blue jeans is coming down the stairs barefoot. She smiles and says, "Good morning."

"Hey." I turn and almost let the screen door slam behind me but catch it at the last instant.

Cage

I slide the old Bronco into the parking lot at Coffin's Marine Supply and leap out the door. Power surging from every sinew, I feel like Attila the Hun come to sack imperial cities and raze ancient monuments. Turning the corner, I see Virginia Folger on the sidewalk, holding a sack in one arm and her five-year-old son by the hand. I'm about to backtrack when she sees me.

"Cage." Her voice is icy. "I waited all morning yesterday for you to show up."

"Mornin', Ms. Folger. Hey there, Ben, little man. How y'all?" I amble up to them with the rolling stride of a seaman. I keep grinning until she smiles reluctantly. Ben rushes up to me and I lift him up and spin him giggling around and around. "I am sorry, Virginia, I'm just so busy, opening up all those houses. I'll be out to finish the deck this afternoon. I promise. I'm going to pick up the lumber this very minute."

"You've broken three appointments this week." She shifts the groceries to her other arm.

I set the little boy down. "You have my word."

She mocks my accent. "I do believe you gave me your word the day before yesterday."

"Captain Cage, when you going to take me fishing?" Ben asks.

"One day soon, when I finish a boat, we'll go shark fishing." I wrap my arm around his little waist and hold him upside down. "We'll go after the god of the great whites."

"What does God look like?" Ben says when his feet hit the ground.

"Hmm." I bend down and peer into his little face, big eyes and bangs. "That's a tough one. Can't say that I've ever seen him. Have you?"

Ben nods, his face serious.

"Really?" I glance up at Virginia, who looks puzzled.

"I think I saw him when he was putting me together," Ben says.

"You're going to be a poet, little man." I laugh.

"What did God look like?" his mother asks.

"A big friendly polar bear," Ben says with a solemn face.

"I don't know where he gets these ideas." Virginia sighs. "But he's sure had a lot of funny ones since you started taking him fishing."

"Children are closer to God because they have more recently sprung from the eternal source," I say.

Virginia nods uncertainly. "Come on, Ben, we're going to be late for school. I'll see you later, Cage."

"Absolutely." I ruffle the boy's sandy hair. "Bye bye, Ben."

"Catch you later, Captain."

Inside Coffin's the plethora of hardware along the walls and shelves, all the colored boxes, is a testament to the ingenuity of man. Since flint was first flaked, man has devised thousands of tools for thousands of purposes. I mean to put many of them to good use on my trip through the vale of tears. I fill a shopping cart with wrenches, vise grips, crowbars and screwdrivers, a power saw, and a package of sanding belts and then order marine paint and lumber to be loaded in the truck.

Bill Tanner glances up from the invoice. "You sure you're not getting carried away there, Cage?"

"Got a lot of work going on at Slade Cottages." I feel bad about charging all this to the Slade account but I'll cover it in time with the rent on the Blake and Treadwell houses because they aren't due for another two weeks.

"What's Slade making that wants thirty gallons of marine paint?" Tanner asks.

"That's for my boats. He owes me for a job and we're squaring it with paint. Sort of tax-free barter."

Tanner looks at me for a long second, then punches a calculator and says, "Three thousand four hundred and sixty-three and change."

"Got to run," I say, signing the bill.

"So little time. So much to do?" Tanner smiles.

"Clocks." I tap the face of my watch. "My grandfather called them the reductio ad absurdum of all human experience."

"Way down South?" Tanner says.

"Away down South in Dixie."

No one is at the Folgers', which is perfect because I want to finish the job before they return and surprise them. It would take most carpenters eight hours to complete the deck but I'm moving in double time, sawing and nailing with no wasted motion, improvising lyrics to the tune of a John Prine song: "Jesus was a carpenter. The best trim m-a-n along the Jordan River. When Jesus hit the zone, an angelic look upon his face, the crew would begin to moan, 'cause they couldn't keep the pace." The last board's in place by one. I realize I haven't eaten anything all day but a bowl of Grape-Nuts, so I throw the tools in the truck and stop at Bartlett Farm to buy a carton of lemon pasta and fruit, which I eat in the sunshine sitting on a railroad tie by the front door. I nod and smile at the housewives going into the big greenhouse to shop. The sight of their legs in shorts fills me with longing, so I decide to head into town to Sylvia's house.

At the junction of Bartlett and the road to town I pause and think of everything I have to do: finish the fence behind the Caldwells', reshingle the hole in the roof of the Congdons', hang a door in the Ellises' cottage, and overhaul the sloop in two weeks so I can sell it and cover all the checks. There are so many checks. A mountain of debt. But surmountable. I haven't climbed a mountain since the funeral.

Suddenly I remember my first big hike. I can see Dad's canvas backpack bobbing in front of me as we climbed up the side of Roan Mountain. I can taste the horseradish and American cheese and white-bread sandwiches that Mom made for us. Twenty years ago. Before we knew what to eat. Where does the time go? Time is a river, flowing into nowhere. So little time, so much to do. I look out the windshield at the wide world. There's not a cloud in the sky, an infinite expanse of blue nothingness, and the sky's the limit. I'm about to turn toward town, go hang the Ellises' door, when I see a black girl hitching the other way and I turn toward Cisco to pick her up.

"Thanks," she says, climbing in.

"Well, you're mighty welcome, young wayfarer."

She giggles.

"Where you going this fine day?"

"Madaket. I missed my ride." She looks at me and smiles, then looks at the pile of papers on the floor of the truck. "Where are you going?"

"Ah, where are we going, where do we come from—these are the eternal questions that have haunted us from time immemorial. They'll haunt us until the end of time."

Her laugh is like a horse whinny. Her hair's cut close to her head and she's wearing blue jeans and a loose sweatshirt. A chambermaid, probably studying in Boston to be a biochemist. "That's funny."

"As it happens, I'm going near Madaket myself."

"Great." She smiles again. "My lucky day. If I don't make it out there by two I'll lose my job. My name's Sarah."

"Cage." Driving, I quiz her about herself, twenty questions, and sure enough she's studying to be a doctor, a serious and heroic young girl, worth an hour out of my way. I tell her that I wanted to be a big businessman, almost got a double L.L.B./M.B.A., but in the end I couldn't focus on the books and got terrible headaches. Sarah frowns sympathetically. I picture her mother at home in the projects, happy for her daughter to take a working summer in Nantucket, home of the first free blacks in the country. Sarah knows all about Absalom Boston, the black whaling captain.

"Imagine when you walked down the streets of Nantucket a hundred and fifty years ago." I become excited by the vision. "It wasn't a homogeneous sea of white folks back then. It was truly cosmopolitan. Sailors from around the world. Polynesians with tattoos from head to foot. Chinese. Africans. Brits and frogs."

"I'd have liked to see that," she says. "There's the house. Thanks for the ride, Cage. I really enjoyed meeting you."

"You, too, Sarah. See ya."

Turning the truck around, I watch her get a mop and a bucket from a van in front of the big beach house. At the junction that leads back to the main road I look at the waves shimmering in the sunshine and decide to take a quick swim before crossing the island to the Ellises' house.

Learning to Lie
1965

Fountain City, a suburb of Knoxville. A sunny Easter Sunday. A tract of identical ranch homes on barren lawns ringing naked Tennessee hills only fifty years before enshrouded by primeval oak forest. The rectory was distinguished from its duplicates by the front door, which Margaret had painted a deep maroon, and by the lush beds of hydrangeas, lilies, and roses that she had planted along the red-brick walls. In the days before child car seats Margaret, twenty-seven, pretty with waves of thick, dark hair, a wide smile, and a slight gap between her front teeth, pulled a '60 Ford station wagon into the driveway. The heavy passenger door swung open, pushed by a pair of little legs, and out came Cage, five, followed by Nick, four, both wearing pale blue collarless blazers over white polo shirts and navy shorts, white knee socks, and black and white saddle oxfords. They ran screaming up the concrete sidewalk holding red wicker baskets full of plastic grass and painted eggs. Margaret, unlocking the door, said, "Change your clothes first thing, sweet boys."

Back in their room the boys peeled off their church clothes, leaving them in a heap, and put on green dungarees, long-sleeved cotton T-shirts, and red sneakers, which Cage had to tie for Nick. In the living room Cage turned on a small black-and-white TV and began to flick the channels slowly, until their mother shouted, not unkindly, from the back of the house, "Turn that off right now and go outside. It's a beautiful day." Still in a dark linen skirt and matching top with three big buttons leading up to a flat collar, she came out and stood where the carpet of the living room met the parquet of the dining area to watch through the sliding glass doors her boys running to the swing set.

She turned to the front window. A white Corvair, the two-door coupe Ralph Nader would declare unsafe at any speed, pulled into the driveway behind the wagon. The handsome young rector, whom the women of the church all agreed could pass for that Virginian movie star Gregory Peck, had come from locking up the Church of the Good Shepherd, a new, small A-frame with forty-foot-high triangular windows on both ends, a mission parish in the young suburbs of Knoxville.

"Jesus loves me, yes I know," Nick was singing on the swing set while Cage was poking a stick through the chain-link fence, trying to draw the attention of an old Lab that was sleeping in the shade of its doghouse.

"Mama says don't bother Scout," Nick said. "The Campbells don't like it."

"I'm not bothering it," Cage said.

"Yes, you are." Nick leaned forward, swinging up, propelling himself higher.

Cage threw the stick over the fence and it landed a few feet from the old dog, which did not stir. Nick said, "Mama might see you."

Cage shrugged his shoulders, held an invisible machine gun, and swept the dog's yard with bullets. "*Ch, ch, ch, ch, ch, ch!*"

Margaret watched them through the plate glass.

"Hello, honey," Frank said, coming in through the front door. He crossed the carpet and kissed her. "What mischief are they up to now?"

"Just being boys." She slid an arm around his back. "When girls are born, they know immediately what the universe is all about. Dolls. Babies. But boys . . ."

Outside, Cage was shooting Nick, who lobbed a grenade down from the apogee of the swing.

". . . just want to destroy everything," she murmured.

Nick fell out of the swing and lay dead on the grass.

The young priest smiled, wrapping his arm around her. "Like *Lord of the Flies*?"

"Like the nuclear arms race," she said.

"I was a child of the Depression. You were a child of world war. They'll grow up under that shadow." Frank slid his hand up her side and cupped her breast. "It will work out all right."

Margaret kissed him deeply and pulled away. "I better start dinner."

Franklin went to their bedroom and changed into a pair of khakis and a gray sweatshirt. Passing through the kitchen to the backyard, he pinched Margaret's bottom. Outside, the boys were digging fortifications in the sandbox, manning trenches with green and gray plastic soldiers.

"Hey, Dad," Cage said.

"*Kboo!*" Nick made an explosive sound and threw a handful of dirt on the German front line. "Papa!"

"Who's winning?" Franklin hunkered on his heels at the edge of the sandbox.

"The Americans." Cage pointed at a green soldier. "Are there any Germans in Knoxville?"

"Plenty. There are lots of German Americans. They're our friends." Franklin tousled Cage's hair.

"Why didn't you stay in the army, Daddy?" Cage asked.

"Because that's no way to live."

"Did you fight Germans?" Nick picked up a gray soldier.

"No. There was no war when I was in the army, thank God."

"God doesn't like war?" Cage asked.

"No, son." Franklin pulled a pack of cigarettes from his pocket.

"Why doesn't God stop war?" Cage asked.

"Because he lets men have free will, son. He lets men do what they want to do."

"Even if they are bad men?"

"Especially bad men." Franklin put a cigarette in his mouth but didn't light it.

"Do you know some bad men?" Nick asked, cuddling up to his father.

"I met some in the army." Franklin laughed and picked Nick up by the waist and raised him high in the air.

Margaret came out on the porch, an apron over her dress, and called out musically, "Cage and Ni-ick, come to diin-ner!"

Franklin brushed the sand off the boys and followed them into a bathroom off the carport, where they washed their hands and faces before going into the kitchen. He went off to work on his tax return while Margaret served the boys. At the end of the meal she said, "All right, little men, it's time to take your baths."

"No, Mama, we took baths before church." Cage slipped from his chair to the floor. Nick was silent, watching Cage, then his mother, then Cage again.

"Cage, you're filthy. Of course you have to take a bath." She called to Frank from the swinging door.

"Not fair! Two baths is not fair." Cage was stomping on the linoleum, lifting his knees high and dropping his feet down hard, circling the kitchen table. "Not fair!"

Margaret put a hand to her temple, crimped the flesh of her forehead against her nose. Nick frowned and held out his arms. Cage kept stomping around the table. Again Margaret called out, "Frank!" She looked over at Nick, who was still reaching for her with both arms, and smiled at him, lifting the boy from his chair and setting him against her hip.

"Cage Malone," Frank's voice boomed. "Control yourself right now."

Cage stood still and cried out vehemently, "Not fair."

"Why isn't it fair?" Franklin brushed Cage's bangs out of his face.

"I had a bath!" Cage clenched his fists, held them by his pockets like a gunfighter ready to draw.

"That was to look nice in church." His father smiled. "And then you got dirty again. So you need another bath."

"It's not fair." Cage started to stomp again.

His father whisked him off the floor by his waist. "Do you want to get spanked?"

Cage stopped struggling. "No."

"Good." Franklin set him down. "Get ready for your bath."

"Let Nick go first." Cage moved away from his father.

"All right." Franklin took Nick from his mother and carried him toward the bathroom. Margaret sighed and turned to the kitchen sink. Cage walked quietly through the living room to the carport and on into the little workshop at the back. He crawled up on a stool and gazed at the half-complete home-made balsa wood model of the NASA Gemini capsule which his father was building him for his birthday. Sounds of kids on bicycles drew him down the driveway and out to the street.

The Magic Hour. When the world changes color. He always wanted to be outside at this time but it was always dinnertime-bathtime-bedtime. The thick bluegrass glowed with a luminous sheen. The air seemed heavy with light. The brick houses looked denser. This was the time when something special could happen, when Peter Pan or Winnie the Pooh or the Wild Things came out to play. The black mountains in the distance rose up from the golden haze like something out of a fairy-tale kingdom.

Hands in his pockets, Cage walked down Mountain View. In the Grabers' yard some older kids, arranged like the points of a star, were playing kick the can in the twilight. Nobody noticed him as he watched them for a while and then moved on. He ambled along, humming a song from *Captain Kangaroo*. The road circled past uniform lawns. Crows flew through the fading light, looking for roosts in the treeless barrens. A car came from behind, slowed, rolled along beside him, a man watching him from the window. "Stranger," Cage whispered to himself, and cut fast through the Shoptaughs' yard, around their house, and on up a steep hillside. At the top was a bank of tall trees and huge round bushes circling an old farmhouse. Cage sat down by a bush and looked out at the sky, which was deep red now with bands of black clouds.

Cage knew he was in trouble. In the failing light he tried to think of something to tell his parents so that he wouldn't get spanked: I went down the driveway to look at a cat and a strange bad man scared me and I ran up to the Heithoffs' hill and hid. Then he remembered what his father had told him many times: "It's always best to tell the truth." He recalled the story of George Washington and the cherry tree. Cage made up his mind and ran down the hill as fast as he could, his legs revolving like windmills.

At the bottom of the hill he heard his father calling him. Coming near Mountain View, he saw lights winking like lightning bugs—the Graber children had joined the search and their flashlights jerked crazily in their hands as they ran back and forth along the street, calling, "Cage! Cage!"

Cage ran toward the tall silhouette of his father, yelling, "Papa! Papa!"

Franklin covered the distance in a few strides and scooped him off the pavement. "Cage. Where were you?"

Cage hesitated. He thought he would be spanked but he trusted his father's promise that it's always best to tell the truth. "I wanted to see the Magic Hour."

"What?" His father looked at him closely.

The Graber children gathered around them.

"Cage sure is a daredevil," a girl said. "He's not afraid of anything."

"Thanks, kids. You were a lot of help." Franklin started carrying Cage toward home. "Good night."

Cage relaxed in his father's arms, sure that he wasn't going to get spanked. A triangle of light fell on the front porch, through the open door.

"Oh, thank heaven, Frank's got him. Good night, Helen," his mother spoke into the phone and hung it up. "Cage, darling, where were you? You were gone for forty-five minutes."

"The Magic Hour," Cage said simply as his father set him down.

"Honey, you should have told me that you wanted to go outside." His mother knelt on the carpet and hugged him close.

Cage looked at his feet.

"I'll take you to see the Magic Hour," she said. "Just promise me you won't run away again."

"I promise, Mama," Cage said.

"Cage, that was very serious, you running off," she said.

Cage didn't say anything, suddenly uneasy.

"We're going to have to punish you." His mother shook her head sadly. "You know you're not allowed to run off by yourself. You can't run off every time that you have to take a bath."

Cage looked at his father.

"I'm sorry, little man, but you broke the rules, rules for your own good," he said.

"I told the truth," Cage said. "Like George Washington."

"That's good, son. You must always tell the truth." His father's voice was soft and slow. "But you still broke the rules."

Cage saw Nick peeking from behind a door down the hallway.

"Not fair." Cage pulled away from his mother.

"It is fair, son. You have to follow the rules." Frank sat down in a chair and held out his arms. "Come here, son."

Slowly Cage walked over and bent over his father's thigh so that he was looking directly at Nick, who saw their father smile slightly when their mother said, "Looks like he's laying his head down on a guillotine."

Cage pressed his lips together, tensing his body as his father whacked him hard three times on the bottom, and he did not scream or cry despite the stinging that surged through him, despite all the fury. He pushed himself up without saying a word and ran down the hall, past Nick, who was wearing a one-piece pajama suit with footies. From behind, their father called, "Nick, back in bed. Cage, get ready for your bath."

"We'll read *Jeremy Fisher*," their mother nearly sang. "I promise."

Harper

On the TV behind the bar, thousands of kids my age fill Tiananmen Square in China. I wonder if they have any chance of bringing down the government. They look much poorer and much braver than the students drinking and shouting around me, oblivious to the demonstration.

"Something the matter with the beer?" Alice asks from behind the bar. She's a kindly local in her thirties. I usually flirt with her after a few drinks, which she tolerates with good humor.

"Nah, I just don't feel like drinking," I sigh.

"Bad day?"

"Waited three hours for my brother to show up for dinner, then hitched out here and now I don't feel like drinking."

"You just missed him. Billy had to throw him out. Cage kept jumping up on the bar with his guitar. Left with that Sylvia girl."

"God, I'm sorry, Alice."

"I like Cage. He's welcome back. But he's out of control these days. Needs to lay off the jack."

"Yeah, I don't understand what's happened to him." I put some cash on the bar. "Night, Alice."

I walk about a mile in pitch-dark before some girls pick me up and drop me off at my place. Bone-tired from six ten-hour days, I read a few pages of *Siddhartha* and fall asleep around midnight, planning on crashing until noon. When I wake up, Cage is staring at me at the end of the bed, strumming his guitar. Freshly shaved, his hair swept back with gel, he's wearing a blue blazer and white pants. His eyes are electric. "Harpo, listen to this song I just wrote."

Nick and Cage are Irish twins
Born in sixties in the very same year,
The sons of a preacher and a Tennessee belle
who met on a Carolina pier.

Nick likes to spend time alone,
an introvert who's kind of shy.
Cage likes to run with the pack,
'Cause he's another breed of guy.

Behind him Sylvia, who would be quite pretty if she wasn't so anorexic, sits in a cloud of ganja smoke, nodding in time. She's wearing a dress and a cashmere coat. Her eyes are just as wild. The wind-up clock on the dresser shows nine-thirty.

Nick's studying to save the world,
Always knew what he wanted to be,
While Cage was a man cast adrift who
Found himself on cold northern sea.

So let them be the kind of men they are,
Let 'em alone and they will both go far,
Let 'em do whatever they each choose
'Cause they're wearing different-size shoes.

"What do you think?" He sets the guitar on the floor.

"It's great." I yawn. "But Nick's dead."

"No, he's living the greater life, that's what Dad would say. You know what today is?"

"Yeah, I haven't forgotten." I rub my eyes.

"Right. We're all going to church."

"I'm a humanist. I don't go to church. Are y'all tripping?"

"We're coming down," Sylvia says.

Sylvia parks her new Saab a block from a little stone Episcopal church. Climbing out, we hear hymns coming through the open front doors.

"Hurry up, sports fans, we're late." Cage pulls his guitar from the open window and starts across the street.

"I'm not going in if you take the guitar." I sit down on the hood.

"It's a legitimate way to worship."

"Not in there it's not." I start to pull my tie loose.

"Leave it," Sylvia tells him. "Harpo's right."

I follow them into the nave, where shafts of light slant through the stained glass, making bright circles on the wine-colored carpet. The church is fairly full. About a hundred people are standing, reading a psalm in unison: "Wash me through and through from my wickedness and cleanse me from my sin."

"Cage, this way," I whisper, nodding toward an empty pew to the side in the transept.

Cage shakes his head. "The front row's always empty." He starts up the center aisle, reciting along with the congregation from memory: "For behold, you look for truth deep within me and will make me understand wisdom secretly."

The congregation sits down before we reach the empty pew. I feel their eyes on us. Cage smiles like a movie star, guiding Sylvia up the aisle with his hand on her elbow. A teenage girl with long blonde hair smiles back at him. From a high lectern a woman begins to read the lesson. Sylvia sits down, Cage kneels beside her. I sit down just as the congregation rises to sing "A Mighty Fortress Is Our God." Nick sings louder than anyone and he sings well. After the hymn everyone remains standing while an old bald priest with a hearing aid comes down the center aisle where an acolyte holds a big Bible open to the Gospels. I'm trying to follow the reading from Luke when Cage whispers, "Didn't you used to hate it every Sunday when the ushers passed the plate and everyone tossed in dollar bills? Like Pop's salary was coming out of the plate, like we were a family of beggars, you know?"

"Yeah," I whisper back. "It made me feel like Dad was inferior, like he became a priest because he couldn't make it in the marketplace."

"Think of what a good speaker he is. He could have been a

great politician. And he was a good role model." Cage smiles. "Did you ever want to be a preacher?"

I laugh through my nose.

"The Holy Ghost never summoned you to the pulpit?"

"No."

"I feel the Holy Ghost creeping up on me now," Cage says a little too loud as everyone in the congregation sits down except for him.

A woman across the aisle glances at us.

"The Holy Ghost is calling me to be its instrument," Cage says a little louder.

"Sit down, Cage," Sylvia whispers.

"Let me by," he says softly, smiling.

"No," I say. "Sit down now."

Placing one hand on the railing, he vaults over the pew front and dashes forward in time to cut off the old priest, the only other person in the church standing, at the steps that lead up to the pulpit.

A few feet away the rector is seated in a tall ornate chair in front of the empty choir stall. A heavy man with a black beard and warm eyes, he looks puzzled. When he rises to his feet, his face grows stern and he says in a salty voice, "Cage Rutledge, what on earth—"

"I beg your pardon, Father Farlow, but the Holy Ghost has summoned me to preach this beautiful summer morning in your stead," Cage says loud enough for all the congregation to hear. Father Farlow must see the light in his eyes, for he suddenly looks cautious and says nothing. Cage bows to him and then to the old priest, who, with a confused expression, is adjusting his hearing aid.

Cage brushes past him and mounts the lectern. He projects his voice the way he did when I saw him at the Vanderbilt theater in *Fool for Love* two years ago: "Good morning, brethren."

I realize my mouth is hanging open. I shut it as my mind goes into a mode akin to once when I was driving Cage's car near Sewanee, spinning out of control on ice, and time seemed to slow down, and I calmly recovered from a couple of 360-degree turns while absorbing every detail. I turn around to gauge the response of the congregants, who appear to have woken up from a day-dream. A couple of young married men are grinning while their wives look concerned and a number of elderly folks can't make out who is in the pulpit. The mother of the girl who smiled when we walked in now looks suspiciously at me.

"I won't keep you long," Cage says in a deep, confident voice. From a distance he appears to be a specimen of perfect health, tan and handsome in his blue blazer as if he had just stepped off a yacht.

Two ushers, who look like they'd played football twenty years before, have come to the far end of the aisle behind the rear pews and stand waiting for a signal from the rector, who looks at Cage with a sympathetic expression. One of the ushers suddenly turns and hurries down a staircase at the back of the nave into the un-dercroft. Across the aisle, one row back, a woman and her three children are craning their necks and looking at me as if I'm about to leap up myself. I shrug and raise my palms. The family all avert their eyes simultaneously.

"How many of you have read *Moby-Dick*? Surely all of you know that Captain Ahab set sail from the harbor down the street in pursuit of the white whale. I've been rereading Melville's mas-terpiece recently." Cage is using his southern senator's voice. "Many of the chapters are themselves sermons of a sort. But there is an actual sermon in the book preached by the ancient black cook to sharks that are in a feeding frenzy on the carcass of a whale lashed to the side of their vessel." He suddenly switches into a black dialect: "Your woraciousness, fellow-critters, I don't blame ye so much for; dat is natur, and can't be helped; but to gobern dat wicked natur, dat is de pint. You is sharks, sartin; but if you gobern de shark in you, why den you be angel; for all angel is not'ing more dan de shark well goberned."

A handful of people laugh.

"Now, look here, bred'ren, just try wonst to be cibil, a helping yourselbs from dat whale. Don't be tearin' de blubber out your neighbor's mout, I say."

There's more laughter, even from Father Farlow. Sylvia is laughing hard, clutching her arms around her concave belly.

Cage switches back to the orator's voice: "Now, if you take the whale to be the world and the blubber wealth, Melville seems to be saying that we should not be so grasping in our pursuit of wealth. Now, most of the people I know, most of the lawyers and bankers and builders I've met on the island, and most of the professionals who visit from New York or Boston don't go to church. Many of their children have no idea what goes on in church. They have only a vague notion of God." Cage points his finger at me and holds it in the air. "My own brother calls himself a humanist. I had to drag him in here with me today. Bet he wishes he hadn't come, huh, Harper? My own brother, the son of a . . . bishop. But I digress. The point is that here, in the last days of the twentieth century, the blubber itself—wealth—has become the religion. *Don't be tearin' de blubber out your neighbor's mout, I say!*"

The congregation erupts as loud as the laugh track on a sitcom. Sylvia's laughter turns into coughing.

"Now, I know that I am preaching to the converted, though no doubt even some of us believers are suffering from a powerful attraction to the blubber, and you blubbermongers should look deep in your hearts, but what concerns me is how we can make our neighbors outside the church aware of the dangers of blubber. In anthropological terms man is no longer a *Homo habilis*, handyman, the Toolmaker. *Homo sapiens* has become the Toy Buyer. For men pursue blubber in order to buy toys, more toys, and more toys." Cage pauses and looks at the back of the church where the usher who disappeared is starting up the aisle with a policeman. "Fellow-critters, dere is a shark swimmin' tow'd me as I speak. I hab yet to conclude da homilie this morning but it high time to heave off." He leaps down from the pulpit, dodges past Father Farlow, and dashes toward the side of the church.

I don't know what to do. I don't take to the idea of tackling him in church. I just sort of freeze. Cage reaches a stained-glass window, which is round like a portal and open, swung on hinges in the middle so the glass is parallel to the ground, with a breeze

passing above and below it. Cage springs up and pulls his head
and shoulders through the space at the bottom of the window.

A hundred hushed voices are murmuring behind me.

Sylvia clutches my arm.

Father Farlow is saying something from the pulpit.

Watching Cage wiggle his butt through the hole, I think of
Nick telling me the story of when Papa taught them the word *but-*
tocks. Cage and Nick were about four or five and getting into one
of the big Ford LTD station wagons. Papa had said, Sit still and
don't let your buttocks leave the seat, and the little boys fell to the
ground, rolling with laughter. In the car Cage kept repeating,
Buttocks, and Nick kept howling with laughter.

"Sir?"

I turn and the policeman is leaning over the armrest of the
pew.

"Yes." I should stand up but I'm still stunned.

"I'd like a word with you two," the usher says over the cop's
shoulder.

"Sure." We get up. Father Farlow smiles kindly from the pulpit.
I wave and smile weakly and follow the usher toward the back of
the church, everyone staring at us from both sides, the policeman
walking behind me as if I might make a run for it.

The usher leads us down to the undercroft, a basement with a
linoleum floor and a table set with a big coffee brewer and plates
of cookies. Sylvia pulls a cigarette out of a small purse. "You can't
smoke here," the usher says.

Sylvia sticks the unlit cigarette between her lips.

"That cowboy who was hijacking the pulpit is your brother?"
The cop takes out a little notepad. His name tag says *Officer Hen-*
derson. He writes down my name, phone number, and address.
Upstairs the congregation is singing.

"Where does your brother live?"

"Right now he's house-sitting out in Cisco. I can't remember
the name of the street."

"You can do better than that," the cop says. "If you want us to
be nice, you should cooperate."

"There's a bunch of boats in the front yard. But I'm not sure where he'll be next week."

"How old is he?"

"Twenty-nine."

"Is he drunk or high on something?" Henderson watches me with eyes that show no sympathy.

"Cage hasn't been the same since our brother died." My voice is thick. "Um, in a car accident two years ago today."

"You didn't answer my question."

"Go easy, Ed," the usher says.

"Well." I glance at Sylvia, who gives me a look like I've already ratted them out.

She takes the cigarette from her mouth, then puts it back.

"He's been hitting the bottle pretty hard."

"If you're any kind of brother, you'll bring him in to the station before we find him. He'll probably get off with a warning." Henderson points his pen at me. "If we have to go looking for him, it won't be no Sunday school."

Cage

It's night. Only a faint glow of moonlight through the windows. Is it closer to dusk or dawn? I hear her breathing beside me in bed. She is here but I feel no connection to her, as if she doesn't know me, that we are two apes who happen to be lying beside each other by arbitrary selection. I can't remember getting in bed. I stare up at the ceiling, try to reach back a few hours, but there is only darkness and the sound of a car on the road. Darkness in the room. Darkness in my head. Why do I get these gaps? Drugs? asked that little, frightened woman at the Nantucket health service when I told her I had racing thoughts and couldn't sleep and I thought that people looked at me as if I didn't belong on the island. No, I hadn't been doing any drugs. She looked more confused than I was and scared of me. I think it was my leather jacket and my earring and long hair. I hadn't done any drugs for months until I walked out of her office.

The psychologists I've met are clueless anyway. I was so depressed at Vanderbilt that I started sleeping all day. I couldn't face the classrooms filled by fumes from the erasable markers they used to cover the walls with graphs. Remembering the fumes gives me a headache. Mankind was born in the forests of Africa and not meant to dwell in concrete and cardboard towers with a random selection of humanity breathing chemical fumes. There I was, burning up my parents' money, going in debt to be a cog in a machine, preparing for a life in an office, my head cracking every time I smelled the fumes. The Vanderbilt counselors were buffoons. They thought I should ride it out. I should never have been there. My grades steadily declined, then fell off a cliff. Toward the end I was unraveling. Stayed in my apartment for two weeks and made soup for myself and read an Elvis biography and thought I was watching the hair fall out of my head every time I looked in the mirror and no one at school even asked where I was. For an international marketing class we had to get a partner or a group of people to do a presentation. I got together with another misfit, a guy from China, and we did this thing on selling crematoriums because they had so many people over there who were dying. Macabre. He used to sell them. I got up in front of the class and couldn't remember what I was saying. We were supposed to be addressing the class as if we were addressing the board of directors of a company to ask for money to do marketing R&D. I had all these prepared notes in front of me and I couldn't think of anything to say. I couldn't organize my thoughts. I finally just put my notes down and said, Look, all I really want is forty dollars from the board so I can buy this directory of international business. The class started howling and the professor reached in his pocket and pulled out two twenties. In front of this whole big group of people. Everybody was laughing at me.

A cold wind stirs the curtains. I stand up to close the window and gaze at the moon. I can remember Vanderbilt a year and a half ago, I can remember two weeks ago, but I can't remember where I was this morning. I try and try but I only see the graphs on the walls and smell the dizzying fumes. *Where was I this morning?* I scream silently. I walk barefoot around the room looking for a clock and the ticking draws me to a heap of clothes and I find it under them. Eight-thirty. It's only just night. Why were we sleeping? I'm wide awake now. I pick up my pants and find something in my pocket, the bulletin from St. Paul's, and I remember the morning with relief—like discovering your location after wandering around lost in the woods for hours.

I laugh and Sylvia mumbles from the bed. From the church I'd run right back here. We'd started tripping around three in the morning, seven hours before the service. I haven't slept much the last month, only a few hours a night, and I was exhausted and crawled right back in bed and slept for eight hours. Now I'm refreshed. Ready to rip. Lock and load.

"What are you laughing at?" Sylvia sits up, the sheets sliding down to her belly, revealing her teardrop breasts.

"My sermon." I crawl beside her. "I don't know what possessed me. Maybe the Holy Ghost."

Sylvia smiles. "It was impressive."

I kiss her breasts for a long time. She arches her back. I wrap one arm around her thin waist, pull our bodies together. We seem to melt into each other. I trace my tongue down her belly, along the blades of her hips until she is grinding her ass slowly.

"Fuck me," she says.

I slide inside her, get up on my toes so my pelvis is pressing against her clitoris.

"I love your cock."

"I love being inside you."

Her breathing grows heavier. She lifts her head and licks my chest. I'm getting too excited, so I picture the waves lapping the shore, skidding back to sea, and rolling back to the beach until she is breathing fast, yelling, "Kill me. Kill me. Oh, kill me!"

I rise up on my arms, drive myself in and out of her, watching her face tense. Then she moans and her body goes slack, her eyes roll up so only white shows through the slits of her lids. A woman's face is most beautiful immediately after coming, flushed and soft, radiant. I watch the flickering transformation, then pull her legs up in the air, her knees behind her head, and hammer my flanks between her thighs, borne on a furious rush, a wind howling up a mountainside, the promise of reaching a new summit, the ultimate peak, a union of souls, and then I come and the climax is a cruel swindle as I fall, down, down, down into blackness, utterly alone. It is the disenchantment that makes a man rush out of a woman's bedroom as if fleeing the scene of a crime.

"That was wonderful," Sylvia says, her eyes open and focused, the ephemeral beauty gone.

"Yeah, it was great," I say, rolling onto my back. "I'm hungry."

Sylvia pulls the sheet up and closes her eyes. I get up, pull on some clothes, and go downstairs. Outside the front windows, Harper is riding up on his bicycle. I go out on the porch. "Hey, Harpo."

"You finally woke up." He comes through the gate. Halfway across the yard he stops and looks at all the boats, shakes his head. "How do you feel?"

"Like I could run a marathon."

Harper comes to the edge of the porch. "Listen, Cage, I think we ought to go to the police station. That cop said if you went in to talk, you'd get off with a slap on the wrist, but it'd be worse if they came after you."

"Why?"

"Disturbing the peace. Public drunkenness. I don't know." Harper seems uncomfortable, like he feels guilty. "The cop called me this afternoon and said that those checks you've been bouncing have caught up with you."

"I'm not going to any damn police station." The idea terrifies me. What if they give me a drug test? They might railroad me into a rehab program right off the island and blow all my plans apart. "I'll cover those checks if I can just keep working."

A squad car rolls out of the darkness in front of the yard.

I walk quickly inside, run up the stairs, and grab my passport—

never leave home without it—and a stash of cash in my sock drawer. Sylvia rouses for a few seconds, squints at me, and rolls over. I kiss her on the back of the neck and tell her I love her but she doesn't stir, so I fly out of the room and down the back stairs four at a time, my feet just barely touching the edges, and run out the back.

A cop is standing in the yard a few feet from the door in the moonlight.

"Hi." I slow down as if I'm just coming out for a stroll. Just beyond his reach I dash to his side. He lunges and tackles me. I hit the ground with a heavy thump that knocks the wind out of me and I see little bursts of color. As the air comes back in my lungs, I try to squirm away from him and he says, "Hold still, asswipe."

"Hey, I didn't do a thing. I'll have you arrested for assault. Tackling me like I was a criminal." Rage fills my body at the injustice and I say, "Would you kindly get off me, Officer?"

He bends my arm around my back until my elbow feels like it's going to break, and says, "Now let's walk slowly around to the front."

"All right." I start walking.

"Hurry up," he says, pushing my forearm to send a shooting pain through my elbow.

I kick him in the shin, spin around in the direction of the arm he's holding and punch him in the face. He staggers back, cupping his chin.

I run across the yard toward a path that goes to the beach.

"Freeze, motherfucker!" he yells when I'm halfway to the bushes. No way he's going to pull the trigger, I think, and keep running when a shot whizzes over my head. I stop and raise my hands. I turn around and see him aiming the gun with both hands. I have to laugh at the serious look on his face. A bad actor playing a cop.

"Whoa now, son, hold on," I say.

Harper and the cop from church come running around the house.

"First this bastard tackles me." I point at the cop who is still leveling the gun at me. "Then he shoves me and then he tries to shoot me. Clear-cut police brutality."

"The asshole hit me in the face." The cop holsters the gun.

"After you nearly broke my elbow," I say.

"Cage Rutledge," says the other cop.

"Yeah."

"I have a warrant for your arrest." He pulls my arms around my back and tightens the handcuffs until they're biting into my wrists.

"You've got to be kidding," I say. "For what?"

"Fraud."

"And resisting arrest," says the other cop. "And assaulting an officer."

The cop from church leads me around the house, reading my rights. Around front I see Sylvia peeking out of an upstairs bathroom window. She's probably flushing her stash down the toilet. "You going to bail me out, Harper?"

Harper doesn't say yes. He looks at me with tears in the corners of his eyes. "I'll follow you down in your Bronco."

One cop shoves me in the back of the squad car, knocking my head against the door frame. I see Harper asking them something. Suddenly I feel trapped in a cage. "You insular catamite pederasts!" I yell and thrash about the seat. The handcuffs cut deeper into my wrists. My plans are crumbling around me. If I can't get out and finish a boat, I'll never cover my debts. The whole house of cards will fall. The postdated checks will come due soon and the mountain of debt will rise up like a volcanic atoll. The space between the wire mesh and windows shrinks until I can barely breathe. I kick the wire but it doesn't bend. "This isn't fair! I don't deserve this! I didn't do anything," I scream as the cops get in the car. I take a deep breath and lower my voice. "Will you please let me tell my girlfriend good-bye?"

"Kiss your own ass good-bye," one cop says from the passenger seat without turning his head.

"Fuck you!" I kick one foot through the door window, spraying the glass outside on the road.

"That was cooperative," the other cop says, opening his door.

"Cage." Harper's face, lit up by the car lights coming up the street, seems to float in the hole in the window. "Get ahold of yourself. You're just making it worse."

One cop opens the other door, drags me out by my collar, and lets me fall on the shoulder. His knee on my back, he grips my head with one hand and grinds my face into the shell gravel, crushing my nose and tearing my lips for a couple of seconds. He says into my ear, "You just lay quiet until the wagon gets here. You're going to love the wagon."

"Cage." Sylvia sits on her knees and cradles my head. Her face is dark, haloed by the red taillights of the car.

"Your face would launch a thousand ships." I remember the first time I told her that. I'd towed the sloop from the harbor and was unloading it in front of the Taylors' house. She was walking down the road toward the beach and stopped and asked what I was going to do with her. Rebuild her, I'd replied. Sail her to Ireland at the end of the summer, pay homage to my progenitors. She laughed and said she always wanted to crew across the Atlantic. You can christen her, I said. Your face would launch a thousand ships.

"God, Cage, why?"

"The checks. Those goddamn checks."

"They'll let you out, right?" She's sobbing. "You'll get out soon."

"I don't know. Someone might have to bail me out."

"Okay," she says.

Headlights from another car suddenly illuminate Sylvia, and the sound of its idling drowns out her sobs. She looks younger than I've ever seen her, only a child. Two more cops walk into the light. One glances down at me, then at the cop I hit, who is leaning on the trunk of the squad car smoking a cigarette. "Fucker broke my finger when I tackled him."

"Another brat too big for his britches?"

The cop exhales smoke and nods. "The waffle treatment."

"Excuse me, miss," the new one says. Staring up from his legs is like sighting up a tree trunk. "Move away now."

He picks me up by my belt and walks me along the road like I was a rag doll, then tosses me face-first through the open rear doors of a van. I twist and take the impact on my shoulder then roll onto my back.

"Don't hurt him!" Sylvia shrieks.

I'm trying to stand up when the doors close and it's dark except in the front, through the mesh, where the glare of the headlights comes through the windshield. The cops get inside. The van pulls away and I fall on my ass. I scoot across to the mesh screen and stand up, hunching over, my head scraping the roof.

"I'm sorry I hit your colleague. I was out of my head. I'm kind of confused these days. Will y'all apologize for me?"

"Shut the fuck up," the driver says.

The big one says, "Heat up the grill."

We turn onto the highway into town and the driver floors the car, goes through the gears like he's in a drag race, sending me sliding backward until I hit the rear metal doors with a loud crash, then he slams on the brakes until I'm rolling forward, head over heels, the tires screeching against the road, and my face smacks into the mesh, the little cop yelling, *Waffled!* and the world is starbursts of red and yellow, the big one's deep belly laugh and the little one's nasal cackle, the grind of the accelerating transmission, then the heavy thud of my back hitting the floor. I can't breathe, my lungs stunned, paralyzed. I skid slowly on my back until my head nudges the rear doors and still my jaw jerks my mouth open and shut like a fish in a dry bucket gasping for water. I must have landed wrong on the handcuffs, snapping the spinal link to my lungs, like pulling a plug from an electrical socket. Dizzy, my brain begins to suffocate.

Everything is clear and simple, though here in the ultimate moment it remains impossible to declare if this end derived from fate or free will. Now is the time for my last thoughts but it's hard to think at all with the vacuum beneath my ribs on the edge of exploding, so I struggle for perspective and see: I'm dying from a freak accident in a police van driven by two utter strangers, the first fatality of the Nantucket waffle treatment. The absurdity of my death strikes me as so funny my chest and knees jackknife together in a convulsion that yanks me up off the floor, and a last laugh escapes my throat with no sound. And then there is air.

My head is spinning from careening from one side of the road to the other, banging from starboard to port and back. I lie curled like a bruised, manacled fetus, timing my kicks to stop the sides from slamming me. When I miss, the wheel well punches me on the forehead. The doors open before I know that we've stopped. I lift my head and see two dark figures, like Klansmen in black robes, blurry in the square of yellow light, speaking a foreign language. One reaches toward me and drags me by the scruff of the neck out of the van and holds me upright. He barks something in Russian and lets go of my collar. I find myself sprawling in grass at his feet, choking back a rising tide of vomit then hurling it all up on one of his leather shoes.

"You slimebag motherfucker."

They're speaking English after all. The shoe jerks away.

"I'll kick the fucker's teeth out." The little cop's voice.

"Not in front of the station," says the big one, lifting me from behind.

The world clicks back into focus in the fluorescent light inside the station. I see for the first time the faces of the two men apprehending me, like escorts to hell who have no connection to you and will never see you again. A new watershed moment in my life. Like graduating from college. A rite of passage. The big one dumps me on a chair and says, "Lieutenant, here's the crazy carpenter that kicked out the squad car window."

The lieutenant's ruddy bald head rises up slowly from behind the counter, a cobra out of a basket, followed by his powder-blue pleated uniform shirt. I'm sure I met him at a clambake last month and strain to remember his name. He looks at me with a bored, deadpan expression, then recognition flickers through his eyes and he says, "The guitar player from New Orleans."

"Baton Rouge," I manage. "How you doing?"

"Fair to middling." He squeezes a pin in his fist and taps it lightly on the counter, concern beginning to animate his face.

"I hear that. *You* ever had the waffle treatment?"

The lieutenant pauses with his mouth half open in a reluctant smile.

"Going back to the Bohners'?" I hurry on, taking control. "They asked me to come play next week." I squirm against the handcuffs behind my back.

The lieutenant nods. "They invited Sally and me, too."

His name comes to me and I say earnestly, "Listen, Bobby, would you kindly tell them to take these shackles off? I ain't no Ted Bundy. I can barely stand up. They waffled me across the damn island. I just threw up outside and I'm feeling sick again."

The lieutenant tells the big cop to remove the cuffs.

"Thanks. Where's the head?" I need to ditch the nickel of pot and the Moroccan pipe in my pocket before they search me. When I take a step, the room lurches into motion like a merry-go-round, Bobby's bald dome orbiting behind the big one's, and the little cackling cop's face farther out there like Uranus. I watch the room revolve a couple of times and repeat to myself, Remember the root of the problem. "Listen," I say aloud, smiling at the circling heads. "Those checks, I'll cover those checks." I try to focus on Bobby's red planet but all three faces swing by faster and faster, blending into one ring.

Harper

A little chapel built for a race of smaller men, the courtroom in Nantucket, erected by anal Quaker millionaires in the last century, seems cramped even with only a handful of people. After two days in a ten-by-ten cell Cage looks scared, like a trapped animal, wearing rumpled seersucker that I didn't have time to take to the cleaners. At the table beside him John Hawthorne, a hand-

some young man in a tan suit, looks like an advertisement for
Brooks Brothers. He handles property work for the Slades, the
one couple from New York who bothered to show up here. Yesterday, when Cage and I met with Hawthorne at the jail, he
seemed like an astute, empathetic guy. He told us he would have
Cage out in a couple of days.

Mom and Dad are traveling in Ireland after a bishops' conference in Canterbury and I haven't been able to reach them. Cage
told me to stop trying. He wants to explain everything himself.
When he jerks his head around to look at me on the bench directly behind him, I raise my arm at the elbow and make a fist.
He doesn't smile. In a dark suit the prosecutor looks like a young
Marlon Brando. He rode up the cobblestone street on a Harley.
After the judge calls the hearing to order, when Brando stands up
to speak, he glares at Cage like he's looking at a hardened killer
and lists a litany of offenses—the checks, speeding tickets I didn't
know about, drunken antisocial behavior in bars, disrupting the
Sunday service at St. Paul's.

Brando calls Dr. Ian Lamb, the one psychiatrist on the island,
to testify whether Cage is sane enough to stand trial. Hawthorne
looks caught off guard. Cage told me that in a bar a few months
ago he had offended Dr. Lamb, telling him that every shrink he
had known socially was alcoholic or deeply fucked up in some
other way, but that yesterday Lamb had been friendly when they
spoke in his cell for fifteen minutes, mainly about Cage's travels in
Mexico. Forty-something and tan from afternoons on his fishing
boat, the good doctor has a kind, sad face.

"Mr. Rutledge has shown himself to be unpredictable and
prone to violence. In my professional opinion he is not fit to stand
trial," Dr. Lamb tells the court. "It is the best interest of the court
to remand him to Bridgewater for further evaluation. He could
well suffer from a deep-seated illness which accounts for his re-
cent erratic behavior."

Hawthorne objects and the judge steamrolls right over him.
Cage doesn't seem to understand what's happening any more
than I do. The hearing is moving too fast.

"I'm sorry I hit the officer," Cage stammers on the stand, his eyes full of fear. "I would be happy to do a long period of community service to make up for it. I'll cover those checks when I sell a sloop that's almost seaworthy. I've let things slip out of control and I'm sorry that others have suffered as a result. I very much wish to begin counseling."

Brando stresses that Cage is too dangerous to run loose on the island and calls again for a medical assessment. The judge orders Cage to be evaluated for forty days at Bridgewater State Mental Institution and ends the hearing. Hawthorne looks aghast and I realize that Bridgewater is not your average rehab clinic, which is where I was hoping Cage would end up. Suddenly I feel terrible about my collusion with the state.

"You dumb motherfucker," Cage tells me as two cops lead him, handcuffed, out of the court. "Why did you tell the cops where I was?"

The next day I follow Cage out to the airport in his Bronco and watch from a distance as two state troopers load him into a single-engine plane. I try calling Bridgewater and they will not even confirm that he is in the place.

Three days later I get a poem in the mail:

> *Dear Baudelaire,*
> *I am writing to you from the bowels of the earth,*
> *Where phantoms on glistening stallions*
> *Charge hi-yo silver away into mists forever forgotten.*
> *The only sound is the memory of the sound*
> *Of their hooves clanking against the cobblestone.*
> *I am in the jungle of mankind, lost without a face,*
> *Near death of self, my soul a lingering grimace*
> *Hanging untethered in space.*

I stay up all night reading it over, feeling like Judas Iscariot, and thinking about calling Mom and Dad, who are due to arrive in Memphis the next day. What a homecoming.

Cage

Beyond the barred windows, beneath a leaden sky, three rows of tall fences topped by razor wire encircle the grounds. The alley of grass between the outer fences is patrolled by rottweilers and German shepherds and a blue K9 patrol car. Inside the white room, twelve men in blue denim sit on plastic chairs in a semicircle while another inmate leads what's supposed to be a discussion but is usually a long silence punctuated by deranged musings apropos of nothing. A couple of Thorazine tadpoles squirm and list in slow motion around the room. An old grizzled guy named Ozanne keeps repeating softly, "Straightaway, straightaway, straightaway to heaven," then he laughs uproariously and points to the ceiling.

Welcome to Schizo Anonymous.

Alcoholics Anonymous, Narcotics Anonymous, Sex and Love Addicts Anonymous, Bipolar Anonymous, I go anywhere to get off the block and away from my cellmate, who murdered a state senator and a hooker and kept them in the trunk of his car for a week. They've yet to diagnose me, so I'm free to attend any group. I started the week on Max 2, the medical wing, but the first day, a giant named Barney told me he was going to rape me on the full moon, so at my first lunch I pocketed a butter knife, not knowing that they were counting. They searched us on the way out and by the end of the day I was moved into Max 1, in with the serious criminals.

"Cage, would you like to share anything with us?" the group leader asks. "What's on your mind?"

"Well, Bill. Let's see." I take a deep drag off a Camel. I started smoking in the week I've been in here and dream of walking into a restaurant and when asked, Smoking or nonsmoking? I'll reply,

Chain-smoking, please. Little vice I picked up in the nuthouse. I blow a smoke ring. I discovered a natural knack for smoke rings. "I keep wondering what the fuck I'm doing in this cage with a bunch of criminal lunatics—ax murderers, grandma-rapers, dog torturers, cat buggerers, sadists, masochists. One moment I'm a carpenter on Nantucket getting more pussy than Jim Morrison and the next I'm in this dungeon which would make the pit of Dante's hell look like a tailgate party at the Super Bowl."

Some of the nuts cackle.

"Do you have anything constructive to say?" Bill is very patient. He speaks in a caressive, womanly cadence.

"Well, I keep telling myself it's a bad dream, worst fucking nightmare of my life, and I'm going to wake up soon." I blow a ring within a ring, figure if I make it out alive, I'll be able to blow a third through the second.

Bill's opening his mouth to say something *constructive* when Ozanne comes out of his private nightmare and asks, "Do you think Jesus was a schizophrenic?"

"Whah?" someone says, while the others laugh. Half the group stops drooling to denigrate the question. Schizo Anonymous is most animated in group criticism.

"What kind of question was that?"

"Ozanne, you're in the ozone."

"Of all the retarded remarks."

"Now, hold on, fellows." Bill tries uselessly to guide the group back to a therapeutic exchange.

"Straightaway, straightaway, straightaway," Rey Rosa, a Latino from Boston, mocks him.

"Straight to hell, straight to hell, straight to hell," an arsonist who looks like an accountant chants in a high, abrasive voice.

I reach over and offer Ozanne a cigarette.

Ozanne smiles and sticks the cigarette between his lips. Within seconds it's covered in spittle.

"Silence!" Bill yells, a little red in the face. "This is not *constructive.*"

Rey Rosa is up on his feet dancing around Ozanne. "If Jesus was a schizophrenic, maybe we should invite him to the group."

"Then it would be a revival." The arsonist titters.

"Straightaway, straightaway." Reynolds, who'd thrown his mother from a balcony, joins in the chorus.

Ozanne sticks out his chin and yells, "Well, Jesus said he was God *and* man!"

That silences them. Even the most deranged, street-born schizos can utter truth. I start clapping.

I call 'em Jacks. You can't go a half hour without seeing one. In the shower, in the bathroom, in the cells, in the doorways, inside, outside, on the ball field, furtively or in full view. At any given minute there must be three hundred guys jacking off to fantasies too horrific to ponder. No telling what's going on in the women's wing. At any given minute three hundred Jacks putting their drool to good use, lubricating their lunatic cocks like randy chimpanzees, enough for thirty self-help sex addicts groups. Unified, the Jacks could take over the joint. If I wasn't crazy when I arrived, I will be by the end of the evaluation.

I'm in the library typing a letter to Sylvia, who wrote she would sell her Saab to pay for a good lawyer, when Rey Rosa walks up with another Latino and starts reading over my shoulder. Turning my head, I ask him, "May I help you?"

"You like to write, don't you?" His eyes are black holes that suck in the light from the room.

"Look, amigo, I'm just minding my own business."

I turn around and start typing. He is breathing in my ear, his breath rancid as dead fish. "Dearest Sylvia," he reads in a faggy voice. "How in God's name did I end up in this hell?"

I lean away. "This is a private letter."

He pops me right in the eye. I elbow him in the gut but it glances off and he smashes my face into the keys. I come onto my feet, screaming and turning over the table, and manage to lift the chair and swing it at him but he jumps clear.

The other Latino stands a few feet away, shouting, "Hit him, Vincente. Kill the cracker!" The inmates at the other tables turn their backs.

I keep swinging the chair around, screaming, "Security!"

Rey Rosa manages to kick one of my legs out from under me and I fall, then scramble under a table, come up on the other side, and flip it over, still shouting. Rey Rosa and his buddy come toward me. The other inmates are quietly picking up their books and walking away. Finally four screws in tan uniforms come running in and tackle all three of us. They put Rey Rosa and me in solitary. It's a dark cell with a sheetless mattress and a toilet without a seat. I feel safe for the first time in days, then the next morning I start doubting they will ever let me out. They do in the afternoon. Walking past Rey Rosa's cell, I see him strapped down, wrenching against restraints and howling.

When I finally make it into the evaluating psych's office, some sort of trusty is sitting behind his desk, a shrimp dressed in lumberjack flannel despite the summer heat. He wipes his mouth with a filthy handkerchief. "Sit down, Mr. Rutledge."

I sit down and take out my packet of Camels.

"No smoking," the man grunts.

"Where's Dr. Willcox?" I ask.

The man looks around the room, sticks his head under the desk, then pops up, smiling. "That's me."

I sit there, stunned. Lunatics are running the asylum.

"Do you know why you're here?" He dabs the brown hankie against his lips.

"Forty days' evaluation to see if I'm competent to stand trial for resisting arrest, assaulting a cop, destruction of public property, and passing bad checks."

"That's correct. Do you think you're competent to stand trial?"

"No doubt about it, Doc."

"Dr. Willcox." His grin reveals particles of food stuck between his yellow teeth. "Why did you assault the policeman?"

"Dr. Willcox, I was stressed-out. I have a lot of debts. I've bounced a lot of checks." My hand trembles, putting the pack of Camels back in my shirt pocket. "But I hadn't done anything to merit being hauled into jail and then this cop shoved me from behind and I exploded."

Willcox stares at a folder on his desk. "You consulted the Nan-tucket mental health service prior to your arrest. Why?"

I tilt my head back and take a deep breath. "I was having prob-lems sleeping and concentrating. My thoughts raced along at the speed of light but I've calmed down a lot since I've been here. I think I just needed to catch up on my sleep. Those green pills they give us at night zonk me out. I think I just needed to sleep for a long spell."

"Hmph." Willcox scribbles something in the folder. "You seem to have a propensity for violence."

"No, sir. I told you. I was just stressed-out and snapped. My friends and family will tell you that I'm not in the least violent."

"Yet you attempted to steal a knife your first day here and yes-terday you got in a fight in the library."

"Doctor, I took the knife because this guy Barney who could play fullback for the Patriots told me he was going to rape me." I struggle to keep my voice calm. Does this doctor ever walk the halls? "In the library a guy from Schizo Anonymous punched me in the eye for no reason. I was simply trying to make enough noise to get the screws—I mean the correction officers—to rescue me. *I* haven't started any fights. I just try to mind my own business, get along."

"Well, you certainly seem to be rational and calm now." Will-cox shuts the folder. "I enjoyed our chat. See you again soon."

Raven, the double murderer who bunks below me, is out getting electroshock treatment, so I'm in the cell skipping the group meetings, reading Faulkner to remind me of my roots. *The Un-vanquished.* Shit. Those two boys never spent any time in a Yankee nuthouse. See how unvanquished they'd be after a week in this place. On the corridor outside, two old inseparable, indistin-guishable black guys known as Amos and Andy, trusties who stick together like Siamese twins, are clattering mops and buckets.

"Ever spied how crabs act in a bushel basket?"

"I 'pose I seen some crabs 'fore in a basket."

"You remark how they act?"

"Reckon they ac' how they always ac'."

"How's that?"

"Crabby."

"Heh, heh, heh. You ain't observe 'em too close."

"Never knowed you was a scientist yo'self. When you making a big study o' crabs anyhow?"

"Back in Carolina, tíme I's knee-high to katydid."

"Surprise' you ken 'member that fah back. So, how's crabs ac' in a bushel basket?"

"Well, when one of 'em crabs works his way from out de bottom of de basket all way through the rest 'em crabs till he reaches the rim and he's about to climb on out, other crabs gang up 'gether and pull his spiky ass right back in."

The Value of Money
1968

Bristol, Tennessee. In the foothills of the Appalachians, Cloudland Drive circled through a neighborhood of colonial two-stories and low-slung Frank Lloyd Wright caricatures situated on wide, shady lawns. The rectory was a large gray-shingled split-level with a maroon front door. On a steep slope flanking it the new rector had built a tree house on stilts like a little fire tower. Nick, seven now, came down a rope ladder hanging from a trapdoor, then climbed up the mossy slope to the driveway that wound around behind the house.

He went inside through the kitchen door, then passed through the dining room, living room, and sitting room, looking for his mother. He followed the sound of the TV up the stairs and found her at the ironing board beside an overflowing laundry basket.

"Hello, Nickfish." She wiped sweat off her forehead with the back of her hand, glancing at the TV, where a casket was being unloaded from a hearse in a sea of black people. "Martin Luther King. He was a minister like your father. Killed by a bad, bad man. Such a shame."

"Why?" Nick stared at the procession.

"For trying to help the Negro people. It's a tragedy."

"Does Daddy try to help the Negro people?" Nick rested his hand lightly on his mother's leg.

She smoothed his hair. "Yes, your daddy has organized a march to remember Martin Luther King. Someday you'll understand how brave your daddy is."

"Will bad men kill him?"

"No," Margaret said. She set the iron upright and bent down
to hug him. "No one will hurt your daddy. Okay?"

"Okay." He nodded.

"How 'bout an Eskimo kiss?"

He rubbed his nose against hers.

"Lord, I have so much to do." She stood up. "All this ironing. We have to drive across town to pick up Cage. Then there's
dinner. And we've run out of milk."

Nick said, "I'm going back to the tree house."

"Okay, honey." She fit one of Frank's shirts on the tapered
end of the ironing board.

Nick went downstairs into the kitchen and opened the refrigerator. Nothing caught his eye. He walked slowly to the sink
and looked up at the windowsill, where the school milk money
stayed in two plastic change wallets, round ovals with splits
down the middle that opened when you squeezed them, a red
one for Nick and blue one for Cage. He hoisted his knees on the
counter and reached over the sink, took two quarters from the
red one, put it back on the sill, and dropped to the floor with a
thump. Holding his breath, he looked over his shoulder at the
sitting room door.

Nick ran outside, circled the house, and streaked across the
front lawn, over the soggy low spot above the septic tank, worrying for a moment that his mother might see him from the upstairs window, and down the bank to Cloudland Drive, then up
the hill, past Martin Parks's house to the Ridgeway Road. He
ran down Ridgeway, past the McInneys', where older boys were
playing football, to the bottom of the hill. A quarter mile from
home he stopped to catch his breath. He knew what he was
doing was wrong. He knew that he would be caught. But he
also knew that somehow he would get away with it. Subcon-
sciously he wagered that the pleasure would be greater than
the punishment. Between hills, Forest Avenue was a busy road
that ran in a straight flat line. Out of breath, Nick walked on
the shoulder, deliberately keeping three feet from the cars that
whizzed past.

Pucket's was a little red clapboard store with a gravel lot. At the sound of the bell attached to the door, Mrs. Pucket looked up from a magazine and said, "Howdy, young feller."

The sight of the grandmotherly woman jolted Nick with a pang of conscience, and he shuffled across the unpainted floorboards deeper into the dim light, where dust floated in shafts of sun angling from the dirty windows to the racks of candy. Silently he surveyed the array. He glanced at Mrs. Pucket, who was absorbed in the magazine. He pulled his hand from his pocket, counted the hot, damp change, then chose his favorite, two long thin straps of taffy in wrappers with pictures from the *Archie* comic strips, and carried them to the counter, which was taller than him.

Mrs. Pucket's head appeared over the edge. "You'ins mighty quiet today. Cat got your tongue?"

Nick had never understood that expression. He said, "No, ma'am."

Mrs. Pucket laughed. "You shore are cute. Look at 'em big brown eyes. Where'd you get those big eyes?"

"The zoo." Nick wasn't sure why he said that.

Mrs. Pucket's laugh sounded much like a cough. "That'll be twenty cents."

Nick was glad that he had a quarter left over to put back in the purse. Maybe he wouldn't be caught after all. He thanked her and left. Outside, Lyman and Otto Jospin, two skinny boys in dirty clothes, were throwing rocks at a trash can. Their father was a gravedigger and they lived in a trailer in the cemetery behind Pucket's. Pausing, Lyman and Otto stared at Nick, who smiled and hurried past. Walking along Forest Avenue, he ate one of the pieces of taffy, then zipped the other in a pocket of his camping shorts.

A station wagon pulled up. Jimbo Eppers leaned out the passenger window and said, "Hey, Nick. Been to Pucket's?"

Nick stopped and put his hands in his pockets. "Yeah."

"Whadya get?"

"Nothing."

Jimbo's mother leaned across the seat. "Nick, dahlin', does your mother know you're down here by yourself?"

"Maybe. It's okay."

"Get in, honey. I'll give you a ride."

"No thank you."

"Get in the car this minute, young man."

"Yes, ma'am." He had to use both hands to pull the door open.

The drive home was very short. Mrs. Eppers parked the white station wagon behind his mother's brown one, which was nearly identical, both with wood decal siding and long silver roof racks.

"I think I'll see how Margaret's holding up," Mrs. Eppers said, dashing Nick's hopes that she would drop him off and drive away. She quickly stepped out of the car and walked in the house through the sitting room door without knocking, calling out, "Mars!"

"You're going to get licked," Jimbo said.

Nick jumped out of the car and ran through the garage and opened the kitchen door. He looked both ways quickly. The kitchen was empty. He was up on the counter, on his knees, placing the little wallet back on the sill when the women walked in. For a moment, glancing over his shoulder, it was hard to tell them apart. Their short dark hair was held back by bands, and they wore tapered slacks that came to their ankles and sleeveless cotton shirts. Mrs. Eppers was trying not to smile and his mother's face was red with anger. Nick lowered himself down to the linoleum floor.

"Nicholas Rutledge, where have you been?"

Nick muttered, "Around."

"Did you go to Pucket's?"

Nick was silent.

"Nick, tell me the truth."

"Yes, ma'am." Nick squeezed his lips into a curvy line.

"I've got to get home and make dinner," Mrs. Eppers said, backing out of the room.

"Thanks, Nancy." His mother crossed the floor and knelt by him.

"Nick, what were you thinking?" Her voice was gentle. She put her hand on his shoulder.

Nick was silent. He looked at his feet, shrugged.

"Nick, you know you're not supposed to walk to Pucket's on your own, a little boy like you. Some bad people might get you."

"Who?"

"Strangers. There are bad people in the world."

Nick glanced up at her face, back at his feet.

"Do you understand?"

"Yes, ma'am." He looked in her eyes and saw that she wasn't angry but worried. "I won't go again by myself."

"You took your milk money, didn't you?"

"Yes, ma'am."

"Oh, Nick, how could you?" She shook her head, put her hand to her brow, and squinted. "We're not like the Eppers. We don't have much money. You can't buy candy whenever you want. You won't be able to buy milk at school. Do you see?"

"Taffy tastes better."

She shook him by the shoulders. "Nick. There's not enough money. We don't have enough money." She raised her voice. "I don't know how we're going to pay our bills. We might run out of money. God, there's never enough money. There's simply not enough. Never enough. Your father doesn't make enough money. They don't pay ministers enough."

Nick had turned his head. His mother was sobbing. She stopped shaking him and held him close. "Oh, Nickfish, I'm so sorry. It's not your fault. Okay?" She looked at him brightly, smiled through tears, her cheeks wet. "You're too young to realize the value of money."

Margaret

Nantucket is like a newly born place. Part of it is the wind from the ocean, and I'm sure the flowers are so beautiful because of all the moisture, but *every* flower—most of them are flowers I'm familiar with and many of them are flowers we grow in the South—is more lush. Just fresher. The yellow Scotch broom is in bloom. It's a shrub up here. I'd only seen it in flower arrangements and to see it growing is thrilling. Annuals like nasturtiums are wonderful and the perennials, like hollyhocks, are just spectacular. And then those beach roses, the *Rosa rugosa*, a pink rose that almost grows wild up here. But the best thing of all is the roses growing up on the rooftops. I've never *seen* anything like that. I borrow Harper's bicycle and ride and ride, looking around for the roses covering the rooftops. I do believe Nantucket is one of the most exquisite places in terms of its climate and visual beauty.

The first morning, exploring Siasconset on the bicycle, I saw the town tennis court and I peered through the shrubs. It was like being in a dream. The ladies had on big straw hats and long white linen skirts and their blouses had big leg-o'-mutton sleeves. The men were wearing long white linen pants and elegant white linen shirts. Just enchanted, I watched them playing and thought, Oh my goodness, this is the world of a hundred years ago, and I felt really weepy, thinking, Oh, I don't want Cage to be in trouble. I want him to make a place for himself up here so I can become a part of this world. Later Beth Slade tells me they were filming the tennis players in period costume for an ad but I didn't see any people with cameras. Nobody else was watching.

There's a tragic irony in Cage going to jail in Nantucket two years to the day after Nick died in San Francisco. I was bracing myself for the anniversary of his death, and Cage's news caught me off guard and brought a double sadness rushing into my heart like a winter wind. The three weeks in England were the first time since his death that I was able to laugh aloud. Nick was the son closest to my heart. Where Cage and Harper resemble their father physically with their blue eyes, Nick had my dark hair and eyes and the shape of my face and my quiet temperament. When he was tiny, I would take him to the Junior League and church committee meetings and give him a little toy and he would entertain himself quietly for an hour, never a nuisance. He was the most loving one, the one I could always count on. A mother may love all her children equally but there is one to whom she feels a special bond. This was the one God took from me and I suppose there is a lesson in that.

Nothing is sadder than parents burying their own child. Nick was cremated and we spread his ashes off the top of Roan Mountain in North Carolina where Franklin had taken the boys hiking from the time they could walk. Like any brothers born so close, Cage and Nick fought often in their adolescence but they loved each other fiercely. Cage wept the whole way walking up the mountain and after Franklin read the committal service and we scattered the ashes, Cage stood on the edge of the cliff for a long time as if he might follow Nick into the abyss.

Now it seems as if he has.

A few minutes after Franklin and I walked in the door back home in Memphis, jet-lagged from the long flights, the phone rang and the operator said it was a collect call from the Bridgewater State Mental Institution. At first I thought it was one of Cage's jokes. But when they put Cage through, I knew it was real from the desperation in his voice. He tried to sound upbeat, asked about our journey, and when I asked him why on earth he was in a mental hospital, he said, "I don't know, Mom. I haven't done anything wrong," and he started crying. He sounded like a little boy, just pitiful. I asked him what the hospital was like and he replied, "You don't want to know. You wouldn't be able to sleep."

Perhaps I should have waited for Franklin to get over the terrible flu that he picked up crossing the ocean—he started vomiting on the leg from Atlanta to Memphis—but trying to be brave and spare him, I decided to come up here by myself. The afternoon I arrived Harper took me to the house, where the yard was full of funny old boats and paint cans. We worked and worked for days to clean up before the owners arrived. Oh, those people, when they got there, they were so cool to me. This is cruel, I thought. Mrs. Taylor thinks that I'm responsible, that I haven't been a good mother or he wouldn't have turned out like this. There's a lesson there somewhere. Never transfer your anger from one person to another.

I spoke to the lawyer that Harper had hired, a boy just out of law school who was apologetic about the terrible outcome, and I spoke to the psychiatrist who had sent Cage off to Bridgewater, a curt man who had trouble looking me in the eye. He said that he suspected that Cage was manic-depressive. That was shocking news to me and Harper, for we had been certain that Cage dropping out of Vanderbilt so close to finishing and all his wild behavior on Nantucket were a result of his depression over Nick's death. I asked if a traumatic event could trigger a manic episode and he said quite possibly.

On visiting day I fly to Hyannis and rent a car. You can get a good deal on a day rental. Bridgewater is a big, fearful-looking place. I park and go inside the waiting room. I'm sure I have everything but *First Time* written on my chest. The waiting room is unpleasant and the staff who ask if they can help you are these hardened people. They tell me I'm early and can't see Cage until midafternoon. A matronly woman who has visited someone inside and is on her way out sees that I'm flustered and comes up and says, "Would you like to go and have lunch somewhere and I will tell you what I know?"

We go to a pizza place in a little shopping center not too far away and she tells me that she's a schoolteacher and comes *every week* to see the man who was her fiancé, a high school principal and very upstanding citizen, an absolute straight arrow. Every day he visited his parents, who were elderly and didn't have much money. He was very concerned what would happen to them if something should happen to him and he decided the best thing to do was not let that happen. He went to their apartment and shot both of them. So he's in the facility for life. The story fills me with a hopeless feeling. I ask his diagnosis and she tells me that he's bipolar, manic-depressive, which is shocking, for I had no idea that manic-depressives could be so violent. She tells me that once you get in Bridgewater, it's very hard for the family to get you out. I think, Well, I have to start working on that right away.

I adhere to the hints of the schoolteacher, who told me to get to the waiting room early so I can be at the front of the line and to get in as quickly as possible because the time passes so fast. She told me to tell my son to be polite to the guards, not to talk back, and to keep a low profile, which has always been hard for Cage to do. They lead us into a big room with all these tables and chairs. It's a shock to see Cage come out dressed like a criminal in blue denim. His hair hasn't been so long since he was a teenager. When he sees me, his face lights up like a tiny child thrilled to see a parent.

"Hey, Mama." Hugging me, he smells like he could use a shower. "Welcome to the nuthouse."

"Oh, son." I manage to smile and hold back the tears. "Is it as awful as it looks?"

"Wretched beyond words." He laughs and sits down across a small table. "I stole a butter knife and for six days they had me in Maximum 1, sharing a cell with a double murderer."

Cage must see the horror on my face because he touches my hand and says, "Don't worry, Mom, after I met with the shrink in charge, they moved me back to the med wing, Max 2. Where's Pop?"

"He'll come next week. He has a terrible flu, can't keep anything down. The break was so good for him. He's been stressed-out. The diocese might be torn asunder by extremists on both sides."

"Fags and bigots," Cage says.

"That's not polite."

"Okay, homos and homophobes." Cage shakes his head at the

absurdity. "Yeah, well, Pop doesn't need to see his firstborn locked up like an animal. How's Grandmother?"

"She's fine. She told me to tell you that she loves you and is praying for you."

"I'm sorry to do this to y'all. But there's been a mistake. I don't belong here."

I put my hand on his. "I know. We'll get you out. Just hang on."

"I'm not sure how long I can hang on." He looks around the room, lowers his voice. "The guards are worse than the inmates. They scream and spit and kick you. They don't like me. They don't like southerners. Once a day we go out on the ball field. There's a tree near a fence. I think I could climb it. Make a run for it."

"Cage, I know one bit of advice I'm going to give you. Don't try that or you're going to be here for a long time." I squeeze his hand. "Remember what your great-grandmother would say: 'You've got to take hold.' "

"Mama, I wasn't crazy when I got here. I don't know why they had to send me here." He looks so much like a frightened little boy that it just breaks my heart. He starts to cry. "But I'm going to be crazy if they keep me in here. These crazy inmates start fights with me. When I'm out on the ball field, I see them huddling together, pointing at me. They know I'm different. They know I don't belong here."

"We know you don't belong here, too, Cage. We're doing all we can to get you out. You'll be out soon. Just pray for deliverance." I want to cry but I know I must appear strong to help him stay strong. I reach across the table and cup his face with my hands, and thinking about what the teacher told me, I say, "We're going to get you out."

Cage

Leaving the visiting room, I wipe the tears on my sleeve and set my face. I pretend I'm tough, pull my shoulders back, set my lips together tight, try to emit a don't-fuck-with-me vibe. Sometimes I try to be invisible. We walk in a line with screws at the front and the rear down the long white corridor. The whole place is white, every hallway, cellblock, meeting room. White. The absence of color. After ten days I'm going snow-blind. Seeing Mom in her green summer dress brings home how far away I am, how deep I've descended into white hell. The shame of a mother coming to visit you in a lockup—imagine your mother catching you jerking off and multiply times a thousand. But praise Jesus for parents. Home is the one place you can count on. Mom and Dad are my only hope. Sylvia has not replied to my last letter and has stopped accepting my phone calls. The last time we talked, she said her parents had told her not to get involved. So much for love.

The line halts at an electric door. A man behind thick, scratched glass nods at the screws and buzzes it open, then we walk through. The sound of it sliding shut nearly triggers another round of tears. Thirty days, I repeat silently. Just thirty days. The screw stops at a T-junction, the corridors that run to Max 1 and Max 2, and divides us into two lines. I'm at the front of Max 2.

"Move it out."

Barney the Giant is sweeping the linoleum with a big push broom. I try to look past him. He stands up straight and runs his hand up and down the broom. "Yo, pretty boy, you watching the moon? Gonna be full next week. Not long now."

"Shut the fuck up, Barney," a screw says.

The reek of madness and misery seeps through the heavy doors and fills the white hallway for a hundred feet, growing stronger with each step. Max 2 is a warehouse for the mindless nuts. The ones who sleep in their shit and have to be bathed with a fire hose. I almost gag when the doors open and the cellblock exhales a stench like the wind off a dump, carrying the noise of a thousand maniacs. Moaning. Howling. Singing. Conversations with God. Dialogues with Satan. Soliloquies to the quick and the dead. It's only quiet in the evening after they've tranqued every-body. The screws stand aside to let us pass.

An old man floats by, catching invisible butterflies with an invisible net, who, if you believe the screws, was a Harvard lepidopterist who mounted one of his students under glass. I walk slowly down the white hall, looking for Mike, the single other semi-sane inmate on the floor, to see if he got the new *Newsweek* and kill some time discussing current events. I glance in the TV room, where a crowd is watching *Atlantic Professional Wrestling*, Horrible Hogan and the Exterminator, by far the most popular show in Max 2. The violent crims of Max 1 prefer *Cops*.

"I have to see my doctor," a wizened little man tells me. "I have to see my doctor."

"It's Saturday," I say. "I don't think they're on duty."

"I haven't seen my doctor for twelve years."

I look at a screw standing nearby. He smiles at me and nods.

"That's true?" I ask.

"Hell, yeah, cracker boy. You think you in the fucking Mayo Clinic? You in the Land of the Lost here, boy." He laughs and moves down the hall, singing "Whistle While You Work."

"You seen Mike?" I ask a tall crew-cut guy standing by the door.

He turns his head slowly toward me from the TV. "Hulk Hogan is breaking us out tonight. Just before dawn. He's coming through the TV."

"I'll be here," I say, backing up.

"Make sure it's on channel thirteen," he whispers, putting a forefinger to his lips.

Down the hall a large man with a noble face and a mane of black hair is gesticulating forcefully, punching holes in the air, his voice booming. "The greatest weapons to fight communism are not missiles but Big Macs. A McDonald's in every city will make the world safe for democracy."

"Mr. Speaker." I wave.

"I recognize our distinguished colleague from south of the Mason-Dixon." He smiles beneficently.

"Haven't you seen the news? We're going to win! Communism is crumbling. It's the dawn of People Power." Passing by, I pat him on the back. "Poland, East Germany, China, the workers are rising again."

His eyes fill with fury and his hand shakes as he points at me. "An agitator!" he screams. "An agitator in our midst. Don't let him escape."

Farther down the white hall, a man sits on the floor, his head between his knees, weeping. Behind him, in a cell, a man is filling a tin cup with excrement, scooping it off the floor. In the next cell a Jack is going at it fast and furious to a photograph of a beagle. I close my eyes and keep walking. We are not responsible for what others do, I think. But are we somehow responsible for what we make ourselves see?

At the end of the corridor Mike's cell is empty. I sit on a bench and look down to the other end, the nuts gradually diminishing in size until the ones at the far end are denim stick figures. Speaker is raising a clenched fist. The lepidopterist's arms are akimbo, beating his wings. The long white corridor becomes the red cinder straight of an oval track. The noise and the stench fade into silence, the nuts blur and disappear. Papa was walking hand in hand with Nick and me, about eight and nine, leading us to the soft foam mattress in the pole vault pit, where we jumped like it was a trampoline while he ran his laps, waving each time he passed.

"Straightaway, straightaway, straightaway to heaven." I open my eyes and see a guy from Schizo Anonymous a few inches from my face, pointing to the white ceiling. He laughs and laughs, hugging his sides like he's freezing.

"You're just a lunatic," I say softly. "Just a fucking lunatic."

He stops laughing and makes a peace sign. "Thanks for that cigarette."

*   *   *

"Up shit creek without a paddle, as they used to say," a voice whispers. I come awake with a start, then keep perfectly still. The room is dark, save a faint glow through the bars. The hallway beyond is quiet. Pringle is snoring on the bunk below. My spine tingles. The voice is familiar, one I haven't heard in a long time. I wonder if I'm dreaming.

"Events sort of got out of your control, swept you along like a flash flood, and dumped you in this place." The voice is coming from the end of the bed. I'm too scared to move. I know that voice almost as well as I know my own. "Well, it's a better place than where I am."

"Nick?" I whisper. "Is it really you?"

"It ain't the bogeyman."

I raise up on my elbows and see a figure sitting on the end of the bunk, dangling its legs over the edge. "Am I dreaming?"

"That's not the right question. There's a fine line between waking and dreaming, life and death, sanity and madness. Who's to say what's real?"

"I must be dreaming."

"You must be . . . or maybe not."

"I'm sorry, brother. I didn't mean to kill you."

"Don't worry about it. It wasn't *really* your fault. It's kind of too late in the game but I forgive you. Okay? Feel better?"

"Is that why I'm here?"

"That's one way of looking at it. Sort of simplistic, though."

"What's it like being dead?"

"Beyond the mirror of your imagination."

"I miss you, Nick. Every damn day. No one knows me like you did."

"I'm with you, brother. Wherever you go. Following you like a fart."

"That's nice to know. Have you seen Poppy?"

"Went fishing with him the other day."

"Fishing? Where?"

"Where else? Old Hickory Lake. You can only go places that you've been."

"Jugs or poles?"

"Poles. Caught a whole mess of bass. But he likes to throw them back now."

"Will you tell him that I love him?"

"He knows that, Cage."

"Can you help me get out of here?" I sit up, lean my back against the cold wall. Nick is transparent, the hallway light filtering through him. I can't make out his features.

"Like what, help you escape? You shouldn't try to escape." His jaw doesn't move when he talks.

"Maybe you could write an order for my release and put it in the right tray."

Nick laughs. "I wish I could help you, Cage. I would if I could. But it's beyond my parameters."

"Nick, is there life after death?"

"I wouldn't exactly call it life."

"Are you in purgatory?"

"No such thing."

"Have you seen the face of God?"

"We're not allowed to talk about that."

"Can you give me a hint?"

"No. Listen, I've got to go. Take hold, Cage, you'll be all right. You won't be here forever. Take my advice and don't tell anyone I was here. They'll think you're crazy."

Then he's gone.

"Nick, come back." I crawl to the end of the bed to see if he had left an imprint on the blanket, and it's flat. "Nick, come back." I wipe tears from my eyes. "Nick!"

"Shut up, you crazy cracker," Pringle says groggily from the bed below. He kicks the mattress. "Don't make me get out of this bed and bust up your face."

"I must have had a nightmare," I say, lying back down.

"Save it for group." Pringle kicks the bed again. "I don't care if you dreamed you were locked in a nuthouse."

Franklin

"If this is the way God treats his friends, no wonder he has so few." St. Theresa of Avila's words resound in my head like the refrain of a hymn, over and over, as I sit down in the kitchen to put on my fortieth, maybe fiftieth, new pair of New Balance, which became my brand in the seventies when Cage swore by them in high school. I wear out a pair every three months, mail-order them quarterly from Runner's Warehouse. The kettle whistles and I rush across the kitchen in one shoe to take it from the burner before it wakes Margaret, who's emotionally exhausted from her trip to Massachusetts. The clock on the stove shows five-thirty. I pour the water over a tea bag and pick up the steaming mug with a picture of a grizzled cowboy and a quotation: *There's a lot of things they didn't tell me when I signed on with this outfit.*

First Nick's death. Now Cage's crack-up. After nearly thirty years of consoling grieving families, after countless accidents, sudden heart attacks, long, slow deaths, hundreds of thousands of hours in hospital rooms sitting with families while the doctors trooped in to recommend further futile treatments whose only tangible results would be protracting the pain and bankrupting the families, I don't know where to look for solace. The trials of Job.

I carry the tea out the back door into the garden. The sky is lightening the palest pink. Warblers, jays, and cardinals are singing as if all is right with the world. I single out my favorite—the ethereal flutelike *ee-o-lay* of the wood thrush. A foreign song, without human meaning, without human feeling, Harper, my youngest, the atheist, would say. After stretching, fifty sit-ups, and twenty-five push-ups, I leave the garden through the gate by the carport and jog up the street toward the country club parking lot.

God has blessed me with good knees. Even after thirty-five years of daily running, after most of my peers have given up jogging for swimming or golf, my knobby old fellows are going strong. Hitting the golf course, I commence my morning prayers. "Almighty and most merciful Father, we have erred and strayed from Thy ways like lost sheep, we have followed too much the devices and desires of our own hearts, we have offended against Thy holy laws," but I break off, remembering Nick as a long-haired, gap-toothed teenager. He came home once from a matinee, a movie set in the future where the world was so polluted all the trees had died, so affected that he spent the rest of the afternoon picking up trash for a mile along the street outside the rectory where we lived in Virginia. Why did You take him so young, so idealistic? Or was it You who took him?

The trees cast long shadows over the fairways beneath the bluing sky as the sun simmers the humidity into a sticky broth. My sweat has soaked through my shirt. I stop trying to pray and follow the high ivy-covered brick wall that encircles the club. Was it something we did, some failure as parents? Through grammar school and junior high, Cage had been the bright one, always one of the top students in his class, a leader, the captain of the football team, while Nick was the shy underperformer. In the first grade Nick had refused to learn to read. He simply didn't want to. In fourth grade, after refusing to do his homework for a week, his teacher whipped him in front of the whole class. That would never happen nowadays, but it worked. He started turning his homework in on time.

Then a clear reversal occurred in high school when we moved from Virginia to Louisiana. Cage became a B student, while Nick logged straight As, was elected president of his class. Cage grew into a mercurial young man, often storming away from the dinner table or the Christmas tree, dissatisfied with his presents, with his lot in life as the son of a clergyman, while his friends got new cars, stereo players, ski trips. Nick was quiet, the peacemaker. The pattern continued on through college. Nick's grades never slipped, while Cage's continued to drop. Cage graduated without a clue as to what he wanted to do, without a sense of purpose. I think the professors at Sewanee these days are as morally confused as Cage is. I suppose Cage was doing drugs.

Marijuana. Cocaine. LSD. They are just names to me. Or even reliable ol' alcohol. What else would set loose Cage's illness? Manic depression. It seems to me the culture of rock and roll music has accounted more than anything else for the moral decline of American society, distracted our children from the serious business of life. When I was growing up, kids didn't blow their minds on drugs and stay out all night listening to music that impairs their eardrums. In the Great Depression everyone was working hard to get by, better themselves, make something out of their lives. Nowadays kids have it too easy. All they're interested in is excitement.

Harper came along nine years after Nick. He was the only one we planned. Margaret badly wanted one more child. He would be perfect, the one with whom she would apply everything that she had learned from raising the first two. She wouldn't make the same mistakes. But Harper turned out to be an angry child.

Across the link Malachi, who looks as old as Methuselah, comes out of a barn on a riding mower, which calls up the image of an old Negro on a mule in Arkansas in the thirties. Every Tuesday, Malachi's and my paths intersect on the eighteenth fairway. Malachi waves and turns along in the same direction, yelling above the engine noise, "Mo'nin', Bishop."

"Morning, Mal. Another scorcher."

"It gets any hotter than yesaday, they gonna have get me some special inshunce for sunstroke, yes suh. Don't sees how you stan' to run."

"Got to suffer a little to stay healthy."

"I know Jesus promised eternal life. Looks to me like you's aiming to have it right here on earth."

"Hell, I ain't that old, Malachi."

"Nah suh, but you ain't that young neitherway be out here at the crack o' dawn every mo'nin'."

Reaching the iron fence, I say, "Good morning to you, sir."

"Always a pleasure talking to you, suh." Malachi grins and turns the mower in the opposite direction.

I remember that today is a diocesan executive committee meeting with the Integrity chapter. Those fellows. They are growing so adversarial one day they'll split the entire Episcopal church. The Great Gay Schism. They are never satisified with our attempts to accommodate them pastorally. That's what I find so frustrating. I empathize with the plea of the homosexually oriented person that they have been excluded from the life of the church and I have tried to make them a part of the Body of Christ, to incorporate them into the community. Regardless of what I do, it's not enough. They want to make everything a legal issue. This year it's blessing same-sex unions, which diametrically opposes the teachings of the church on holy matrimony. I don't know what to do except to liturgically recognize fidelity practiced between same sexes. But you cannot call it marriage. Hell, it ain't marriage. And what will they want next year?

I wish I was hiking alone along a high, cool ridgetop, deep in the Appalachians.

Harper

In late August the Magic Hour comes earlier and doesn't last as long. Late in the day, up high on a ladder on the side of an old shingled two-story, I watch gulls wheel and shriek over the shore. I look across the water at the gray horizon as if I can see Cage locked up in the asylum. The more I think about it, the more Cage's crack-up scares me. Can I suddenly go crazy? Can I change into a conniving, charming con man? For all I know I'm carrying the bipolar time bomb.

I still feel terrible about telling the police where they could find Cage. When Dad was up here in July, he told me that I did the right thing, that there was no way to know that the judge would throw him into that hellhole. Mama has been up three or four times over the summer. She is a stoic. Each time, she's come back from Bridgewater shaken up by the scary place and more determined that we will get him out soon. She despises the lawyer in Bridgewater. "He is a coarse man, well acquainted with the system and clever. But, my land, is he coarse. He is not a gentleman. Never forget you are a gentleman, Harper. Manners are morals." I scrape peeling paint under the eaves and think about that. It seems erroneous to me; a perfectly mannered man could be a crook. Manners are exterior forms, habits of good behavior, at best an awareness and consideration of others. But are they morals? Yes, if fine manners means thinking of others before yourself, then it is a moral imperative. Like love thy neighbor. Mama expects me to be a Christian gentleman.

It would have been good manners for me to have gone to Bridgewater with her but I used work as an excuse because I was ashamed to see Cage, since I felt like I had put him there. I keep making up my mind to go to the mainland on the next visiting day, then wussing out.

Bipolar. Manic-depressive. I thought Cage was simply being selfish and partying too much, that he'd gone over the deep end. Dr. Lamb told Mom and me that he was self-medicating. After her first visit to Bridgewater, Mom insisted on seeing him again, scheduled an appointment. He wasn't apologetic about his recommendation to send Cage for an evaluation. He said, Cage had shown a capacity for violence; the legal system required his evaluation. I felt like punching him in the nose. Mom responded, I hope you have the capacity to appreciate the damage that you've inflicted on my son and experience some feeling of regret, though you have the look of a psychiatrist who has exorcised guilt from his vocabulary of emotion. I was impressed. Lamb was silent at that one.

Looking back at Cage's life, you wonder if the illness was there all along. The fits of anger. The wild escapades. The depressions in college and grad school. Was what had appeared to be normal adolescent turmoil really the slow arrival of his madness? "When they figure out the right drug to control manic depression, to allow them the manic energy without the psychosis, the bipolars will rule the world. They are often very bright," an orthopedic surgeon from Charleston told me one day while I was painting his house. It's easier to talk to southerners. I told him I was thinking of staying through December, maybe longer, and he said I could look after his huge place right on the bluff, looking out at the ocean, until next June.

Sylvia's Saab comes down the street. She slows down and waves. She's started running with some guy from Rhode Island, another hard-partying trustafarian. I don't run into her much. I raise a paintbrush and start to come down the ladder. She rolls on by.

I'm thinking of staying because I'm not sure what I want to major in, what I want to be. Hanging out in a fraternity house with a bunch of drunks getting fucked up and chasing trim has lost its appeal. I've been seeing a therapist, a guy named Jack, since a couple of weeks after Cage went into Bridgewater. Jack says my not wanting to go back to college stems from an adjustment disorder. He's trying to adjust me. I think the long silences of painting houses are more valuable than the fifty minutes a week with him at a dollar a minute. He did introduce me to the tool of stepping out of myself and drawing back from my family, watching all of us interact as if I was watching a play. But he doesn't have much else to teach. I'm getting more out of a book on Gestalt therapy. I need to take some time off and think about what I want to do.

Mom and Dad are against it. The unspoken subtext is: Look what happened to Cage when he took time off from college. With their oldest son in the loony bin, their middle son dead, their youngest son appearing to drop out of college, they're fairly freaked out. So I tell them that I'll pay my own way, including the sixty percent of the therapy not covered by the church medical insurance. Mom guessed right away that there's a girl involved.

I'm falling in love. Savanna heard about Cage long before she met me. He was famous across the island. Even now in late August they're still talking about the sermon at St. Paul's and the yard of boat wrecks and his arrest. The boatbuilder who bought Cage's sloop for three grand, twice what Cage had paid for it, said the work Cage had done was first-class. I used the money to pay off the Slades' account at Coffin's Marine. There's a consensus across the island that Cage got shafted by the doctor, the judge, and the prosecutor. Cage is remembered fondly, especially after Mom rode all over the island apologizing to everyone and covering the rubber checks—enough to send me to Tulane for a semester.

Mom hasn't met Savanna. She was in Boston or the Vineyard when Mom was around. Mom doesn't know that she moved into my attic. She goes to Wellesley, just a ferry ride away, studies political science, wants to be a lawyer, like half the people I know. I started therapy because of her. She's very pragmatic. "You've got to do it, Harper," she told me about dawn the night I met her. We stayed up talking all night, not even drinking much, just talking. "Your family is obviously dysfunctional. Everyone's is. It's too bad there's not a Jungian analyst on the island. I had a great one in Atlanta."

She taught me how to sail a Laser. Sometimes at sunset we cast into the surf on an isolated beach. One week we read *The Moviegoer* and the next *The Last Gentleman*. I like Walker Percy. He's funny and captures the upper-class South in the sixties but I don't buy his theism. Savanna believes in God. We lie on the sand under blankets, half naked. We didn't make the two-back beast, as Cage would say, until after a month of hanging together constantly. She's slender, like a ballerina. She has dark skin and short dark hair and barely comes to my shoulder. The first time we made love I thought I was going to hurt her. She just seemed so small. She had slept with two other boys. But once she decides, she's into it all the way. After the long gentle warm-up of soft kisses, half-clothed bodies entwined, tender caresses, tentative wandering hands, we fucked like alley cats. She leaves marks. It's the first great sex of my life, the first without awkwardness. I get a double bed that takes up most of the attic. We live on that bed.

So I'm going to weather the family storm on Nantucket, ponder the future and the past, try to find a path.

The End of the South
1969

"Nick. Wake up." Cage nudged his shoulder. "Sompin's in the corner."

"Huh?" Nick yawned and squinted in the darkness at the bedroom ceiling. He rolled over and hid his head under the pillow.

"Nick," Cage whispered. "It's floating."

Nick kicked his legs under the sheets but they were not long enough to hit his brother on the other side of the big four-post bed.

"Nick." Cage's voice was trembling more now. "It . . . it's . . . it's an old wo-woman. She's *floating*."

Aunt Benda, Nick thought, coming awake with a start. By instinct he lay perfectly still like an orphaned cub in tall grass. Before he went to bed Granddad Cage had told them that he'd heard Aunt Benda in the attic the night before they had arrived. Even in the daylight when Nick was in the upstairs of the old house he felt Aunt Benda watching him from the corners where the walls met the ceiling.

"Nick. She's get . . . get . . . getting close."

What do you do? Granddad had never said what to do. How do you make a ghost go away? Nick's heart was racing. He couldn't bring himself to turn over and look at Aunt Benda. He pictured her in a white nightgown, shriveled like his great-grandmother, with long gray hair, holding a candle. He wanted to cry out for his mother but she wasn't in the house. The other upstairs bedrooms were empty.

"Nick," Cage said in a whispered shout, "she's on the bed! Aaah! Aaah!"

"Mama!" Nick yelled, pushing himself up on his arms. "Granddad!" He jerked around to look but there was only darkness.

"She's gone," Cage said. "I thought she was going to kill me."

Nick was panting, squeezing the sheets in his fists, his eyes wide, listening to the crickets outside in the night. The curtains billowed in a breeze and faint moonlight.

"Aunt Benda?"

"Yeah," Cage whispered. "What's that? Hear sompin?"

The floorboards squeaked on the staircase down the hall. Footsteps getting closer, the creaking louder. Someone was coming up the stairs.

"She's coming back." Cage pulled the covers over his head.

Nick couldn't make himself move. His heart pounded louder, seemed to rise up in his throat as the footsteps reached the top of the stairs and came slowly down the hall. He started sobbing. He heard the knob turning and saw the door swing open. He thought God would protect him from the ghost but where was God now? He didn't want to see Aunt Benda. He squeezed his eyes.

"You boys okay? One of you had a bad dream?"

Nick heard Granddad Cage's voice and opened his eyes. The room was bright from the chandelier hanging from the ceiling. Granddad walked toward the bed and stopped by the fireplace in front of a portrait of his father, a gray-haired man with a stern face in black old-timey clothes who seemed to look out at them from the world of ghosts, an unhappy place where Nick never wanted to go. "Poppy," he said, leaping out of bed. "Cage saw Aunt Benda. Here in the room. She almost got him."

His grandfather raised him off the ground and clutched him to his chest. His breathing slowed as he felt his grandfather's hand smoothing his hair, smelled the reassuring fragrance of Old Spice. Granddad set him down and looked him in the eye. "Nick, Cage was just trying to scare you." He pulled a handkerchief from the breast pocket of a pressed khaki shirt and wiped his tears. "I reckon there's no such thing as ghosts."

"But you said you saw Aunt Benda," Nick said.

"I was just having a little fun," Granddad said. "Cage has taken this too far."

Already in a T-shirt and shorts, Cage was putting on a pair of worn-out sneakers without socks. He looked up when his grandfather said his name. "Cage Malone, don't you ever let me catch you scaring your little brother again. I'll give you the first real hidin' of your young life."

"Yes, sir." Cage grinned.

Granddad leveled his stare until the smile disappeared from Cage's mouth, though it lingered in his eyes.

"I'll look after him," Cage said.

"That's right, son. You two have to look after each other. Never forget that."

"Yes, sir." Cage's eyes were serious now.

Nick was silent. He looked from his brother to his grandfather, a tall tower of khaki.

"Grandmother has breakfast ready," Granddad said, leaving the room. "Wash up and come down."

"Yes, sir," they said in unison.

"Wipe the sleep out of your face, Nick." Cage tossed him a pair of cutoffs.

In half-light Cage led them on the path from the backyard through the boarded-up quarters down to the lake, where a gray blanket of mist floated a few feet off the black surface. Granddad cinched tight the straps on the boy's orange life jackets, then told Cage to let Nick go first to the front of the boat. The last into the flat-bottomed metal skiff, Granddad pulled the starter cord on the outboard while Cage scrambled about, untying the lines. The woods two miles away on the far side of the lake grew distinct as the sun burned through the mist. Nick yawned, wishing he was still in bed. The droning outboard pushed them across the dark, flat glass. Nick leaned over the side, dangling his fingers just above the smooth water. Cage shouted above the engine noise at Granddad, asking him questions about inlets and bait.

About a mile from the dock, in the middle of the lake, Granddad cut the engine. Nick sat up, wondering why he'd stopped the boat far from the coves where they always fished. The sun was high enough to illuminate the tall white house sheltered in a copse of towering oaks on a quarter-mile-wide shoreline hemmed on either side by clusters of low brick ranch homes. Granddad tore off a plug of tobacco and stuck it in his cheek. He looked at Nick and asked, "What's the name of our place over yonder?"

"Cage's Bend," Nick answered.

"Where's that name come from?" Granddad looked at Cage.

"A bend on the Cumberland River which ran right here below where we are now." Cage smiled. "Before the TVA dammed the river up to make the lake."

"Morgan Cage was our great-great-great-"—Nick counted on his fingers—"granddaddy."

Cage cut in, "He moved here in 1824. The bend in the river got named after him."

"Smart boys." Granddad nodded and shot a jet of juice over the side. "Look at those subdivisions. Like cancer, eating up the country." He shook his head. "Used to be our land, boys. A thousand acres. Now we're down to twenty acres and the house. We had to sell the land off over the years, to pay our bills, to pay our taxes, to send your mama to college. The Cages didn't adapt well to modernity."

"What's motornity?" Cage asked.

"Modernity." Granddad spelled the word. "Modern times, Cage, modern times."

It was hot now. Nick could never understand how Granddad wore long pants and sleeves and a hat on the lake in the middle of the summer. He leaned over the side, splashed water on his face, and looked back at his grandfather.

"No, boys. We didn't adapt well to changing times." He spit expertly over the stern. "I never put the time I should into practicing law. I spent too much time fishing and hunting."

"And drinking," Cage said with a mischievous half-smile.

A flash of anger passed through Granddad's eyes, then a look of sadness. "Cage, ol' son, you're wise beyond your nine years." He smiled and shook his head. "Yes, boys. That's been a problem, too. I remember when I was about sixteen, after a football game we used to go out and get corn liquor and see how much we could drink. That's the height of foolishness, the summit of stupidity. Promise me that you will never drink to excess."

"I promise," Cage said.

Nick wiped the water off his face. "I promise, too, Granddad."

"Well, the long and short of it, Cage Malone Rutledge and Nicholas Morgan Rutledge, is that you two are the last men in Morgan Cage's bloodline. He was a pioneer who came here from God knows where and carved out a farm from the wilderness."

"And killed a lot of Cherokees who lived here first."

"I'm afraid that's true, Cage. The soil of our nation is bathed in blood." Granddad laughed sadly. "Do you get whipped often in school for your tongue?"

"No, sir," Cage said. "But Nick got whipped this year because he refused to do his homework for a week."

"Nick? You sound like me all over again." Granddad raised one eyebrow. "My point, boys, is that Morgan Cage came with nothing and built something. He was a close friend and associate of President Andrew Jackson, worked for his administration in Washington. And look at me now, I'm nothing but a country lawyer, not a very successful one at that. I'm afraid I've squandered Morgan Cage's legacy."

Nick raised his hand. "What does that mean—squandered his doohickey?"

"Son, it means that I've wasted what was left to me." He raised an arm toward the dock and the house and the tall oaks. "I haven't held on to the land that we had. I haven't made the most of my opportunities." He lowered his arm. "Now, I'm afraid, there won't be anything left for you. All I can pass on to you is my name."

"It's a cool name," Cage said. "All the girls like it."

"Boys must grow up a lot faster today," Granddad said. "When I was nine years old, I had no more interest in girls than I did in mathematics. I worry about your generation. Rootless. Look at that blight of ranch homes over there. Kids who grow up there have no more connection to the land than a tumbleweed. People don't live in one place hardly long enough for the mail to catch up to them."

Nick's eyes followed a dragonfly skimming the glassy surface of the lake while Cage, head tilted to one side, watched his grandfather closely, the frown lines on the corners of his mouth, the furrows across his brow.

"The South is finished." Granddad Cage expectorated in a high arc that landed some distance from the boat and sent ripples radiating out in circles. "Whether it stood for any worthy agrarian ideals is a matter of debate. Now it's no different than anywhere else. That might be one reason I drank, Cage—to the memory of the wilderness in which I was born."

"Amen," Cage said.

The old man laughed softly and tousled the boy's hair.

"Let's go fishing, Poppy," Cage said.

"Indeed, let's go." Granddad Cage pulled the starter cord, splintering the silence.

Cage

I walk up the center aisle at St. James Church. It's empty. Light streams in through the Tiffany stained glass. Approaching the altar, I'm surprised to see Jesus with his legs crossed and his hands on his knees in lotus position where the chalice usually stands. Getting closer, I see that Jesus has my face. I stare at him quietly for a long time until he opens his eyes and I see myself reflected in them. I realize that he is meditating me, that I am his dream, and that when he wakes up, I will cease to exist.

I hold my hand in front of my face, watch it shake—lithium tremens. Through the barred windows the near-full moon sluices lanes between the treetops across the fenced fields. Avenues of light that promise escape. Pringle is snoring. I sit up in the bunk, ponder the dream. Another week has passed with no word from Dr. Willcox, who makes and breaks appointments to see how I will react. Sylvia is incommunicado, nothing more than a memory. Harper sent a postcard saying that he bought a dune buggy. Got one from my cousin Rutledge Jordan, who's in the Peace Corps in Africa. Seven college friends have written to express their shock and support, which gave me a moment of warmth but mainly heightened my isolation—all of them through graduate school, married, homeowners. Locked away in the nuthouse, I'm an aberrant miscreant, a fuckup, a failure. The moon rises higher. Pringle turns and mumbles in his sleep.

"Dear Mom and Dad," I whisper to myself. "You have shown me love and I have only soiled my hands and learned to hunch my shoulders and avert my eyes. Know this has been my choice, a stubbornness and not a lack of training."

"Buck up, brother," the voice comes from the end of my bed.

"Nick?"

"The one and only." The moonlight passes through him, glows around his edges.

"I thought I'd dreamt you. But now you're back."

"Feeling sorry for yourself again. I told you last time you've got to take hold."

"I'd like to see *you* stay calm in a hellhole like this."

"Yeah, but you were always the toughest of us, the only one who could survive a joint like this. Remember when you hitched across the country after your freshman year at Sewanee, sending back cards you signed 'High Plains Drifter'?" Nick laughs so loud I think he will wake up Pringle. "I never had the guts to hitchhike. You're a tough son of a bitch. You can handle it."

"I must have been half crazy already. Ten years ago."

"Maybe. But you can't blame yourself for your illness. I've met a lot of manic-depressives on this side. Byron. Shelley. Dylan. All our heroes. Just be glad they've made medical advances in the field. Imagine the Gothic asylums where they were locked up." Nick laughs. "They're still traumatized."

I laugh involuntarily, almost against my will. "You know those guys?"

"Well, let's say, I, uh, sought them out to make their acquaintance. Generally they despise Americans. Other day I ran into some of the victims of the Jonestown Massacre." Nick's voice carries a smile, though it was impossible to make out the mouth on his indistinct face. "Reminded me of your Jonestown party in high school. Remember in the backyard in Baton Rouge while Mom and Dad and Harper were at the beach? The grape Kool-Aid with grain alcohol? You put up a sign that said 'The People's Temple.'" Nick laughs loud and slaps his knee, which makes no noise, then shakes his head. "You always had a great sense of humor."

I haven't thought about the Jonestown party in years. It doesn't strike me as funny anymore. "That was so decadent and morbid."

"Oh, come on. Don't be hard on yourself." Nick pats my leg. I can't feel his hand but an iciness shudders through me.

"Nick, have you attained enlightenment?" Shivering, I hug myself.

"No, Cage. Consciousness after death continues at the level of consciousness attained by humanity. One does acquire a more ironic perspective."

"How disappointing." Suddenly I'm hot again, feel sweat beading on my forehead.

"I would have thought you would be gratified to know that consciousness survives death."

"I was always a believer, Nick. You were the agnostic."

"Well." He seems momentarily at a loss for words. "Strange dream you had. Really gave you a start."

I stare at the ghost, wondering if he is real or something my mind has conjured up to console me.

"Have you ever wondered," Nick goes on, "if unconsciousness, rather than consciousness, is the real existence, if our conscious world is an illusion, a false reality constructed for a specific purpose, like a dream that seems real while you're in it?"

"That's the sort of stoned speculation we indulged in in college," I say. "Are you saying that those bars aren't real? That this nuthouse is here for my edification? That I am here for a purpose, which, though hidden now, will ultimately be revealed?"

"Clearly," Nick says. "How did you get here? You have to do some soul-searching. You must try to figure it out."

"I got here because I passed a lot of bad checks and freaked a lot of people out. That's how. I shouldn't be in a maximum-security lockdown with killers." I press my temples between my palms as though my brain will explode. "Let me fucking out!"

"Shut up, Rutledge," Pringle yells from below. Nick is gone. I stare out at the near-full moon, so big it's surreal, and try not to think about Barney the Giant and his broomstick.

Franklin

The guards wheel a young man into the visiting room. Both his legs are cut off at the knees, his hair is close-cropped like a marine's, he has an appealing mild face and a huge smile. His mother and father stand up, looking at him expectantly. They look like kind, innocent folks and they greet him with great love and he smiles and greets them. Within three minutes he flies into a rage, just a rage, cursing them with the most horrific language, and the parents just sit there silently, their faces fraught with sadness and despair. They try to calm him down but he only grows more angry and slaps at his mother, missing her nose by about an inch. He's shaking with fury in his chair. A guard comes rushing in and wheels him out and, my God, the parents are devastated. I squeeze Margaret's hand and she shakes her head and looks more resolute.

A few minutes later the guards bring Cage out in his prison blues. My mind winces back involuntarily like an engine jerking suddenly at the freight cars behind it and I glimpse him as a baby in my arms, a little boy with a satchel headed off to school, a striking sun-golden teen holding a string of fish, breaking the tape in a track meet, tall onstage in a cap and gown receiving an award, and I think, What did I do wrong? Where did he jump the tracks? How do we get him back?

His eyes light up for a moment. As your gaze telescopes in so that you see only his face and not the appalling room and the miserable people on every side, you forget the circumstances and for a comforting instant you are inside the pure, undiluted love that bonds you to your child. Then you exhale and the world comes crashing back.

"Hello, son." I hug him close.

"Oh, Papa, I'm sorry." His smile seems out of place beneath his anguished eyes. He looks like he has aged years in the weeks since I have last seen him. "I mean, I don't think I deserve to be here. But I'm sorry you had to come all the way up here again and again."

"Oh, Cage," Margaret says, hugging him. There are tears in her voice, though her eyes are dry. "We know you don't deserve to be here."

"Son, we're doing everything we can to get you out." I pat him on the shoulder.

"I'm sorry to cost you so much time and money," Cage says, sitting down at our little table.

"Don't you worry about that," Margaret says. "You just keep telling yourself that you will be out of here very soon."

"I believe it when I see you or talk to you on the phone but when I'm alone in there, I start to think that I'll never get out." Cage's hands dart from his thighs to the tabletop. His fingertips are newly stained by nicotine. "This place is not part of the world that we come from. It's a world of its own with its own rules and rulers and—"

"Cage, Cage," Margaret pleads. "Keep the faith. We *will* get you out. You just remember that."

"That's right, son."

"That's not what the guards say." His face suddenly looks more terrified than I have ever remembered. "They say that no one ever gets out. Same with the inmates. No one can remember the last time anyone got out."

I clasp his right hand with both of mine. "No, son. The lawyer says it's difficult and it does take time but it is not impossible. He thinks the best strategy is to get you transferred to a lower-security facility where the patients are less, uh—"

"Crazy?" Cage is smiling now, a glimmer of his old self.

"Chronic," I say.

"That sounds reasonable." He suddenly seems to relax. "Let's not talk about this place anymore. We only have a few minutes. It must be a hundred degrees in Memphis right now. I can't believe

I missed a whole summer in here. You know, I think I would have gone off the deep end if it weren't for Nick."

"Nick?" Margaret glances at me, then back at Cage.

"He visits me at night after lights-out." Cage does not appear to be joking. "Isn't that exciting? I mean, I always had problems with 'life after death,' but there you are. Nick is still alive. Or his spirit is. Like you, he keeps telling me to take hold."

"You mean he comes to you in your dreams? There are many biblical precedents for dreams as forms of revelation." I try not to sound as if I doubt him or suspect that he has indeed gone completely crazy.

"No, Papa. Sometimes I wake up from a nightmare or just wake up in the middle of the night anxious and sweaty." His smile is skeptical as if he himself doubts what he is saying. "And there is Nick, sitting on the end of the bed, ready to comfort me in his old smart-ass way."

"I wish he would visit me sometime." Margaret laughs.

"Son, have you told this to your doctors here?"

"Are you crazy, Dad?" Now Cage laughs. "Obviously they would assume I was raving."

"That's wise," I say.

"You don't believe me, do you?" Cage peers into my eyes.

"I do." Margaret smiles.

"Two minutes!" a guard says from the far side of the room.

"I think you might be dreaming, Cage." I shrug and smile. "But who knows? The ways of God are manifold and mysterious. Anyway, keep it to yourself if you want to get out of here quickly."

Around the room, patients in blue denim are rising from the tables. The babble of low conversation rises and a few women begin weeping all at once.

Cage chuckles and says, "This place is like a misery factory, huh?"

I nod, coming around the table, hug him. "Keep your chin up, Cage."

Margaret squeezes him like she's holding on to a tree in a windstorm, her head on his chest.

"Let him breathe." I laugh uncomfortably.

The guard by the prisoners' door glances over at us and shouts, "Time to go, people!"

Margaret finally lets him go.

Cage walks backward, slowly, holding us with his eyes, until he reaches the door, where the guard puts his hand on Cage's shoulder and spins him around, not ungently. Cage glances back over his shoulder, raises his fist high in a sixties Black Power salute, and disappears through the doorway. I remember when he stunned an audience at the Fourth of July follies at the country club as a boy with that gesture. Cage, always the provocateur. We are the last to file out of the room. No one is talking.

Outside, along one end of the parking lot on the gray brick wall of the administration building is an enormous sign two stories tall that reads *Bridgewater Correctional Center*. Why on earth did they have to send him here of all places? The individual is powerless against the state once it has you in its grip. Even Ted Kennedy is powerless against the bureaucracy of Massachusetts. Rowan Patrick, Nick's old high school friend who may well be elected the youngest congressman ever from Louisiana in November, is a friend of some of the senator's staff from his years at Harvard and his work with the Democratic Party. Ted Kennedy's office sent a letter and made some phone calls. Nothing happened. It seems possible that Cage will languish in there for years, the evaluation periods extended again and again.

A black gentleman wearing a white coat and carrying a clipboard walks up the sidewalk toward the crowd of visitors slumped and defeated, making their way toward their cars.

"I'm going to talk to that doctor," Margaret whispers to me.

"Honey, leave the man alone. You can't just accost him on the sidewalk."

"Well, we still haven't been able to see a doctor." She pats her hair. "I don't see how it could possibly hurt."

The young doctor comes closer, looking at his feet as the crowd parts around him like a school of fish, then closes behind him.

"Beg yah pah-dun, Dahkta." Margaret's voice must sound like

Blanche DuBois to this New England Negro, who looks up with
a slightly annoyed, hurried expression.

"Yes?" He slows down but doesn't stop. We move a few steps
with him back toward the wall with the sign.

"I wonder if I might take just a moment of your time?" Margaret's smile is her strongest feature. It's so open and sweet that it
can't fail to hit the heart of its target. It was her smile that caught
my eye in 1957.

The doctor glances at his watch, then says, "Yes, ma'am?"

"Why, you're from the South, aren't you?" Margaret brushes
her fingertips lightly on his white sleeve, then brings her hand
back to her heart, as if she's saying the Pledge of Allegiance.

"Yes, ma'am." The doctor is smiling now. "Lafayette,
Louisiana."

"Why, how providential. We lived in Baton Rouge for ten
years." Margaret laughs at the lucky coincidence. "I'm Margaret
Rutledge. This is my husband, Bishop Franklin Rutledge."

"Frank," I say, sticking out my hand.

"Hubertus Plauche." His grip is firm. "What can I do for
y'all?"

Margaret looks at me, so I begin. "Our son has been here for
three months. He was remanded for a forty-day evaluation from
Nantucket, where he assaulted a police officer who was trying to
take him in because he was acting peculiar and writing bad
checks. His current diagnosis is manic depression. He's twenty-
nine years old. He has no previous criminal or psychiatric history.
He clearly doesn't belong in an institution for the criminally insane. We are trying to get him transferred to a more therapeutic
setting. We—"

"What's his name?" Dr. Plauche takes a pen and notebook
from his breast pocket.

"Cage," Margaret says. "Cage Malone Rutledge."

"It's a big organization." He scribbles on the pad. "Mistakes
happen all too often, I'm sorry to say. But eventually we sort them
out." He hands me his card. "I'll look into it. Call me on Friday."

"Oh, Doctor, I just can't thank you enough." Margaret touches
his sleeve. "You're so kind."

"I hope I'll be able to help. Try not to worry." He smiles. "I know that's impossible. I can just imagine my own mama if she were in your shoes."

"She must be very proud of you, Dr. Plauche." Margaret's smile would melt ice in Antarctica. The doctor shakes our hands and hurries toward the big main doors.

"I do believe that man will help us," Margaret says as the sadness rushes back into her face. "He seems like a mighty fine doctor."

Cage

The small courtroom at Bridgewater reminds me of Dad's office in the parish house in Virginia—tall ceilings, dark paneling, ornate trim from another era. I'm sitting with Dr. Plano, an MIT forensic psychiatrist who's costing Dad about a grand an hour, and my attorney, Wainwright, who's costing Dad four hundred bucks an hour. Mom and Dad are behind us, the only people occupying a few rows of metal folding chairs. The presiding judge is a very distinguished gray-haired gentleman who looks like he will see right through me. Dr. Willcox is there, not in one of his flannel shirts but a button-down and a corduroy jacket. Willcox is so odd that I'm scared he will tell the judge some complete fiction about my behavior. I have seen him a total of two hours in the four months I've been locked up in this hellhole. Either dealing for years with thousands of lunatics has rubbed off on him, or, as they say, the reason that he went into psychiatry was that he was crazy to begin with. As far as I can fathom, Willcox is an enigma.

Some functionary from the state of Massachusetts calls the hearing to order and the judge asks for Dr. Willcox's evaluation.

"Your Honor"—Dr. Willcox's voice is lower than the grating screech of the one-on-one sessions in his office—"it is the opinion of the evaluation team that Mr. Rutledge requires further psychiatric treatment. We assert that he suffers from a schizoaffective disorder with potentially violent tendencies."

I hear my mother gasp softly behind me, though I doubt that the judge does.

"He has displayed violent episodes as recently as June and we believe that he continues to harbor hostile, antisocial attitudes," Willcox goes on while the judge listens with a stern poker face. I want to shout out, What in God's name are you talking about, you fucking quack? Tell the judge that you've hardly seen me in the last four months, that I was only defending myself, but I keep quiet while Willcox rattles on. Then Wainwright stands up, introduces our distinguished MIT shrink, and sits down, and then it's Dr. Plano's turn. He is a tall guy with gray hair a little longer than most businessmen wear theirs, sort of professorial hip, and he has a rich voice.

"Your Honor," Dr. Plano says, with his hands resting on the edge of the table, "Mr. Rutledge suffers from textbook bipolar disorder, a disease that commenced some years ago and has gone undiagnosed until now. I understand the June episode here, an altercation with a patient with a record of harassing others, to be a situation of self-defense. He is not given to violence. He is, in fact, a sensitive person with great powers of empathy. He needs therapy more than incarceration in a prison. He needs therapy which is not available here. In fact, his incarceration in Bridgewater is counter to his recovery. I believe very strongly that he should be transferred immediately to a therapeutic facility."

The judge nods and says, "Mr. Rutledge, do you have anything to say?"

"Your Honor," I say, thinking, It must go to their heads hearing everyone say, Your Honor, Your Honor, Your Honor, all day. I clear my throat. "Your Honor, I understand now that I was spinning out of control in Nantucket and caused a big mess but I am not a brute beast. I am not dangerous to society. I am not a criminal. I am not a killer. This is the scariest place that I have ever been, one not conducive to pulling oneself together, and I very much need to get out of here."

The judge nods and shuffles through a file on his podium. "It is the judgment of this court that Mr. Rutledge is neither a danger to society nor to himself and that he should be transferred to the Taunton State Hospital to undergo therapy for bipolar disorder as soon as a space is available in said facility."

"Thank you, sir," I say. That's it. Ten minutes to put an end to months of torture. Dr. Willcox doesn't look at me. He studies a folder for the next case coming before the judge. Mom is beaming and Dad looks relieved. We all leave the courtroom together. A guard gives me just enough time to shake everyone's hands and hug Mom before leading me back to Max 2.

Coming onto my unit, I run into Barkely, the friendly guard whom I'd told about some pot plants that I'd seen growing in abandoned fields beyond the perimeter of an exercise yard that's rarely used. I say, "Yo, Barkely, I think they're sending me to Taunton soon. It ain't freedom but I hear it's like a college campus."

"Oh, yeah?" He doesn't smile, which is odd. I thought he liked me.

Lunchtime, gentlemen, a loudspeaker says. *Everyone out of your rooms and line up.*

Barkely walks off and I stand by the electric door. Thirty uniformed lunatics line up behind me and the guards run a count. Boyles and Jones, two guards who are never nice, come up and Jones says, "Rutledge, come with us."

For a second, walking between them toward a stairwell, I think that I'm being transferred but I know that it would take days or weeks, not minutes. "What's going on?"

Boyles shoves me from behind into the dim light, then pulls the door closed and stands in front of its little window, while Jones slams me against the cinder-block wall. He lifts me up by the throat so that only the toes of my sneakers are touching the floor.

"If you ever talk back to us again, we're going to kick your ass down five flights of stairs," Jones says.

I try to say okay but it comes out a gurgle. I nod my head enthusiastically.

"If you ever say anything to anyone about what you think you saw out in the fields, we're going to kill you." Jones squeezes my throat harder.

I choke out a few sounds and nod my head again. Jones lets go of my neck and I drop to my feet, gagging and wheezing. Boyles presses my shoulder against the wall and says, "We're watching you, corn bread. Remember that." He grabs me by the collar and throws me out of the stairwell into the hallway, which is empty now, with everyone gone to lunch. The door clanks shut behind me. My gut growls, since I missed breakfast, waiting around for the hearing. When my stomach is empty too long, I start to feel queasy from the lithium. I pick myself up and stagger into the TV room and collapse on a lumpy sofa in front of *Days of Our Lives*.

Independence Day
1973

From the pool the blue fairways fell down to a shaggy carpet of treetops that ran across the flats to the green ridges of the Appalachians reaching into a clear sky where the summer sun cast long afternoon shadows from the high dive and tall poles with speakers playing "Sha Na Na Na, Hey, Hey, Goodbye." On one side of the pool, under a canopy where the greasy odor of frying hamburgers mixed with the acrid chlorine off the water, kids pushed french fries through little puddles of ketchup on paper plates. On the other side, at the edge of a slope that angled down to the parking lot, a line of lounge chairs in the grass was occupied by sunbathing women.

Just below the top of the slope Nick walked slowly behind the chairs, darting between them occasionally to steal a half-smoked cigarette from an unguarded ashtray. With a handful of butts he circled the hill beyond the deep end and sat down with two boys on the concrete slab over the big humming filters. He cracked the bottom of his fist and let the butts spill out one by one like gold dust.

"No one saw you?" Billy Kimball asked.

"I think Mrs. Thomas saw me but didn't say anything."

"Mrs. Thomas is cool," Norman Blevins said. "But Mr. Thomas is scary."

"We don't have any matches," Billy said.

Nick dug a white pack with the country club logo from his cutoff shorts and flicked it with his thumb onto the little pile.

Billy lit three-quarters of a Virginia Slim and coughed.

"Greedy creep," Nick said. "That was the best one."

"Here, take this." Norman handed Nick half a Camel, then selected a slightly shorter Pall Mall with lipstick marks. "Who was smoking this?"

"Mrs. Reynolds." Nick coughed.

"The one with the big bazooms?" Billy asked.

Nick nodded, inhaling. He felt dizzy.

"Nick's mother has the biggest boobs of all," Norman said with a tone of awe.

"I fingered a pussy yesterday," Billy said.

"Really?" Norman said.

Nick pumped his jaw to blow a ring and the smoke only curled out of his mouth.

"What's it like?" Norman asked.

"Warm and slimy, like . . ." Billy tapped the ash, sighed. "Like Play-Doh with warm baby oil."

"Jenny Wright?" Nick tried another ring, failed.

"Yeah."

"Never kiss and tell," Norman said. "That's what my brother told me."

"Jenny Wright lets anyone finger her." Nick ground his cigarette into the concrete.

"Try to be gentlemen." Norman waved his pudgy arms back and forth like a referee.

"You never fingered her," Billy said.

"I've never tried." Nick looked hard at Billy. "I don't want to."

"You're scared. Scared of girls."

"I'm scared of girls." Norman laughed. "Especially my sisters. Hey, did you hear that next year we won't be able to wear cutoffs in the pool anymore. The threads clog up the drains or something."

"I won't be here next year," Nick said. "We're leaving next month for Virginia."

"Really?" Norman didn't inhale. He blew out a mouthful of smoke that hung motionless in the humidity. "That sucks. When did you find out?"

"My parents have known for a month. They just told Cage and me last night."

"Is Cage mad?" Billy lay down flat on the slab and blew smoke up at the sky.

"He's really mad. He doesn't want to lose his friends. He wants to stay here, live with the Campbells."

"Will your parents let him?"

"No way."

"Your dad got transferred?" Norman asked.

"The church is not like a company." Nick let his legs dangle over the edge. "They don't transfer you. When a church needs a new minister, they go out looking until they find one that they like."

"Oh," Norman said. "So why did he take it?"

"It's a bigger church. More salary."

"Norman's always changing the subject," Billy said. "Let's go."

The men's changing room was damp and smelled of disinfectant. Norman, peering around a wall at the outside door, gave them a thumbs-up sign behind his back. Billy and Nick scrambled from a bench to the top of the lockers, slid aside a board of thin plywood, from which Cage and some of his friends had removed the nails the year before, and crawled into the darkness on the top of a cinder-block wall. Nick slid the board back almost in place and moved slowly behind Billy, who scraped his knee and cried out. Nick whispered, "Shsh!" Billy rose up and looked through a hole in the plywood.

"Shazaam," Billy whispered.

Nick clenched his fists. He remembered seven years before, in kindergarten, where the girls' and boys' bathrooms were adjoining stalls, and he and Norman had climbed over the top to watch a cute dark-haired girl sitting on the toilet. Where is it? What happened to it? he'd asked Norman after the girl left. Girls don't have wee-wees, Norman had said with the authority of having sisters. Wow, Nick had mumbled, dumbstruck by the great revelation, which was his first lesson in the differences between the sexes.

"Golly, they're huge." Billy's voice was shallow. "Like cantaloupes."

"Lemme see." Nick pinched Billy's butt until he moved farther along the top of the wall. Through the hole he could see Mrs. Miller, a woman about his mother's age, stooping over to put her legs through a bathing suit. She stood up, revealing round white breasts with pink nipples the size of saucers, and pulled the suit up her fat legs to the mysterious dark triangle, then stretched the navy fabric up her white belly and wiggled her arms through the holes, shaking her breasts. A heat rose up from his toes until Nick's whole body felt feverish, a strange, overpowering sensation to kick through the thin plywood, dive from the locker tops onto Mrs. Miller, rip the suit off her, and bury his face in her breasts.

"They're big bosoms, huh?" Billy said in the darkness.

Nick opened his mouth but no words came.

"One is the loneliest number that you'll ever do," Cage said, standing on the edge of the pool. Beside him Nick held his breath, watching a sixteen-year-old swim the ninety-foot length of the pool underwater. The boy reached the wall of the deep end, smoothly flipped, and swam back toward them. Nick exhaled and shook his head. The crowd hushed as the boy reached the blue line marking the deep third of the pool. He swam on, breaking last year's record. Nick looked up at Cage's sandy hair and fierce blue eyes, then back at the pool, as the crowd applauded.

Midway between the two ends the boy stood and raised his arms over his head. On either side lifeguards moved a rope of floats stretching across the pool to mark the position. The noise ebbed and the crowd looked back at the shallow end to see if there were any more contestants. Cage waved at the chief lifeguard.

"You?" a high school kid said to Cage. "You're just a freeloader. Preachers get a special deal."

"Lay on, Macduff," Cage said coolly, looking the kid calmly in the eyes before turning and walking away from the pool.

"What?" the boy said.

"Ever heard of Shakespeare?" Nick didn't know the boy, only saw him in the summers at the country club.

"How old's your brother?" the boy asked.

"Thirteen." Nick crossed his fingers and glanced at the swimmer, who had just climbed out of the pool. He looked a full foot taller and twenty pounds heavier than Cage.

With one hand behind him touching the wall of the club-house, Cage turned his head slowly to the lifeguard, who nod-ded, raised a thumb, and smiled. Cage breathed in deeply, filling his chest three times, then shot across the concrete, his bare feet slapping the puddles. He reached the edge and dove long, seemed to hang in the air an instant before slicing the water. He swept his arms back and held them to his sides, glided to the middle of the pool, then breaststroked smoothly to the far end, kicked off the wall, and moved toward the blue line on the bottom.

"I hope he doesn't pass out," Nick's mom said, appearing suddenly at his side. "Cage is so stubborn."

Nick said, "Oh, Mom."

Crossing the line out of the deep end, Cage seemed to slow down. Nick imagined his lungs bursting, the pain that cried out for air. The floats were impossibly far, another twenty feet. The high school kids on the edges stopped talking. Cage inched along, stroking then gliding, kicking slowly. Nick watched his mom, her lips pressed tight. He put his hand around her back, then quickly dropped it and stepped away. Cage was coming to the surface. The back of his head came out of the water, then he jerked it back down and kicked wildly. His head grazed the bottom of the marker rope and he popped up on the other side. The spectators cheered louder than before. Cage held one hand on the rope and kicked to stay afloat, too short to reach the bottom.

"I wish your father were here to see this," Margaret said.

"Why does someone at St. John's always die on the holi-days?" Nick's face was serious.

His mother laughed, examined his small face with marvel and affection.

Out in the middle of the pool Cage raised his right arm above his head and clenched his fist in the Black Power salute. Suddenly everyone by the pool was quiet.

"That boy," Margaret said. "One day he's going to go too far."

Cage

"Nick, do you hear me?" I whisper.

Under a cloudless autumn sky a guard cradling a shotgun with a German shepherd at his knee walks past on the gravel road between fences. A bunch of the inmates are playing baseball but I never feel comfortable with them. The grass is soft and warm. A hawk climbs an updraft in widening circles, his eyes scanning the ground as he rises. The buildings of Bridgewater, the thousands of wretched inmates, the millions of dark insane thoughts, getting smaller and smaller, until all that is left is a blur of color from a great altitude.

The guards don't want to let me go. Every day they fuck with me for no reason. Before I came out here one of them told me that I was wanted on a phone over in Max 1. They were going to beat the hell out of me as they walked me over, so I refused to go and tagged along with the baseball detail. Last night after lockdown, Pringle was watching his little black-and-white TV and I asked him to turn it down. He turned it off. Then he starting jacking, going, Yeah, baby, oh yeah, suck me, bitch, suck hard, yeah suck on this, suck away, mmm, mmm, mmm. I put the pillow over my head but I could still hear him, Yeah, baby, that's right, lick my balls, lick my asshole, put your tongue up my ass, yeah, just like that. I yelled down, Pringle, turn your damn TV back on. He screamed, Fuck you, faggot, or I'll jump up there and come in your face. I yelled back, You try it and you'll never jack off again. Later on while I was asleep, two guards grabbed me and told me they wanted me in solitary until the next morning. I hadn't done anything. Outside the buildings, they took turns throwing me up against the wall with no explanation, never said a word. Weird stuff. I don't know what's going on. I think they want me to get in a fight so that my holding order is extended. I'm trying just to be cool. Right, brother? What else can I do? But how can months of this not leave you with a heavy case of shell shock—post–traumatic stress disorder? These months are scarring me for life. Invisible scars. Grooves in the brain. I have seen so much that is squalid, depraved, evil. It's part of me now. I am, after all, the sum total of my experiences. That's all anybody is. A compilation of experience. And now I am stuck with this. I am Cage Malone Rutledge, the max-security-nuthouse inmate. I will carry that with me to the end of my days. My time here has wrought itself into a cage to hold me back from living a normal life. How can it not?

Margaret

Well, praise the Lord, this is the last time I will enter these gates, I think, driving into the hospital. What a misnomer. More a cruel warehouse of insanity.

"I won't miss it," Harper says, parking the car, though he has only been here once before. "But it's kind of exciting. I mean, the armed guards. The dogs. The electric gates."

"You can bet Cage won't miss it." I hand Harper a breath mint, put one in my mouth. "Oh, how I have been praying for this day. You may believe yourself to be a humanist, Harper. But look at the miracle of today. So many people have told us that it is nigh impossible to get someone out of Bridgewater and it is happening today. So many churches are praying for Cage in Baton Rouge and Memphis and Bristol. You should pray, Harper. Even if you don't believe. Belief can come through practice."

"I'd rather practice Buddhism."

Harper gets out of the car and puts on the navy linen blazer that he reluctantly agreed to wear over his polo shirt. I pick some lint off one sleeve. He has grown so tall. The top of my head doesn't reach his shoulder. He is our only boy who is larger than Franklin. So proud of them all. Such handsome boys. Suddenly I remember Nick is dead. More than two years later, when I picture the boys collectively, I still take Nick as among the quick for a few seconds before the bottom falls out of my heart. Oh, Nick, I pray that you are feasting with the saints for eternity.

Harper opens the door and follows me into the dreary reception area.

"Good morning, Mrs. Beasely." I smile at the hard woman with a bird face and thinning hair who has not so much as grinned in the last quarter of a year.

"Good morning." She doesn't smile.

"We've come to collect my son." I smile. She looks rather surprised. "Cage Malone Rutledge."

"What's his number?"

I have it memorized. "R. O. O. O. Three. Five. B."

"Take a seat."

"Thank you." I smile.

Mrs. Beasely leaves the desk.

Harper says, "That woman is a real bitch."

"She must have a very hard life, son," I say. "Imagine the legion of angry, desperate relatives passing through her office every day."

After half an hour Harper glances at me and goes up to the desk.

"Beg your pardon," he calls out. My boys are all—both—polite.

Mrs. Beasely comes to the desk.

"Do you have any idea how long this will take?"

"No." She spins on her heel and walks off.

Harper tries to read an old, tattered *Islands*. I only read waiting room magazines with gloves and it's too warm for gloves. I fret about Franklin in Memphis, the pressures on him from so many people, then I see a picture of a beach in the magazine that looks like Pawley's Island, where Harper fell through a rotten screen on a front porch headfirst ten feet down into sand when he was four. That was the summer when Nick insisted on spending most of his time in the shade of water oaks with a young Cherokee wood-carver, learning to sculpt tiny owls and dogs. Cage spent all day in his little metal fishing boat on the ocean, a boat built for a lake that had no business out on the open sea. Instead of motoring around the island to the calm water of the inlet, he started coming in through the breakers to the beach in front of the house. I can still see him in the stern as a wave spins the boat broadside to the shore and rolls it, see his dark, skinny body diving through the spray. How many times did Cage nearly give me a heart attack? And Nick. Once I was reading the evening paper on the porch of the house in Bristol. It was my favorite of all the rectories. Nick was pedaling fast down the steep road at the foot of our yard, the day he put on high-rise handlebars and a banana seat, the new fashion amongst the kids at the time. I had told him to wait until Franklin got home but he didn't. I watched the handlebars swing forward and Nick catapult over the front wheel and hit the road with his face, his mouth open. I thought he'd cracked his head but he only chipped his teeth. Then Harper. Harper was an angry child. Once, driving him home from school on the freeway going seventy miles an hour, Harper just opened the door wide open and threatened to jump out. For a moment I thought he was going to do it. That was only five or six years ago. Boys. My Lord. How often have I wished that I'd had girls?

"It's been two hours, Mom," Harper says. "What can be taking so long?"

"I don't know, honey." I pat his leg. "They told me to come here today when they opened. The wheels of this bureaucracy obviously need oiling."

The reception room has filled up with a whole spectrum of people from various socioeconomic brackets, from couples dressed up as if they are going to church to an unshaven man in coveralls to a filthy man who may very well be homeless. Mental illness is very democratic.

"Maybe Cage doesn't want to leave." Harper's smile is strained.

"Maybe your father will be consecrated the archbishop of Canterbury." I think of how my grandmother always made light of grave situations, which was never easy for me. I have a tendency to obsess.

"Everyone who has registered please proceed to your numbered table," Mrs. Beasely announces from behind the desk, and the crowd files into the visiting room, leaving us alone again. I try to make eye contact with Mrs. Beasely and she looks right through me, then disappears into her office. "Thank goodness for Dr. Plauche. Without his intervention I think Cage would have languished here for years."

"I thought you said it was prayer." Harper yawns.

"How do you think I happened to bump into the good doctor as Frank and I were leaving last month? What made me decide to talk to him?"

"Happenstance." Harper smiles.

"Providence." I pat his leg again.

"I wish Providence would speed up the bureaucrats."

"Patience."

"Patience is a virtue," Harper says, "but I don't have the time."

"Humor and grace. Those are Cage's favorite virtues."

"That's what he says."

"He was quoting your father's favorite saint, Francis of Assisi."

"The nature boy. Talked to animals. Birds landed in his hands. I remember the statues. Mythology, Mama. That's all that is."

"Doubt is the companion to faith."

"Yeah, yeah." Harper goes back to his magazine. The waiting room starts filling up with visitors for the next session. Harper keeps glancing at a very pretty brunet who looks like a young Audrey Hepburn. I don't think he noticed her wedding ring. He asks, "Who do you think she's visiting?"

"Whom," I correct. "A friend, I hope, and not a sibling or her husband."

Harper nods silently. The adjacent room exhales the first round of visitors, who look more defeated now than they did going in, then it inhales the newcomers. After a few minutes Harper gets up and peers in the small glass window in the door. Sitting back down, he says, "She's visiting her husband, I think. Wonder what he did."

"I don't want to know. I don't think I can bear any more despair. Where on earth is your brother?"

Harper squeezes my shoulder and walks up to the counter. "Mrs. Beasely? Please excuse me. We've been waiting for over three hours. We were told to pick up my brother first thing this morning."

I can't hear or see her from my seat.

"What?" Harper glances over his shoulder at me with an expression of horror and incredulity. "You're kidding, right?"

My God, I think. They're not going to release him after all. He got into a fight. Every day on the phone he said how the guards were provoking him so that they wouldn't have to release him. Or he's injured. The guards beat him up and his body is so bruised that they can't show him to us. Oh my Lord, maybe he's dead. Some murderer could have killed him, jealous that he was going to be transferred. The air leaves my body like a punctured balloon and I can't catch my breath. The room is suddenly fuzzy, my head light as a feather, the air feels a hundred degrees.

"They can't find him." Harper is at my side, his voice sounding far away. "Mom, are you all right?"

I nod and breathe in through my nose, slowly pouring air down deep to my abdomen, recalling Mrs. Swinivasha, my yoga teacher for a year in Baton Rouge. I wish that I had kept up my yoga, found a teacher in Memphis. It certainly would help me deal with the stress. Through my nostrils I breathe out calmly. Harper is saying, "It's okay, Mom."

"They can't find him?"

"That's what she says." Harper shakes his head. "They're looking for him."

Somewhere *in there*, those massive wings, the place as big as the Pentagon. "They lost him?" I stand up, smooth my skirt, and cross the room with Harper at my elbow. I raise my voice and keep it calm. "Mrs. Beasely!"

She turns from a filing cabinet ten feet behind the counter and looks at me.

I do not smile. "Do you mean to say that we have been waiting half of the day while you looked for my son?"

"We're a big institution. We're understaffed. Takes time to process people. If you would—"

"Where is my son?" I cut her off.

"They're looking for him. His unit thought he was in protective custody but he wasn't. He may be in one of the recreational areas. We'll find him."

Behind us a number of people have arrived to register for the next visiting session. I turn to them, smile. "Pardon me for one more minute. They've kept me waiting for hours and now they say that they've lost my son." Looking back at Mrs. Beasely, who has come to the counter now, I say, "Mrs. Beasely, I wish to see the director." I pull an envelope from my handbag. "This is the judicial order for the transfer of my son from this negligent disorganization. I want my son."

"We're looking for him, lady." Mrs. Beasely is looking through me again. "Just take a seat and we'll find him."

"When?" Harper looks as if he is enjoying my performance. "Tomorrow?"

"Very soon." Mrs. Beasely looks at Harper, then the growing crowd behind us.

I turn around and smile. "I'm very, very sorry. What would you say if they lost *your* son?"

"Lady—"

"Mrs. Rutledge." I cut her off again.

"Why don't you come back after lunch?"

"Why don't you put out an all-points bulletin? Why don't you call the director for me? Why don't you do something to find my son? I want my son!" I no longer give a damn about politeness, scream as loud as I can, "*I want my son! I want my son!*"

"Okay, okay, Mrs. Rutledge." Mrs. Beasely crosses to her desk and speaks into a phone, then comes back to the counter. "I'm sorry for the delay. A supervisor is going back to his unit."

I step aside for the visitors to register, stay by the counter.

Harper looks at me with a proud smile. Mrs. Beasely gives cards to a young couple and an elderly woman, who smiles at me and says, "I know just how you feel." Mrs. Beasely answers the phone, then looks at me and says, "They're bringing your son up now."

The young couple starts to clap and in a few seconds all of the visitors, about a dozen of them, are applauding, strangers, bound together in despair, cheering each other on.

Cage

Taunton. No walls. No dogs. No armed guards. Shady trees turning yellow and orange. Tall, gabled red-brick Victorian buildings laid out like a college campus. The most famous "mental health consumer" to matriculate here:

> *Lizzie Borden took an ax*
> *And gave her mother forty whacks.*
> *When she saw what she had done,*
> *She gave her father forty-one.*

The oldest wing, where she stayed, which has huge long glass conservatories and puts me in mind somehow of London's Crystal Palace, is an alluring ruin, encircled by a high chain-link fence, a nest of rats and ravens. These days Lizzie wouldn't be here but forty miles away in the women's wing of Bridgewater, just one of many homicidal maniacs. I haven't seen Nick in a while, but if he visits me here, I want to ask him if he can find Lizzie in the afterlife. Ask her if she did it.

I feel extremely lucky to be at this gloomy, peaceful haven, one of a few hundred residents out of thousands of indigent mental health consumers in the state of Massachusetts. I can see clearly now how I was out of control in May. Full-blown manic. Woke up in Nantucket and took off like a harpooned sperm whale, Moby-Dick, ramming speed right off the pillow. Woke up in Nantucket with a sense of endless possibility, gigantic optimism. It started off as simply feeling good for the first time in so long. After feeling sad for years, even before Nick's crash, back to Grandfather Cage's death and further, the anger Dad quietly carried around in him, the background melancholy of living in such a sad, fucked-up world. At first there was the elation that came with the decision to forget corporate America and become a boatbuilder. I would be a craftsman, an artisan. I could be happy doing that. It would take the family some time to accept it, after all the years of saving and borrowing to put me through Sewanee and Vanderbilt. But they would come to appreciate a quiet life on a beautiful island.

For the first time in eleven years I felt I had a purpose and a tempting destiny, since I was the Louisiana state champion miler and headed off to a Tennessee mountaintop to run and write poetry, wear a black gown at the pseudo–Oxford University of the South. The real darkness began on the cold Sewanee mountain the first winter, a few weeks of dark depression, which, the next winter, grew into two months of lassitude. I dropped off the cross-country team in November and in February failed to show up at track practice. The next winter, junior year, Meriwether, my housemate, had to pick me up and shake me sometimes to get me to the dining hall. I wasn't suicidal. I was just paralyzed. The world seemed too sad and pointless.

My last winter was saved by a woman, Carlin Heather, a tall premed lacrosse player from Connecticut who could quote Yeats. If love can't conquer depression, it can at least keep it at bay for a while. She was a year younger and I hung around Sewanee after graduating, working as a carpenter and studying for the LSAT. When Carlin graduated, we traveled through Central America, then came back to the States, stayed with Nick in San Francisco the spring of his first year of grad school. Carlin decided I was too unfocused on my future, which was true. I hadn't a clue.

Though everyone expected me to get an M.B.A. or a law degree, I knew that simply wasn't me. Carlin went back East to med school at Yale and I stayed on in San Francisco, working as a carpenter. Nick kept telling me to buck up, that I'd find another Carlin. In the fall I went to Vanderbilt to appease my parents, who were exasperated at my aimlessness.

The first couple of years went okay; just the structure kept me occupied. I was building decks on the side to partly pay my way. Spent a fair amount of time visiting my grandmother outside Nashville. After Nick's death I slowly came unglued. I was going through the motions but every day feeling more distant and alienated from my peers. I didn't know then that my mind was already chemically unbalanced. I was deep in a clinical depression and I thought it was because of Nick's death, my broken heart, the discontent with the course of my life. I had no idea that it was a built-in dysfunction, some cross-wired part of my own mind, something inherited, that was plunging me deeper and deeper into a black hole. No doubt it was both brain chemistry and experience.

The jagged pieces of the puzzle fall in place in Taunton in group. While Bridgewater is a rabid menagerie of wild dogs and feral cats, Taunton is a big warren of damaged hamsters so harmless and shy there is no need for cages. Veterans of many groups, everyone listens attentively, respectfully, and adds their considered remarks to the sad life story of the day. Seems like seventy percent of them were sexually abused by fathers, uncles, or neighbors, who were sexually abused by their daddies, granddads, or great-uncles, who were sexually abused by . . . *ad infinitum.* The meek victims of two thousand years of perversion. Surrounded by them in group, I feel like a member of the privileged minority of the undefiled.

So I tell them my story a couple of times over the next month in group and one-to-one with a psychologist, rooting out more details, gaining perspective. At last I understand the pattern, the cycle down, down, down into darkness, followed by the mania which arrived at first in Mexico after I quit grad school as if to save myself from the black hole. A pleasant light breeze, the first feelings of simple joy in such a long time, a year ahead of the coming hurricane of rapture, hubris, delusions of grandeur. Now I am back, somewhere in between, tenuously balanced between the two poles on the fulcrum of a simple salt, lithium.

Nick never visits me at Taunton. I want him to. He would like the huge trees, the old buildings, and the access to the therapists. In high school he was sort of envious of his friends who saw psychiatrists regularly. He wanted to explore his psyche with a pro but thought that it was too much to ask of Mom and Dad. Of course I'm not sure if I really saw Nick's ghost. Maybe he was a construct of my mind created to comfort me in that house of horror. He surely seemed real but he might have been a dream. A dream within a dream.

Harper

The island empties the first week in September. Twenty thousand people shut up their houses and fly out, spread across America like migrating birds. Savanna goes to Boston. Even Jack, my therapist, leaves. I stay on with two thousand local souls, move into the big free house on the edge of the bluff, and settle in the converted attic, the warmest room in the house. The windows are portals. I stick my head out in the morning and feel the spray from the sea crashing on the rocks a hundred feet below. I look east over the Atlantic. With the sloping walls and round windows, the sound of the waves, it's like being in a big ship.

I signed contracts to paint two big houses. At least two months of work. One of the owners joked, Don't let me come back in June and find the yard full of boats, Harper.

You might find it full of tombstones, I said to freak him out. He just laughed.

I take on two part-time helpers, Bob, a tenth grader who is keen to work after school and weekends, and Sean, a blue-collar kid from Boston who's working as a waiter five nights a week, saving up money to go back to college. I clear it with the owner, the doctor down in Charleston, and let Sean move into one of the five bedrooms. I only see him the days we paint together.

Most weekends I leave instructions for Bob and Sean and go to Boston. Savanna shares a small two-bedroom apartment with a girl named Lindsey from Atlanta. Three young southerners in the North, we feel slightly superior to the Yankees, more gracious, better mannered, slummers from a more exotic locale. Since I'm averaging thirty bucks an hour, I treat them to movies and dinners. Sometimes we go to college parties. Watching the pointless revelry, listening to the students talking about what they were studying as if it's a waste of time, makes me glad I'm not just burning through college on a long ecstasy rave.

On the island I am alone most of the time. Bob and Sean cover all the tedious scraping, so I'm free to paint, roll it on and then touch up with a brush. Easy, rhythmic work, conducive to morbid introspection. If you died today, I wonder, what would be the epigraph on your tombstone?

Harper Henley Rutledge
1970–1989
An Angry Young Man

In middle school I had a pugnacious reputation. When I was thirteen, I broke a kid's nose when he cut the lunch line. I wasn't particularly big, pretty skinny really, but my fist packed a lot of fury. Where does *that* come from?

Just last spring I was walking down Bourbon Street with a date. Two Cajuns slowed down beside us in a pickup. One made a V with his fingers and stuck his tongue through it, then said, I'd like to suck your lady's cunt. Reflexively I spit a glob of snot that splatted right on his forehead. The guy jumped out and came running at me. Cool as a Popsicle, I reared back and flattened his nose. He hit the ground, out cold. By this time his friend was rounding the front of the pickup. I had grown into a fair-size boy, six-two, one ninety-five, but this guy was much bigger than his friend, thirty pounds bigger than me. I panicked. If I'd stayed cool, I might have punched him out, too, but instead I grabbed him and we rolled around until some cops broke it up and sent us in opposite directions. That anger is as old as I am.

"I miss jogging through the streets of Nantucket town. The roads're so bumpy and uneven it's like running on a dry riverbed," Cage says as we walk the smooth winding asphalt between the red-brick buildings of Taunton in October. He's been here for a couple of weeks. He looks far better than he had in Bridgewater, where he must have forgotten to brush his teeth or the bathroom was too scary or someone stole his toothpaste, something. He refuses to speak of Bridgewater, not a word. Now he can look you calmly in the eye. "They let me run here. I'm running every day again. But the meds make me sluggish." He pokes me in the belly. "You're getting a beer belly, boy. You better start running yourself. You let that injury beat you, you know."

He's talking about when I was a junior at Louisiana Episcopal in Baton Rouge. I pulled a hamstring my sophomore year, which kept me out much of the season, and even as a sophomore I never got back to the times I was running as a freshman. Cage's records in the mile, half-mile, and two-mile were still hanging over the bleachers in the gym. Midway through my junior season, when it was clear that I was no longer a star, that I couldn't compete with Cage's ghost, I quit.

"Why am I so angry, Cage?" I ask. "Why have I always been angry?"

"Dad carried around a lot of anger. I remember once when he took Nick and me to a fair before you were born. In one of those booths with a pop gun that shot corks, Nick knocked over a cigarette box with a five-dollar bill, which was a lot back then. The carny running the booth said that you had to knock the cigarette box completely off the shelf, which was impossible. Dad was irate.

He looked ready to leap over the counter and wallop the guy. Instead he said, 'This is a farce!' Nick and I both cracked up because we thought that he said, 'This is a fart!' "

"Why was Dad angry?" Tree limbs, trickling orange and yellow leaves, track overhead.

"You should ask Dad," Cage says. "I think maybe he thought he was being misled. Every time we went to a new church the search committee led him to believe that there was a lot more going on at the church than there was."

Cage is quiet for a time. We walk by a greenhouse where a few residents are potting plants. Cage suddenly starts riffing on Kipling's "Gunga Din," which Dad would recite to us as we walked along the beach in South Carolina, me on his shoulders and Nick and Cage wingmen on either side:

> In Taunton's sunny clime,
> Where I us'd to spend me time
> In service of her majesty, the brain,
> There was greenhouse therapy,
> A fine activity we all agree,
> For those of us headed down the drain.

I start laughing, then he joins in, and we both fall over howling on the lawn outside the greenhouse. Blurry behind the glass, a resident comes to the steamed-up wall and smiles. We lie on our backs in the grass, looking up at the sky, getting our breath back. After a long silence Cage says, "Dad was angry because he didn't have a dad."

I impose a new routine on the days when I'm painting alone. An hour when I have a large space to roll out becomes my own private therapy session, where I play shrink and client.

Visualize the family member who pisses you off. Picture him in a memory that makes you feel angry. Picture it until you feel the anger. See what you can dig up. Then let him have it. Everything you've always held back.

Her thick black hair showing lots of gray, sweeping high off her forehead, long waves framing her face. Her wide, kind, constant smile. Lipstick. Pearls. White hose stockings. Dressed up for church. She's holding a purse and car keys.

Hurry up, Harper, she shouts up the stairs. We're late. We're late again because you dawdled in the shower. You do this deliberately.

You'd never be late if you didn't make me go to church, I say, coming down slowly.

As long as you live in this house you're going to church. You're twelve years old. You've got six to go.

I reach the bottom of the stairs and we walk together into the kitchen. I stop and open a cabinet and pull out a glass.

Dammit, Harper, don't do this now. Please, you've made us twenty minutes late already.

I ignore her and turn on the faucet.

She reaches over and turns it off.

I turn it back on.

Harper, dammit. Why do you do this to me? Don't you think I have enough stress in my life? Nick would never do this. Why can't you act more like Nick?

"Why do you always compare me to Nick?" I yell, pushing the paint roller hard against the clapboard. " 'Nick was so sweet. Nick won a scholarship. Nick never complained. You can do better. You've got the same genes. You're as bright as him. Cage and Nick always made the headmaster's list. You can do it, Harper. Just try harder!'

"Well, I studied until my head hurt but I never measured up!" I catch my breath and load the roller up with paint, slap it on the wall. "Get it, Mama? You made me feel ashamed that I didn't make the headmaster's list! You made me feel like I didn't live up to your expectations. You made me feel like I wasn't as good as them. They were the stars who got the glory and the attention and I was Mr. Average."

I glance around to see if anybody is looking—if they see me screaming at the wall they'll think I'm as mad as Cage—then clean the mist of paint off my sunglasses. I climb a few steps up a ladder for the roller to reach the top of the wall. I'm leaning to one side, stretching as far as I can, when the ladder slips and I tumble from five feet, hit the ground, and stumble to my knees.

Leaning over to reach for my shades, I see Dad ten years before, bending over to pick up his glasses. His hair was already turning gray. He was wearing a seersucker suit and dog collar. His eyes were furious. I had just pulled the glasses from his face and flung them on the floor. I can't remember why. I was just angry. He had just gotten home from work. He was in a bad mood. When I was growing up, I'm not sure he was happy being a minister. He's been happier since he became a bishop, maybe he was happy as a young minister, but he was in a bad mood a lot when he came home while I was growing up.

Throwing his glasses, I must have broken the camel's back.

If it weren't for you, he said, I could be doing what I want.

A buried memory excavated! See, therapy works.

A kid can't understand those circumstances. Dad had a bad day at the office. He was trying to be the best dad he could, but he was remote, like most industrial dads. He was struggling to put his first two sons through college and his nine-year-old was always angry and out of control. No doubt biting his tongue later, in one short sentence he told me what a pain in the ass I'd been, how he'd sacrificed his own desires for me, and he confirmed what I'd known unconsciously but never understood all along: he didn't want a third son. He wanted to focus on his career, become a bishop, get ahead in his profession. In anger he expressed the very source of my anger. He loved me—he was always at my track meets, took me hiking and fishing, made the effort—but he wasn't a hundred percent behind conceiving me. I was a concession to my mother, who wanted another child. Back then I knew unconsciously that he didn't want me, and it fueled my anger.

I lift the ladder, slide it a few feet down the wall, move the paint tray, load up the roller. Climbing up, I feel lighter, like I can fly.

One night up in my attic in late October while I'm reading Robert Bly against the background of crashing waves, while I'm feeling pretty good about paying my own way, about my bank account, about starting to understand myself, about forgiving my parents for what they have done to me and what they have left un-done, about my beautiful girlfriend and the coming weekend, my phone rings.

"Harps," she says in a voice I've never heard.

"Hey, Savanna. I was just thinking about you."

"I'm pregnant."

The sea pounds against the rocks as if it will shatter them into a thousand pieces.

"I'm flying to Atlanta tomorrow. My mother has arranged everything."

"I'm so sorry." Thanks for taking me into your decision.

"It's your fucking fault."

"I beg your pardon?"

"You knew I forgot my diaphragm the last time I came out to Nantucket. I begged you to come in my mouth. And you said, 'I'll pull out at the last second.' "

"God, Savanna, I'm so sorry. I want to come to Atlanta."

"No. I've thought about it and I've made up my mind. You're sweet. You're cute. You're a baby. You're three years younger than I am. You need a lot of therapy. You're lost. And my mother says you've got no prospects."

"Thanks a lot."

"I told her that you would be successful one day. I love you, Harper."

The waves crash upon the cliffs.

"Would you want me to keep it?"

I hesitate. "I don't know if I ever want children. I surely don't need one right now."

"That's what I told my mother."

"I'm sure she was relieved."

"She likes you. She said, 'At least it would be good-looking.' "

"I really want to go with you to Atlanta."

"You can't. I want to do this with my mother."

I'm silent.

"Listen, Harper. I should do this my way. I want to keep talk-ing, to try to work through this, but I've made up my mind."

I don't say anything for a few seconds, then, "I'll pay for it."

"Mama thought you would offer to. She says you're a gentle-man. She told me to tell you not to worry about it."

"I want to pay for it."

"You can't."

"Then I'll give you a present. How much is it going to cost? God, I'm so sorry, Savanna." I'm not sure how I feel, if I feel anything at all.

"I have no earthly idea. It's not your concern. I'm leaving to-morrow. I've got to pack."

"I love you."

"I love you, too. Bye, Harper. I'll call you from Atlanta."

"I'll be with you in spirit . . ."

She laughs strangely and hangs up. It was a lame thing to say.

November is the coldest month of my life. At night it drops to zero. Polar winds howl off the Atlantic. It hurts to be outside. Growing up in South Louisiana, my blood is thin. I've finished the two houses, turned down contracts on others. Too cold. I start waiting tables at a restaurant that gets a lot of weekend traffic from the mainland and working as a bouncer at the Chicken Shack, where the regulars call me Little Cage. In the summer the place is packed and the bouncers are burly fuckers who take shit off no man. In the winter there are a few dozen locals, and the medium-size bouncers like me have no control over the flamma-ble mixture of alcohol and cabin fever. My income is quartered.

Savanna hasn't returned my calls in two weeks. I do some phone sessions with Jack, who assures me that women always have a lot of anger when they go through an abortion. He tells me not to take it personally, not to beat myself up about it. He commends the work I've done on my own, suggests that I think about going back to school instead of freezing my ass on the is-land. The only action I'm getting on the island is winks from des-perate old fishermen who've been months out at sea. One night a grizzled salt grabs my ass. I spin around and am just about to smash his face when I see what a pitiful old guy he is. I drop my fist and say, "Lay off, you old queen."

I start writing Savanna letters. I tell her she is the love of my life. I tell her I can't live without her. I tell her that I can't sleep. I go into Boston but her roommate won't let me in the door. I put some Tiffany pearl studs in her hand.

The first day of December is two below zero. Riding in the dune buggy from the house on the bluff to the Nantucket post office is like dogsledding across the tundra. The wind rips the tattered top off the car, nearly blows the car off the road into a cranberry bog. In my mailbox are the earrings and a letter:

Dear Harper,

The pearls made me cry. It was so sweet of you. I almost ran after you on the street, but Lindsey held me back. And she's right. There is no point in seeing each other again. It would only be painful. You are a dear, sweet boy. I will never forget you. But there is no future for us. This terrible thing has made me realize that. You have to figure out your life. I'm ready to get on with mine. I do want babies one day, and I believe you when you say that you do not. It's hard to say all this. Don't think I'm cruel. I've started dating a guy here in law school. Take care of yourself, Harper. You're a good soul. You're a great lover. You'll always have a place in my heart and I hope that I have a place in yours.

Love,
Savanna

I open up the box and look at the pearls. Three hundred bucks. The most expensive present I've ever bought. I wonder if they will take them back. I moan, "Oh fuck." In the afternoon I telephone the registrar's office at Tulane. I decide I will major in philosophy. Go to law school like everyone else.

Cage

I am rescued from Taunton by a debonair young Ivy League psychiatrist named Peter DeJarnette of Baton Rouge who convinces the Massachusetts Department of Mental Health to release me into his personal care. Dad married him and his dreamy wife, Louise Spencer, who was a couple of classes ahead of me at Louisiana Episcopal. I remember her as smart, sweet, and slightly shy. They look like the perfect couple. Peter heard about my predicament, called Dad, even offered to put me up in their pool house. A friend of the family, a developer, Walter Fairfield, offered to give me a job running a crew. They laid out a little map of the future for me. Harper came over from Nantucket and drove me to the airport in Boston.

It's humiliating, going back to Baton Rouge after seven years, after five months in state asylums, a fuckup, a nutcase, a twenty-nine-year-old carpenter. I feel diminished, spiritless, unworthy of anyone's help. Everyone is warm and kind and I am tentative and hesitant with old friends and strangers.

Peter and Louise are having terrible fights, sometimes right in front of their three-year-old. This is depressing in itself, overhearing the psychiatrist screaming at his wife while little Phoebe cries.

"Do you realize how hard I work? I don't need to come home to your paranoid suspicions!"

Louise's voice is always too low to hear across the patio and pool.

"So what if I bought a motorcycle? I'm thirty-eight. Just because I'm a shrink doesn't mean that I'm not allowed to have a midlife crisis. This one's premature. Better a motorcycle than a mistress!"

Louise's voice doesn't carry but Phoebe's cries do.

"I ride alone, goddammit, get it? Alone!"

I'm pretty sure Peter is fucking a nurse or an old girlfriend or both.

After a couple of weeks I move into a little converted garage only a quarter of a mile away from our old house on Chatmoss, in a neighborhood of several square miles of massive live oaks, most more than two hundred years old, permanently green canopies the size of circus tents, great curling limbs like tentacles of monster squids swooping down to the ground. When I'm feeling particularly lonesome, I climb up into the top of a live oak next door the way Nick used to do when he was nervous about a race or down about a girl.

I run a Fairfield crew of three black carpenters building a small, faux Victorian clapboard on a narrow lot not far from my garage studio in the part of town covered by the grand water oaks. The crew resents the fact that I came in from nowhere and was placed above them because I'm white and a friend of the big boss. I try to be egalitarian, divide the tasks evenly and always work as hard as they do, which they probably take as a mark of weakness. I'm the one that Mr. Fairfield always talks to when he comes around. I'm younger than everyone by ten years.

I look up from where I'm framing-out a window and see that Oranjello and Limonjello, twins in their late thirties, and Erasmus, a grizzled guy in his fifties, have just finished framing the roof over the short bar of the T-shaped house, the first section up top to be finished, what will eventually be the kitchen and dining room. As they drop to the ground, I walk around the house, look at the big rolls of tar paper, and decide that with a few more we could cover this part of the house and be able to store materials safely out of the rain by the end of the day. I tell Limonjello, who is the fastest carpenter, to hang the exterior kitchen door and Erasmus and Oranjello to move tar paper from around on the other side of the house to the kitchen. I drive over to the lumber store to get a few more rolls of tar paper.

Forty-five minutes later when I get back, the three of them are framing windows in the other part of the house. The tar paper is still on the ground, the kitchen door on top of it. I park and get out and walk up to Limonjello. It's difficult to tell the twins apart, but Limonjello has a gold incisor you can just barely see and at seven every morning when they arrive smiling, I mark his clothes. He's about my size. He has on a Grambling Tigers sweatshirt.

"Limonjello, why didn't you hang that door?" I ask him calmly, trying not to let fear creep into my voice.

"Why you asking me? Ask Limonjello."

I smile. "I am."

"No, you ain't. That's Limonjello over there. Ask him. Can't you tell the difference?"

"Stop foolin' with me, Limonjello." Is he fooling with me? Suddenly I'm not sure. "Well, whoever you are, hang the damn kitchen door," I say low enough for Oranjello and Erasmus not to hear.

"Yes, sir, big boss man. I'll jump right on it. Didn't know nothin' 'bout no door. Which do'?" He raises his voice: "Did boss say something 'bout a do'?"

"What do'?" Erasmus chimes in. "Front do' or back do'?"

"Nah," says Oranjello—or is it Limonjello? "Boss ain't said nothing about the do'."

"What about the roofing paper? I told you two to move the roofing paper."

Erasmus and one 'Jello look at me for a beat and then at each other and then start shaking their heads. "No, boss, you told us to frame these windows."

"That's not what I remember. Come on y'all, get the tar paper over the kitchen and the dining room before it's time to knock off." I speak slowly, confused about my place in space and time. "I'll hang the door."

Once the crew sees that I'm weak, they are on me like a pack of hyenas cutting a deformed calf away from the herd. I think I am losing my mind. They are making it worse. When I try to speak to people, I stutter and forget what I'm trying to say. I'm losing my coordination, dropping tools. I am scared of seeing people that I used to know, scared that they will see what a pitiful weakling I have deteriorated into.

After work I go home to my shitty garage and make some pasta or eat something from a can and then sit spellbound by the TV, oblivious to what is on, trapped in my head, dreading going back to the site the next day, too ashamed to call any of my old friends who have real lives, homes, children, careers. I start going to bed too listless to bother to shower. Sometimes I forget to take my lithium. Sometimes I double the dose to make up for it. The crew start holding their noses when I come around and leaving bars of soap on the hood of the company pickup I'm driving. When I shower, I zone out and focus in on the present moment only if the water suddenly turns scalding or freezing. Peter puts me on Zoloft. I'm not sure if I remember to take it. Mom and Dad call most nights to see how I'm doing. I have already caused them so much grief I don't want to tell them that I'm not sure how long I can keep it together. One day I stop going to work.

"Cage," Mr. Fairfield says from the door. It's about eight o'clock on a warm December morning. It's probably sixty degrees, green outside like midsummer in Massachusetts. I can hear a mourning dove cooing. I'm lying on my bed with my work clothes on from yesterday. I know that I have had them on for days but I don't care. I don't have the energy to change them. I can't remember the last time that I did the laundry. I'm too tired to call out to him.

"Cage, are you awake?" I hear him open the kitchen door.

I sit up on the bed. "Walter?"

"Hey, son." He comes out of the kitchenette into the room, a silhouette with the sunlight behind him. "How you feelin'?"

"Scared, Walter."

"It's okay, Cage. Can you get out of bed?"

"Yeah." I stand up, waver on my legs for a moment, steady.

"It's almost Christmas, only a couple of weeks away. You want to go up and see your parents for Christmas?"

I don't say anything. Yes. No. What's the difference? I don't know.

"I think you might as well go on up to Memphis. They miss you. You sure have a sweet mother and a fine father, you know."

"I know."

"I tell you what." Mr. Fairfield moves around the room, opening the windows. He's a big man but he has been nice to me for fifteen years and I'm not scared of him. "You take a shower and I'll pack up a little bag. I can have the rest of your clothes sent up later. Peter DeJarnette's on his way over."

I move stiffly like a robot into the little shower. I can hear Mr. Fairfield moving around in the room so I remember to soap up and rinse off without drifting into a fugue state. I come back in the room with a towel wrapped around my waist.

"These're the only clean clothes that I can find." Mr. Fairfield nods to a pair of gray flannel pants and a blue button-down and a black V-neck sweater. "You'll look like a banker." He laughs.

"It's not funny," I say. "I could have been a banker."

"You can still be a banker, Cage." He hands me the button-down. "You could finish that degree easy."

I laugh because that's preposterous. "My brain is damaged."

"Nah," he says. "Your thinking may be a bit foggy, but you'll come out of it. You've got a good mind."

Outside, I hear Peter's Porsche pull into the driveway.

Margaret

"He's withdrawn into himself," Joanie Fairfield tells me on the phone. "It's so strange. Just two weeks ago I ran into him at Calandro's and he seemed just like that ol' charming, good-looking devil everybody loves, not quite as exuberant, but that's understandable. Now he's just not there at all. Hardly says a word."

"Frank and I will come down and get him," I say. She is a good soul, Joanie, and practical.

"Don't make Frank go to all the trouble changing his busy schedule," Joanie says. "Walter thinks he and Peter should just put him on the train. Cage will be okay until he gets to Memphis. He'll just sit there, the poor dear."

"Tell them to put him on the train today, Joanie. That's the best thing to do. I've got a psychiatrist ready here, a nice man who goes to the cathedral. I've got a room made up upstairs."

"Cage will be fine, Mars. Don't you worry. Every good southern family has a manic-depressive." Joanie Fairfield has a lovely South Carolina low-country accent. "Fine old families often have more. They all learn to get by. They often distinguish themselves."

"Thanks for making me laugh, Joanie. Love you."

"Love you."

I hang up the phone and walk into the garden. My head starts to hurt right behind the eyes. Six weeks ago Peter DeJarnette warned us that a severe depression would follow the manic period that ended just six months ago, after running unchecked for a year or longer. He'd said if we were lucky, we could pick it up early and avert it with the right combination of drugs. "New drugs are coming out all the time. If we get the right mixture for Cage, we can control it." It looks like they haven't found the right mixture. Or caught it in time. Nick would be such a comfort right now, levelheaded, understanding. How many times have I wished that I've had him beside me through Cage's crisis? I do not believe in a God that says, You will die in a car crash. You will get cancer. You will be manic-depressive. I do not believe in a God like that. Suffering is still a mystery to me. I wonder how many generations of women in our family have pulled everyone through struggles such as this. Mother with Father's drinking. Grandmother Madora with Grandfather's early senility, whatever that would be called today. Great-Great-Grandfather Cage was surely a manic-depressive. He built up a steamship company on the Tennessee, Cumberland, and Mississippi rivers, then gambled it all away. The original Cage to settle on the river was probably a bipolar Cherokee killer, that's what it took to thrive back then. I feel weighed down by generations of illness, a heavy sense of futility.

I call Frank at his office and tell him to expect Cage in the afternoon. His voice sounds tired. He says he will meet the train.

Cage

"You're diving now in the downward part of the cycle, Cage. It's awful. But you will come out of it." Pete is wearing his white lab coat. He is driving his Porsche Carrera ninety miles an hour along the yellow concrete highway through a vast expanse of tall reeds due east of Baton Rouge. "It won't last long. I'll consult with Dr. Fielding in Memphis. We'll figure out the right meds."

I can barely hear him across a vast plain of apathy, as wide and dreary as the flat marsh that runs to every horizon under gray light. I don't feel like myself, like anyone. I don't care. I watch the approaching green signs grow larger, then swoop over the open sunroof without reading the words. I think the letters are scrambled but I'm not sure.

"Cage, are you listening to me?" Pete squeezes my thigh.

"Are you obeying the speed limit?" my mouth says on its own.

Pete laughs, cuffs my shoulder. "You're going to be okay."

Pete is out of his mind if he thinks that I am going to be okay. I'm not sure where I'm going but it's not okay. I say things by pure reflex. I make people laugh by reflex. It's not me who is talking, making you laugh. I don't know who it is. I don't particularly care. It takes too much of an effort just to scratch my nose. I look at Pete and I can see his skeleton through his skin, a death's-head grinning skull shining through his tan face. Pete is Dorian Gray, a facade of virtue—the brilliant young psychiatrist—cloaking a coke-snorting philanderer with a miserable wife and child. *But he cares about you*, I hear Nick's voice in my mind in stereophonic Dolby sound. *He cares. He has his problems, he needs to do some soul-searching himself, he might even need medication, but he cares about you.*

In the Hammond station parking lot he watches me swallow a Xanax capsule and three little lithium pills. He puts his arm around my shoulder as we watch the *City of New Orleans* barrel out of the swamp and pull into the country station.

"Thanks, Dr. Pete," says the part of myself that talks automatically. "Can't say you didn't try."

"Cage, you're bright. You're going to beat this illness. It's just an illness, like diabetes. There's no shame. No stigma," Peter says, walking along the platform. Nobody is riding the train that carried the black diaspora out of the South no mo'. Which is fine with me. People make me nervous. "And you can beat it just like hundreds of thousands beat diabetes."

He grabs my bag from me and I follow him into an empty car. I stand still as he puts the bag in the rack overhead, then pull out my wallet as if to tip him. "My doctor, my chauffeur, my porter."

Peter smiles and pats me on the back. "If you want to come back to Baton Rouge, I'm your man."

I have the sense that I'll never get off the train. I stare at him, uncomfortable, wishing he would leave, afraid for him to leave. The talking part of my self is quiet. Over his shoulder reflected in the plate glass my face is twisted in a knot, my eyes fear-shot. The talking part says, "Last train to Memphis."

Family Conference
1974

*S*end *it to* Zoom, *send it to* Zoom*!* kids in their early teens sang on TV. Nick watched them, thinking how they looked happy and confident like Cage. *Zoom, Box 350, Boston, Mass. 02134.*

"Nick." Margaret stood in the door of the sitting room. "Turn off the TV and finish your Latin."

"*Zoom*'s almost over."

"Remember we have a family conference after supper, so you have to do your homework now."

"Okay, Mom," Nick mumbled without looking at her. As the words between programs zipped up the black-and-white screen, he thought how everyone he knew had gotten color TVs. His mother said color was a waste of money and if he kept complaining she would throw out their old one. She never stopped worrying about money. Her latest cost-cutting measure was powdered milk. Every day Cage and Nick took turns mixing water in the powder and stirring forever until all the globs were broken up. Harper hated that milk and he was not even four. This morning at breakfast he had thrown his on the floor. Nick could see his mother was trying hard to smile. He thought she was going to cry but she just laughed. Cage had jumped out of his chair and used a paper towel to wipe it up.

Before Harper was born their parents told Cage and Nick that they were going to have a new brother or a sister. They said that it was a hard decision for them to make because there were already too many people in the world and a family should only have two kids, one to replace each parent, so the population wouldn't get bigger, but they thought that maybe this new Rutledge would turn out to be a great scientist who could help the problem of overpopulation. Nick used to look at Harper and wonder what kind of scientist he would be. Lately he decided that it was just something they thought up to make themselves feel better.

"Nick." His mother was back in the doorway, wearing an apron now. "Did you hear me? Turn that off."

"Okay." Nick crawled slowly toward the TV.

"Mr. Haley is such a nice man," she said. "And he really likes you. You're lucky you have a Latin teacher who went to Harvard. He's so disappointed when you don't do your homework thoroughly."

"Yeah." He switched off the TV.

"Yes, ma'am." His mother smiled.

"Yes, ma'am." Nick went upstairs and sat at his desk and looked out the window at the church. Darkness gathered over the empty lot across the street. In Tennessee they didn't have to live downtown right next to the church. All of their friends lived way out off Mulberry Road and only kids who went to public school lived around them. Nick wished that they had never left Tennessee. The kids here said *ta-mah-ta* instead of *to-may-toe* like they were from England or someplace, snobs, and when the Rutledges first moved to Virginia the year before, their classmates would lick their fingers and touch Cage's and Nick's necks, making a sizzling sound that meant the Tennesseans' necks were so red that they fried the spit on their fingers. One day on the bus when Kyle Kent, the biggest guy in the eighth grade, a lot bigger than Cage, touched Nick's neck and said, "Tsss," Cage went crazy. He jumped up from across the aisle and punched Kyle so hard in the nose it sounded like a basketball hitting the backboard. Cage screamed, "Never touch my little brother again or I'll kill you!" He kept on hitting him until some tenth graders stepped in and pulled him off. After that everyone respected Cage. He and Kyle were good friends now.

Nick turned on the desk lamp and opened his Latin book,

then watched his own reflection in the window. He pulled a spiral notebook out of a desk drawer and wrote, *Cage has always been at the top of his class and I am what they call an underachiever. I think it's my lack of confidence.*

He conjugated Latin verbs for half an hour and then went back to his diary: *Every seventh grader at Westminster has to make a speech at morning assembly to the entire school, all the students and teachers from the first to the twelfth grades, like three hundred people. Last year Cage did his on smoke jumpers, the firemen who parachute from airplanes to put out forest fires, because Dad was a smoke jumper in the summers between college. Cage looked really relaxed like Dad does in the pulpit, standing in the gym in front of the whole school. Just like Dad, he started out with a joke. The headmaster and all the teachers gave him an A. I'm doing mine on Sir Francis Drake because Granddad Cage told me that he was our ancestor, and because he was a pirate. It's in a week and my palms sweat when I think about walking from the packed bleachers across the gym floor to the microphone.*

"Nick, get Harper," his mother sang from the bottom of the stairs. "Dinner's ready."

In his room Harper was rolling Matchbox cars along an orange plastic track. He looked up and smiled at Nick, then sent two cars speeding toward each other. A tiny Camaro knocked a Firebird off the track. He raised his arms toward Nick, who picked him up, swung him onto his back. Going down the stairs, Nick told him, "Listen, Harpo, don't go throwing your milk on the floor, okay? None of us like the powdered milk. But we have to drink it."

"Why?" Harper said into Nick's ear.

"Because Mom and Dad don't have money for real milk right now."

"Why?" Harper moved his little hands to Nick's neck.

"Because ministers don't make very much money."

"Why?" He stuck a finger in Nick's ear.

"Just because."

Harper said, "Dad should be a fireman."

"Firemen don't make a lot of money."

"Why?"

"I don't know."

In the kitchen Cage had just come home from football practice. He was standing by the sink, smiling, his hair all mussed up, smudges of black cream under his eyes. "Nick, guess what? I'm the starting cornerback on Saturday."

"Hey, that's great." Nick set Harper on a chair at the kitchen table with a pile of worn cushions. He was proud of Cage and jealous at the same time.

"You want me to help you with your Latin tonight?" Cage smiled and poured the powdered milk into a tall pitcher.

"Nah. I finished it already." Nick walked over to the counter. "It's my turn."

"I'll do it." Cage smiled.

"Nick," his mother said, "please set the table."

"In the kitchen or the dining room?"

"In here."

Franklin Rutledge came in just as his wife was removing a casserole of ground beef and red beans from the oven. At forty-five Frank had hair that was still boot black, his weight—one eighty-five—the same as it was in the army. "Hey, Mars, my love. Evening, boys."

"Hey, Pop," Cage and Nick said in unison. Harper was singing to himself on the chair with cushions.

"Been visiting parishioners in the hospital?" Cage asked.

"All those who travail with trouble, sorrow, need, sickness, or any other adversity," Frank said with a faint smile. "How was football?"

"Fantastic." Cage pushed his long bangs out of his face. "Made the starting squad. I'm the only ninth grader to make varsity."

"You are a prodigy." He patted Cage on the back, walking out the door, then came back a few minutes later, still in his black shirt but without the white collar. Sitting down at the head of the table, he held out his arms to Nick and Cage. While they all held hands, he tilted his head down, closed his eyes, and was opening his mouth when Harper said, "Don't make it a long one, Papa."

Cage laughed. Nick stared morosely at the floor. Their mother sighed and their father smiled, then said quickly, "Bless this food to our use and us to Thy service. Keep us ever mindful of the needs of others. In Christ's name we pray, amen."

Every time their father blessed the food, Nick felt guilty about cheating in confirmation class. The class was supposed to read Bible lessons each day for weekly quizzes. His father told the class he would stop quizzing them if they promised to do the readings. All twenty pledged but not a single soul read the Bible verses. Silently Nick prayed, Dear God, please forgive me for not reading the Bible like I promised, knowing that he wouldn't read it later on either, wondering, Why does God let us sin and ask for forgiveness and be forgiven again and again? It seems like a license to sin. He watched his father eat, thought he saw sadness in his father's blue eyes. Ever since they had moved to Virginia his father hadn't seemed as happy as when they lived in Tennessee. Cage had told Nick it was because the rich people in the church treated their minister like one of the employees at their furniture factories.

Nick cleared the table and handed the dishes to Cage, who rinsed them before putting them in the dishwasher. When they finished, Franklin said, "Well, boys, last week I asked you to give some thought to how we all get along in the family. It's important to be open about what bothers you about other family members, not to quietly harbor resentments toward one another. Cage, why don't you start?"

"Okay." Cage dried his hands and set the towel on a hook over the sink. "The only thing I resent is the ten p.m. curfew on weekends." He walked to the table. "Buck and Slim Jones, everybody else, get to stay out until eleven."

"You're only fourteen, Cage," Margaret said.

"So what? I made the varsity football team. Most of those guys don't have a curfew at all."

"I think he's grown-up enough to stay out until eleven,"

Frank said. "But the first time you're late, the curfew is going back to ten."

"Eleven-thirty," Cage said.

"Eleven. No argument," Frank said.

"All right." Cage dropped into his seat. "That's a deal. GFI, Nick."

"I hate it that I'm always compared to Cage and told to act like him. Like at the coffee minute after church, Mom always says, 'Why can't you be more like Cage. Look at him out there talking to adults.' I don't have anything to say. I don't like to talk to adults."

"It's for your own good, Nick." Margaret placed her hand on his. "You need to learn to be comfortable socially."

"But I'm not Cage. He can do that. He's confident. I'm not."

"You'll never gain confidence if you don't try," Frank said.

"You can talk to people." Cage patted him on the shoulder. "Just ask them questions about themselves. Everyone likes to talk about themselves. Then just nod and smile and when they finish, ask them another question."

Nick looked at Cage and nodded. "Okay, I'll try."

"What about me?" Harper waved a spoon around from the high chair.

"Yes, Harper?" Frank said. "What don't you like?"

"Mama smiles at me too much."

Everyone laughed. Margaret stopped smiling. She said, "I'll try not to smile at you so much. Anything else?"

"I don't like Dad's farts or the smell of his pipe."

Cage leaned over the table laughing. "Yeah, Dad, you fart like a donkey."

"Cage Rutledge." Margaret raised her hand to her mouth.

"Harper," Frank said with a straight face. "I have been meaning to give up the pipe as it's hazardous to my health. As for the flatulence—"

Cage interrupted. "It's in God's hands."

Cage

I don't have much time left. They're coming. They'll be here soon. I lie in bed looking up at the ceiling, listening. I hear a siren in the distance, growing closer. They're almost here. My transgressions are infinite and follow me like my shadow. My sins have become a legion of ghosts that populate my dreams and crowd the room, hundreds of vaporous forms, like Nick was in Bridgewater, but he is not among them. I cannot escape. The ghosts moan softly like angry souls in hell beckoning me to join them. I have repented a thousand times but there is no forgiveness. Dr. Fielding doesn't believe in Evil but I know it exists. The old monk Father David told me you can smell it. He says when the Son of God was tempted by what he called the devil, he was speaking of personalized Evil. Even when he's consecrating communion, he feels slammed by temptation and says, Satan, get the hell out of here. In the name of Jesus Christ I command you to go. And Satan leaves. I try it now. I yell out, "In the name of Christ I command you to go!" But the ghosts just move in closer and the stench thickens around me, filling my nose until I can't breathe and I lie on the bed, gagging.

Harper comes running into the room, saying, "What's the matter?"

The ghosts withdraw when he enters. My brother. I love my brother. What if they get him, too? They might take the whole family because of me. They'll kill us all. Of course. On the night before the Son of Man was born. "Do you smell anything?"

"No. Are you okay?" Harper leans over the bed and pats me on the shoulder. "Brother, it's good to see you. What smell?"

"Evil."

"What?" Harper squints at me.

I know that he will not understand, so I say, "Eggnog."

"Come on, get out of bed." Harper buttons the neck of his shirt and starts to knot a red tie. "We're leaving in fifteen minutes."

"I'm not going. We'll die if I go. We might have a wreck."

"That's crazy, brother. Nothin's gonna happen," Harper says. "Now come on."

He drags me out of bed and I walk into the bathroom, where I know the ghosts will be waiting. I turn the hot tap and hold my hand under the tub faucet waiting for the water to warm before I mix in the cold. I picture Monica kissing Nick, then hugging him and at the same time smiling over his shoulder at me with a look in her eyes that said he never has to know until I realize that the hot water is scalding my palm. At the foot of the stairs Mama sings up, "Come on, boys! We don't want to be late!" Harper yells down, "Cage's in the shower, Mom. Five minutes."

I dress in my blue Brooks Brothers suit that I've worn maybe twice in the two years since I dropped out of business school, a symbol that I'm a fuckup, of my failure to become a productive individual. That's one of my sins. I have taken and taken and taken from my parents and I shall be punished by forces older than mankind. Memphis is an ancient city connected by a river of time to the Egyptian city on the Nile and there is an order of old families that is as ancient as the forces. They condemn and destroy depraved miscreants like me. Tonight, on the eve of the birth of the Son of God, they will strike me down. By dawn they will boil me in oil.

"Come on, brother!" Harper yells from the bottom of the stairs.

I don't want to go but I don't want to be alone either. They might come for me when I'm alone. I want to be with Harper. I never see him anymore. Downstairs I get an overcoat and go out the kitchen door to the carport where a cloud of toxic exhaust is billowing up in the cold night. Mom drives and Harper sits in front. In the dark in the back I listen for sirens. The police might not come for me. The car could crash, explode into flames. But I say nothing and try to focus on the conversation in the front.

"Some people who've been through a lot of therapy become so . . . *selfish*," Harper is saying. "They do exactly what they want to do with no regard for others. Their therapist told them it's okay."

The last stretch of Union before you reach St. Mary's runs past a row of pawnshops and I think of my grandfather's Belgium Browning twelve-gauge and the power tools and guitar I pawned on my manic spree and I know that I'll have to pay for these, too. Every action is remembered forever and the culpable shall perish in ultimate pain. Past the pawnshops, the cathedral towers up in the night like a Gothic fortress. Hunkering by the cathedral, Dad's office looks like a haunted house.

Harper

I never lived in Memphis, so going there is always an exotic trip. St. Mary's rises out of the abandoned no-man's-land between the renewed downtown on the river and the middle-class neighborhoods of midtown. The diocesan headquarters was originally the bishop's rectory, a Victorian limestone mansion with gables and tall, narrow windows. The parking lot is full but there is one space marked *Reserved for Clergy* near a side entrance to the church.

"We shouldn't park here," Cage says from the backseat. "We don't have the right."

"Of course we do, Cage," Mama says cheerfully. You might accuse it of being a voice of false cheer but it isn't. Constant but never false, evidence of her determination.

"Mom works as hard as most of the clergy," I say. "She organizes events, writes for the diocesan newspaper, helps out with all sorts of things. I think she deserves to park here."

"Thanks, Harper." Mom pats my thigh with her gloved hand.

"But why do they call this a cathedral?" I say. "Notre Dame is a cathedral. It's pretentious. This is just a big church."

"The seat of a bishop is a cathedral, Harper," Mama says. "If you had paid any attention growing up, you would know that."

We're late. For as long as I can remember on Sunday mornings we always arrived late. Dad would drive in before for the eight o'clock service and Mom would be left to get Cage and Nick woken up and into seersucker suits and me dressed in shorts like Christopher Robin, all of us into the station wagon and across Baton Rouge to St. James downtown by the river. Invariably we were late. Mom would lose her temper when we dawdled stubbornly. More than once she swatted me on the butt with a hairbrush when I refused to dress.

"Hark the Herald Angels Sing" resounds through the wide space when we enter the cathedral. The acolytes are already leading the procession up the center aisle toward the altar. The church is crowded with Christmas and Easter devotees. "Merry Christmas," we say to the ushers, who greet Mom by her first name and smile at Cage and me. Only in the far wings of the transept, the arms of the cruciform shape of the church, are there any seats.

During the service Cage's face is contorted with pain, his cheeks squashed up in worry lines from the corners of his eyes. I try to get him to sing. He has a good singing voice and I think the hymns might take him out of his misery for a few moments but he just shakes his head. I put my arm around his shoulders but he shrugs it off and mumbles, "They'll think we're gay."

"Who will?" I say. "Nobody will."

Cage nods at four men in colorful sweaters sitting on the pew in front of us.

"So what? They're gay and nobody cares."

"You don't know," Cage whispers, his face drawn like the agony of Christ.

"Gays aren't damned for their sexuality anyway," I say.

"*We* are damned," he whispers.

"No, we're not. Nobody's damned. Just repent for whatever's tormenting you and you'll be forgiven."

Cage shakes his head. Mom says softly from my other side, "Shush."

Dad mounts the pulpit in his robes and the pointed miter hat. He begins the sermon by quoting from the Gospel of St. John: "And the Word became flesh and dwelt among us, full of grace and truth. We have beheld his glory, glory as the Son of the Father." It never made much sense to me, an omnipotent God who sent a savior two thousand years ago into a world full of pain, disease, and violence to bring us eternal salvation, and whose arrival did nothing to diminish everything terrible in the world.

"From after Thanksgiving to before New Year's, the stories of Christmas are told and retold. They are read to wide-eyed children from large illustrated books or heard on the radio or seen on television." Dad preaches without notes, gazing out into the congregation. Nick used to say that Dad would have made a good politician. As a boy I wished that he were more important than a preacher, a word Mom disliked. Call him a minister, not a preacher, she used to say. I think she was embarrassed to be associated with Baptist fundamentalists.

"They range from the heroics of Rudolph the Red-Nosed Reindeer to the death and resurrection of Frosty the Snowman, from the reformation of the Grinch Who Stole Christmas to the repentant Scrooge of Charles Dickens's *A Christmas Carol*," Dad goes on in his ridiculous hat. I've heard this sermon several times over the years.

The men in front of us whisper to each other. Cage leans toward me and says, "See? They're mocking Dad because he isn't the real bishop."

"Oh Jesus, of course he's the bishop." I wonder how God could have inflicted this disease on Cage. Is it a trial to test Mom and Dad's faith?

I flunk the test.

"The secret of these stories is that they are maps of the human heart. They tell us about basic human responses." Dad's voice is deep and sincere, magnified by speakers through the nave. "They cut through the adult world of moral ambiguity to state basic truths that have the power to renew the human spirit. How many times have we heard Charlie Brown proclaim that the true meaning of Christmas is the love that gives life to a broken-down tree? How many times have we followed the dastardly doings of the Grinch knowing full well that no one can resist the grace of a star? And how many times have our hearts warmed when Scrooge finally sees the errors of his ways and responds to the spirit of Christmas?"

Too many, I think. Too many times have I heard these stories, for now they fall on deaf ears.

Cage

At the end of the service, while Mom and Harper are greeting parishioners, I know with certainty that my end is nigh. My fears were confirmed again and again through the midnight mass. The ushers placed us in the far left of the church like outcasts. The trumpets sounded like snorting pigs. The fags poked fun at Dad's sermon. The reading said that a light would be focused on the wicked. After the reading I had waited for a spotlight to shine down on my pew but it never came and I understood that they were teasing me, drawing out my capture, telling me secretly that they would come in the night and find me and drag me away and boil me in oil. I see myself tossed into an enormous bubbling pot, the oil scalding my flesh and flaying it from my body until my skeleton floats in the thick yellow liquid, all the impurities, all the sins of my flesh burned away with the flesh, the final cleansing which destroys as it purifies.

Harper is standing in the aisle talking to the McFarlands. He

smiles at them as if they were not among the old families, part of
the old order that has condemned me. They smile back so as not
to betray the secret. They will not tolerate the profane and the
unproductive. The old order will crucify me for the common
good. The world will be better off without me.

Harper walks over. "How you doin', brother?"

I can think of nothing to say that he would understand.

"There's the Jenkinses. They like you. Let's go say hello."

"They smile but they don't like me." I sit back down in the pew
and pray, Dear God, make it fast and painless.

"Come on, Cage. Get up. Let's go say hello to the Jenkinses."

"Look deep in their eyes, Harper. Look deep and you'll see
they're part of it."

"Part of what?" Harper asks as Mom arrives beside him.

"The old families."

"Old families?" Mom asks.

It is time now to tell them. "I can see something that has been
hidden from us forever. Now I can see the design. Memphis is
named after the ancient Egyptian city because there is an ancient
order that runs thousands of years back to the city on the Nile,"
I say slowly so they can follow. "Everyone who is not a productive
member of society, everyone who has not had children and raised
them well, everyone who has violated the laws of nature will be
boiled in oil."

"You've been productive, Cage," Harper says quickly. "You've
worked hard and you've helped a lot of people. You haven't committed any unforgivable sins."

"We are not one of the old families. Our whole family will be
put to death."

"We may not have much money but we come from one of the
oldest families in Tennessee," Harper says.

"Very old families," Mom says.

"Besides," Harper says, "they wouldn't crucify the bishop."

"Dad is not the real bishop. Dad is an impostor."

Harper smiles in disbelief but he will see. Soon he will see for
himself. Dad has gone back to the sacristy to change out of his

vestments. The church is nearly empty now and I apprehend that when it is vacant they will come for us. "Let's go."

"You boys go on." Mom gives the keys to Harper. "I'll come with your father."

I walk warily at Harper's elbow outside into the cold, watching for the hooded figures who will come to take me away. I see one standing in the shadows by a stone wall and I break for the parking lot, too scared to look over my shoulder. Behind me Harper yells, "Cage, what's up?" I hear footsteps behind me and I run harder but my overcoat is slowing me down, so I shed it where the lot meets the street and turn right onto the sidewalk, heading for the lights of the Mississippi River Bridge. Harper shouts, "Cage, stop! Where are you going?" Ahead on the sidewalk the hooded men move slowly toward me, cutting off my escape. I slow down, looking right and left at the bare trees and derelict buildings. The footsteps behind grow louder, like hammers hitting the concrete, hammers that will smash my skull open and spill my brains over the sidewalk like a broken jar of jelly. Running is pointless. They will find me. They know where I'm going even before I do. I fall to the sidewalk and sit up on my knees, looking up at the few stars visible through the glow of the city lights. I beg for forgiveness but God is not listening. The footsteps are upon me now. I twist my head around expecting to see an angel of death but it is only Harper. He sets my overcoat on my shoulders and pulls me to my feet and hugs me.

"Cage . . . Cage . . . why are you running from me?" Harper looks into my eyes. "Why are you sobbing? Everything's going to be okay. Look, your hands are bleeding and you've torn a hole in your pants."

Behind him the three figures come out of the darkness. I whisper, "Harper, watch out!"

Harper turns and gazes at the figures, three old black bums, weaving unsteadily in a row, and says, "Merry Christmas!"

"Merry Chris'mas, chief," says one in front.

"Looks like yo' frien' done had too much Christmas spirit already!" another says, tittering, and the others guffaw like a chorus.

"Running like he saw a ghost!"

"Christmas kind of a rough time of year, ain't it, chief?" one of them says to me.

I open my mouth but no words come.

"Got the Christmas blues," a bum croons. "Ain't nothing sadder than the Christmas blues."

"Gentlemen, we wish you a happy holiday." Harper laughs. "But I must be getting my brother home."

"He be your brother, huh?" One peers intently from Harper's face to mine. "A brother be a lot of trouble sometime." He looks at me hard. "You mind your brother, now. Don't be running off into the street in the middle of the night."

"Bes' git 'im on home." One of the black men offers a bottle toward Harper. "He don't look right in the head."

"How 'bout a little Christmas gif' for three pilgrims on a cold night?" the tallest asks Harper.

"Yeah," the shortest one says. "We ain't even got a manger to lie in."

Harper pulls out a wallet from inside his coat and holds out a ten.

"Merry Christmas, chief," the tall one says, snatching the bill, his hand darting out from his ragged ski parka like a piranha. "And a happy new year to ya, too!"

The other two crowd in on the tall bum, the shortest yelling, "I'm the treasurer of this outfit, remember! We voted on it. I'm the only one can be trusted with cash." Harper turns me around by the shoulder and we walk back to the church parking lot, the sounds of the bums' argument fading behind us. As we reach Mom's station wagon, Harper puts his arm around my shoulder and says, "What were you running from? There's nothing to be scared of."

"Nothing!" I shout. "Harper, if you think hell is simply some sort of symbol, then just look at me!"

Harper

We drive all the way home from the church in silence. Waiting for Mom and Dad, I turn on the cable and surf until I find some soft porn.

"What are you watching?" Cage asks with a horrified expression.

"Cinemax."

Cage says, "It's evil."

"You're right." I start surfing through the channels aimlessly.

Cage ascends the stairs in slow motion, as if with each step he cannot make up his mind whether to go up or stay down. When he's halfway up, I switch back to Skinemax. Watching two half-naked, fake-titted blondes kissing and fondling gives me the urge to go to the guest room and choke the chicken to memories of Savanna's small breasts, her mouth on me. I resist for five long minutes and I'm about to scout Mom's cabinets for some hand lotion when I hear the sound of the side door opening and Mom singing out, "Boys, we're home!"

Ever since I was ten and Nick and Cage were both at college, the family has opened our gifts after the midnight service. I persuade Cage to come downstairs and join us in the living room, where old oil portraits of Rutledge preachers and Cage planters glower at us as if the latest generation of their progeny has bitterly disappointed them. Which one of them passed on the gene of Cage's illness? I suspect it was the first Morgan Elijah Cage, who carved out a little frontier empire. Family lore says he was a generous man who donated land for a church and reared a Cherokee boy orphaned on the Trail of Tears. Then he lost it all in whiskey and poker chips. Must have had a lover or two if he was anything like the last Cage.

The Christmas tree, beautifully decorated as long as I can remember, even after Nick's death, looks like Mom sort of threw on a few ornaments. Wearing a bathrobe over his pajamas, Dad sits in a wingback chair, sipping a glass of wine. Cage slouches on the sofa, staring at the reflection of the room in the window, and Mom, still in her church clothes, perches on the other end, holding a steaming cup of tea. The only sound is the crackle of the fire.

"Well." I stand in the middle of the room. "Shall we begin?"

"Yes," Mom says brightly. "Christmas brings back so many lovely memories."

I start passing out the gifts. I think of Cage and Nick, before I was born, their matching bicycles and identical UT football uniforms, Granddad quarterbacking plays in the big living room at Cage's Bend, the pictures of them sledding in the mountains of East Tennessee, the huge bonfires of Christmas trees they used to have in front of the church in Bristol, all photos in an album older than me. One Christmas in Baton Rouge, Cage stormed off because the bronze statue of a Labrador like his dog Trapper that Mom had given him didn't measure up to the gifts his rich friends would receive. That was the rub of growing up Episcopal minister's sons. We were thrown in with the wealthiest kids in any given community but we were basically poor by comparison. Cage was angry in high school that he didn't have a car or a stereo or as many clothes as his friends. Was that simply adolescence or was the anger made deeper by the illness, years before it was detected, before it blossomed like a poisonous flower?

"I have a special gift for Cage," Mom announces after the last boxes have been opened. She leaves the room, then returns with a large, baggily wrapped parcel.

Cage runs his hands along it, says, "I know what it is. But I don't believe it." His hands shake as he tears it open and reveals a wooden sled, a Flexible Flyer with red runners.

I laugh. "It never snows in Memphis and when it does there's not a big enough hill to sled for a hundred miles."

"You were so upset when we moved to Baton Rouge and left yours behind in the attic in Virginia," Mom tells him.

"You're trying to heal my inner child." Cage smiles at the futility of the gesture.

I'm a little stunned at the absurdity of giving a thirty-year-old man a sled and saddened by the desperate logic of replacing something that they had taken from him a decade and a half before.

"Thanks, Mom," Cage says hollowly. "I've been so scared." He laughs with some of the old glimmer in his eyes. "The other day in Baton Rouge, Walter Fairfield sent me to a store to buy some ice for the Christmas party he throws for all his crews. There was a big black man behind the counter. I tried to speak and my voice came out all high and trembling, May I have a bag of ice? The man nodded toward a cooler across the room. I got a bag and set it on the counter. Walter had given me a twenty and I was worried that the man couldn't make change for a dollar-fifty bag of ice, so I asked him if he had change. He looked at me as if I were mentally defective. He made the change, pushed it across the counter, and my voice came out a little peep, Thanks. He followed me to the door and said, Come back again, big money."

Everyone laughs at the sad little anecdote, grasping for holiday cheer.

On the first day of 1990 Dad, Cage, and I are watching a bowl game while Mom is cooking in the kitchen. During some commercials, Dad changes to CNN. An anchorwoman is talking about the execution of Ceauşescu. Cage's face is twisted with fear or horror, impossible to say exactly what.

"She's watching me," he says.

Dad and I look at Cage, then at each other, then back at him.

"No, son, she's not watching you," Dad says.

"Come on, Cage," I say. "No one's watching you."

"You don't know. You think you know," he says, suddenly rising out of his torpor. "You think you know how reality works. But you don't. I know. I can see it now. She's watching me. She's part of the Order."

"There is no fucking Order, Cage," I nearly shout. "Sorry for my language, Pop." I'm sick of his obsession with the Order, the

secret society of vengeful old families who control everything and
are going to punish him for being a fuckup, for all the sins of his
life. His conscience is turbocharged, out of control, its Sunday
school morality taken to paranoid Old Testament extremes. The
psychiatrist is dosing him with antipsychotics to dispel his delusions but apparently they take weeks to kick in. You can talk to
him till you are blue in the face but you can't break through.

"You can't see it because you're not a part of the Order," Cage
rattles on. "They spurn our family."

"You know what I just figured out?" I look at him and Dad and
at Mom, who came to the door of the den when I yelled. "His
delusion is about not really belonging to his circle of friends in all
the cities he lived in because he wasn't as rich as any of them. He
felt like he never really belonged. We never belonged. We weren't
as respected because we weren't rich. That's the root of it."

"That's very insightful, Harper," Mom says.

"Yes, it is, son," Dad says. "That could be it."

Mom puts her hand on Cage's shoulder. "Do you see, Cage?
Do you see the root of your delusions? You were always ashamed
that we didn't have as much as your friends."

"Oh, you just don't see." Cage shakes his head. "I can see because they are letting me in on it now. They let you know before
they come for you. Part of the punishment. I'll just disappear. You
won't ever know what happened to me."

"Cage." Mama is crying. She bends down and hugs him. "No
one is going to come for you. Nothing is going to happen to you."

Dad moans a deep animal sound of despair, changes the TV
back to the bowl game.

I spend the next week with Cage, trying to get him to go outside
and take a walk around the Chickasaw Gardens lake near the
house. The most I can get him to do is go out in the backyard,
which Mom in her grief over Nick turned into a lovely garden of
azaleas, camellias, ferns, and shrubs. There is a moss-green statue
of Buddha that was in the garden when they bought the house
that she chose to keep. This is the first house that they've owned,
the church having abandoned the rectory system for a mortgage

allowance to give ministers equity in real estate. I try to get Cage to meditate. He will only talk about the Order. Every hour he thinks they are coming. He thinks the mailman is watching our family. He's convinced that he has a womanly body, that he is a ninety-pound weakling, though he is a fit hundred and seventy-five pounds. He will be exterminated because he is so puny. He runs upstairs whenever the doorbell rings. Every football bowl game could be the occasion when they come for him. Every public holiday. Or the middle of the night. His obsession is endless, unceasing, his every waking hour hell.

Cage refuses to go with Dad to take me to the train station. At the kitchen door he tells me, "They're going to take me after you go, brother."

"No, Cage. I'll see you on spring break. Or you can come down to New Orleans and visit me."

He laughs grimly at the outlandishness of the idea that he will still be alive in March, shakes his head. "You don't know."

I hug him and he hugs back in a bear grip, still strong from all the carpentry and swimming of his long manic run. He whispers in my ear, "Be good, Harper. Don't waste your life like I have. They could come for you one day."

Back in New Orleans I get a single dorm room while I look for an apartment. I'm still sick over Savanna. Not an hour goes by when I don't feel like screaming. I've never felt so low in my life. The nights are excruciating. But having a beautiful older woman love me for a time has given me new confidence. Now I realize girls find me attractive and I talk to girls I wouldn't have dared approach when I was a freshman. They laugh at my stories of the horny old fishermen at the Chicken Shack. I think I've matured some over the last six months. I'm no longer impressed by the antics of the guys at the SAE house, the parties with strippers, the drinking contests. I drop my membership and focus on the books. For the first time in my life I'm getting all A minuses and B pluses. When studying philosophy, it's easy to find a book of criticism that explains the text and then kind of plagiarize. I'm not proud

of it but it works and I'm learning something. I sleep with a couple of girls, date a few, and spend a lot of time by myself. I start
writing songs, imitating R.E.M. But I suck because I don't play an
instrument. An ad on a bulletin board advertising a band inspires
me to go by the address, where four grungy-looking guys from
San Antonio are hanging out on the porch of a run-down house.
I vaguely remember seeing them around freshman year, when
they were preppie.

"So what do you do, man?" one of them says.

"What's the name of the band?" I reply.

"Body Count," another one says. "What do you play, man?"

"I'm kinda learning guitar," I lie. They sort of smile. "I write
songs, *dude*."

"Cool," one of them says. I catch another glancing me up and
down disdainfully. I'm wearing worn-out jeans and a red sweatshirt that says *Nantucket* in bold white letters. My hair is much
shorter than theirs.

"You got some on you?"

I hand him some typed sheets of paper. "Maybe I could listen
to you jam."

"Not now, you can't, man. We blew the power in the house,"
says the one who's done most of the talking. "But we'll read these
and get back to you. You got the number on here, huh?"

"Yeah. Okay. Hope you get the power fixed." I get the feeling
they don't really want me around, so I step off the porch.

"Me, too, dude."

"Later." I cruise. I never hear from them. My songwriting career ends.

I call home every couple of days. Cage thinks the phone's
bugged, so he won't say much. Half the time, Mama sounds on
the verge of tears. She keeps asking me what they did wrong. She
believes what the doctors tell her, what they say at the Alliance for
the Mentally Ill, that it's not her fault, that it's genetic, but that
doesn't alleviate the muddled guilt she feels. She says that Cage
sleeps most of the time, drugged up. Though I don't want to go

up to Memphis and see Cage a broken shell of himself, I promise to catch the train at spring break.

Cage has the same haunted look in his eyes that he had at
Christmas. He babbles on about the Order. The last traces of
his famous sense of humor have vanished. He is anguished
every waking moment and all his dreams are nightmares. He
sits mute at the dinner table. There is little conversation among
the rest of us.

"How are preparations going for the flower festival?" Dad
breaks the silence, then looks my way and says, "Two years ago
your mother started a flower festival at the cathedral. It's beautiful. Thousands upon thousands of flowers."

"It's going to be more beautiful than ever this year." Mama
smiles. My high school girlfriends always remarked upon her
full-on smile. A smile that says here I am, ready to help you, listen, understand, empathize. Used to bug me when I was in grade
school. There she was around me all the time smiling. I wonder if
it haunts Cage, gets twisted into something like the floating smile
of the Cheshire cat in his tortured imagination.

"That sounds cool," I say. "Flower power. The azaleas are
starting to bloom in New Orleans now."

Mama gushes, "Oh, I'll bet it's beautiful now."

Cage says, "Do you think if you look at a flower, it weeps for
you?"

We look at each other.

"What a poetic thought," Mama says. "I'm always finding
scraps of paper with his jottings. Many of them are just insightful."

"I was very proud when you won the Sewanee poetry award,"
Dad says.

"A thousand bucks," I say. "I remember that and I was only
twelve. I thought you were going to be a famous writer."

"You might be still," Mom says.

"I had to pay back dues at the KA house." Cage laughs. For a
split second the haunted look vanishes. "The treasurer went with
me to pick up the check."

Everybody laughs. Cage smiles for a second, then falls back into himself.

"Oh, it's good to see you laugh again," Mama says. "Must be the first time in a month. No, you laughed two weeks ago, Father David told me."

Everyone looks at Cage for a second waiting for a response but he doesn't see us. Dad looks at me and explains, "Father David is a hermit who has taken a vow of silence but his phone is always busy. Sometimes I can't get through for hours. He has raised a whole lot of money for his leprosarium in Liberia and he calls our bookkeeper almost daily to check on his account." Dad is trying to keep the humor going. He chuckles and Mom laughs. "He's eighty-five. He longs to go back. Frankly I'm glad for him to go. I said, 'Father, if you want to go back to Africa to die, it's okay with me.' 'Die?' He raised his staff in the air like John the Baptist. 'I'm going back to serve!' "

Mama's smiling. Cage is somewhere else.

"What's the matter, Cage?" I ask.

He looks at his plate, shakes his head.

"What?" I reach across the table and take his hand.

Cage nods and returns the pressure on my hand. "When Father David leaves, they will come for me."

"No one is coming for you, Cage." I fight the urge to scream, Stop it! Just stop it! Snap out of it!

"You're safe here," Mama says.

"Here?" Dad says. "You're safe anywhere, son. No one's coming after you."

Cage shakes his head. We finish the dinner in a hopeless silence.

Pushing the Envelope
1978

Baton Rouge. Midnight. Ninety-two degrees, ninety-eight percent humidity. Cage, Nick, Rowan Patrick, and Tad Beauregard,
squeezed in the cab of a pickup, slowly cased the back of a
small hospital. Nick was the driver. He'd altered the license
plate number with black tape. Cage, Rowan, and Tad were all
wearing black jeans and black T-shirts and holding suede
gloves and wire cutters. Nick parked in the shadow between
two tall streetlamps. The boys in black piled out of the car and
ran for a small chain-link cage enclosing a metal door. Following carefully choreographed maneuvers, they each clipped several feet of fence, one on top of the other, so a six-foot-tall slit
appeared within seconds. Two of them slipped inside and
picked up a 175-pound pressurized tank, leaning it forward quietly, until one boy had the front and the other strained to lift the
rear. The third held the fence open and the two waddled out,
then the three of them labored the tank twenty feet to the car.
The tank made a huge bang as they slid it onto the bed of the
truck.

"Let's go," Nick whispered through the truck window.

"One more," Cage said.

"Fuck that. One's enough." Nick raised his eyebrows at
Rowan Patrick, his best friend, a gangly redhead with a Roman
nose, the son of a hard-drinking senator, the smartest guy at
Louisiana Episcopal, whose word carried weight.

"One was the plan." Rowan raised the gate of the pickup to
shut it.

"Come on, Tad." Cage ran back toward the fence.

Tad Beauregard, the tall son of a psychiatrist, was Cage's best friend. This snatch was his idea, conceived while working part-time in the hospital. He shrugged his shoulders and ran after Cage. Rowan lowered the gate of the pickup and loped back to hold the fence open. Cage and Tad lugged the tank through. Rowan grabbed the middle, and Cage, carrying the rear, stumbled twice on the way to the pickup. They strained to lift it onto the bed. The two tanks colliding sounded like a car wreck. The door behind the fence swung open and an orderly yelled, "Hey, you!"

Rowan slammed the gate closed and climbed over the back. The orderly was through the fence, dashing across the lot. Cage and Tad rolled over the sides on top of the tanks. The orderly nearly grabbed the gate of the pickup as Nick peeled out with a screech of rubber. The orderly yelled, "Got your number, assholes!"

Cage sang, shouting, playing air guitar on one knee, "Thanks for the cure for the summertime blues."

They took the tanks to Tad's house outside the city in hilly oak woods near the levee. A sixties hacienda, photographed in *Architectural Digest* and *Southern Living*, it featured a two-bedroom apartment separated from the main house by a long covered walkway. This was where Tad and his brother Nelson lived. It was known among the drug-using half of Louisiana Episcopal as Party Central.

"Don't worry. Henry and Virginia were sloshed at sunset," Tad said after they banged a tank loudly, carrying it down a winding flight of brick stairs to the front door. Inside, the central air was almost icy. They set the tanks on the shag carpet of the living room. Tad cranked up the Alan Parsons Project on his B&O stereo. By one o'clock a dozen friends, mostly girls, had dropped by with eight-packs of Miller Lite and bottles of Bacardi. Everyone was taking turns inhaling from the tank, then bursting out laughing. Lenny, a big linebacker with a mean streak, came out of one of the bedrooms with his big-boned, heavy-breasted girlfriend, smiling and theatrically tucking in his shirt. Condor, an amateur ornithologist, was gliding around the room with his long arms outstretched at shoulder height, navigating through thick currents of cannabis smoke.

"Careful, don't let your lips touch the valve. It's so cold it will burn them." Nick was stationed by the tank, assisting the process.

". . . because the only people for me are the mad ones, the ones who are mad to live, mad to talk, mad to be saved," Cage was saying to a blonde called Buffy, who listened, enraptured, "desirous of everything at the same time, the ones who never yawn or say a commonplace thing but burn, burn, burn like fabulous yellow Roman candles exploding like spiders across the stars."

"You wrote that?" Buffy asked.

"Nah." Cage smiled. "Jack Kerouac."

She nodded slowly. "I've heard of him."

Tad came out of the kitchenette with a garbage bag. He poked a hole in the bottom and attached the bag to the tank with rubber bands. Lenny was the first to try the bag. He kept his head in for about a minute, then hit his knees, laughing convulsively.

"Don't stay in so long," Nick said to Tommy, the one gay guy in their circle who was out of the closet. After about thirty seconds he tried to pull the sack off Tommy's head but Tommy held on. Tad was gay, too, but none of his straight friends would know until after graduation. By the time Cage went manic on Nantucket eleven years later, Tommy would be dead of the plague, Tad would be an engineer in San Francisco, Lenny would be a real estate lawyer in Baton Rouge, Condor a high school science teacher in Atlanta, Buffy a child psychologist in San Antonio, and Rowan would be campaigning for the U.S. House of Representatives.

"They mix this stuff with eight parts oxygen," Rowan was saying. "It's too rich. He's pushing the performance envelope."

"Beyond design specifications." Nick laughed. "Ninety seconds and counting. His ship is starting to burn." Nick tore the bag from the tank.

Tommy collapsed on the rug. Rowan pulled the bag off his head. Tommy had a huge smile, his eyes closed, his head wobbling in circles. Lenny grabbed the tank and sucked straight from the valve until his lungs were full. Pulling away, he screamed, leaving a thin layer of his lips behind on the valve. He glanced down, smiled slyly, and pushed the tank over onto Tommy. Rowan caught it just before it crushed Tommy's head. Lenny stumbled off, touching his lips with his fingertips. Raising the tank upright, Nick and Rowan looked at each other and said at the same time, "What a motherfucker."

Rowan attached the bag back on the tank. "Just try it for thirty seconds."

Nick stuck his head in. Breathing slowly, he felt as if he were in a deep-diving suit, dropping through a black sea. Rowan pulled the sack off his head. Nick was laughing harder than ever before, hearing only a loud ringing in his ears: *Nying . . . nying . . . nying . . . nying!* The ringing filled his head and he passed out. Rowan caught him and lowered him to the floor, shook his shoulders till he opened his eyes.

"So in America when the sun goes down and I sit on the old broken-down river pier watching the long, long skies over New Jersey and sense all that raw land that rolls in one unbelievable bulge over to the West Coast, and all that road going, all the people dreaming in the immensity of it," Cage was reciting to a pretty brunet named Laura, who was smiling, holding a drink in one hand and a cigarette in the other. She would end up a yoga teacher in Santa Fe. ". . . the evening star must be drooping and shedding her sparkler dims on the prairie, which is just before the coming of complete night that blesses the earth, darkens all rivers, cups the peaks and folds the final shore in, and nobody, nobody knows what's going to happen to anybody besides the forlorn rags of growing old . . ."

Margaret

It's a beautiful spring day, everything so green. I try to remember if this is the fifth or sixth time that I've driven Cage out to the hermitage on the grounds of a retreat center in the woods northeast of Memphis, St. Columba, named after the sixth-century Irish missionary, Colum, who brought Christianity to northern Scotland. It's the only place he'll let me drag him besides Dr. Fielding's office, which is harder. Father David has lived here for six months, after thirty years in African missions. The monk has been Frank's spiritual counselor since before he was ordained, when Frank was a deacon at the cathedral downtown in '56. I didn't know them then, but I can almost picture the two of them, Frank, about Cage's age, in a black suit and collar, and Father David, a bear of a man in his mid-fifties in a long brown habit. Unusual men for their time, men called to serve in an age of dwindling faith. Squaresville.

Cage used to sit up so straight. Now he's hunched over in his seat, staring at his hands.

"It was good to have Harper here for a week," I say. "Don't you miss him?"

"Yes," Cage murmurs.

The green woods of St. Columba are scattered with stands of trees simply burning from their lowest branches to their peaks with pink and cream flames.

"Look at all the dogwood, Cage. It's the first thing to bloom in the spring."

Cage looks silently out the windshield.

"A folktale about the dogwood says that it was used to make the cross on which Christ was crucified," I say. "The tree was stunted and the tips of its flowers stained red with his blood. The four large white petals are the shape of the cross and in the center the circlet of tiny yellow petals is a symbol of his crown."

"I'm familiar with that," Cage says woodenly.

The hermitage is a white colonial house that used to belong to an old woman who left three hundred acres to the diocese. On the other side of the property is the new conference center and all the little cabins for meditational retreats. I park in the sunshine. Father David is standing in the front door smiling. He has flowing white hair and a long white tunic over his stooped six-foot-six, broad-shouldered build. He resembles an Old Testament prophet. He holds a staff the size of a shepherd's crook but without the hook.

"Greetings, Margaret," he says as I get out of the car. I have to walk around and open the door for Cage.

"Come on, son." I tug at his sleeve. "Smell the fresh country air."

Father David is halfway down the walk by the time Cage has gotten out of the car. "Hello, Cage. Welcome."

"Hey, Father." He squints in the bright light. I put my arm through his and walk him up the sidewalk.

"You're looking better." Father David engulfs him with his big arms and the folds of his habit. "Your eyes are clearer."

Cage looks up at the old monk's face with his brow furrowed.

"I think I'll walk to the pond, see if the water lilies are in bloom," I say. "I'll come back in forty-five minutes or so."

"You don't want to take communion?" Father David asks.

"No thank you. It's just so beautiful out in the woods today. The dogwood just makes my spirit soar. You two go ahead without me."

Cage

"The doctor told me that I must wear these outside all the time now, especially as I am going back to Africa." Father David puts on those big, square sunglasses that eye clinics give you and leads me around the house to the garden, with his arm around my shoulder.

A raven is watching me from an elm tree. Father David sees me trapped by its eyes and says, "He comes here every day about now. He scares the other birds away from the feeder. A greedy fellow but not a demon." He leads me to a wrought-iron patio chair. "Is that what you were thinking?"

I nod, sitting down on the edge of a seat.

Father David pulls the sides of his robe, settles in the chair opposite. "St. Anthony was the first Christian hermit, a wealthy young man who took Christ literally. 'Go, sell what you possess and give to the poor, and you will have treasure in heaven.' He gave it all away and went off to scrabble in the desert. His disciples saw the bruises from the nights he wrestled demons."

"You have to admit that sounds depressingly like a bunch of Deadheads on acid freaking out in the Mojave," some part of my brain says, then I hear myself half laugh.

Father David doesn't smile. "Well, I don't know about any Deadheads, but St. Anthony was also a guerrilla in Alexandria who defended Christians persecuted by Emperor Maximinus. Are Deadheads some variety of hippie?"

I clear my dry throat. "Yes. Sort of."

"Well, back in the sixties, when I first read about the communes, the orgies, LSD, I thought there were demons at work. Why can't a demon take the shape of a little pill? Demons are archetypes. They reside in everyone. Perhaps St. Anthony's bruises were psychosomatic or self-inflicted as he was flung about by his inner demons. The point is that demons exist in some form."

"Can you perform an exorcism, Father?"

"I could, but I don't think it would work on your particular demons. No, I think a confession and reconciliation would be more effective." His big fingers make a little steeple over his chest. I wish I could see his eyes. Red coals glow through the dark plastic for a second, then I tell myself, No, it's just Father David. You've known him since you were a boy. He used to stop by the house in Virginia. "Cage, is there something that you've been keeping back that's burning in your conscience? A sin for which you have not forgiven yourself? Perhaps that is your demon."

He leans forward, takes off his glasses, and holds my eyes for a long time, as if his eyes were searching my soul for the dark secret I have carried with me for three years. He knows it's there, something I've never told a soul. He can see its shadow in my eyes. The proof of my wickedness, the sin that shall damn me forever unforgivably.

I open my mouth. "I . . ."

"Yes." His eyes do not blink. He smiles and reaches his long hand across and pats my knee, then makes the steeple on his chest, leaning back in his chair but holding my eyes.

"I . . ." I can't reveal the degenerate act. "I confessed to you last time, Father."

"You confessed everything?" He smiles and raises his arms in the sunshine. "Doesn't spring smell wonderful, all the new life, the rebirth and regeneration?"

The sky and trees, everything is black and white. I glance across the flagstones at the crosses he has fashioned from wood he found rotting on the forest floor. Not symbols of resurrection, but the idle amusement of an old fool. I don't want to share this secret with him. It won't change anything. Maybe he will report it to the Order. More evidence to condemn me.

"Ah, look," Father David whispers. A chipmunk pauses in a ray of sunlight across the garden, just basking for a few moments, hawk food. "It is a shame that you can take no pleasure in the light, the coming of spring. Must be hell to walk through life with no joy, only sorrow and regret."

"I feel like Munch's guy etched in the eternal howl in *The Scream*, fixed in a landscape of horror."

"Poor soul." Father David shakes his head. "Did you share everything with Nick?"

How does the monk sense that Nick has been coming to me while I sleep, not to comfort, but to accuse?

"What are you thinking about, Cage? What was that strange expression?" Father David shakes my leg.

"A dream." I try to relax my face.

"What sin is troubling you, dear boy? You can be absolved."

I start at a noise in the woods, twist around.

"It was only a deer." Father David hands me a small leather-bound Book of Common Prayer and stands up. "The rite of reconciliation, shall we begin?"

I open to a page marked with a ribbon attached to the spine.

"Have mercy on me, O God, according to your loving kindness," he begins, and I join him, my voice halting at first but then starting to flow. "Wash me through and through from my wickedness and cleanse me from my sin, for I know my transgressions only too well, and my sin is ever before me."

"Pray for me, a sinner," I read.

"May God in his love enlighten your heart, that you may remember in truth all your sins and his unfailing mercy," Father David says, watching me.

"Amen," I stutter.

"Now in the presence of Christ, and of me, his minister, confess your sins with a humble and obedient heart to Almighty God, our Creator and our Redeemer." He sits down in his chair and I kneel a few feet away on the slate flagstones.

I find my place on my page, begin, my voice shaking more as I go along. "But I have squandered the inheritance of your saints, and have wandered far in a land that is waste." I catch my breath. "Especially I confess to you . . ."

I glance up. The old monk's kind eyes catch mine, plead for me to tell the truth. "Especially I confess . . . I killed Nick."

"No, Cage." Father David leans forward. "Nick was hit by a drunk driver. You were on the other side of the country."

"This isn't a delusion. I'm not saying that I was there. I talked to him the night he died. He was a mess. Monica, the girl that he'd been living with, had just moved out. He was heartbroken. Wrecked. He kept going on about how good she was. I was trying to make him feel better. I told him that he would find someone better. He was better off without her. She wasn't perfect. I told him that she had slept once with me when we were both drunk. I knew as soon as I said it that I was killing him. Nick went dead quiet. Then he told me I would pay and hung up. That was the last time that I spoke to him. He wouldn't have been on the bridge driving at four in the morning if—"

"That's not true, Cage." Father David puts his hands on my shoulders. "If he was heartbroken, he was upset and restless and could have been anywhere. A drunk could have hit him anywhere. It wasn't his fault. It wasn't your fault." He shakes me gently. "Believe me." He nods toward the book in my hand. "Your only sin was fornication."

"Therefore, O Lord, from these and all other sins I cannot now remember, I turn to you in sorrow and repentance." My voice wavers. "Receive me again into the arms of your mercy, and restore me to the blessed company of your faithful people; through him in whom you have redeemed the world, your Son our Savior Jesus Christ. Amen."

Father David stands, says, "Do you then forgive those who have sinned against you?"

"I forgive them."

Father David places his hand on my head. "Our Lord Jesus Christ, who has left power to his Church to absolve all sinners who truly repent and believe in him, forgive you all your offenses." He makes the sign of the cross on my forehead. "In the Name of the Father, and of the Son, and of the Holy Ghost, I absolve you from all your sins. Go in peace. The Lord has put away your sins."

"Thanks be to God." I feel my forehead. It tingles where the monk touched it as if he had rubbed Tiger Balm on my third eye.

The tension gripping my body floods away all at once. I look around the woods and realize that I am no longer afraid. It's just the Haldol and the placebo effect of the confession, I think, just the irrational rapture that any other yokel feels when he's baptized and born again. It won't last. I stand up and smile. I laugh and hug the big old monk. I am forgiven.

Margaret

As I walk through the blooming dogwood and laurel onto the lawn of the hermitage and see Cage standing tall, his hands on his hips, smiling, some maternal instinct makes my heart leap, telling me that he's come to a turning point. I'd begun to abandon hope and imagine that he would spend the rest of his life in an institution. Now, suddenly, his old self's returned, my son, the boy I bore into this world, the son who exasperated me the worst but made me laugh the hardest. There he is. Reborn. Born again in Christ, if it's Father David's work. The miracle that I have been praying for, that churches across the South have been praying for every Sunday for so many months. Cage is back. I can feel it from fifty feet. I want to dance a jig.

Drawing closer, I see him laugh from deep down, the way he used to, his head tilted back.

"Hello, pilgrims," I call out, carrying branches of dogwood dripping white flowers that I have clipped for a centerpiece on the dining room table. They turn and watch me approach, both of them smiling. "Cage, I haven't heard that delightful sound for such a long, dry spell."

"Ol' Father David is a shaman," Cage says. "He's got the cure for evil."

"After all those years in Africa." Father David smiles slyly. "Where man was born."

We all laugh. I look at the joy on Cage's face and it's hard to believe the transformation. It's as if he's shed an old, dry skin and come out in color. The muscles in his face have relaxed and there is light in his eyes, which were caves of despair. Dear God, I pray silently, thank You. Please give us the strength and wisdom to help him heal and carry on. We are grateful and we thank You from the depths of our souls.

Father David pulls back the sleeve of his habit and looks at his cheap black digital watch. "I have another visitor arriving shortly. See y'all soon."

Cage

The day after my confession I borrow Mom's car and drive myself over to a shopping center to get a haircut. It's the first time I've driven since Baton Rouge in December, five months ago, the first haircut I've gotten since leaving Taunton six weeks before that. I drive farther downtown to Dr. Fielding's office. He decides to reduce the antipsychotics by three-quarters and keep the lithium level steady. He asks about the side effects. I tell him my hands still tremble. He tells me that will go away eventually. After the appointment I walk out to the wide brown river gathering America's water from the Appalachians to the Rockies. Harper is down on the mouth of the delta. I picture Dad and his brother Uncle Ned across the river in Arkansas in the fifties, home from college, working on Granddad Rutledge's sawmill, Dad dreaming of going out West halfway through the summer to become a smoke jumper in Montana, Uncle Ned, hungover, dreaming of the country girl he met the night before in a bar. Farther west, Nick's soul left us at the edge of the continent.

There are only a few new towers on the skyline: Morgan Keegan, First Tennessee, National Bank of Commerce. The rest, the tallest, built in the Roaring Twenties, look like prewar buildings in New York. Some are empty, others under renovation. Track is being laid for a new trolley line to go down Main Street, a wide brick boulevard, a twenties look, nostalgia for the country folk come to the big city from Mississippi and Arkansas. On the southern tip of Mud Island, which is really a peninsula hooking out into the river, there's an amphitheater and the World War II B-17 bomber, *The Memphis Belle*. Farther north on the peninsula is a new zero-lot-line neighborhood of skinny Mark Twain two-stories with a lot of scroll trim mixed in with wider Cape Cod–esque clapboards. I laugh aloud and say to myself, "You'll fit right in."

In the want ads I circle jobs in sales—everyone keeps reminding me how personable I am but it's hard to remember—and construction management, which I'm conversant in, following Dad's advice to get out of carpentry and use my mind, to get something with security and benefits. He offers to cosign a loan for a car as soon as I find a job. I wonder what to say to prospective employers about being just a semester short of a Vanderbilt law degree *and* an M.B.A. I decide to tell them that I was crushed by student debt and plan on going back but not for two years. Just the thought of the fumes from those marking pens gives me a headache. Typing my résumé out on Dad's old manual, I laugh to myself at the idea of listing Bridgewater and Taunton.

On Sundays I start going to church with Mom. The first couple of times, I leave before the coffee hour after the service, let Mom ride home with Dad, then I begin to stay and mingle. In the parish hall of the cathedral, which is furnished like a living room with great Oriental rugs across the floor, plump sofas, and wing-back chairs, the walls are lined with oil portraits of bishops, back to before the war, one of a Confederate general. Back then they all knew Latin and classical Greek, as Dad does still. It's easier

than I thought to play the role of bishop's son, exchange pleas-
antries with the businessmen, make the old ladies laugh, to engage the attention of the single white female Episcopalian.

"My, Mrs. Crawford," I say to a woman in her late seventies in
a floral print dress, her steel-gray hair cut in oval tufts like a poo-
dle's. "Don't you look ravishing today?"

"Thank you. That means something coming from a handsome
young man. Still, no reason to break the commandment 'I shalt
not lie.' I know I look an old fright." Her laugh sounds older than
her voice. "How are you settling in Memphis?" She pretends that
I have just arrived a few weeks ago, dismissing the months of
cowering in my parents' converted attic.

"I like Memphis. I always liked coming here to visit Dad's parents and the cousin about my age, Rut Jordan. Do you know his
family?"

"That devil. He's a charmer." She fixes me in the eyes. "Last I
heard he went off to Africa with his tail between his legs after
stepping out on that lovely Demange girl."

I smiled. "Yes, ma'am, he's in the Peace Corps now, in Tanza-
nia."

"I would no more set foot in Africa. All the AIDS—those people ought to keep their diseases to themselves."

"That's not fair, Mrs. Crawford." I'm not sure if she's joking.
"Well, I'm dying to go. Next time I get the urge to wander I'm
going to see the Serengeti."

"You just stay put and watch those wildlife programs on the
TV. You've done enough wandering for a while." She pinches my
cheek with her little diamond-studded claw. "You're a fine young
man."

Mrs. Crawford hobbles off and I see Katherine Horn talking
to my father and a middle-aged couple. Katherine's a single accountant and aerobics instructor about my age. I angle to the coffee table in the middle of the hall, pour a cup, then stand around
smiling. Mom waves and smiles from across the room.

"The prodigal son," says a hoarse voice.

"Hey, Katherine." I turn and smile. "What did you think of
Dad's sermon?"

"Very inspiring." Her brown hair is cut at her square jaw, parted on the side. She has alert, shrewd eyes. She's handsome, not pretty, definitely sexy. You imagine she has a real no-nonsense manner in the office . . . or in bed.

"I thought it was sort of lame." I laugh. "I'm sure I've heard it before as a kid."

Katherine laughs and touches my sleeve for a moment. "What are you doing for fun now that you've come out in society?"

"I'm not allowed out after dark." I frown in a mock pout.

Katherine laughs again. "You look like a picture of health to me."

"They all know, don't they?"

Katherine just barely nods.

"They all know that I've gone crazy and back."

She rests her hand on my sleeve. "Most of them know that you were having a rough time for a while."

"They don't have a clue." I chuckle uncomfortably. "But of course they couldn't."

"All of them are pulling for you to prosper now."

"I want what they have," I say.

"What's that?" She takes her arm off my sleeve.

"What they have?" Please put your hand back, I think. "The goodness of God, going to church, the joy of living in the sub-urbs, cooking out, coming home in the twilight sky, having three stiff cocktails, and assaulting your wife in the armchair."

Katherine laughs and touches my sleeve again. "You crack me up."

"No, I'm the one who cracked up." I sweep my arm around the hall. "Young and old, upper and lower middle class, a smattering of blacks, they all look content, like they know their place, where they came from, where they're going."

"Yes," Katherine says. "I see that. But I see Mrs. Crosby, who has cancer. And Mr. Nichols, who just lost his wife. Old Mrs. Rathburn, who sits alone at home all day. I see a lot of suffering in that crowd."

"No doubt." I nod earnestly. "But they belong."

"That they do," Katherine says. "And so do you. Want to go to a movie tonight? I want to see *Pretty Woman*."

Construction manager. Twenty-four thousand bucks a year. I made more as a carpenter on Nantucket but the DA told me never to go back there, so it's not exactly an option. William George, a heavyset guy in his fifties who's building five faux Victorians on Mud Island, hires me to do his legwork, save him from hanging around the sites all day so he can go fishing. Mom gives me her credit card to go buy khakis at the Gap, rugged button-downs at Patagonia, dress the part. Dad drives me in his new LeSabre with a car phone, a far cry from the sedans he would drive into the ground the first thirty years of his ministry, out east to the Buick dealer who gives the diocese a break on the clergy's cars. We pick out an '87 Jeep Cherokee, three years old, thirty thousand miles, clean. They let me drive it off the lot on Dad's word that he'll organize a loan with First Tennessee the next day. I'm ready to go to work. Instant yuppie.

The main crew is three first-rate trim carpenters a few years older than me: Steve Sullivan, Garland Webb, Lane Edge, graduates of the Memphis College of Art, who paint and sculpt on the side. At the end of the first week Garland invites me on a river trip. We meet at the yacht club, three roofed docks with about forty boats on Mud Island. People are drinking and picnicking on the decks of the houseboats, which look like floating trailers. Garland and his wife, Carol, who works at a real estate agency downtown, take me upriver in their ski boat to an island near the Arkansas bank. We collect shells and interesting bits of driftwood. Smoking a joint, they offer me a toke. I'd like to take a hit. I'd like to feel completely alive. The meds seem to level off my emotions, no pain, but no real joy. I miss the magic, the wonder of the river and the wide horizon, the lust for life. I feel like I'm not really here. I reach for the spliff, and the AA groups at Taunton, at Bridgewater, the doctors driving in the idea that drugs, even grass, can trigger a manic episode, all comes flashing back and I just say, "Nah, thanks."

William George lists me as the sales agent for the properties and I take the real estate exam and get my license. My days pass quickly, staying on top of subcontractors, making sure all the supplies are on the job at the right time, jawing with the crew, meeting prospective buyers. In the evenings I start going to hear live music, blues at a tiny juke called Wild Bill's, and folk-rock journeymen like Steve Forbert and James McMurtry at the High Tone. Lane Edge plays guitar and sometimes I go over to his house and jam. I'm not sure if I want to buy a guitar, too many humiliating memories of jumping up onstage in Nantucket. Lane's better than me so I pick up a few licks. Two weeks pass, I collect my paycheck, mail in the car payment, put a couple of hundred dollars in the bank. I know I'm lucky. I ought to be out on the street.

"Seems like I never meet any girls that I can connect with in Memphis," I say loudly over bar noise at the Blue Monkey to Lane Edge.

"You want something unusual, a one-off, a unique specimen." Lane is six-three and very skinny. He holds his long arms in front of him, fingers interlaced, palms out, and cracks his knuckles.

"Aren't we all one-offs?" I sip a beer. Dr. Fielding says a couple of drinks a day is okay, now that I'm off the antipsychotics. I drink two glasses of water between each glass of beer or wine and spend a fair amount of time in the toilet but I never get more than a mild, comfortable buzz.

"Oh, no, some people come off conveyor belts." Lane grins and nods at some women at a table, all of them with heavy makeup, fake tits, bleached hair.

"Memphis's finest," I say.

"Maybe you need an earth mama."

"I do respect canoeing skills in a woman."

"An artist?" Lane holds his chin like Rodin's thinker. "No, artists have egos. If I trade Lynn in for a new model, I'm mail-ordering an Oriental who doesn't give me any lip, or better yet doesn't even speak English. That's my advice to you. Start hang-

ing around Saigon Le and all those Cong shops over on Cleve-
land. Find a nice Vietnamese girl."

"You'll never leave Lynn." I find myself taking everyone literally even when I know that they are joking. "You're lucky. She's
smart, sexy, funny, everything a man could ask for."

"You're not listening to me, boy. Ego, lad. You have to consider
the ego." He tilts his long neck back and drains the last swigs of
a bottle of Tecate, then sets it on the counter and turns it very
slowly, whispers, "You want someone you can dominate down to
the last drop."

"I don't want a slave." I tilt an empty glass of ice water to my
lips, catch the slice of lemon in my mouth, and say almost unin-
telligibly, "I want a goddess."

"You mean like a *Sports Illustrated* swimsuit model?"

"Naaa." I spit out the lemon. "Lame-, I mean Lane-brain, I
mean someone like her."

Two girls come in out of the night and wait by the hostess station. One's tall with long brown hair and a gentle, bemused face,
while the dark eyes of the other, who only comes to her chin, are
striking at twenty feet, maybe green, so rare that color. She wears
her hair short, almost like a boy's, a simple white button-up
blouse with no sleeves or collar, slim-cut khakis, and red cowboy
boots. As she turns to speak to her friend, I see that her ass is like
a small melon, hardly there at all. I say, "Holly Golightly."

"Those two dykes?" Lane raises his hand for the bartender.

"You think they're lesbians?" I crush some ice in my mouth.

"Know for a fact. The tall one's the catcher and the short one
with the butch haircut is the pitcher. Don't go getting between
two lezzies. Get your balls chopped off."

The hostess leads them to a table not far from where we're sitting at the bar and I say, "You're full of shit, Lane. They're not
lesbians."

"Famous lesbians," Lane says. "Most famous lesbians in West
Arkansas. The tall one's called Bonnie and the little one goes by
Clyde."

"Those two?"

"Yep." Lane pops a lemon slice into the tall neck of the Tecate bottle.

"I heard of them."

Lane scrutinizes my face.

"Yeah." I take a swig off Lane's beer. "One night they took a guy hostage who'd beaten up his girlfriend, a friend of theirs back in Polecat Junction. At gunpoint they took him to the local shit-kicker dive and made him and his best pal, another wife-beater type, give each other blow jobs in front of a crowd of rednecks. The biggest one started to cry."

"You heard about that way up in Nantucket?" Lane laughs.

"Yeah." I'm conscious of how I'm enjoying myself, the simple pleasure. "The big one cried when he came in his pal's mouth in front of fifty of his farmer buddies. The girls left the gun on the doormat of the bar on the way out. Turns out it was plastic. Obviously they haven't been back to Polecat since."

I see that Bonnie and Holly are watching us, drawn to our laughter. I catch their waitress's eye and when she comes over ask her, "Would you ask those young ladies if they would like a drink for their heroics in West Arkansas."

"Their heroics in West Arkansas?"

"Yes, ma'am."

The waitress crosses to their table. They look over at us with indifferent expressions, speak to themselves, shake their heads emphatically. The waitress returns looking grim. She says, "They say you must have mistaken them for someone else."

"I told you they weren't Bonnie and Clyde," Lane says.

"They refuse your drink," the waitress goes on.

"Ouch," Lane says.

"Unless you go and sit at their table." She smiles, darts off.

"I'm a married man," Lane says, moving toward their table.

"Doesn't mean you can't read the menu."

"Evening, ladies." Lane sits next to the tall one. I sit down next to Holly Golightly. "I'm Lane and this here reprobate is Cage."

"Alli," the tall one says, "and my friend Samantha, or Sam."

Lane raises his eyebrows at me discreetly at the mention of the masculine name. He calls the waitress over and we order, then he

says, "Yeah, Cage was trying to convince me that y'all were famous lesbians from Arkansas."

"Now, hold on . . ." I feel myself blushing. I expect them to be
offended but they only look at each other and smile. Lane keeps
going, the whole fish story, and the girls are laughing and Sam
keeps glancing at me. Soon all four of us are laughing.

"My, what an imagination," Sam says. "What does that say
about you?"

"I've been feminized," I reply. "I'm close to my mama."

"That's a good quality." Sam's eyes aren't green after all but
brown. Her heart-shaped face has a delicate nose and a pretty
mouth with full lips. "You from Memphis?"

"Nah, I just moved here a couple of months ago." I'm not
telling anyone about the long stint in my parents' attic, any more
than I would carry around a banner with *Mentally Ill* sewn on it.
"My parents are here. My dad's from here. What about you?"

"I live here with my little boy." She watches my eyes. "I grew
up in Mississippi and went to Rhodes, went back to Jackson and
got married. Came back here after I got divorced. I've got a sister here."

"How old's your boy? What's his name?"

"Ray. He's five."

"Ray, that's nice. What a great age. I had a blast when I was
five. We lived at the edge of the mountains, outside Knoxville.
My dad used to take us up in the Smokies. Does Ray like the
woods?"

"Ray loves the woods." She has a calm presence. She tells me
she's gone back to her maiden name, Samantha Anne Carr. She
owns a vintage clothing place called Time's Arrow at a shady in-
tersection in midtown which has a number of cafés, antique
stores, gift shops, restaurants, a couple of blocks of pastel Haight-
Ashbury ambience. She and Ray rent an old house in midtown,
a converted duplex. Ray spends most of his weekends down in
Jackson with his father, a lawyer who has remarried.

"I've seen Time's Arrow." For some reason I don't want to
think about her husband, ex or not. "Looks nice. Never been in-

side, though I think I've seen you blurry through that old plate glass floating around in there."

Sam's laugh is delicate. She's a hummingbird. She leans her head forward and slides her hand from her forehead through her hair, holds it back.

In August the unfinished tin-roofed structures in Harbor Town are like the hot boxes used to torture prisoners in *Cool Hand Luke*. Lane Edge tries to convince the crew that they should arrive on the job at first light, take a long siesta from noon to four, then work again until dark falls after nine, but no one else will go for it. Lane begins to work solo, on Mexican time.

In the long summer twilight we carry a canoe out the front door of Garret Stoval's converted warehouse loft through his little yard, over the Illinois Central tracks, down a hundred and fifty feet of sloping grass levee, across Riverside Drive, and down another fifty yards of broken stone levee.

"Pick it up, Huck." Garret has red hair and big square-jawed good looks. He was a college friend of Nick's, once went camping with Nick and Harper and me, when Harper was about fifteen, and he used to run around Memphis with my cousin Rut. Several times Garret came by and tried to talk to me while I was hiding in my parents' attic. Now he never mentions my madness and there is an unspoken sense that he's looking out for me, that a bond of brotherhood was transferred from Nick to me.

"All right, Jim," I drawl, and move faster through the sharp rocks to the river's edge.

In the late light, out in the middle of the river, the surface of the water is a frothy pink. The wind and the slap of water against the fiberglass are the only sounds. The Memphis skyline looks like a flimsy set, a row of false fronts, perched on the top of the massive levee wall. On the other side a row of ragged trees, flood survivors, curtains off the marshlands of Arkansas. We paddle against the current, inching upriver toward Mud Island.

"You heard anything from Rut?" My cousin writes Garret from

Africa about as much as he does his own parents but tells Garret more amusing stories. "Has he gone native?"

"He *says* he's only fucked one girl in a year and a half, a white girl." Garret stops paddling and looks in my face to see if I believe that.

"Why don't we like black girls?" Sweating heavily now, I'm cooled slightly by a downriver wind. "None of us do. Everyone I went to college with at Sewanee, all Nick's friends at Vanderbilt. None of us ever tried to fuck a black woman."

Garret's face is dismissive, like the answer's obvious. Different colors.

"It's because we were segregated," I continue. "There were barely any blacks in the postintegration private schools we all went to. The only blacks we knew at all were our maids. Whoever wanted to fuck his big old fat maid?"

Garret laughs. "I know a guy."

We paddle hard quietly for ten minutes until a river current swirling into the mouth of the cove on the north side of the Mud Island peninsula takes the canoe and we hold our paddles across our thighs. Coming out of the wind into the cove is like stepping into a steam room. The canoe stops in the middle by itself. It's quiet. The C-shaped shore of the cove is a parking lot set on a steep slope. This is where the annual Memorial Day canoe race will start.

"Three hundred canoes," Garret says. "Think we can take 'em, Huck?"

"Yassuh, Jim, I reckons we can." I swat a mosquito on my neck. Clouds of gnats move in over our heads.

"How's it going with Samantha?" Garret starts to paddle toward the mouth of the cove, out of the steam and bugs.

"Great. Going great. I moved in two weeks ago."

Garret looks back over his shoulder. "Must be a relief to be out of the bishopric." He smiles. "I always wanted to use that word. Bishopric."

"That's not a bishop's house." I laugh. "That's his office."

"Whatever. What about the kid?"

"Ray's a kick. I got him a redbone coonhound, beautiful auburn puppy. "

"What's the dog's name?" Garret spits, takes a slug of bottled water.

"Ray started calling him Jonathan, I think from the Bible. Then the dog loves biscuits, so I started calling him Jonathan Seabiscuit-Eater, after the racehorse my grandfather loved so much."

"Happy little family." Where the cove opens onto the mighty river, Stoval says, "Let's see how fast we can make it to the end of the course."

"Full speed ahead," I say. Knifing the paddles into the water, we run with the current along the shore of Mud Island, switching sides in unison. I imagine Nick sitting in between us keeping cadence, with one of the big drums we beat with our fathers in Indian Guides, before we were even Cub Scouts, a strange thought that chills and reassures. I almost tell Garret my dark secret, then paddle faster, watching the stone foundations of the bridge to Arkansas loom larger until the bridge fills my field of vision and we rush into the half-light under the span.

The house on Vinton is a beautifully built twenties Tudor divided into upstairs and downstairs flats like so many of the fine old homes from Memphis's glory days of high cotton. The trees are the only thing the city can brag about, as Mama says, and the tallest, the ones over a hundred feet, all the old oak species, are here in midtown, shading the remains of the city, circa 1890 to 1935. Dad grew up in this neighborhood, first in an apartment just a few blocks away, with his grandmother, mother, and older brother, his father having hightailed it while his mother was pregnant with him. Granddad Rutledge was the black sheep of his family, the son and grandson of Episcopal bishops, who left his wife in the Depression for a beautiful, wealthy woman with lumber mills in Arkansas. I never really knew Granddad Rutledge. He used to visit us once a year, when we were on Pawley's Island. I think he paid the rent for the beach house. As a teenager Dad lived in a house a few blocks in the other direction on Peabody with the alcoholic doctor who married his mother. When they were boys, Dad and Uncle Ned must have wandered the alleys that parallel most of the streets in this part of town, separating backyards. Squirrels, rabbits, chipmunks, ringneck doves, robins, cardinals—wildlife flourishes in the old trees and hedges. Coyotes have moved in since Dad was a boy.

No moonlight makes it through the trees, so it's pitch-black in the alley between Vinton and Carr. Dim house lights wink through hedges, but you can't see your feet. Ray and I walk quietly behind Jonathan Seabiscuit-Eater, who ranges back and forth across the cobblestone and grass, patches of concrete, sniffing loudly. He stops and claws at something, whines quietly. Ray turns on a midsize Maglite that I bought him for his birthday. Seabiscuit's on his hind legs, his front paws on a tree trunk, his nose and tail held perfectly straight, pointing up. Ray raises the beam of light into branches thirty feet high where an animal is frozen.

"Is it a coon, Cage?" Ray holds the beam steady with both hands. "Is it a coon?"

"I can't tell, Ray. Might be." I don't want to disappoint him.

Seabiscuit starts barking and leaping around, scratching the trunk as high as he can reach.

"Sit." Ray scolds the dog like I taught him, making his voice deep like a man's. "Sit."

Seabiscuit sits down at the base of the trunk.

"I think it's another cat," Ray says. The dog barks again and leaps at the tree. The cat screeches and races higher, out of the light.

"Come on, Seabiscuit." I turn back toward our house. "Ray, you're a good hunter. I think it's nicer to hunt with flashlights than guns. I used to hunt a lot with my grandfather, doves and ducks mostly, and I don't feel so good about killing those animals."

"Just another cat," Ray says. "I want to get a raccoon."

Seabiscuit realizes we're on the way back and starts to trot up the alley ahead of us.

"Maybe tomorrow night we'll get lucky and bag a coon with

your light." I take him by the hand. A rusty wrought-iron gate leads to our backyard. We go several steps up onto a deck that I built against rent. Samantha has citronella candles burning in a mosquito-free halo around a lounge chair, where she lies looking up at the patch of stars between the treetops.

"The great hunters return," she says, sitting up. "How many did you get?"

"Three cats," Ray says, disappointed and proud.

"I think Jonathan Seabiscuit-Eater is not a redbone coonhound after all." I pick Ray up, hold him in one arm.

Ray puts his hands around my neck. "No, Cage?"

"Nope. He's a redbone cat hound!"

Ray and Samantha laugh. I think, This is it. This is what it's all about. This is what you've been missing. It doesn't get better than this.

1999

Harper

Walking down the corridor, I try to remember the times I've seen Dad's brother Uncle Ned. Some holiday dinners at Cage's Bend since Honeywell moved him from Baltimore to Nashville and then downsized him when I was in high school. Before that I don't remember him. He never came to Baton Rouge. A sad fact of modern American life is that families are spread over such vast distances that relatives see each other seldomly. In the end you can look back and count the times on your hands.

The door to the room is open. Uncle Ned is sitting up in the bed, his back against a pillow, several tubes dangling down to one forearm, gazing at Dad and Mom on a sofa against the wall. On the far side of the bed, Ned's wife, Aunt Rhonda, digs in an overnight bag on a table. Through the window behind her a gray sky hangs over a park of green trees and a full-scale Parthenon, just the way it looked in classical Greece, seventy-five yards of aggregate concrete pillars erected in the twenties to proclaim Nashville the Athens of the South. Over the trees somewhere is Parthenon Pavilion, a mental hospital where Cage stayed a couple of times when suffering paranoid delusions. No one is talking.

"Hey, y'all," I say, coming in the room.

"Hah-puh Henley Rutledge!" Uncle Ned calls out in a deliberately exaggerated drawl. He's thinner than I've ever seen him, but still a heavy man with large jowls. He calls out convivially, "Glad you could make it!"

"Hey, Uncle Ned, Aunt Rhonda." I set my suitcase down and hurry to the bed. "I jumped on a plane as soon as I heard."

"Look at you, boy. You worth a million dollars yet?"

"In stock," I mouth silently. Careful of the tubes, I hug him. I feel the heat gathering in the corners of my eyes, the first tears start to slide down my face. "Uncle Ned."

"Are you in pain?" Ned smiles. "I don't get it."

I smile back.

"Here you are, sir." Ned hands me a tissue.

"I wanted to take you golfing in Hawaii. I wanted you to see me get rich."

"I'll see you, son."

My cousin Lila comes out of the bathroom carrying a little blonde girl, Zoe, who looks around the room with a peaceful, expectant expression. Lila kisses me on the cheek. "Thanks for coming."

"Oh, don't thank me." I hug her. "I didn't know he was so sick. He never told us about the other surgeries."

Lila smiles sadly and turns to her father. "Are you hurting, Dad?"

"No." Uncle Ned wags his head back and forth. "The morphine's taking care of that." He looks at me. "So nobody knows where the High Plains Drifter is at the moment?"

I shake my head. "Safe, I hope."

"Go look for him." Uncle Ned sets his hand on mine at the edge of the bed.

"Uncle Ned, you know that I would. But if I find him, it won't do any good. I'll be powerless. He won't listen. We have to let him bottom out. That's what the pros have been telling the family for years. Tough love. I hope he doesn't crash and burn."

"Go find him." Uncle Ned closes his hand on mine. "Promise me."

I hesitate. I'm never sure when my uncle is joking. He glances at Lila and Rhonda. Lila is bouncing Zoe in her arms. Aunt Rhonda has a strained smile.

"Promise you'll go after him one more time." His voice is even, strong.

"All right, Uncle Ned, I'll go after him." I wonder if I will.

"Until you find him."

"Dead or alive." I smile out of regret for saying it.

Uncle Ned laughs. "You never learned to watch your mouth."

"I'm going to miss you. I'm more like you than Dad, you know."

Uncle Ned laughs. "He's the better role model."

"Har-puh." Mom stands up.

"Hey, Papa." I walk over and hug them. "Mama."

Looking over my shoulder at Ned, Mom says, "Your nephew came all the way from New York."

Uncle Ned nods and says, "He's a good boy."

"What do you remember now, Ned?" Mom asks.

Uncle Ned holds up his arms in a big V for victory. He looks around the room and says, "We're a very close family."

"We certainly are, Ned." Mom tilts her chin high and smiles resolutely. She wears a wool skirt and matching jacket, a Junior League matron. I watch Aunt Rhonda answer the phone, trying to imagine her thirty-five years ago, the sexy stewardess she was when Uncle Ned met her. "It's for you, Frank." My father walks behind the women encircling the bed.

"Hello." Dad speaks softly in the phone. "His kidneys aren't working and he has a ruptured aneur— We're here in the room."

"Aneurysm," Uncle Ned almost shouts. "Ruptured aneurysm on the aorta."

Dad finishes speaking and hangs up.

"Franklin." Uncle Ned raises his eyebrows, widens his eyes.

"Neddy?" Dad says.

"That's the way you look," Uncle Ned says. "Like you're startled."

My gaze drifts between my uncle and father, the younger brother by two years. Uncle Ned's hair is gray, Dad's white. Ned's face is heavy from decades of drinking, his nose bulbous and veined, while Dad's face, despite a large nose swollen by seventy years, is lean from decades of training and moderation.

"Why aren't you in your dog collar?" Uncle Ned asks Dad.

"I didn't want to wear black today," Dad says. He's in khakis, a tweed blazer, and a blue button-down with a white T-shirt showing at the neck. An old country theologian. "This isn't official business."

"Oh, but it is, Frank." Uncle Ned smiles.

"Neddy was quite a boxer in the navy," Dad says. "Everyone in Memphis knew that he could take care of himself."

"Oh, come on, Frank." Uncle Ned looks annoyed.

"I remember once we were in a booth, talking about Mother and Dr. Jacobson. There was always some kind of critical situation and Neddy and I rarely had any time together. A young man who was a contemporary of mine, a bore, came in and forced himself on us." Dad cleans the lenses of his glasses with a handkerchief and chuckles. "He sat down and started chattering on and on. Neddy stood and picked up the man's raincoat off the back of the booth and said, 'Put this on and leave. My brother and I have private matters to discuss.' Neddy just dismissed him." Dad laughs. "I wanted to be polite. I felt sorry for him slinking out of the diner like a dog dragging its belly. But it was impressive." He whistles. "Oh Lord, Lord. Oh gee."

"Oh, Frank, good God." Uncle Ned stares into space for a moment, then says softly, "Yeah, I remember that."

Lila sets Zoe on the floor. The little blonde girl walks quietly around the bed toward her grandmother, Aunt Rhonda. Lila says, "Want some more water?"

"Your timing is perfect," Ned says. "Ol' Lila." When he finishes drinking, the room is silent. Everyone is sitting down around the bed. Ned looks up and grips his gown as if he were holding the lapels of a jacket, about to speak from a stump. "This meeting will be called to order."

"What are you going to tell us?" Mom smiles.

"I love you all," Uncle Ned says. I see a sadness in his eyes for the first time.

"I've got to run out for a few minutes," Lila says.

"Please leave," her father says. "You need a break from this. I need a break from this."

"Be back," Lila says.

"Okay, darling." He smiles. "Come back when the people who really care about me come in."

"I'm going to take a shower. I didn't have a chance this morning," I say. "See you later, Uncle Ned."

"Okay, son."

I pick up my suitcase and follow Lila out of the room, thinking that you cry not for the one who is dying, but for your own loss. I put my arm around Lila's shoulder.

"I heard Mama say things that I thought would never come out of her mouth," Lila says. "She told him that he was a good husband and a good father."

"Wow," I say. "How long does he have?"

Lila's face is dry and calm. "No telling. A few hours. A few days. "

When I come back to the hospital, Uncle Ned is asleep, leaning against the headboard. Mom and Dad are sitting quietly. Zoe is sleeping on Aunt Rhonda's lap. I kiss Lila and she tells me, "They're letting us take him home."

"That's good," is all I can say.

"He's just as cheerful as ever," Dad says.

I glance at Uncle Ned.

"He's not listening," Dad says.

"Yes, I am." Uncle Ned opens one eye.

"I took a nap and a shower," I say.

"Now you feel good like me," Uncle Ned says. "So you're a programming whiz?"

"Uncle Ned was a big shot with IBM in the sixties," Dad says.

"You know what IBM stands for?" Uncle Ned says. "*I've been moved.*"

Everyone laughs.

"Like the job?" he asks me.

"Yeah. The wages are good."

"Let's do it," Uncle Ned says.

"What?" I ask.

"Let's do it. Let's put it together, man. I think this will really fly," Uncle Ned crows, sealing a deal with clients over cocktails in an imaginary bar. A nurse comes in and checks the level of the IV bags. Uncle Ned asks her, "You in the designer business or the accounting business?"

"A little of both," she says, laughing on her way out.

I watch my father, whose eyes are puffy and nose red from a cold, take a handkerchief from his breast pocket.

"Don't get so emotional, Frank," Uncle Ned says. "You've been through this many times before." He looks at his grandchild, Zoe, who is now awake and quietly straddling her grandmother's hip, and says, "Hey, gal." The toddler smiles and plants her head in her grandmother's neck. He tells Aunt Rhonda, "Zoe's wild about you, honey." He smiles, masking pain, leans back against the headboard, and shuts his eyes. Suddenly, without opening his eyes, looking almost asleep, his breathing becomes labored and then, a half minute later, there's a low gurgling in his chest, the sound of air mixing with the fluid rising in his lungs. Everyone gathers close to the bed.

"I think he's going," Lila says.

Everyone is leaning over the bed, touching him, clasping his arms and legs.

"We love you, Uncle Ned," I say. "We love you, Uncle Ned."

"I love you, Neddy," Aunt Rhonda says, crying.

Uncle Ned opens his eyes and glances at Aunt Rhonda and says, "I'm not dying."

Denial or a declaration of immortality?

"I know," Aunt Rhonda says.

"Hey, Ned," Dad says.

"Yeah, brother?" Ned is staring past all of us.

"We're going to make it," Dad says.

Ned doesn't answer. There is no sound of breathing anymore, just gurgling.

"Are you in pain?" Lila says.

"Yes," Ned says through his teeth.

"Where's the morphine pump?" Lila, holding Zoe in one arm, pats the sheets with her free hand.

Uncle Ned, with a lost look in his eyes, says weakly, "Don't pump it."

Lila squeezes the pump once anyway. With her small hands Zoe brushes tears off her mother's face.

Staring into the distance, Ned says with force, "Good night! Good night!"

"Good night, Ned," Mama says.

"Oh please," Uncle Ned says. "Oh golly. Oh golly." His arms begin to shake violently.

A nurse rushes in and Lila tells her, "He doesn't want any heroic measures."

Dad begins the Lord's Prayer, "Our Father, who art in heaven," and everyone joins in, weeping as they recite. Then Dad recites the Twenty-third Psalm, "Yea, though I walk through the valley of the shadow of death."

"O God, oh please, oh please," Ned is saying, his arms still shaking.

"I love you," everyone is saying. "I love you. I love you."

For a moment Ned's eyes focus in from the distance onto Lila's face. "I love you, Lila."

"I love you, Dad."

"O God." The pain seems to block his vision as if his open eyes can see nothing.

"Let go, Dad." Lila hands Zoe to her mother and tries to smooth Ned's eyes shut. "Let's close your eyes."

Aunt Rhonda, with Zoe on one hip, sponges his face. "Does that feel good?"

"O God." Ned opens his eyes again and looks at nothing. "O God."

"Close your eyes, honey," Aunt Rhonda says, "and let go."

"We love you, Uncle Ned," Mama and I are yelling.

"We love you," everyone is saying into the gaps of silence.

Lila shuts his eyes but they pop back open.

"Tell Mama hello and Dad," Dad says.

"And Nick," Mama says. "Tell Nick hello."

"We love you, Uncle Ned."

The gurgling rises into his throat and Edmund Henley Rutledge closes his eyes. His body shudders and stops and is suddenly quiet.

"Seven o'clock straight up," Lila says.

The toddler Zoe looks around the room and back at Ned with the same expectant expression in her eyes, as if he is still alive. I notice her rosy cheeks and Ned's dead skin and think, She is his only immortality.

"Gosh, he's beginning to get cold already." Dad lays his hand on his brother's forehead.

"I'm sorry, Harper," Mama says. "We just have to cherish each other the years we have left."

Aunt Rhonda fixes her eyes on my face. "I'd gone home to wash the sheets to get ready for him."

Staring at the corpse, Lila is hit by another round of weeping. "Oh, Dad, I love you so much."

Aunt Rhonda puts her arm around her. "He was proud of you, you and Bob and Zoe. He was proud of Frank's boys, too."

The undertaker, a crew-cut man wearing a bright brown suit and a silver tie, knocks on the open door of the room. Mama says, "Let's leave while they cover him up." I keep studying Uncle Ned's face and its expression of peace or the absence of expression, while everyone leaves the room. The undertaker pulls off the blankets, exposing the pale white legs below the hospital gown, then covers him with a sheet. He and an orderly pick up the corpse and load it on a gurney and push it out of the room. The undertaker works for an old Nashville funeral home, the last independent in town, Cage, Taylor and Williams, which Granddad sold when Cage and Nick were in college to help put all three of us through.

The family is standing in front of the elevators. Aunt Rhonda says, "He never once complained about pain."

"He showed us how," Mom says. "He was carrying a banner all the way with a big grin on his face."

I think that he looked terrified in the very last moments when he was saying, Oh golly, O God. "That's the way I want to go," I say. "With my family all around me."

"We were all with him in the very end," Mom says. "Or should we say, the beginning. The older I get, the more convinced I am. Remember Ned said, 'I'm not dying.'"

"A lesson in dying," I say. "I keep thinking of that. A gallant way to die."

"He died with real dignity," Dad says. "I ought to know. I've seen a lot of people go."

"About an hour ago," Aunt Rhonda says, "Dr. Finch told Ned, 'You've been a good patient and a good friend,' and Ned said, 'I've certainly seen enough of you.' "

"He was a joker to the very last," I say as the elevator door opens.

A plague of cicadas fills the woods with an alien screeching, a sound effect from a Hitchcock movie. Millions of locusts, risen from the ground after seven years and doomed to live for a single cycle of the moon, cover the trees, the house, the drive, all of middle Tennessee. Legions of males screech over and over, screaming to mate, their drumlike abdominal organs pulsing ceaselessly. I sit on the front porch of Cage's Bend listening to the demonic orchestra invisible in the twilight. Closing my eyes, I see Dad with his arm raised in a blessing and Lila putting Uncle Ned's ashes under a tree in her front yard. Something lands on my sleeve. I open my eyes and see a locust crawling down my arm. "Get back to your insect orgy," I say, thumping it into the air with my forefinger. How many generations of locusts have lived so briefly in the front yard? I think, looking out at the lawn, the four huge oak species, white, yellow, red, and pin, planted by Cherokees for some reason—a lacrosse field, a religious site, a curse on the white man?—in a perfect square long before Morgan Cage came here in the 1820s and planted the oak alley along the drive.

The first Cage built a log cabin which grew into a rambling warren of added rooms, floors, and porches. In 1838 his fellow Nashville attorney and horse racing buddy President Andrew Jackson ignored the Supreme Court's decision in favor of the Cherokee Nation when Georgia started throwing them out after gold was discovered, and Morgan Cage rode with the federal troops evicting the natives, fourteen thousand of them, herding them along the Cumberland River toward Oklahoma, the tribe sold out by its leaders for six million bucks and the promise of some much less impressive real estate in the prairie. The Trail of

Tears passed between the log cabin and the river. Four thousand died, mainly women and children, on the forced march of eight hundred miles. Morgan Cage must have felt some guilt, for he adopted an orphaned Cherokee.

Mom thinks that we have some Cherokee blood. She insists Nick looked like an Indian, his dark eyes, hair, and skin and his hawk-shaped nose. Her theory is that while Morgan was off gambling away his fortune, the young brave comforted his lonely wife, injected the genes of the conquered natives into the blood-line. I think some black blood made it as well because of the full lips and Bantu noses of some of the Cage women. Be interesting to do some DNA testing. I'd welcome some color in the family gene pool. I remember a Pueblo chief who said, How cruel the whites look! Their lips are thin. Their eyes have a staring expression. They are always seeking something. What are they seeking? They are always uneasy and restless. They don't know what they want. We think they are mad.

Cage is mad right now, wandering the streets of San Francisco, playing his guitar on the sidewalks, begging for change, his speech as rapid-fire as an auctioneer's, his mind in overdrive, completely lost in the moment in a world of endless excitement on a five-month manic run that started around Christmas. A shooting star about to burn up in the atmosphere. I cannot ignore Uncle Ned's deathbed command but I truly believe that there is nothing I can do.

I tried so many times over the last ten years. It's hard to keep the chronology straight. After he first went manic on Nantucket and then six months later fell into a deep, dark, delusional depression, he pulled out of it and started making a life in Memphis. He was working as a construction manager and living with a very nice girl and her little boy. For about a year he was stable. The whole family thought he might go back for his last semester and finish off his joint degree. Then when the recession in the early nineties hit and he lost the job, he started gradually, so slowly that no one really saw it coming, going manic. Sometime in that year he went off his lithium, or maybe he didn't even go off it, maybe the dosage needed to be increased but Dr. Fielding didn't catch it.

Probably he was still on his lithium but it wasn't enough to hold off the high spirits, a warm wind after a long winter that presaged the coming shit storm.

Think about it: You've felt so bad for so long, even when you were stable, haunted by the humiliating memories of your manic behavior, all the destruction, and then you finally start to feel good. You wake up singing in the morning. You're hopeful again for the first time in years. Life spreads out before you like a land of dreams. What you should do is run to your shrink and say, Emergency, Doc. I'm feeling *too good*. Better give me something to take me down before I spin out of control.

But you don't. You tell yourself that the lithium is working. You're productive. You're happy. You're fun to be around. What could possibly be wrong? The little fire smoldering in one part of your brain catches flame. There is not enough lithium to put it out. It inflames one hemisphere of your mind, then jumps across the ditch to the other side. In a couple of months your skull is an inferno. All restraint, your very conscience, goes up in smoke.

Cage broke up with Samantha, said good-bye to little Ray, moved into an apartment in midtown, where he entertained different women—older divorcées, young waitresses, college girls— every night. He was working with his carpenter buddies and dabbling in real estate. He talked our stepuncle Jack into signing a contract that gave him six months to renovate and sell the split-level twenties "airplane bungalow" where Granddad Rutledge's second wife had lived. Granddad had spent most of his time at the lumber mill in Arkansas away from his second wife, though he came back to die in that house when I was a kid. Jack had just moved his sister, Granddad's childless wife, who was still beautiful in her eighties, into a nursing home, and agreed to sell the house to Cage for a song. Cage could've doubled his money, could've pocketed forty grand or more if he pulled it off.

By the time I came up from Tulane for the summer, Mom and Dad were stressed to the breaking point. Families are powerless now. It's impossible to put someone away anymore unless you can prove that he is a danger to himself or to other people. Cage was clearly gone, replaced by a fast-talking con man who was bouncing checks all over town, getting in fights in bars, exploding at Mom and Dad whenever they tried to talk sense to him, up all night, jumping up onstage with his guitar. He had stopped making payments on the Jeep, so Dad was covering them. At the house on Carr he had torn out walls and ceilings but hadn't begun the renovation. There were only a few weeks left on the contract. I tried to help him get the house presentable enough to sell, Sheetrock the walls and the raised cathedral ceilings, get it painted. Cage would work for a couple of hours, say that he was going to the lumber store, and never come back. Turned out that he was tripping on acid while I was slaving away for free, trying to help him salvage the house.

When the contract was up, we had a conference with Jack, Dad, me, Cage, and some investor who had put up some money for renovations. Jack took the house back. I remember after Cage dashed off somewhere, Jack told Dad, You know I lost Jack Junior when he was eighteen but I think that was easy next to what you're going through. Jack Junior, Dad told me later, was hit by a bolt of lightning on a baseball field. I remember taking the Jeep away from Cage, punching him out in the street in front of the Carr house after he hit me, but I can't remember how that manic spree ended. Not in jail, not that time. I remember Mom and me cleaning up his apartment, which was like a hurricane disaster area, Mom saying, A psychologist told me that the state of his room reflects the state of his mind. If that's true, his mind was like a dump. Sometime after he came down, he ended up in Parthenon Pavilion, terrified again, scared of the Order, watched by the television, the remorse over his manic sins amplified a million times.

When he got out, he went to Rugby, where Great-Grandmother Cage had given my parents an 1880s Victorian cottage for their wedding. Dad used to drive Cage and Nick up there on weekends from Knoxville in the sixties, while he was renovating it. It had an outhouse, bedpans in the bedroom. It's called the Owl Nest. All the houses in Rugby have names. Originally it was a utopian experiment for the younger sons of English aristocrats, educated but disinherited by primogeniture, somewhere they could be car-

penters or farmers without shame, but they were playboy pio-
neers long on tennis courts and short on elbow grease, so the
colony failed. Cage went to live in the Owl Nest and work for Historic Rugby, the restoration association. He was stable for a year
or so, had nice girls coming to visit him from Nashville and Baton
Rouge, spent a lot of time riding mountain bikes through the
woods and canoeing the white-water rivers. He relaunched the
Rugbian, the utopia's newspaper.

I graduated from Tulane while he was at Rugby, started writing code for banks. I just picked it up. In Memphis I was broke
after college, so I ordered the parts to a computer through a
friend who worked for a systems contractor. He was going to
show me how to build it and I would save a few hundred bucks.
The parts arrived and he was out of town, so I built it by myself.
He said I should go talk to his boss. I went into the guy's office
and within five minutes he said, I like the cut of your jib. You've
got people skills. Most of my programmers are total nerds. Yeah,
I want someone who looks like you. I'll tell you what. I've got a
system down in Milwaukee. If you can get it up, I'll give you a job.
He called out to his secretary: You know that ticket to Milwau-
kee? Change it to, uh—he looked at me—what'd you say your
name is? I worked for him for about a year, designed programs for
FedEx, then found a headhunter and got a job with a bank in
Philadelphia.

Two years later I moved to New York. The most fun I've had
was six months in Moscow on a team upgrading the Russian
stock exchange. I make three times as much as my father, and
bishops make over a hundred grand. I want to cash out one day
with ten million. I like my toys, my Harley, my Jet Ski that stays
out at the place I rent in the Hamptons, my Lexus, my one-
bedroom on University Place in Manhattan. Call me shallow but
it's fun to gratify your whims. And I tithe like my daddy does, just
not to the church. I give ten percent of my pretax gross to Conservation International, Amnesty International, and Planned
Parenthood. After a deprived childhood relative to my peers in
the Episcopal schools I attended since kindergarten, I'm still get-

ting used to what it feels like to be rich instead of a poor man in a rich man's house.

Cage ended up in jail in a little town twenty miles from Rugby. The last few biweekly issues of the *Rugbian* were progressively weirder—a strange tribute to Nick, rants against people he had pissed off at Historic Rugby, enemies he had made among the moonshiners and pot growers, American foreign policy, multinational corporations. Once again he'd left a trail of bounced checks.

When the deputy sheriffs came, he punched one in the face and disappeared into the woods. A couple of hours later a half dozen deputies and their hunting buddies were on his trail with a pack of hound dogs. Cage was Butch Cassidy. He was having a fine old time. He swam down streams and backtracked and climbed sheer rock faces. The posse broke into three groups and chased him for two days, came very close but never ran him down.

They got him when he came back to the Owl Nest for his passport. He was hightailing it with the idea of planting trees on the eroded island of Haiti but he ended up in the Fentress County jail. Mom and Dad went up to see him. So are you going to bail me out? Cage asked, smacking on gum. No, son. You're manic right now and you would just get in more trouble. You've got to get back on your medicine. Cage spit out the gum. You're no father! You son of a bitch. You don't care about me. You motherfather! Mom and Dad dutifully paid his debts, cleaned up the Owl Nest, and took him back in their home after he spent a month in the county jail and another one in a county hospital chilling out.

And a couple of months later he was back in Nashville in the Parthenon Pavilion riding out the tortured psychotic hangover, which comes like clockwork after the long manic highs. Back in Memphis he got it back together, built a huge house out in the country with his carpenter-artist pals, moved into another little apartment in midtown, started dating a nice, sexy girl ten years younger than him. Then, ten or twelve months later, it all started again. Dad saw it coming and took the Jeep away again, since it's in his name. A few weeks ago Cage took off for California, hitching with his guitar, the return of the High Plains Drifter. I might have left out a complete bipolar cycle, possibly two. It's hard to keep track. The cycles from mania to depression and back seem to accelerate over time, come with more frequency with a briefer gap of stability in between.

The locusts shriek in the dark. If you can't tune it out, it's maddening. I take a long swallow of iced tea and get my ThinkPad out of its case, set in on my lap, wake it up, click on a file. The other day Cage called me at my office. I recorded the conversation on my laptop and translated it into text:

Black guys jumped me, took my money and tried to take my guitar, and hit me with a broomstick. Come on, Harper. You've got plenty of money. Help out your old brother when he's down on his luck. I've found this hostel. Tomorrow I can sell my guitar and get my plane fare and hit the road, go back to Memphis. First thing I'll do is see Dr. Fielding. Just wire me some money.

I'll get you a hostel for one night with a credit card and then you should go check yourself into a hospital. Dad pays your medical insurance.

Hostels don't take credit cards. I checked about thirty places. My face is bleeding so I guess I'm going to go to an emergency room and spend the night there.

All right, Cage. I'm sorry. Tell them to dose you up on lithium.

It just makes me so angry.

Well, you shouldn't have gone out there. You're manic. The whole family thinks you should go into a hospital.

A little mania never hurt anything. We've got a problem. We'll fix it. Hear this (rattle of pills)? I've got my lithium. I've got my cotton sweater. I've got my suit, fuck the family. Who are you to talk? You're a sex addict.

I think we're both promiscuous. So was Nick. I'm not sure if I'm a sex addict but if I am, there are a lot worse things today.

I've got no money. I was mugged. I've got nothing to eat.

Go to a homeless shelter. Go to a soup kitchen. Check yourself into a hospital.

Fuck you . . . fuck you . . . fuck you . . . suck my dick.

I'm sorry, Cage. You should go to a hospital.

I shouldn't. Harper, you are a cunt-sucking pussy.

You chose to hitch across the country.

It was an instructional ride.

He hung up. In a few days he turns thirty-nine. Maybe I should fly out to San Francisco for his birthday on another pointless rescue mission. Over the years I've been to two family weeks at the end of two drug rehab programs, visited him in two jails and several hospitals, given him money when he was stable or depressed. Each time he emerges from black suicidal months and starts pulling himself up by his bootstraps, I believe that he is going to finally Keep It Together. Maybe now is the time to really practice Tough Love. Stop Enabling him. Let him Bottom Out.

"Isn't it a lovely evening?" Nanny interrupts my thoughts, coming out on the porch.

"Except for the cicadas." I stand up automatically.

"The infernal racket. But the birds are happy. Feasting every day." Nanny moves slowly toward a rocking chair. She's ninety now, outlived her husband by twenty-five years. She has a leaky heart and two strangers' corneas and she still lives alone. "Everything is so green. We had so much rain this spring. There was flooding across the county but we're up on a hill. We're always okay."

"I forget how green the South is." I take her arm.

She shakes it off gently and continues across the porch. "I hope your cousins understood that I really wanted to go to Edmund's funeral. He was a gentle man."

"Of course, Nanny." She is the soul of Christian charity, always kind, always optimistic. Only once as a kid did I glimpse

Granddad on a binge, slugging down bourbon until he became a raving beast. She hung in there for forty-five years. I try to picture a young Poppy belting a young Nanny with the back of his hand but I can't clearly. I wonder if one day someone will invent a device to watch people's memories like video. Record their dreams. I'd like to write software for that.

Nanny's voice is high and soft. I have to listen hard to hear her over the cacophony of insects. She was always a good storyteller. Nick used to follow her around asking for stories. "Tell me a story, Nanny."

"I don't have any news. I called some people from church today who don't have anyone to look in on them." Slowly she brushes a locust from her sleeve. "I talked to Grace Adel for two hours. She enjoys my calls. I could call her more often. She has nothing left to talk about but old Thebes. She's ninety-five. Everyone we talked about today is dead. I'm not scared of dying. There's a lot of things worse than dying. I don't want to be a burden."

I plug a mic into my laptop, aim it at her, watch her words appear on the screen.

"After your mother was born, just above us in the room with the dormer windows, I began to run a very, very high temperature. They took me to St. Thomas hospital in Nashville and there were no antibiotics, no sulfa drugs, nothing. They could give you blood transfusions but at that point they hooked you to somebody else and they didn't type the blood. They didn't know what they were giving you. I would go into convulsions after the transfusions. I was very ill for a very long time, was down to about eighty pounds. My mother could even pick me up and she was a little sparrow of a woman."

"I remember her."

"Of course you do. When I left here, there was snow on the ground. When I came back, the leaves were on the trees, the flowers were blooming. During that time, Mary Frances Washington, who was a tall *wonderful* black woman who lived here on the place, came and stayed here in the house and took care of Margaret." Nanny stopped gliding and sank in thought for a minute. "During the six months I was in the hospital . . . I never told anybody this until after I had heard that other people had similar experiences, because I didn't think that anyone would believe me. They were all standing—there were three doctors on the case, they were all friends of mine and contemporaries of my grandfather and they were wonderful doctors. They were doing everything they could for me. The day I remember is the day they gave up. There was nothing else they could do for me. They were standing around the bed with my mother and Morgan and they were looking at me and I was hovering over them looking at them with the most wonderful feeling of peace and I thought I'll just go on now. Then I decided no, I can't leave that baby behind. She needs a mother. I've got to go back. I didn't want to. I felt so good. It was so wonderful, it was just . . . a feeling of having everything just right." Nanny laughs. "I can still feel myself over that bed, looking down at myself. They thought I was gone. I didn't hear what they were saying. They were just very somber. I was looking down on this woman who was me. I remember it so plainly."

"So you believe in life after death?"

"Oh, yes, I know there is something wonderful waiting for us."

I hit the keys to save the document.

Cage

I came out here to return to the scene of the crime twelve years ago. Something keeps me from going the last little way, across the Oakland Bay Bridge and up into the Berkeley Hills to stand outside his old house where I spent spring break in '87 and fucked his girlfriend—the two-backed beast that killed Nick. He wouldn't have been out driving all night if I hadn't told him. And I can't get myself across the Golden Gate either. Nick died just about in the middle, on the side heading back to the city. Every day I have stood in Golden Gate Park and studied the bridge, the parapets and superstructure. I wonder when I get my nerve up to catch a bus across the bridge if I will feel Nick's ghost when I pass over the spot. I'm not sure he really visited me in the place I never name. I doubt that he has forgiven me.

After four days back in San Francisco I know the city from the Golden Gate to Lake Merced, from the Pacific Ocean Esplanade to China Basin on the Bay, the whole seven-square-mile nail of the thumb-shaped peninsula on which the city perches uneasily, straddling the tectonic fault. I've crisscrossed the city on foot, bus, and trolley. I know where to busk. I know where to cadge free meals. I know where to buy pot. I know where to sell pot for street dealers. I know where to score heroin. I know two dozen people to hang out with.

The Great American Manic-Depressive Novel—how's that for the title of a third-person memoir? I'm out here exploring the San Francisco underworld on an anthropological expedition, gathering anecdotal info about survival on a freaky, urban scale. I've got chapters from Mexico eleven years ago and childhood sketches I wrote to remember Nick and make sense of the past when I was incarcerated and when I was inspired on the road. On the Greyhounds between Memphis and Denver, I just wrote one about Harper in junior high. I always keep a spiral notebook handy, got twenty-three full ones in Memphis. I've got an eye for detail, an ear for dialogue, and plenty of empathy. All my travels, the loony bin sojourns, all the stories from the damaged and the damned have given me a well of empathy as deep as any saint's. And I've got a substance abuse problem, another hallmark of a great writer.

The sun breaks through the rolling fog, illuminates a row of pastel Victorian frame houses on Haight Street. San Francisco is the most beautiful city in America and the city with the highest suicide rate. The jumpers from the Golden Gate all leap from the Bay side, looking back at the city, never out into the emptiness of the ocean. I stop on the corner of Haight and Ashbury and climb up on a streetlamp, one leg on the base, one arm holding the pole. Swinging above the passing heads, I yell, "Out of some subway scuttle, cell, or loft, a bedlamite scales thy parapets."

Only a few people bother to turn their heads.

"Tilting momently, shrill shirt ballooning, a jest calls from the speechless caravan. Hart Crane."

A white girl with blonde dreadlocks smiles and passes by.

I drop down from the lamp and move on into the throng of humanity flowing along the sidewalk. The sun disappears behind sea fog and instantly I'm shivering. The coldest winter I ever spent was a summer in San Francisco. Mark Twain, aka Samuel Clemens, fellow southerner of note. I put my guitar down on a bench by a bus stop and dig a Patagonia vest out of my backpack. Across the street is a pretty, dark-haired girl with the gaunt frame and the haunted eyes of a junkie. She's sitting on the sidewalk trying to sell a pair of high-heel shoes displayed on a box that says *Prada* in glossy navy against matte navy. She's wearing a thin black cocktail dress, something out of *Vogue*, over a pair of faded jeans. Interesting combination. No coat in sight. Spanish canvas fisherman slip-ons with rope soles. She must be freezing. I've seen her around before, always selling something expensive. I pick up my guitar, sling my backpack over my shoulder, and cross the street.

"How much do you want for those shoes?"

She raises her head in slow motion and blinks. "At Bergdorf's they sell for twelve hundred."

"What sort of crazed fashion victim would shell out that many greenbacks for a pair of shoes that won't get you across the road?" I squat down beside her.

"My mother." A faint smile flickers across her lips, then her eyes cave in.

"You sell much stuff this way?"

Her eyes focus in on me for an instant. "I'd do better right outside Prada."

"I think I could jazz up your marketing strategy." I smile, try to keep her attention from dissolving.

"Yeah? How?"

"You watch." I set my backpack by her shoes and sling the guitar strap around my back, tap one suede cowboy boot a few times in a basic blues beat, and start a song I've been writing since I got to San Francisco, loud and deep and full of soul:

You might trip, you might fall,
Might feel like you hit the wall,
But don't ever let no man
Hold your spirit down.
'Cause you're heading on to paradise
Can't let no one spin you 'round.

If you were blindfolded, you couldn't tell the difference between me and Robert fucking Johnson. I sound so black Harper must be right about the family gene pool. Maybe I'll be discovered on the streets of San Francisco.

You may live in a palace,
You may live in a slum,
All men got something to teach,
Even a dirty old bum.

I repeat the paradise refrain, pull the harmonica out of my pocket, carry the chords through to the next stanza, then go back to guitar. A crowd has gathered. A few dollar bills float to my feet. The girl grabs them languorously, slips them in her bra.

Well, I'll sing songs that's weird to you,
I'll sing from the Bible 'cause it's all true.
You're headed up to paradise, folks,
Can't let no one spin you 'round.

Change cascades against the concrete, a few greenbacks waft in the cool mist, at least nine bucks' worth of paper and silver as I start over from the top. Selling songs. Forty, fifty bucks a day if you're ambitious, move around the city to stay in a crowd. I'm a troubadour. Very important in medieval days and the Renaissance. The messengers. Spreading vital information, news that stays news, with their mandolins.

"You can sing." The girl finishes picking up the last of the change, puts it in her jeans.

"Muddy Waters seduced my great-grandmother."

She laughs. Her teeth are in good shape.

I lift her up, cupping her armpits. "Save your mommy's shoes for tomorrow. I'll give you enough to score if you've got a place to take a shower and crash."

"Fifty bucks?" She's suddenly alert.

"I'll top off what you just took of mine. I'm feeling generous."

"I got a room in the Tenderloin." She bends over and picks up the shoes. "Let's go see an old friend." She starts along the side-walk.

"Where you go, I go. My name's Cage," I say to her back, put-ting my guitar down so I can pull on my backpack. Fully loaded, I jog to catch up.

"Cage. That's a nice name. You sound southern."

"Yeah. Raised all over the South. What do you call yourself?"

"Emma."

"Jonesin' Emma. You sure are pretty. What you doing out here selling yo' mama's shoes?"

"Better than selling myself."

"That's for sure."

"Could you put them in your pack?" she asks.

"Yes, ma'am." I stop and hand her the guitar and put my pack on the ground. "How old are you?"

"Twenty-two. You?"

"Thirty-nine in a few days."

"No shit. You don't look it."

"That's what they all say."

"Ready?"

"Lay on, Macduff." I slide my arms through the straps, center the pack on my back.

Emma hands me the guitar, starts down the street. "You've been to college. "

"The hard road has taught me how to live." I stroll along beside her. "The soft road has taught me how to love."

"Where'd you go to school?"

"You've never heard of it. A little school on a Tennessee mountaintop."

"Sewanee?" Emma is walking fast.

I stop dead.

"My father's an Episcopal minister," she says over her shoulder, turning onto Masonic. "Not that I see him much."

I catch up. "I'll be damned. My father's a bishop."

"Maybe God made you come over and play guitar for me." She laughs.

"Providence."

Emma is really striding now. She can't have been a junkie for very long. Maybe God did send me here to save her.

"Where'd you go?"

"Technically I'm a philosophy major at UC Santa Cruz."

"Really? So was my little brother. At Tulane."

She stops listening. Weighted down with the pack and the guitar, I struggle to keep up. Finally after about a half mile, when she turns onto McAllister, I say, "This town has a fine public transportation system."

"Yeah. It's kind of far still." Emma plumps down on a bus bench. I slide out of the pack, pull out a liter bottle I keep filled from water fountains.

I offer some to her. She shakes her head. I say, "You should always stay well hydrated. Best thing you can do for your body."

She rolls her eyes and sticks out her hand, takes a tiny sip, and tosses the bottle back to me. Her knees and calves are rising and dropping like sewing machine needles. When the bus comes, she takes off the bench like a sprinter out of the blocks. I carry the guitar in one hand, my pack in the other. The bus is nearly empty. I sit across from her, the guitar on my lap.

"You know how to use that thing," she says.

"I learned on the knee of B. B. King."

"I don't like the blues. It's so repetitive." She looks away and starts biting a fingernail, then jerks her hand from her face, slides the dress up to the top of her jeans, and digs out all the change. She pulls the dress down and drops the change in her lap, counts it. "Eleven dollars and forty-seven cents. That means I need, uh—"

"Thirty-eight fifty-three." I hand her two twenties. "Knock yourself out."

Heading east on McAllister, all the cars suddenly change from Toyotas and BMWs to Impalas and Cadillacs. Most of the pedestrians are black. We get off in front of some run-down buildings.

"Yesterday over there I asked a big black guy if he was selling ganj and he said no but we could smoke some and go in and buy some," I say, scrambling to keep up. "So we walked over to this corner and he lit up a bowl and I thought, Man, there's something shaky about this, so I ran away, and when I ran, I hit his elbow and I heard his pipe fall and crack on the ground."

"That was hella uncool." Emma walks in long, confident strides like a model on a catwalk.

"Yeah. He started chasing me, yelling, 'That man stole my five dollars. That man stole my five dollars.' I didn't even have a five-dollar bill on me. So I just kept running and a cop stopped me about five blocks away. Undercover guy who happened to step out of a liquor store at that moment. A cruiser arrived with the black guy in it. They ran a check on my license and then they made me sit in the back of the cruiser. Then they interviewed the black guy. Between the cops they pulled together five bucks and gave it to him. Sent me on my way."

"Those were nice cops," Emma says. "Most are fuckers."

There are small clusters of rapper-style black dudes in high-tops and baseball caps, sitting on the steps and milling around the courtyard in front of the main entrance. I ask Emma where we're going.

"You're hanging out on that bench over there 'cause if you go up inside, someone's going to take your pack or your guitar or both." Her eyes are clear for the first time. "I'll be back." Emma starts for the door.

"Will you be okay?"

She pauses, half turns. "The guy I'm going to see would kill anybody who robbed me and no one wants to rape me 'cause I'm a junkie. "

I watch her walk up the steps. A couple of brothers nod and smile at her. One jumps up and cruises over to her. They go in through the front door. I walk back to the bus stop, uneasy now that I'm alone. Few white men would feel comfortable here. I collapse against the bench. I can't remember the last time I slept. Not for at least forty-eight hours. My watch reads *4/10/99.* I dig a hotel receipt out of the pocket of my backpack. April 7. Seventy-two hours. Emma better come back soon before all the energy drains out of me and I pass out on this bench and get picked up for vagrancy and she loses an easy mark. I'll gladly share my busking earnings with her. I'd like to hang out with a pretty Episcopalian for a few days. After fifteen minutes I begin to worry. I'm heading down the street to circle the block and see if there is some sort of back entrance when I hear her yell my name. I stop and she catches up.

"Tired of waiting?" She hasn't shot up yet, still looks jittery.

"Just tired. I haven't slept for three days."

"Crystal meth?"

"Natural brain chemistry." I yawn. "Where's the doss-pad?"

"What?" She brushes hair out of her eyes, looks likes she's about twelve for a moment.

"Your room."

"Not far." She takes the guitar from my hand and turns onto Laguna. The sun comes back out and I have to stop and take off my fleece. I follow behind her, watching her switch the guitar from one arm to the other, cradling it like a shotgun, and then we turn onto O'Farrell, a row of fleabag hotels with winos and hookers. On the steps of the El Dorado is some sort of purveyor of flesh, a black man-woman dressed up in a sequin gown like a Supreme.

"Howdy, Emma." Its voice is deep.

"Afternoon, Tiffany."

"These people living in this town have their own little network of freaks," I say as we pass by the empty desk and head up a dark, malodorous staircase.

"Yeah?" Emma says.

"Even if you got them out in the mountains, you could never get the freak out of them."

"Suppose not," Emma says. Several flights up she opens a door and we go in a fairly big room with a window onto the street, a kitchenette and a bed, a desk, a wardrobe.

"You keep it pretty neat." I set the guitar and pack down.

Emma laughs. "Other night I couldn't score, so I shot some speed." She gets her works out of a drawer by the sink, lays them on the counter by a little camping burner. "I couldn't sleep and about dawn I was thinking about painting the place red like hell, so I mopped everything, even the walls."

"How long have you been here?"

"Couple of months." She pumps up the stove, lights it with one of those sticks with a trigger that sparks.

I don't want to watch. "Can I take a shower?"

"Sure." She doesn't look at me, picks up a big spoon.

I cross the room and open a door. Maybe forty women's dresses hang on a short rung, compressed by the vise of the walls. I glance at the labels—Issey Miyake, APC, Armani—then find the door to the bathroom. There are reasonably clean towels hanging from the shower curtain rod, a pile of fashion magazines by the toilet. I turn on the water, strip. When I take my boots off, the little room fills with a terrible stench. My feet are rotting. I forgot to air them over three days of pedestrian peregrination. I bang the frame and push on the tiny window for several minutes, finally manage to lift it a few inches, then I step into the shower, find no soap but a bottle of eco-friendly dish-washing liquid, and wash off days of sweat and grime. At dawn this morning I was at a Bible study service in Golden Gate Park. A hundred homeless parked their grocery carts in orderly rows in a lot nearby, like minivans around a suburban church. "May God hold you all in the hollow of His hand," I pray aloud, scraping my scalp with my fingernails. The hot water washes away the last of my energy. I turn off the shower and hear loud pop music that I don't recognize. Wrapping the towel around my waist, I go into the other room. Emma is spread out on the bed staring up at the ceiling. In my pack I find a semiclean pair of baggy drawstring pants and a sweatshirt. I walk slowly to the bed. Emma's eyes are open. She glances at me from the other side of midnight, then her eyes go back to the wagon wheel lamp hanging from the ceiling. When I turn off the boom box, Emma makes no protest, so I lie down on the bed, careful not to touch her. I shut my eyes.

Harper

The locusts screech on and on. Nanny glides quietly in her chair. I wonder where Cage is, what he's doing. The phone rings distantly in the house. Nanny starts to push herself up.

"I'll get it." I walk inside through French doors, cross the living room, a thousand square feet covered by antique Persian carpets illuminated by chandeliers hanging from sixteen-foot ceilings, then the dining room, past an oval table that seats twenty, huge old sideboards with china displayed on the shelves, to a phone hanging on a wall in the kitchen, which is the size of my Manhattan apartment.

My stomach drops as I pick up the phone. I brace myself for the manic version of my brother, Mr. Hyde. "Hello?"

"Harper."

"Hey, Mama. You and Dad back home safe?"

"There was no traffic. It was a nice drive. Have you heard from Cage?"

I hear Nanny pick up the phone in the sitting room.

"Margaret?"

"Hello, Mother. How are you feeling?"

"Fine. We were just on the porch. Everything is lovely and

green and the cicadas are making an infernal racket. Has Cage called you?"

"No, Mother. All we can do is pray."

"Every minute," Nanny says.

"Have you given him any money since he went to San Francisco?"

Nanny hesitates. "About a week ago I wired him money for a bus ticket to come home."

"I remember that and I begged you not to do that again."

"I know. But he was my first grandchild. When I hear his voice . . . A few days ago he said that he didn't have a place to sleep, so I had him find a hotel that would take my credit card. I gave it to the man at the desk."

"No, Mother, you can't do that. Under no circumstances should you do that again," Mama says. "I know it seems harsh. It scares me to death to have him on the streets. The only way he's going to get well is tough love. Harper, explain it to her."

"I know what it is," Nanny says with a hint of irritation.

"We're not going to give him the money to come home because he'll spend it on drugs or sushi, God knows." Mama is talking rapidly, all wound up. "He's got to want to be well so badly that he'll take measures. It breaks our heart. We have to treat him as we would an addict. If we send him money, it will reinforce the idea that we will support him. We can't enable him—"

"I know all this, Margaret. If a hotel man calls me tonight, I'll tell him that we can't help Cage. I'll ask him to suggest a shelter or a homeless place."

"You absolutely must, Mother. We must not enable him."

"I know all this. I know all this. You don't have to tell me all this. I won't do it. When the hotel man called the third night, I told him no. Cage called back really upset. Said he'd spent his last dollar getting to the place. I said, 'Cage, I've talked to your parents, you must check yourself into a hospital.' He said he was taking his medicine and had seen a doctor—"

"Unlikely," I say.

Nanny goes on, "Cage said, 'Well, you promised.' I said, 'I know. I'm real sorry, Cage.' You never heard such cussing."

"The really horrifying thing to me," Mom says, "is that he pressured a ninety-year-old woman. After Harper leaves, I beg you to take the phone off the hook."

"I'm not going to answer," Nanny says. "It will hurt too much to turn him down."

"He's not helpless for getting home," Mama says.

"He can always sell his guitar," I say. "Where will he come home to?"

"I can't have him here again," Nanny says. "I'm just an old lady."

"He'll have to go into a hospital until he stabilizes," Mom says.

"He'll never agree to that," I say.

"I think he'll come back to Tennessee," Nanny says. "I think he's coming."

"I've been thinking all day about him," Mom says. "I have a sense of profound sadness that's with me all the time. We're going to have to let him bottom out in San Francisco."

There's a long pause.

"The last thing . . ." I hesitate, thinking that the last thing any of us should do is help him, because it's not help but a complete fucking waste of time. "The last thing Uncle Ned asked of me, um, was to go out and find Cage."

"Will you go, Harper?" Mom's voice is a mixture of relief and eagerness.

"That would be a fine thing for you to do, Harper." Nanny's voice is calm again.

"And probably pointless," I say. "I don't know. I'm in the middle of a project. If I can organize some time off. What the hell. I promised Uncle Ned."

"Oh, Harper. You're such a good son," Mom says.

Nanny says, "Your brother's keeper."

Car Pool
1983

Harper hated his mother's car. It was a Buick Century with a bizarre hatchback box shape, a style that was only made for a year due to abysmal sales, which Franklin had bought new for half price from the dealer who gave discounts to the dozen Episcopal clergy in Baton Rouge. Over the years since they'd bought it, from the age of nine to thirteen, Harper's loathing of the car grew with the onset of adolescent hormones until the sight of his mother standing by the hunchbacked Century in a shining line of Mercedes, Cadillacs, Thunderbirds, and Broncos filled him with resentment. So did her smile, the big smile always glued to her face twenty-four hours a day.

Standing by the flagpole at Louisiana Episcopal School, Harper watched a thousand uniformed students swarming out of the long pink-brick and white-columned buildings, encircled by verandas on two stories like giant South Louisiana plantation homes, fanning across the lawn for yellow buses on the boulevard and mothers parked along the oval drive by the chapel. In the midst of the teeming uniforms, Harper could see the Century and his mother's smile at fifty yards.

Father Crewes couldn't get her on the phone, Harper thought; she wouldn't be smiling if he'd told her. He walked toward her with three classmates, Robert Crespo, Trent Nightengale, and Rebecca Mornier. The boys wore blue trousers and white polo shirts with gold knight logos over their hearts, Rebbeca blue plaid, which reached her knees and hung by thin straps over her shoulders. The weather was so hot only a few of the girls wore white blouses under their dresses.

"Nice ride," Crespo said for the hundredth time since September.

"Watch out." Trent pushed Crespo from behind. "He'll break your nose."

"The blood was all over his face." Crespo sidestepped a few feet to avoid Nightengale so that the two shorter boys bookended Harper, bobbing at his shoulders while Rebecca trailed quietly along a few feet behind.

"One punch," Trent said.

"Sounded like smashing a pumpkin," Crespo said. "You could be the first thirteen-year-old to knock someone out. I've never heard of a kid KO'ing anybody. Have you?"

"I'm sure Ali did when he was a kid," Harper said. "Any number of people."

Margaret Rutledge waved from thirty feet.

"My mother hasn't heard."

"What do you think she'll do?" Trent asked.

"Yell a lot," Harper said. "Ground me. I don't know."

"Averatte had it coming."

"Thanks, Crespo."

"He's an asshole," Trent said. "I'll tell your mom you were right."

"Execute with extreme prejudice," Harper said, echoing a phrase he'd heard Cage use. Crespo and Nightengale laughed.

"Extreme prejudice," Crespo said between cackles. "That's what you did. Fist to nose. *Whap!*" Crespo stopped laughing and tried to look serious as Margaret Rutledge called out, "Hello, boys. Hi, Rebecca."

Harper set his jaw. Margaret saw the brooding in his eyes, wondered vaguely why he was always so smoldering. She glanced at her watch. The damn car pool always fell on a day when an important visitor wanted a tour. Margaret was the most charming and knowledgeable guide at the Louisiana Historical Association, the first one to be called when VIPs were coming to town, often at the last minute. Today a group of Exxon executives from the Houston headquarters suddenly wanted to see Magnolia Mound and Oak Alley. If the traffic didn't catch her, she could be at the Hilton without keeping them waiting.

"Pile in, boys. I'm late for an appointment." She opened the driver's door and brought her seat forward. Trent and Crespo crawled into the backseat.

"Let Rebecca ride in front, Harper," Margaret said. "Where are your manners?"

"It's his turn." Rebecca spoke for the first time in five minutes.

As Rebecca climbed in the back, Harper looked down her uniform, glimpsed the top of her bra and a sliver of round flesh. Sometimes during car pool Rebecca felt his eyes on her and nervously covered her throat or adjusted her dress.

Margaret sat rod-straight behind the wheel. She craned her neck to see the traffic on Robin Hood Boulevard, gunned the heavy car across the oncoming lane, and swerved around the break in the median, a strip of grass with spindly young live oaks planted in the sixties every thirty feet for a mile to the gate of Sherwood Forest. The developers cut the original oak giants. The largest now looked like big broccoli spears. Perhaps in a hundred years these would shade the land again from the deadly ultraviolet heat of the Gulf sun.

"How was school?" Margaret asked. No one answered. "Harper?"

"Long." Harper adjusted the radio from NPR to KISS FM.

"Robert, how was your day?" Margaret moved on brightly.

"It was okay," Crespo said. "I think I failed the science test."

"I'm sure you did better than you think." Margaret smiled at him in the rearview mirror. "Rebecca, how was your day?"

"Fine."

One-story homes with the odd low-sloping Louisiana roofs flashed by on either side, identical except for the color of the brick—brown, yellow, red—and the trim around the windows and gutter line. Margaret's attempts at conversation failed. She wondered why they were so quiet today. Usually she had to raise her voice to make them quiet down or stop Trent from beating on Robert. Outside the subdivision, after passing a

Denny's and McDonald's, several gas stations, she forced the Century with the pedal to the metal up the ramp to the freeway, off-white concrete divided in short sections that thwapped the underwheels every few seconds.

"Why on earth is everyone quiet?" Margaret asked as she reached cruising speed, seventy miles an hour, fifteen over the limit.

Harper looked out the window. He might as well go on and tell her. Still gazing at the cars in the slow lane, he mumbled, "I hit Joey Averatte."

"Beg your pardon?" Margaret said.

"Harper broke Joey Averatte's nose," Rebecca said clearly. "Knocked him out cold."

"Averatte had it coming," Crespo nearly shouted.

"Just one punch," Trent said.

"You should have seen the blood," Crespo crowed.

"He deserved it," Trent said. "Everyone hates Averatte."

"He's not popular with the guys," Rebecca said. "But all the girls like him."

"He's a jerk," Crespo said.

"Hush, now," Margaret shouted.

Elton John sang "Island Girl" into the silence. Margaret reached over and flicked the radio off.

"Harper," she said calmly, "tell me exactly what happened."

"Joey Averatte has been bugging me all semester, teasing me about being on a clergy scholarship." Harper massaged the knuckles of his swollen right hand. "He cut in front of me in lunch line today. I told him to get in the back of the line. He said, 'Make me.' We squared off and I hit him once in the nose."

"Knocked him out cold." Crespo leaned over the seat. "With extreme prejudice."

"Robert, sit still and shut up!" Margaret dropped her mask of southern grace, which rarely happened in public.

Crespo inhaled loudly, clutching his backpack to his chest, and leaned back.

"You broke his nose?" Margaret's voice, meant to be calm,

was low, strained. She glimpsed Harper smiling and raised her voice, whispering, "It's not funny, young man. This is very serious. My Lord, they could sue us, though I don't think they are that kind of people. Though you never know. Jim Averatte is a lawyer. What did Father Crewes do?"

"He made me apologize to Joey in the infirmary. The nurse told me if the swelling in my hand doesn't go down, I should have it X-rayed." Harper blew on his hand.

Margaret glanced at his hand. "What did Father Crewes do?"

"He called the disciplinary committee. Commander Lirt, a few teachers." Harper didn't say that he had started crying in front of them, that Father Crewes had kindly pushed a box of tissues across his desk. "Father Crewes asked me if I learned that punch from watching TV." Crespo and Trent laughed and Harper fought back a smile. "I thought I should agree with him, so I told them that I saw those cops punching out bad guys on *CHiPs.*"

Trent and Crespo laughed again.

"It's not amusing, young men," Margaret scolded. "Harper, continue."

"I said there's a lot of anger on TV shows and I think it affects the way I express anger. They bought it hook, line, and sinker." Harper tensed his chest to keep from laughing.

"Harper, are you saying that you lied to the committee?" She looked ready to slap him.

"No, ma'am. Um . . ." Harper tried to think of the best thing to say. "I am affected by TV."

"What's the punishment?" Margaret glanced at him.

"They gave me three days of in-school suspension. I have to eat with the fifth graders. I have to spend all my free periods in a little room under the staircase doing homework."

"The hole," Crespo said.

"I wonder if that is enough," Margaret said coldly.

"Don't ground me," Harper said.

"We'll talk about it with your father," Margaret said. She looked at Rebecca in the rearview and said, "You don't know how many times I've wished for girls."

"Girls. You'd like Cage and me to be girls," Harper said angrily. "Except for Nick. Your precious one."

"Nick is certainly more restrained than you." In the heat of the moment Margaret forgot Dr. Spock's injunction to never compare your children to one another.

"Nick is sweet-tempered." Harper sprayed flecks of saliva. "Nick is perfect." He pulled up the lock and pushed the long door open. "Nick is God." Wind rushed into the car. "You don't love me like you love Nick." He held the door wide open with his leg. The edge nearly scraped a Volvo station wagon–load from Episcopal in the slow lane.

"Close the door, Harper," Margaret shouted over the wind. She checked the traffic behind her, started braking, then looked back at Harper and wasn't sure if she caught the last of a smile at the boys in the backseat as she swerved in front of the Volvo. "Shut the door, Harper."

Harper glared at his mother.

"Please, pull the door shut."

Harper turned to watch the yellow line along the shoulder and the grass bank that swept down to tract homes and a shopping center. Margaret was slowing the car down. The yellow line disappeared underneath the floor. She was pulling onto the side, had slowed down to fifty, when Harper removed his leg and leaned forward, stuck his hands on each side and his head out the door like a parachutist, turned his face into the wind, and let slip a rebel yell that would have impressed Cage. Margaret lunged over to grab him, but her short arms wouldn't reach without letting go of the wheel.

Harper turned and looked back at Rebecca. With her shoulders slightly hunched she was leaning forward, with one hand on the seat by his mother's shoulder. He could see down her dress, two perfect young breasts, the cup of the bra fallen forward revealing the two rings of darker skin. Harper gawped and swung back into his seat, pulling the door closed, in one smooth motion.

"Harper, you nearly gave me a heart attack." Margaret checked the mirror, accelerated back on the freeway, deciding it was best to stay calm, think pragmatically. She thought he was bluffing, histrionic. Still, there was a moment when she believed he was ready to jump and a cry from her soul filled her with a strong adrenaline rush. In any event it was peculiar behavior and she decided right then to put him in therapy. Crespo and Trent thought it was the eccentric bravado of their hard-hitting hero. Rebecca was in love. Without conscious decision she had pulled the front of her dress forward, raised herself up a few inches off the seat, and tilted her shoulders to loosen her bra, giving Harper a glance at what he'd been trying to see all year. Feeling his eyes on her nipples made her tingle between her legs. Mooning over him since she moved into his neighborhood two years before, she described him in her diary as funny, cute, and nice. Now she would add brave, strong, and kinda crazy.

"Sorry, Mom." Harper stretched his right hand open slowly, winced. "I think I need an X-ray."

"Do you have your medical insurance card?" Margaret pushed the Century up to seventy-five. They passed a Monte Carlo full of upper-school girls smoking cigarettes who ignored them as Harper fished around in his wallet.

"Yes, ma'am. I've got it."

"Good. I'll drop everybody at Robert's house and take you to Doctors' Hospital across from the Hilton, where I'm picking up a tour. Maybe Trent's father will examine you." Margaret brushed her wind-swirled hair back into shape with one hand. "You may call your father from the emergency room."

"Are you driving them around in the Century?"

"Don't be sarcastic, Harper. You've seen the association's van." She touched his thigh. "I'm sorry I can't stay with you at the emergency room. It's always a long wait." She thought of when Cage turned over the thirty-five-gallon vat of boiling water on his leg while removing crawfish, the time he nearly cut off his toe with a lawn mower. "I'm sure Dad will get there before the doctors see you."

"It's okay, Mama." Harper heard Crespo giggling about something in the backseat. He turned and raised his eyebrows at Crespo and Trent, did his impression of Jack Nicholson in *The Shining*.

"I'll swing by the hospital after the tour." Margaret patted his thigh. She felt morose. Harper's anger perplexed and saddened her. "I hope you haven't fractured it."

Rebecca leaned over the seat to look at his hand.

Harper clutched it in a loose fist, released it again slowly. "*Fu . . . udge!*"

"I'll wait with him at the hospital," Rebecca said.

Harper looked up, surprised, and blushed slightly.

"That's very kind of you, Rebecca, but you should get home." Margaret had long suspected that the girl had a crush on her son, though she wasn't sure if Harper was aware of it. "Harper's father will meet him."

"It's like a balloon now!" Crespo said.

"It's broken. You're getting a cast," Trent said with the authority of an orthopedic surgeon's son. "I told you that at two o'clock."

Rebecca thrilled at the image of her beloved in a cast.

"Well." Margaret cleared her throat. "We're almost home."

After a big green sign for Acadian Thruway, she angled the Century down the ramp toward a stoplight.

Cage

I open my eyes into half-light. Something in my dream scared me but I can't remember what. What is this room? Blank white walls. Institutional. Where am I? Am I in a lockdown? I yell out, *"Nooooo!"* Then I see my backpack and guitar on the floor in the red neon light glowing through the curtain and I remember the Tinker Bell junkie who brought me here from Haight-Ashbury in her black cocktail dress and the terror stops. I laugh. "Take hold, son." I press the button on my watch, which lights up *7:13 p.m.* I turn on a lamp and climb out of bed. Her syringe is in a pan of water on the single burner, still warm, boiled not that long ago. There's a full packet of yellow-brown powder. She hasn't gone out to score. She must get money monthly from her parents, which runs out before the first, so she sells some of her mom's clothes. "Yes, Dr. Watson, that is how it appears to me." In an empty cupboard is a box of Kashi cereal, some soy milk in the minifridge. I wolf down three bowls in under six minutes. Now I am calm. I sit in lotus position on the floor and breathe through my nose, filling up the bottom of my belly, not moving my chest, slowly, as if through a straw. One hundred breaths. I like the way I feel now—light, at ease—so I dig in my pack for the lithium and take a couple, wash them down with some soy milk, and start to look for some socks before remembering that I threw them all away because they were stinking up the pack.

The clothes I took off last night are soaking in the bath. Emma is the tidiest junkie I've ever met. I drain the tub, turn on the tap, and rinse the clothes out, wring them dry, hang them from the shower curtain. I put my boots on barefoot, grab my Patagonia coat, and leave the room.

There's a hunched old guy at the desk who looks like William Burroughs.

"Evening," I say.

He looks up with no expression.

"Emma said you'd have a key for me. Room 411."

"What's your name?"

"Cage."

"Get it when you come back."

"Okay. Ciao."

He looks back at a catalog of guns.

Wearing a bathrobe, the transvestite smokes a cigarette on the stoop. Stepping past her, I say, "Good evening, Tiffany."

She looks up and smiles. With her wig crooked and her long lashes gone, the illusion isn't working. "Hey, baby, take a walk on the wild side."

"Hadn't heard that in a while," I say. "Can I bum a cigarette?"

"Sure, darling."

I sit down beside her. It's chilly, the stone cold and damp against my butt.

She lifts a pack of American Spirits toward me, one flicked out longer than the rest. "You're from the South."

I nod as she holds out a lighter, lean forward, and navigate the tip into the tiny flame.

"I got a ear for accents. The southern men I know, white we're talking, are heavy drinkers. Yeah, I think they must drink heavier back there than out here on the coast. You like to drink?"

"I've been known to. What I'd like to do now is smoke some herb."

"Burn a bone? Why didn't you say so?" Tiffany pulls a little banana-shaped spliff from her gown pocket, hands it over. "Don't be shy. Go on. Light it up. This is San Francisco."

I start it off the end of the cigarette, pull in a deep toke, pass the joint, let it go.

"You know where I can buy some socks?"

"Hosiery? Condoms?" She blows smoke in my face and winks. "What you mean by socks?"

"Tube socks."

She laughs, hands me the joint.

"Seriously I need some athletic socks. You know, a five-and-dime." I hold the end in my fingers so her saliva won't touch my lips.

"Five-and-dime," Tiffany says. "Talkin' in code, like you're trying to score something."

"You know a Walgreens or Kmart, a store with cheap socks?"

"Settle down, handsome." She sucks in a toke and blows it out the corner of her mouth. "Corner of Gough and Turk, not far."

I stand up.

"Go get your guitar and croon for me," she says.

"My feet are cold. I got to get some socks."

"I got all the condoms you need," she says.

"Thanks for the smokes." I head up the hill. My legs are springy, my thighs strong, my step light. I just needed a straight twenty-four hours to be good as new. The whole night lies in front of me. Endless possibility. All of human nature on display. All the races of the world washed up in this port city. On Gough I find a Rite Aid that sells tube socks in packs of three. I buy two packs and some Dr. Scholl's medicated powder. Outside on the sidewalk, I take off my boots, powder up my feet, pull on a pair of socks, pour more powder in the boots, and pull them back on. Preventive medicine. I pass St. Mary's, a Catholic cathedral, then stop in an empty Jefferson Square. The night is clear. I lie back on a bench and try to see the stars but the city lights let only a few show through the glare.

"Hi." A guy in a business suit appears out of nowhere by my head.

I sit up quickly, leap up to my feet. "You shouldn't sneak up on people like that."

"I thought you were sleeping."

"What if I was? What were you going to do?"

"Put your cock in my mouth."

"Oh, you San Francisco boys. Not quite so many of you back where I come from."

He laughs. "Where's that?"

"Planet organic." It's too dark to see his face. Mid-fifties?

"I'll pay you twenty bucks to let me give you a blow job."

"My cock is worth twice that. It's big and sweet."

"Is it?"

"You've never licked a cock so big in your life."

"Really? Can I see?"

"No money, no honey."

He pulls out a wallet, takes out two bills, holds them out. I grab the cash out of his hand and sprint across the square, thinking, Don't look back, they might be gaining on you. He never says a word. When I hit the street, I glance over my shoulder and see him halfway between the bench and the street, not moving, his head hanging down, so pitiful that I almost go back and return his cash. Ill-gotten gains. A shudder of creepiness shakes my body. I jog on down the street.

I swing by the El Dorado to see if Emma has returned. Tiffany has gone from the stoop. William Burroughs hands me the key without a word. The room is empty. For a few seconds I panic because I don't see my pack and guitar and then I find them under the bed where I'd left them. I put my new socks in my pack, wet my hair and comb it back, early Elvis style, hold it down with a little hand lotion. Then I grab my guitar, fly back down the stairs, and drop the key on the desk. I tell the old man, "Got to put a little work in every day or you just can't feel good about yourself."

He grunts.

"Like you. Earning the daily bread."

"I'd rather be on a range firing ten rounds a second." He purses his lips together like an asshole.

"Very violent hobby. Don't you golf?"

"Do I look like Tiger Woods?"

"No, you look more like the trainer in the ring corner who sponges the boxer's face, slaps grease on his cuts. That kind of thing."

His mouth flashes gold, rows of fillings, as he laughs.

"Whom do you imagine that you're shooting on the range?"

"None of your business."

"Remember, you can sin by thought, word, or deed."

"That's who I shoot. The fathers that fucked me up."

"Therapy," I say. "Later, gunslinger."

I head out into the evening to ply my temporary trade. The Tenderloin is more crowded now. People are milling around the garish entrances to the strip joints, sex shops, and dive bars. I catch a bus on Geary east toward the Bay and stay with it as it turns north on Kearny. Watching the blocks flash by, I feel buoyant with eighty bucks in my pocket and Tinker Bell's doss-pad. There are only a few mute, defeated, gray riders on the bus, so I start strumming Muddy Waters songs, singing above the engine noise. When I get off at Columbus, the old black driver says, "Son, you ain't bad for a white boy."

"Thank ya, cap'n." I tip an imaginary hat, then swing off the stainless-steel pole over the three steps and out onto the street.

I walk up to City Lights bookstore and through the windows watch a handful of lonely people browsing the shelves. I stole a copy of the *Tao* the morning I arrived, put it back the same afternoon with a flower pressed in its pages. I try to think of some Ferlinghetti lines and I can't, so at the mouth of the alley across from the front door, I lean against a post that holds street signs that say END and JACK KEROUAC and try to conjure up a passage from *On the Road*. I used to know so many.

A businesswoman about my age comes out of City Lights and walks to the point of the sidewalk where Columbus meets Kerouac, right across the alley. She raises her hand for a taxi. I strum the opening of "Jumpin' Jack Flash," then chant, "Because the only people for me are the mad ones, the ones who are mad to live, mad to talk, mad to be saved, desirous of everything at the same time"—she listens, amused, smiling slightly—"the ones who never yawn or say a commonplace thing but burn, burn, burn like fabulous yellow Roman candles exploding like spiders across the stars."

"Bravo!" She digs in her handbag, then throws some change. "Bellisimo."

"Thank you, gorgeous." I start playing "Blowin' in the Wind." She looks out at Columbus.

"How many miles must a bipolar man fly," I sing, "before he can settle and land?"

She looks back at me. Everyone knows someone bipolar and they're usually very interesting people. People are curious.

"The answer of my end." I go through Dylan's refrain, playing the guitar loud.

She glances at the street, sees a taxi coming, flags it down, looks back at me.

I launch into an old Eagles tune, improvise the lyrics. "Come on, gorgeous, stop and think twice."

The taxi pulls up and she opens the door, gets in slowly.

"Take a chance you won't regret," I sing.

A lonely career girl, she watches me through the open door until I finish the line.

"Better than dinner with a TV set."

She blows me a kiss and pulls the door shut.

"You're not a bad musician," says someone on the other side.

I wave good-bye at the woman, then turn and see a guy in his late forties with a goatee and corduroy blazer, total beatnik look, a ghost from the fifties. "You've got a good voice."

"Thank you."

"You just need to train yourself more." His tone is kind. "I can see that you're out here paying your dues as a musician."

"Haven't come very far in eight years, I guess." Sixteen really, but I never played geetar in the black dog days.

"I wouldn't say that," he says quickly. "And I ought to know since I teach music in a high school nearby."

"Well, thanks."

"Say, would you like a coffee or a sandwich next door?"

"At the famous Vesuvio, where Kerouac and Dylan Thomas drank themselves under the table?"

"That's the one." He sticks out his hand. "Karl."

I can tell he spells it with a *K*. "As in Marx?"

"Precisely."

"Cage." I shake his hand. "Yeah. I'm hungry."

We cross Kerouac Alley and pass under the stained-glass sign. Yellow light pools beneath the lamps, reflects off the surface of dozens of framed pictures on the dark paneling. A campy young waiter sucks on his pen while I order an Anchor Steam and an avocado sandwich. Karl orders a coffee and carrot cake.

"You AA?" I ask after the waiter leaves.

Karl says, "Twelve years."

"Thank God for Dr. Bob," I say. "He helped me a few times."

"But you fell off the wagon again." His face is calm, concerned.

"Some time ago." I shrug. "My life is particularly disorganized at the moment but alcohol is a symptom, not the root. I'm not drinking much. I'm naturally high."

"You're manic-depressive?"

"The current terminology is 'bipolar,'" I say as the drinks arrive. The beer's tasty.

"I have friends . . ." Karl nods. "You should go back on your meds."

I'm starting to get pissed off. "Listen, dude, thanks for playing the Good Samaritan, but you can back out of my kitchen right now. You're starting to rattle my pots and pans."

"It's cool," Karl says. "Ah, here comes the carrot cake."

"And I'm not gay, okay?"

Karl laughs. "Neither am I, man. I was just complimenting your singing by buying you a meal. All right?"

"Thanks, Karl. You're a good guy."

"If you get hungry, there's an AA breakfast every morning at St. Francis of Assisi right up Columbus."

William Burroughs smiles when he sees me come inside. Handing me the key, he says, "The young lady is entertaining, sir."

"Thank you, Jeeves." I bound up the stairs. There's music inside the room. I knock on the door. "Carlin—I mean Emma?" Nothing. "Em!" I turn the lock slowly. Inside is dark and still like a tomb with U2 songs for hymns. The only light is the glow from the gas burner on one side and fluorescence falling in from the bathroom on the other. I slip in quickly, shut the door quietly.

In the kitchenette corner a man, hard to see in the orange light, has a bare foot up on the counter. As my eyes adjust, I see he is sticking a needle between his toes. From the bathroom come the sounds of vomiting. Across the dark room, Emma's cradling the toilet. The guy says, "Cotton poison," without looking at me. I go into the bathroom and find a rag, wet it with warm water, and lift her gently up by the chin to wipe off her face. She looks like she just ran a marathon. Her eyes are less remote. She mouths a word I can't make out.

"Can I get you anything?"

She shakes her head.

"Are you sure?"

The corners of her mouth turn up in the beginning of a smile and then a convulsion racks her body and she turns away. I hug her from behind until she is quiet, then wipe off her face. I walk back in the room where the music is much louder now and the guy is sitting cross-legged with his back to the cabinet doors, swaying to his own beat. I kneel by him and say into his ear, "How can I help her?"

"You can't." He doesn't open his eyes.

"Will she be okay?"

He doesn't answer, keeps swaying off time.

"*Will she be okay?*"

Emma's body shudders but I can't hear her. I shake the guy by his shoulders. "Hey, will she be okay?"

He looks at me from across the canyons of his mind. I shake him hard once more. He opens his eyes, says, "Fuck off," and closes them. I go back to the bathroom. With the side of her face resting on the toilet seat, Emma is sobbing. Her white Issey Miyake crimpolene gown is drenched with sweat. I raise the hem up, lift her by the waist an inch to get the dress over her knees and up her legs. She's wearing faded Patagonia stand-up shorts. I pull the dress over her head. She puts up no resistance, just raises her arms. She's not wearing a bra. Her breasts would fit perfectly in champagne cups. She is beautiful. I wrap her in a towel, lean her against the tub, then go to the kitchen and get some water from the tap. She shakes her head as I put the glass to her lips.

"Keep yourself hydrated," I tell her.

She takes a sip.

"We can wash that cotton poison away," I tell her.

She takes a swallow. Then another.

"Imagine your body washing that poison away." My voice is slow, soothing. "Wash it out of your blood."

She finishes the glass. I fill it up from the bathroom sink, hold it back to her mouth. "Wash it out of your body. Wash it all away and you'll feel better. You'll keep feeling better."

I talk her into a trance, almost hypnotize her, get her to drink several glasses of water before she throws up again, and then I make her drink several more, talk soothingly to her for a long time as she leans against the bathtub.

She speaks for the first time: "I'm sleepy."

I lift her out of the towel and carry her in a fireman's hold to the bed, lay her down. The other guy is gone. I take her Patagonia shorts off. The size of her bush surprises me. I lift her legs up high in the air by her ankles, pull the bedspread out from under her, lower her to the sheet, cover her up. "You are deep, deep within yourself," I tell her. "You are completely relaxed, completely at harmony. Go in your mind to Yosemite. Picture the sheer face of El Capitan rising up tall and straight, a granite monolith high against the sky. You are as calm as the mountain. The poison is going, flushing from your system." I keep talking, checking my watch. After twenty minutes I pull back the sheet, reveal her beautiful body, pick her up. She puts her arm around my neck. "You're going to pee now, flush it all out of your body. After you pee, all the poison will be gone."

I set her down on the toilet. I can see her face clearly in the light. Her eyes are closed but she is smiling. "Let it out!" I command, like my hypnotherapist used to do to me, and she starts to pee a steady stream like a garden hose filling up a pool, for a full ninety seconds. "The poison is going, going out, out, draining from your body." She dabs herself dry and raises her arms. I pick her up, flick the flush handle down with my foot. "Now you're going to sleep, a deep, deep sleep, such a deep sleep, and when you wake up, you will want to go clean. We'll go camping in Yosemite. You can flush it all out. I'll help you through it. Providence brought us together, two PKs on the streets of San Francisco. You can beat the monkey." I lay her down on the bed and keep talking, painting a picture of a clean future in the mountains, her blood as pure as a mountain stream, after she has fallen asleep, embedding those hypnotic suggestions. Together we can make it.

Harper

"Do you have the authority to clear this trade?" I ask an asshole at Merrill who equivocates. I spit a jet of tobacco juice. "Well, get me the organ-grinder. I'm tired of talking to the monkey!" I hang up on him in midsentence, spin my chair to my third screen, and search a medical database for "nymphomania":

Nymphomania signifies a woman's excessive or pathological desire for coitus. There have been few scientific studies of the condition, but those patients who have been studied usually have had one or more sexual disorders, often including female orgasmic disorder. The woman often has an intense fear of losing love and attempts to satisfy her dependence needs, rather than to gratify her sexual impulses, through her actions. This disorder is a form of sex addiction.

From my window on the eightieth floor of the World Trade Center is a blighted landscape of factories and freeways. Light flares off the glass towers of Newark. Every time I look up from my screens, I wish we had an office on the north side and a vista of the Manhattan canyons rather than the depressing collage of postindustrial Jersey. The office is an oven. The record heat caught the tower's air-conditioning off guard. It's ninety-four degrees outside. Must be ninety-eight in here. My hands ache and I wonder if I'm getting carpal tunnel syndrome. I set my glasses on

the desk, push the lever to lean back in my Aeron chair. Two ker-
nels of pain about six inches apart radiate from my spine. I lean
forward and push the lump of Copenhagen out of my mouth
into the throat of a Snapple tea bottle, gargle with Evian, and spit
it all in the bottle.

Standing up, I see my reflection in the window, the bulge
around the middle visible under my shirt. My StairMaster has
been dormant for weeks. Make that months. I walk toward Asgar,
an Indian programmer we picked up cheap.

"How's it going, Asgar?"

"Hi, Harper."

"You are a living legend," I say slowly.

"Okay, Harper." Asgar smiles uneasily.

"We're going out of business. We'll all be ruined." I pat him on
the back, smiling widely like an idiot. "You'll be deported."

"Okay, Harper." Asgar smiles and nods, embarrassed that he
doesn't understand. He's a whiz at what he does and he can read
instructions fine, so we tell him what to do by e-mail, but he
doesn't comprehend one word we say.

"Leave the man alone," Dooner calls from his desk without
glancing from his screens.

"Hi, Aidan," Asgar says, then goes back to his screen, testing a
new part of the program to project tiny changes in stock price.
Through the day Asgar tracked ten thousand stocks, tick by tick,
as many as a hundred thousand ticks per stock from every kid
who bought a share to every mutual fund that bought five thousand, and now he's collating the results.

Dooner pops up from his chair and shouts across the room at
the trading desk. "How many shares left of IBM?"

"A hundred grand," Ronbeck yells back.

The other four traders turn to watch Dooner, a redheaded hulk
who could have been an extra in a *Braveheart* battle scene, who
screams, "The specialist smells you like rotten meat. You held on
too long all day. Buy twenty-five thousand right fucking now.
They want to be fully long by the close. You got twenty minutes."

"On it, Mom," Ronbeck mutters, hitting speed dial to the market maker.

"Don't let him hear the fear in your voice," Dooner yells, dropping down in his chair. "Or we're royally fucked."

Supply and demand, testosterone and poker make a market. The gospel according to Dooner. I tell the back of his head, his thick freckled neck bulging out of a stained Thomas Pink collar, "I can't take the heat."

"Get out of the kitchen," he says impatiently, furiously typing away on the keyboard. "Global warming."

"I think it's part of a natural heat wave," I say. "My grandma's first memory is sitting on the back porch at Cage's Bend with my great-grandmother, who had just barely survived the flu epidemic of 1918 when tens of thousands of Americans dropped like flies. It was Christmas and so hot that the roses were blooming four months early."

"Roses are late bloomers." Dooner sighs, glances over his shoulder, keeps on tapping keys. "They weren't blooming early. They were blooming late."

Aidan Dooner and I designed a black box that assures institutional investors trading large blocks of stock that they will get the volume-weighted average price, or better than VWAP, on any trading day. Pennies a share add up to millions. Our team is the program trading desk of the Union Bank of Luxembourg, which guarantees our trades with a two-billion-dollar intraday credit line. There are only eight of us, nine counting Asgar, but he's on a short-term contract. We're a plug-and-play operation. We've been with other houses, we're going to a Hong Kong bank soon, taking a lot of our clients with us. Dooner's the senior partner. He had the prototype. Two and a half years ago I got an equity stake in the start-up by quitting my job and writing code for nine months, then helping him pitch it on the Street. Dooner's the Heavy Quant, the mathematical genius who sees market applications in fractal sets, stochastics, the Fibonacci sequence. I'm just a glorified Asgar.

"Asgar." Five feet from his desk I raise my hand toward the windows, several hundred square miles of New Jersey, and say slowly, "One day all this will be yours."

Asgar frowns, furrows his brow.

I peer into his eyes. "If you give me your soul."

"Okay, Harper." Asgar smiles. "E-mail, okay?"

At my desk I adjust the chair and consider e-mailing him Satan's proposition but I want to get out of here as fast as possible. I ought to run home along the park by the Hudson, sweat out some of last night's toxins in the sticky breeze. Every afternoon I think of jogging in the twilight but never remember to bring shorts and shoes. By the time I make it home by taxi or the subway, all I want is a beer. Dooner follows the important baskets through the day, intervening at times to lock in a trade, but lately I've been letting the box do it. He says I've developed a lame-duck attitude while the negotiations are going on, and he's right. As soon as we jump ship, we'll be working twice as hard trying to impress our new partners with our execution quality. I tell him that I'm saving my ammo for the firefight on the horizon. I watch the box closing my last trades, then stand up in my chair and look out the window. A thousand feet below, someone by the Merchant Marine statue has collapsed in the heat. A crowd is gathering. I hear the traders shouting as the markets close, sink back to my chair, pack a dip in my lip, start clearing the eight thousand trades from my station.

"Ronbeck!" I hear Dooner yell.

"Yeah, Mom?"

"IBM?"

"It's on the tape," Ronbeck says.

The elevator is crowded and a virtual sauna. Dooner seems to take up most of the space, dripping in the middle like he just walked off a rugby pitch. Descending fast through the tower, he says loudly, "Remember flying into Kyrgyzstan?"

"Fadies and gentlemen, ve are about to set down in Bishkek," I mimic the Lufthansa pilot. "To adjust your vatches to zee local time, please set zem back zirty years."

Dooner laughs.

The other twenty people in the sauna are silent.

Dooner hasn't mentioned Kyrgyzstan in ages. Five years ago he hired me for a team he led to set up stock exchanges in

Moldova, Ukraine, and Kyrgyzstan. Dooner's thirty-five, six years older than me.

"Gets old doing the same thing every day," I say.

"Not to me," Dooner says. "It's war. The fucking Big Board. Protecting their stocks from the world. One day those licensed thieves are going to fall like a house of cards."

Dooner believes if he can perfect the box, we can sell it for ten million, plus a million a year for the two of us to keep adapting it to subtle changes in the markets. We split seventy-thirty. I believe Dooner. I'm his highly paid apostle. If we cash out big, Dooner will go on to create something bigger. I'll just travel for a few years. Theoretically I would like to sleep with women of diverse ethnicities in their original environments. A Nubian in the Nubia, for instance. A Roman in Rome. Ideally you would live with them for a few months, a season, for, as the Italians say, a story. I picture Tatiana brushing her pale hair off her blue eyes in Moscow, Katinka's dark eyes and sweet smile in Bishkek. They were both carefree, lusty girls. We still correspond. They're married now. They still long to come to America. Now with their families. Right up front I told them I wasn't looking for a wife but for someone to share my bed, dinners, weekend getaways. They hoped first secretly then openly that I would fall in love—the ambition that the expat exploits. I send Katinka's kid to kindergarten. Got pictures of her little family on my refrigerator. Maybe if we cash out big, I'll help them immigrate to the promised land.

"What you up to tonight?" Dooner has circles of sweat beneath his armpits. Rivulets stream out of his thatch of red hair down his forehead and sideburns.

"Drinks with one girl and dinner with another."

"Hundred bucks both of them have dark hair and big tits like that picture of your mommy on your desk."

A woman beside Dooner looks at him distastefully. The elevator door opens. The lobby is still crowded at six o'clock but slightly cooler.

"Keep your money." I angle a shoulder between two guys in suits going too slowly.

"Am I right?" Dooner doesn't slide through the throngs of

suits. They seem to sense the big silver back from behind, give him wide berth. He always steps aside for ladies.

"No. Two blondes." I give up and stroll behind him, let him run interference through the crowd.

"You're making a conscious effort to break the pattern." Over his shoulder he asks, "Betsy Sloan?"

"Bat Girl Betsy," I say. "Fast creature of the night."

"I've got to stop introducing you to dangerous older women. It's starting to fuck with your work ethic." Outside, Dooner offers me a Marlboro Light. "Thinking stick?"

"I've switched to dip entirely now," I say, trying to decide if it's hotter out here.

"Statistically I'm not sure that's a good move."

"Right, Mom." Walking across the plaza, I tell him, "I'm going out to San Francisco to track Cage down."

Dooner draws on his cigarette, then pushes his hand away from his face, a sell signal on the floor, which means he thinks it's a bad idea. "He could be in Mexico or Canada by the time you get there."

"Yeah, statistically it's useless but I feel obligated. I promised my mama. And my granny. And my uncle right before he died."

Dooner nods, perhaps thinking about his own brother who has been in and out of rehab clinics. "Bad timing with Hong Kong hanging in the balance." A block east of the towers, he flags down a cab on Church Street.

"You don't need me to close the deal."

"When are you leaving?" He opens the door.

"Monday. Tuesday. Cage hasn't called for money for ten days. I might hear from him Saturday. It's his birthday."

"Want a lift?"

"Nah, I want to sweat like a pig. Walk up the river."

"Like Jesus?" Dooner smiles, tosses his thinking stick.

"Where you going?"

"Dinner at Cipriani in SoHo with Nicola," Dooner says, tall against the taxi. The great silver back is a serial monogamist. In the five years I've known him he has only been unfaithful to his girlfriend twice, two years apart, both rare coke-fueled nights with a billionaire client who forced a goddess-for-hire on him, more out of desire to accept the man's hospitality than to fornicate. He's faithful to an attractive, smart girlfriend for a year or two and then he can't close the trade. They leave because he's too obsessed with his work. Maneuvering his wide frame into the cab, he says, "Get in early."

Betsy Sloan has a huge natural rack, not unlike my mama's, Dooner would point out. Across 10th Street, at thirty feet, those two globes dominate your field of vision, then your eyes take in her hourglass figure in a tight skirt and matching jacket and helmet of light hair set in the CNN studio that frames her wide cheekbones. Betsy may very well be a textbook nymphomaniac but she doesn't suffer from female orgasmic disorder. She's the most orgasmic girl I've ever met. She comes six times a night, minimum. She was the attack forward on the Stanford lacrosse team. Two weeks ago we were boogie boarding sizable waves off Bermuda. I was getting hammered, rolled over and crushed, thrashed against the bottom, and nearly drowned. Betsy would watch as the wave peaked and started to curl over her head, then paddle fast, screaming, *"Come on, motherfucker!"* and ride the big ones all the way to the shore. Bat Girl Betsy, the roving reporter. She was an investment banker at Goldman. Lust for fame took her to CNN. Twenty feet away she doesn't look in my direction and I don't call out. She prances on high heels like a Tennessee walker three steps up into Il Cantinori.

I follow her in. The air is icy, the first Louisiana-style air-conditioning I've felt all day. When I come in, Alfredo is kissing both of her cheeks, letting his hand glide down the curve of her back and her ass in the Italian fashion. I'm fairly sure he's gay. He must figure that the female clientele like to be groped. Or maybe he likes the light, quick touch of a woman's flesh through the safety of fabric. He spots me and says, "Ciao, Harper."

"Ciao, Alfredo."

Betsy turns and beams. Her eyes look naughty, like she's already done a couple of bumps. She could have already fucked one of her ex-boyfriends, too. I don't care and I can't take the moral high ground. I'm freshly showered after wrestling a long, tall twenty-year-old debutramp named Laura Day from Tuxedo Park. It took about an hour to get her off. The girl must achieve orgasm. That's my guiding principle between the sheets. Truly, I feel absolutely miserable if she doesn't.

"Look at his jeans, Alfredo." Betsy nods at my knees, the blue denim almost white. "I've got to buy this boy some Levi's."

"Ah, but his jacket." Alfredo runs his hand down the lapel of my green Otesta linen blazer. "More than makes up for them."

"Hungry?" Betsy pulls me against her bosom, kisses me on the mouth, tracing her tongue across my lips.

"Starving."

Alfredo leaves us at a table by the window.

"Geraldo invited me out to his beach house next weekend."

I have no reason to believe that is true. "Bring back a lock of his mustache."

"He's married."

"That never stopped you."

Two Stoli greyhounds arrive at the table, anticipating our order.

"Thanks." Betsy bats her eyelashes at the waiter, then turns to me. "Don't be unkind."

I take a big swallow of my drink. Betsy's father squandered a fortune and looked down on her for going to Harvard Business School. He was an alcoholic who never worked a day in his life. Betsy's mother left him for a girl who cleaned their pool. Her dad died of a heart attack a few years ago. I spit an ice cube back in the glass and say, "Do you think that you like sex so much because your father didn't love you?"

"What do you mean 'like sex so much'?" Betsy still has on a thick layer of TV makeup. It's disconcerting, almost like talking to a mask.

"Let's face it. We're both sex addicts. Us. Clinton. We're a sign of the times."

"Clinton is slime and scum. And I'm not talking about cigars. He and Hillary are evil. They've had people knocked off."

"Bat Girl, my darling." I lift the hem of the tablecloth from the floor to my knees and reach beneath for her right foot, take off the shoe, start massaging. "I believe that I am a sex addict because I'm angry at my mother, who put a lot of pressure on me to succeed. I think that's why I cannot settle down with one woman and be true to her, this anger at my mother."

"Sounds simplistic." Betsy purrs as I massage. She runs around all day in high heels covering the Street on camera. I don't see why she can't wear trainers. You never see TV reporters' feet. Vanity over sanity. I stuff a piece of focaccia in my mouth with one hand, take a swig of my greyhound, then use both thumbs to knead her arch.

"Were you always worried that your father didn't love you as much as your other sisters?"

"Yes." She sips from her glass, closes her eyes.

"When you think of your father, what images come to mind?" I rub two of her toes at a time with my thumbs and first fingers.

"I see him cuddling Jenny." Without opening her eyes she raises her left foot to my thigh. As I begin to rub it, she grinds her right foot in my crotch.

"How far away are you from them?"

"Harper, do you want to make me cry?"

"Not here."

She opens one eye.

"I never want to make you cry," I say. "I want you to feel good."

"You're such a sweet boy." She smiles with her eyes, her lips slightly parted.

"Boy, who you callin' boy?" I imitate Grandpa Cage's gracious baritone. I've lost much of my Louisiana accent in the six years since I left the South. "My dear Elisabeth, you are a mere five years my senior." Which is a lie. I peeked at her passport in Bermuda. She's thirty-seven. I'm starting to get hard, so I put her feet gently back on the floor. "I do believe you have aroused me something considerable."

Betsy sits up perfectly straight, anchor posture, leans forward, and smiles. "Want some of that bad stuff?"

"It's almost eight-thirty. Sun's long over the yardarm," I say. "A bump before dinner can be stimulating to the appetite."

We are about to go to the toilet together when a waiter arrives. I order a Caesar salad. Betsy orders the fifty-dollar veal. Then we get up and meander through the tables, smile at Alfredo, and go down the steps to the basement. I open the door to a toilet for her, then lock it behind us.

Betsy is at the mirror, her head tilted back, holding a key to her nose. I move beside her, watch her scoop another bump from a plastic bag on the sink, hoover it up her sharp nose.

"This morning Dooner made me promise that I wouldn't get dirty tonight," I say ruefully.

"He's a genius, your partner." Betsy presses her cleavage into my sternum, holding the key high.

In the mirror I see that my face has not begun to fatten up like the rest of my body but my eyes look puffy from a week of vodka nights. In the bright light and heavy makeup Betsy looks like a parody of herself, sexy in a strange circuslike way. I tilt my head back, glide the key to my nose in the mirror, clamp one nostril shut with my left forefinger. It burns as it hits the sensitive red skin inside. I grimace and load up the key. Betsy slides her hand softly down the back of my head. I numb out the other side of my nose, feel the little lift of energy, and my palms begin to sweat.

"That's it." I kiss Betsy's cheek, put my arm around her waist. "Don't want to ruin my appetite."

She loads up the key. "You sure?"

"Yeah, baby. Go for it."

Betsy whips the key to her nose, snorts it up, then puts her key and the gram bag in her change purse. She turns and places her arms around my back, slides her knee under my crotch, and squeezes my leg between hers, which are nearly as heavy as mine, all toned muscle, and rolls her hips round and round, rubbing against my zipper.

"I thought so." She stoops, unzips my pants, and pulls my dick out. "You have a great cock."

You ought to be an informed judge, I almost say. "You had me hard back at the table."

"Why did you think I wanted to come down here?" She laughs. "Blow?"

Hunkering on her high heels, one hand on the sink, she puts me in her mouth.

"You like them circumcised, don't you?" I look down at the top of her head. The only dark roots are in the center, the little round spot where the hair grows out in all directions, the same medium brown as her bush. She probably spends a thousand a month on her colorist uptown.

"That's not a courtly question." She glances up. Her unguarded smile is unusually warm and friendly. Her eyes seem to say, I love you. You are just like me. Don't we have an exciting time together? "But, actually, yes, I do."

She takes it deep in her throat. Her warm saliva feels heavenly.

"Are you sure you want to do this?" I touch her shoulder. She draws slowly up, raises her head, and I fall back into myself.

Someone turns the door handle from the outside.

"Do you?" She licks her lips.

"I'm hard as a rock and you look so beautiful down there."

She pushes me over to a little padded bench opposite the mirror. I slip off my linen blazer and spread it on the floor.

"Such a southern gentleman," Betsy says as I sit down on the bench and lean back. She kneels on the jacket and parts my legs, unbuckles my Levi's, and pulls them down to my knees.

"How pretty you are. Such a big boy." Betsy cups my balls with one hand, leans forward. "Shame that Harper never named you." She places her mouth on me, slides slowly up and down. "*Mmmmm.*"

"*Aaahh.*" I rest my head against the wall, letting the tension of making Laura come without coming myself—after an hour I simply couldn't release—wash out of my neck down through my shoulders and chest into the head of my penis. I open my eyes and glance down at her cleavage, the breasts touching, swelling beneath her jacket. I wonder, as I have countless times, why the image excites me. Did I imprint on my mother's so young that the image is embedded, deep and strong in my subconscious? The only tangible reason I can muster as proof of the existence of God is that some higher power must have created the beauty of the breast. Scientists describe tits as secondary sexual characteristics. A therapist told me that they are designed to resemble buttocks, which *Homo sapiens* are programmed to target for the perpetuation of the species. Breasts are butts. The little dimple on my chin is a little butt. That's why Betsy likes it so much. A cross-species comparison is the bladder that a female camel blows out of her mouth and inflates, a big red balloon, to attract randy male camels. Secondary sexual characteristics.

I reach down and unbutton Betsy's jacket, pull down her bra. Her breasts bulge out, pinched along the rims of the cups. I focus on her brown nipples and her white, untanned tits, pitching up and down, as the hot blood surges into my dick, lathered in her warm spit. The heat gathers as her breasts sway. I grasp one in my hand, compress it into a narrow ridgetop. Locked in the moment, the present instant, I stroke her hair, push her lips to my pubic hair. I don't care what the professionals say, I like this. This is what I want to do. Am I a sex addict? Is there such a thing? Aren't males programmed to disperse their seed through the gene pool? *Mmmm*, Betsy gurgles, taking me deeper. I almost dig my hand into her breast. She goes up and down faster. My body goes limp, the last of the life force sapped into my prick. I feel the advent, deep from the base, surging upward like molten mercury. "Aaaah," I cry out, scalded. The heat pulsates into her mouth. Suddenly I am back in the world, with my pants at my knees and a nymphomaniac swallowing my seed. The rush is spent. I close my eyes and try to salvage the afterglow, stroking her back, clinging to the warm calm.

Someone tries the door.

What kind of girl likes to get down on her knees in bathrooms? The kind of girl I like to hang out with. Why? To degrade herself? Just to make me feel good? What made her that way? I wonder, buckling my pants. Did she come to confuse her father's criticism and distance with love? Betsy stands up and rubs her knees. Was his degrading treatment her main form of interaction with him, his only expression of love, of the connection between them? So Betsy reenacts the emotional dynamic with her dead father on the floor of a toilet in Il Cantinori?

Someone rattles the doorknob louder. As I'm putting my coat on, Betsy opens the door.

A big black woman with strong facial features and an enormous Hydra of dreadlocks is waiting outside.

"Loved *Beloved*," Betsy says, walking past the woman.

"Thank you," the woman says.

I smile, following Bat Girl.

The woman's eyes seem to look right through mine.

Going up the stairs, Betsy says, "That was Toni Morrison."

"Who?"

"The novelist. Toni Morrison."

"Oh, yeah. I heard of her. "

"You ought to try reading a novel."

"I've already read one."

As we reach the table, the waiter delivers our salads. I spear a piece of Parmesan and ask, "Aren't males programmed to scatter their seed? Or is that biological reductionism?"

"You fucked someone earlier, didn't you?" Betsy dangles a baby leaf on the end of her fork.

"I won't stoop to reply to those allegations." I'm not sure why I don't just admit it and describe the act in detail. Because she doesn't really want to hear about it. "What makes you suggest such a thing?"

Betsy smiles. "Easy. Your obsession tonight with sex addiction."

"There are two kinds of people. Those who are faithful, like my parents, and those who are not, like me and you." I lift her left hand off the table, kiss her fingers. "We're *hungry*." I bite her thumb. "It's easy for the faithful. They choose to be true. So they are." Her hand against my cheek is hot in the icy air. "You and I need excitement, variety. We're true to our nature, though we feel guilty about it."

"The curse of the good-looking man." Betsy pinches my face. "It's easy for you to get in trouble."

"Not as easy as for a sexy chick."

Betsy laughs, pulls her hand away. "Are you in therapy?"

"Bat Girl, how little we know each other. Off and on for years."

"Don't worry, then. You'll settle down." Betsy's eyes look almost misty.

"Hey," I whisper kindly. "Harry wasn't such a great catch. You'll get a bigger fish." Harry's an English merchant banker who dated Betsy for six months, asked her to marry him down on one knee with a ring, then dumped her a couple of months later for her best friend, Carrie, another blonde bombshell, who had lived in Betsy's summer house in Bridgehampton for years.

"I ran into Carrie an hour ago," Betsy says.

"No shit. Where?"

"Outside APC in SoHo."

"Did you speak?"

"She's crazy. She called me a coke whore."

"That's terrible," I say, thinking, You're not a coke whore, Betsy. More of a blow nympho. There's a distinct difference. You don't fuck a guy for blow. You can afford your own. I frown compassionately, say aloud, "What did you say to her?"

Betsy widens her eyes. "I said, 'Carrie. It won't last. He won't stay with you.' She says, 'Why?' and I said, ''Cause you're a dried-up old cunt.' "

I laugh. "What'd she say?"

"That's when she called me a coke whore."

"Catfight." I whistle.

"What do you think I should do?"

"Well, as practicing Episcopalians, I advise you to pray for her soul."

"You're not a practicing Episcopalian. You just like to take a few tokes and belt out hymns." Betsy laughs. "Want to go to church on Sunday?"

"Love to. I like the way you hang on my arm like we're a young, pure married couple." I smile, then shake my head. "But I'm off to San Francisco to find Cage."

"Poor Cage," Betsy says. "I pray about him."

"Thousands of people pray for him—he's on the prayer list at churches across the South." I sigh. "Scientific studies show that prayer has a positive affect on illnesses, cancer patients in particular. They don't know why. Probably mind over matter. The people believe in its efficacy, so it works. Doesn't seem to be working with my brother."

"Maybe it is," Betsy says. "Otherwise he might be dead."

Busted
1986

Steele Boulevard in Baton Rouge was two yellow concrete streets divided by wide islands of Bermuda grass, boxes for giant live oaks. Hidden behind a tall wall of camellia hedges was a modest two-story Cajun-style cottage and a tennis court with a superb green clay surface and high-powered lights for night play, owned by the Patrick Company, on the books for corporate entertainment. Mostly it was used for Patrick family tennis. Nick had spent many afternoons playing doubles with the Patricks, and he and Rowan often brought their dates here for drinks after all the bars had closed. After Rowan and Nick finished college and stopped coming back in the summers, the house sat idle every night for more than two years, until Harper came of age and began to use the key, which stayed in the same place, stuck to the exterior central air-conditioning unit in a little magnetic box, for at least a decade.

After a party one spring night when he was sixteen and had just gotten his license, Harper took his girlfriend, Rebecca, back to the cottage, where they had been going on weekend nights for months. Rebecca possessed centerfold curves. Harper was in heaven. Drunk, they made love several times, though Rebecca came only during the penultimate coupling. Harper put the rubbers in a little pile on the carpet by the twin bed in one of two upstairs bedrooms. They fell asleep naked in one another's arms.

About a quarter of a mile away, at five in the morning, Franklin rose without waking Margaret and put on a T-shirt and baggy running shorts. He boiled tea in the kitchen, double-tied the strings of his running shoes. Outside in the garden the purple dawn air was seventy degrees, scented by the blossoms of tall magnolias and squat banana trees. The fifty-five-year-old rector followed a series of push-ups, sit-ups, and hurdler stretches. After fifteen minutes he passed through a screen of slatted doors onto the drive and saw an empty space in the carport. Margaret's Buick Century was missing.

Well, there was nothing to do about it now, Franklin thought, setting off jogging down the drive. This had happened a dozen times with Cage and once or twice with Nick. The boys always said that they had had too much to drink to drive safely, so they spent the night at their friends' and retrieved the Century the next day. It was impossible to verify and they appeared to be behaving responsibly. What more could you possibly do? Take away the car and endure a long siege of resentment? You have done your best to instill values and good judgment. At adolescence, in the turmoil of hormones, instinctually driven to break away from us and everything we stand for, trying to become their own individual selves, they are going to push the limits of authority. All you can do is pray that they survive. It's in God's hands. You must have faith that Harper will come home eventually. Before his mother wakes up if he wants to escape the scorpion stinger of her righteous indignation.

Franklin laughed to himself, turning off Chatmoss onto Steele. He loved this shady boulevard of perpetually green oaks, the branches swooping down from fifty feet and swerving up again—the trees were nothing short of a testament to the beauty of God's creation. The branches filled his mind, a latticework filtering out Harper missing in action, all the grieving of the congregation, its factional conflicts, endemic cash shortfalls, church and family, the long lists of tedious tasks in the week ahead . . . breathing deeply, his stride nearly as long as it was at the peak of his competitive days thirty-five years before, he ran up the yellow concrete road. In the half-light he jogged past the cottage, ran on another three miles, passed the cottage again in full light on the way home, and never saw the Century behind the tall camellia hedge.

Margaret woke as usual at six-thirty, when she heard the shower. She came into the bathroom and stuck her head in the curtains and Franklin leaned out of the spray and they kissed, then she went into the kitchen, put the kettle on, spooned freeze-dried coffee crystals in a mug, and looked out the window over the sink at the carport and saw that the Century was missing.

She retied the strap of her bathrobe and marched back to the bedroom, where Frank was pulling on a pair of boxers. Her mouth was set, her jaw held high. She said, "That boy."

Franklin tried not to appear amused. He popped open a safety pin that kept his socks together in the wash. Harper was irresponsible, mainly for making his mother worry, but the sight of his compact little wife on the warpath struck a chord in his heart that made him smile. "He'll come home."

"Doesn't he think about how I will be tormented until he comes home? Until I know that he's safe? He could have the courtesy to call." She put her hand to her forehead. "He was out with Rebecca last night."

"He'll be fine." Franklin stepped into a pair of seersucker trousers.

"Not when I get my hands on him." Margaret laughed.

"I wouldn't want to be Harper when he gets home."

"He'll probably make me late for church." Margaret clenched her hands into little fists.

"Leave him." Franklin pulled on a white shirt, reached in a tall dresser for a collar. "That boy marches to the sound of his own drummer."

"That's letting him off too easy."

"Mars." Her martial nickname seemed appropriate at the moment. "Mars, don't let it work you up. Why don't you take a power walk?"

As Franklin set off for St. James, Margaret walked briskly down Chatmoss. She charged up Steele Boulevard, pumping her arms. The air was already eighty degrees. The camellia hedges of the cottage reminded her that years ago Pamela Patrick said that Rowan and Nick had used the cottage for necking with their girlfriends. She crossed the island and went down the drive. There was the missing Century, the big aquamarine box that Nick used to say looked like a landing craft that ferried soldiers to Normandy Beach. She shook her head. The side door of the house was unlocked. She called, "Harper?" She counted to ten, then walked inside.

At the foot of the stairs she picked up a flimsy red cotton shirt and beneath it a bra with a 34D cup. She stood up slowly, her back perfectly straight, and screamed like a drill sergeant, "Harper, get down here this very instant!"

"Holy shit," Harper said when he heard his mother at the door.

"Oh my God." Rebecca sat up in bed. "Oh God, my mom is going to kill me."

Harper was zipping his pants and Rebecca was still looking for her panties in the sheets when his mother screamed from the bottom of the stairs.

"My shirt. My bra." Rebecca was frantically moving around the room. She found her pants between the twin bed and the wall.

"I don't want to go down there," Harper whispered.

"Don't make me come up there!" Margaret yelled from below.

"Coming!" Harper pulled on a blue Izod, shoved his feet in loafers, and loped reluctantly down the stairs.

"Hey, Mom." A foot and a half taller, he looked down into her eyes, which were like dark landscapes, two twisters on the horizon.

She put her hands on her hips and glared up into his face silently, then held out the bra and shirt.

Harper smiled, took the clothes from her hand. "Thank you. One moment."

"I want to talk to you outside," she said as he ran upstairs.

Rebecca looked like she might cry. He kissed her forehead, hugged her for a moment, then walked back downstairs.

His mother was outside in the sunshine. "Can you imagine Rebecca's mom right now? She must be worried sick."

Harper looked at his watch. It was seven-twenty. "Sorry, Mom."

"Sorry, Mom," she mimicked him. "I'm ashamed of you. Taking advantage of a young girl."

Rebecca came quietly out the side door. Her face was blank. Margaret saw her thirty feet away and said sternly, "Beautiful morning, isn't it, Rebecca?"

"Yes, ma'am," Rebecca replied.

Harper looked from his mother to Rebecca and noticed for the first time that they were built the same—short, a little fleshy, major boobs. His name jarred him from the little reverie.

"Harper! Pay attention. Give me the car keys. Go and strip the bed, make sure everything is in place, and bring the sheets home. You're going to have to wash them and call Mrs. Patrick to apologize."

"Yes, ma'am." Harper yawned.

"Rebecca, get in the car. We're going to go call your mother. She must be frantic."

Harper loped back inside as they got in the car. Margaret had to sit up tall for her neck to be higher than the dashboard. Rebecca slouched in her seat as the car left the driveway.

Margaret said, "I don't believe in free love. Sex should be a part of a marriage of souls. Franklin and I were virgins when we married. I believe that making love is sacred. Don't take it lightly. You'll be happier in the long run."

"Yes, ma'am." Rebecca squirmed in her seat. "I think it's sacred, too."

Margaret glanced over at Rebecca and smiled skeptically.

Margaret parked the Century in the carport. Passing through the garden, Rebecca said, "Oh, your azaleas are so beautiful."

"Yes." She had the sense that Rebecca was buttering her.

In the kitchen Margaret poured them both glasses of orange

juice. When Rebecca finished hers, Margaret nodded toward the phone on the wall. Rebecca crossed the linoleum and picked it up slowly. She dialed the round plastic disk, which revolved back with each digit.

"Mama. I'm really sorry. I fell asleep. I'm at the Rutledges'." Rebecca kept her back to Margaret. "Um, no, we didn't spend the night here." She twisted the long cord with one hand. "We were, um, at the Patricks' tennis cottage."

Margaret watched Rebecca with sympathy, hoping this would teach her to respect her body. She didn't want to know whether they had intercourse. But she hoped that if they had, this would put a stop to it. It was just too serious, too connected with emotions, too intimate to be treated lightly by children.

"Oh, Mama, you don't have to come over here." Rebecca lived alone with her mother, who was a local news anchor. "Harper can drop me off."

Margaret said, "Charlotte should come over."

Harper put the laundry in the washing machine, which was in a room by the carport, connected to the house by a roofed walk, then came in the kitchen door just as Rebecca hung up. As Margaret topped off their juice glasses, he and Rebecca exchanged glances that asked, What's next? They drank silently. Then Margaret delivered another sermon on the sacredness of sex.

Cage

It's midafternoon when I get back. The oversize pockets of my cargo pants jingle with change as I jog up the stairs. At the door I take a deep breath, prepare to block a flying spike-heel shoe. I picture her in the morning, waking to learn that I threw out her syringes, wrestling her to the bed, pinning her down. She raked my cheek with her fingernails. No. That was two mornings ago. Hard to keep track. She might have shot up again by now. I turn the lock quickly and throw the door open, ready to charge in and tackle her fast. Always be prepared.

The room is full of tobacco smoke, a strange, nutty, burned smell, shadows, and soft light filtered by the curtains. Emma is lying against the headboard, smoking. She doesn't look angry. She looks distant and bored.

Jingle-jangling like a joker, jester, Deadhead, I dance into the room and pull handfuls of coins from the cargo pockets, let them drop to the floor, slide the guitar from my shoulder, strum a blues riff, and say, "Nigga rich again, bitch."

Emma giggles. "Guitar man."

"Let's go to Santa Cruz for my birthday."

"Why?"

"I told Carla the White Witch that I was contemplating a birthday sojourn in Santa Cruz and she read her Tarots. The gist—a good omen. She wants to go with me!"

"Take her." Emma sucks in noisily, holds the smoke in her lungs.

"I want to take you."

"So what?"

I cartwheel across the floor and dive onto the bed and brush my lips against hers.

"You really care about me?" Emma's eyes look almost normal.

"Yeah, sometimes you're sweeter than Tupelo honey. You're very pretty. You're smart. You're Episcopalian. You—"

"No, I'm not." Her eyes flash like lightning bolts against a clear blue sky. She blows smoke in my face. "I'm not a fucking Episcopalian."

"If thy mistress some rich anger shows"—I take her hand—"let her rave and feed deep upon her peerless eyes."

"Another dead poet?"

"Keats. Paraphrased. What did your father do to you?" I ask her for the twentieth time.

"Nothing. He was never there." Her voice is detached. "Not for me. Not for my mother. He's a lunatic. I think he fucked half the women in his church."

"The lonely ones. The ones whose husbands died or dumped them?"

"Yeah." She exhales smoke and smiles sardonically, which makes her face look forty years old. "The lonely ones and the horny ones."

"He made you and your mama miserable." I lie on my back and watch her over my forehead.

"I grew up watching them fight. When I was about ten, Mom told me, 'Never marry a handsome man.' It took me about a year to figure out what she meant. Then Dad up in the pulpit. Please. Whiskeypalians. Cocktail Christians."

"They were sticking it out until you left home?"

"Yeah. Living a lie." Emma takes another drag, chokes back a cough.

"Did he get nailed?"

"No." Emma smiles again ruefully like a middle-aged divorcée. "No. When I was sixteen, Mom moved to Hong Kong with an old boyfriend and dumped me in Portland with my grand'rents, you know, these nice old alcoholics who spend their golden years playing bridge and golf. They tried to help. They found a therapist to help me deal with my anger and rejection."

"That obviously worked beautifully." I reach up and touch her cheek.

Emma laughs, a sad sound.

"Your dad's still in Seattle?"

"Negative. Rumors flew after Mom cruised. The vestry let him know that he should bolt at the first opportunity. He left Seattle, moved to L.A. St. something. He's probably up to his old tricks."

"I'm sorry. My parents have been faithful to each other for forty years."

"You sure?"

"Pretty damn. Let's go to Santa Cruz."

"I lost my car."

"I got us train tickets to San Jose. Bus tickets to the Cruz."

"You've been up for two, three days."

"I know. I'm *über*dude."

"Did you fuck me five ways to Sunday the other morning or was I dreaming?"

"Might have been me. Might have been my doppelgänger."

Emma laughs, her face young again. "Your what?"

"The other Cage, my alter ego."

"I like him." She holds out the hand-rolled cigarette. "Smoking it's not so bad."

I shake my head. "Don't want to be smackified. I've got principles. Besides, tobacco makes me cough like a man dying of tuberculosis. You think you can get by just smoking it?"

"With your alterbanger by my side." Emma smiles and strokes the hair out of my eyes. "I might even go cold turkey. I've got a friend in Santa Cruz. Her name's Alisa." Emma laughs gleefully. "Yeah. We should go and see her. Last time, she told me not to come back until I stopped shooting up."

"It's been thirty-six hours." I kiss her and roll off the bed onto my feet. "That counts."

Just after midnight I feel a positive, mystical vibe in Santa Cruz, the hippie surfer enclave nestled between the mountains and the sea. Maybe it's the full moon. Maybe it's because I just logged another orbit around the great gasbag in the sky. Or maybe it's the acid that we dropped as the bus descended the steep mountain pass on a serpentine road, leaving Silicon Valley. Or all of the above.

"Wow. The stars," Emma says. "It's kicking in. Definitely kicking in."

"What do you see?"

"Well . . ." She looks at me, then back at the sky. "Whoa. There it was again. You know . . ."

"No. Tell me."

"It's not doing this to you?"

"Doing what?"

Emma looks at me again. Even in the pale moonlight her eyes have a strong electric gleam. Then she drops her head back on her shoulders. "Whoa. There it goes. The stars all streak at once."

"Like going into hyperspace on the original *Star Wars*?"

"Exactly." Emma laughs.

"No," I say. "But the moon is so bright and soooo 3-D. You can see how much it *weighs*."

"I know what you mean." Nodding her head like a serious child, Emma starts moving along a path by a stream that winds toward the sea beyond a big sixties roller coaster that looks derelict in the dark. In the still night the sound of waves hitting the shore carries for a quarter mile. The bicycle path climbs out of the river bottom away from the fun fair into curving rows of little houses set on a hill, follows an alley between backyards to the point of a peninsula that sticks out into the Monterey Bay. Emma stares in silence at the crashing waves. I take her by the hand and lead her on the path which curves along the sea cliffs for a time, then swings inland uphill to a bridge crossing another little river coming out of the mountains. In the middle of the bridge Emma stops and points at hundreds of poles sticking up out of a low blanket of fog, like needles in a pincushion. Moonlight colors the fog top a swirling yellow. Lightning spears the blackness of the bay but the thunder is too far to carry and overhead the sky is still clear.

"Masts," I say. "Santa Cruz Harbor."

"Boats are cool," Emma says.

We cross the bridge, then walk downhill into the fog, lit inside by a few tall lamps, past some hulls on scaffolds and a closed taqueria toward three long docks that run out into the small harbor. On the bay side, surf pounds against a barrier wall.

"Look how the fog hangs just a foot over the water," Emma says.

"Like a curtain."

Not a soul is around. The wind slaps the halyards against the masts like chimes. Only a small square of chain-link fence framed by barbed wire blocks off the entrance to each dock. I set my guitar by the chain-link door and walk on the rocks to the edge of the water, where I climb up on the fence, then swing myself around, ripping a bit of my sleeve and pants leg as I pull myself to the other side.

"So acrobatic," Emma says.

"Cat burglar." I open the door. She laughs and hands me the guitar.

"Look at her. What a beauty." Most of the sixty boats berthed along the dock are expensive and well kept. Silicon Valley sailors. "That ketch is all teak and mahogany."

At the end of the dock Emma says, "Play a song, Cage."

I strum the guitar and start making up words. "There's a part of me that's a part of you, there's a part of you that's a part of me, too, like the moon in the fog, like the salt in the sea, I'm faithful as a dog, but you sting like a bee."

Laughing, Emma starts to sing, "There's a part of you that's a part of me . . ."

Strumming on, I look around, expecting to see a rent-a-cop or Harbor Patrol or the poe-lice but there's nobody. Emma dances around with an air mic as if onstage. "There's a part of me that's a part of you." Her voice is not bad. Big raindrops splatter on the wood and the water, a storm from nowhere. I shout through the downpour. "Shit, I left my case at what's-her-name's."

"Alisa's." Emma raises her arms into the air and dances in a small circle, catching raindrops in her mouth.

"Yeah, Alisa's." I sling the strap over my shoulder and dash for the stern of the nearest boat I see with a canvas cover over the cockpit. *Day Tripper* is written in scroll across the stern. "How apro-fucking-pos!" I shout. The strangest coincidences always occur when tripping. Synchronicity. Climbing up a rope ladder slung over the starboard gunnel, I hum the Police song and try to remember the words. That song must be sixteen years old now, B.E. Before Emma. At least her rock and roll cognizance.

Rain plops on the canopy. It's dry underneath. There's a towel on one of the cushions. Synchronicity, *mon amis*. I wipe off the guitar. Emma dances around in the rain, laughing, then climbs on board drenched, her hair stuck to her cheeks. I throw her the towel and say, "Maybe there's another one around here."

The door to the cabin is unbolted. I am the man they warned you about when they told you to keep your doors locked. Stepping down inside, I paw blindly until I find the switch to three low-voltage bulbs at intervals along the ceiling. Inside it's ship-shape. There are ramen noodles and canned soups above the gas stove, a closet full of storm gear. Emma comes into the weak light, stands dripping just inside the door, and looks around, turning her head in slow motion. I pull off her Prada cashmere sweater and T-shirt and wrap a dry towel around her. She flops onto the narrow bunk built against the port hull at chair level. The rain on the deck overhead sounds like galloping horses. Stretching out on the starboard, I find the bunk's too short for my boots. The intricacies of the wood grain are a world of dimensions and hue.

"Cage."

"Yes."

"Sail us someplace."

"How'd you know I can sail?"

"You look like the sailor who fell from grace with the sea." Emma laughs.

"That movie was definitely B.E."

"Cable seems to be A.C." Emma laughs.

"Like Kris Kristofferson?"

"Yeah. You look like him. A young him."

"You said I looked like Jeff Bridges."

"You do!" Emma laughs. "Except when you're on acid. Then you look like the sailor who fell from grace with the sea."

She crosses the cabin, letting the towel fall, and leans over me, her small breasts more triangular as they hang down. "Come on, Captain Cage. The gods have sent us here. We're supposed to sail somewhere. It's our destiny."

"Hello, gorgeous." I stroke her cheek. "You know, LSD turns off my libido like flicking a switch. Maybe it's fear . . . while you're fucking, your partner might transmogrify into a large reptile."

"Fuck your libido." Emma's eyes burn like little gas flames. "Who's talking about libidos? Let's go for a cruise."

"Where do you want to go?"

"Back to San Francisco."

"I've done a lot of stupid things in my life, but I'm not going to steal a sailboat." Swinging my body under her chest, I manage to stand up. "Sorry, I was suddenly claustrophobic." I bend over, pick up the towel, drape it around her thin shoulders. "You don't want to get too cold. I doubt your immune system is operating at peak efficiency."

"Let's sail back to the city."

"I don't have charts. I've never sailed in the Pacific, which is a different ocean than the Atlantic entirely."

"Brilliant observation." Emma is very pale, her face bluish around the lips. She's probably getting hypothermia and doesn't feel it.

"You know what I mean." I search the drawers below the bunks until I find a polypropylene shirt, which I pull over Emma's head. "Put your arms in those sleeves. You're acting like a four-year-old."

"I'm sure there's a chart of the coast. There's everything else in this boat."

"No way, Emma."

"Listen." She cocks her ear toward the ceiling.

"The rain's stopped."

She smiles. "Another sign."

"You've got a death wish, little girl."

"Another brilliant deduction."

"Well, I'm not going to be the vessel of your destruction." I put my hands on her shoulders and shake her gently. "I'm trying to help you."

"Baby," she sings, "you'll never be the one who saves me."

I let her go and leave the cabin. Outside, the passing storm took the fog with it. The moon splashes mercury across the surface of the harbor, which is starting to rise with a swell. A ten-knot wind rattles the lines. I haven't sailed since I sort of soloed from Nantucket to Martha's Vineyard. Jack Ransom was on board but he sat back and let me make every move. Ten years ago to the month. A sign? The wind is perfect. How nice it would be to tack across the wind, the boat heeling at a steep angle, nothing but water in every direction.

Without saying anything Emma comes up and wrings water from her sweater onto the deck, then hangs it on a line to dry in the wind. She turns and holds out a key attached to a small yellow float like Eve with the apple.

"Tell you what." I take the key. "If she starts, we'll take *Day Tripper* out for a run in the moonlight and have her back here before dawn."

Emma claps her hands together in delight just like a little girl.

The engine turns over a couple of times and catches.

"Untie us from the starboard cleats." I unhitch the lines on the port, then leap off the stern to unclip from the dock and jump back on board with the rope, wind it in a figure eight around my hand and elbow, then tuck the coil under the deck. "All set?"

"Aye aye, Skipper."

Behind the helm I engage the prop and the boat moves slowly out of the berth into the harbor. Approaching the gap in the barrier walls is like nosing up the Mississippi. I push the throttle lever forward a bit. The foam of the breakers sprays white on top of the rocks, disappears, sprays higher. The storm kicked up a swell and the waves are getting bigger. Emma moves to the bow, leans over the water, a junkie figurehead. I yell, "Hold on!" As we pass through the gap, the waves pound the hull and we ride up the curling face of the breaker that cascades across the deck, then we rush down its back into the trough where another breaker towers above us.

Knocked back on the deck, Emma lies laughing on her back. Stupid of me not to have clipped her in a harness or a life jacket. Too risky to tell her to come back to the cockpit now. "Hold on, Emma!" She doesn't move. I push the throttle full forward and hold the helm steady as we drive up the steep face. Emma slides backward toward the front cabin windows out of my line of sight, then the bow soars over the top like a leaping whale, momentarily airborne, and plunges down the back of the wave, flinging me to the side of the cockpit as the hull leans suddenly port.

I bang my jaw, scramble to stand, get back to the helm. "Emma!" I have a terrible feeling that she coaxed me out here to die. I struggle with the helm to point the nose dead-on into the wave rising higher overhead. "Emma." I can't see her in the chaos and darkness. The wave breaks over the cockpit and we are suddenly surfing down its back side into choppy water.

The dangerous set of breakers behind us, I almost start to relax before my gut contracts into a ball of fear when I don't see Emma on deck. Grabbing a stay, I stand on the stern rail and search the black water. "Emma! Emma!" Water slaps the hull and the surf behind sounds softer by the second. I race back to the helm, pull the throttle back to a near idle, and jump up on the cabin roof. "Emma!"

With the moon behind a cloud I can't see a thing. Peering into the darkness, I hope she's a good swimmer. Shit. What now? Turn around? Shit. "Emma!" I drop down in the cockpit, put the throttle up, and jerk the helm hard to starboard into a long circle to come around. If I don't see her, I'll put the boat back and go for help. "Emma!" You were so sweet, really. Pretty fucked up. But full of potential. You had nowhere to go but up. Dammit. I was trying to help you. And you used me to kill you. How dare you? Looking over my shoulder back at the harbor mouth, straining to see in the darkness, I realize that I'm crying. "Emma!"

"Baby, you'll never be the one to save me."

Startled, I spin around and see Emma standing by the mast. "Where were you?"

"Up there under that sail bag." She jerks her head behind her at the jib bag in the bow.

"I could kill you!" I shout.

"You just said you wanted to save me."

I smile as Emma unties the main from the mast and draws the sheet through the crank.

"You've sailed before."

"A little," she says. "With my dad."

Running with the main, *Day Tripper* clips along at eight knots. After the storm swells, the bay is pretty smooth, more of a big lake than the perilous Pacific. It's almost like daylight under the full moon. With Emma beside me in a yellow slicker I feel like an advertisement in a Peter Storm catalog. The half a hit of acid's tailing off, burned maybe by the adrenaline of the big waves. They used to say that only Thorazine could shut down a trip. I was a Thorazine tadpole for a couple of days. That tranq could shut down a charging rhino. Suddenly I realize that I'm very tired.

"Coming out of the harbor, that freaky set of big breakers," I end a calm silence, "I thought about my father telling me not to take my pint-size fishing boat out into the Atlantic. I was thirteen, 1973. South Carolina. He told me to stay in the high-tide inlet between Pawley's Island and the mainland. I longed to get out into that wide-open space. It was scary out there in the big water. I was never comfortable. I just went for it. Maybe I just wanted to disobey him."

Emma listens without the usual faint sardonic curl at the corners of her mouth. Maybe our little adventure will wake her from her junkie stupor, the ocean spray wash away some of her pessimism.

"Dad didn't know that I was going out with my little flat-bottomed skiff and one-horsepower outboard a mile or so offshore. Then I started coming back to the beach instead of the inlet, riding over the breakers to the sand right in front of Mom and Dad and Nick, God rest his soul, and Harper, who was tiny at the time. I don't remember Dad giving me hell. He must have thought it was pointless to try and stop me, just wanted to keep the peace during his two-week break from the grind."

Emma nods and puts her arm around my shoulder, one of her rare small gestures of affection. I pray that she can become human again.

"Then one time I got broadside to the wave and it flipped the boat. Ruined the little engine." I yawn loudly.

"My sentiments exactly," Emma says.

"You had me going," I say.

"I know," she says with her old smile.

"I'm exhausted," I tell her.

"You've been up, like, forever. Take a catnap. I'll keep us on course."

"Thanks, sweet pea." I kiss her on the cheek and go down in the cabin, luxuriously exhausted, as if I had just swum the English Channel. It's a little after one. "Wake me up in a couple of hours."

I hear myself moan, then see the lights on the cabin ceiling. I'm lying on the floor in several inches of water. Rain pelts the roof like a million fingers. The boat heaves and I fall back onto the bunk, bounce against the ceiling. We are going to capsize. Then I fall farther, curling up instinctively before I bang onto the floor. I crawl to the storm locker, wrest myself up with the handle, pull on a life jacket, grab a smaller one for Emma, and stumble up the steps to the cockpit. She's not at the helm. "Emma!" The sail luffs. The boat's trying to come around. "Emma!" A wave washes over the deck. The rain whips in from the aft, then port. The wind's rotating. A flash of lightning shows Emma in the bow packing a jib back in its sail bag. The boat heaves forty-five degrees, throwing me down, and water splashes in my eyes. Then she rights. With my left hand I steer her into the waves while I sheet in furiously with the right. "Emma, get back here!" I can't see her, have no idea if she can hear me. A bolt of lightning flashes off port, illuminating black rocks standing tall like the big heads on Easter Island, then the world is howling blackness. The thunder sounds like bombs. "That's not real." I paw around for the ignition. That can't be real. Where the fuck is the key! Calm down. Those weren't rocks. That was a trick of light, fog, rain.

The wind changes direction and carries the sound of surf lashing rocks. I find the key. The engine doesn't seem to crank up. "Dear God, please help." We start plowing forward into the waves, so it must be working. I try to steer away from the sound of the surf but there's no way to be sure in the darkness. Emma's shadow steps into the cockpit by the Plexiglas windshield. I glance at her, see that she is wearing a life jacket, then stare into the dark, straining to hear the danger.

"Sleep well?" Her voice is nervous.

"Like fifteen minutes?"

"Like hours."

She's right. My watch says five. In Memphis, Dad is coming in from his jog and Mom is leaving for her morning swim and in New York, Harper is hungover on his way to work at the World Trade Center, while I'm about to sink a sloop in the Monterey Bay. "Why are you trying to kill us?"

"I thought we were in the middle of the bay," Emma shouts over the wind. Her voice sounds scared. "You can't see shit through the rain, no city lights."

"Blindman's bluff." I start to laugh. "With a wall of rocks." I roar hysterically.

"You're not helping."

I manage to stop long enough to blurt out, "Sorry. Just thought of a Conrad line about the merriment men feel when they see that events are about to end in utter disaster." The laughter doubles me over onto the helm. Our roles have reversed. I find some Shakespeare to express my feelings: "By my troth, I care not. A man can die but once . . . and let it go which way it will!"

"Cage, snap out of it!" Emma grabs my arm. The soft light of the instrument panel lights up her face enough to see real fear in her eyes.

I stop laughing. "Nice to see you care about something besides getting high." I put her hands on the helm. "Keep us pointed into the waves. Maintain the compass heading. Let's hope I guessed right. Keep your eyes and ears open." I pat her on the back and leap onto the deck, start to lash down the mainsail, then decide to leave it loose should we have to come around quickly with the wind in a workable direction. Hugging the mast with one arm, I slowly scan the darkness in a circle around the boat. With only four hours' sleep, I feel ready for the watch. I yell out into the night, "I'm the king of the world!"

A chilly northwesterly blows the squall from the bay, leaving in its wake gnats' eggs of light along the coast, the glow of Monterey on the southern curve, the lights of man that obscure the constellations in the opening heavens. Beyond the wall of mountains the sun begins to ascend over the edge of the continent, casting shadows of three hundred million souls haunting the anthill of America. Light brims over the jagged horizon in royal purple, then forty shades of pink, and the escarpment below—shaggy forest tops, bald glades, zigzagging roads and rivers—gathers density and depth. In the darkness to the west the black sea brightens gloamy blue before the night sky begins to lighten. The steady whir of the freeway travels miles across the water in the gaps between the wind, breaking the spell of the Magic Hour. I'm in California, at least its territorial waters. Leaning around the cabin door, I see Emma asleep sprawled facedown on a bunk.

I bring *Day Tripper* around and angle into the wind, decide that it could take a couple of hours to tack north back to Santa Cruz. So much for slipping her back into her slip and slipping away before the harbor is crawling with yachties. Possibly even the owners. It's Saturday after all. April 17, 1999. Maybe they'll let me off if I say it's my birthday. Thirty-nine years after I arrived on the planetary surface, early one Sunday morning away down South in Dixie.

"Yo, dude, like you should anchor along the coast south of the Cruz. Batten the hatches and abandon ship," I suggest to myself in California stoner. "Ditch ol' *Dawn Treader*. The water cops'll find her, totally. No worries. Like, that'd be semirighteous."

"Now, son," I answer in my father's voice, "your impulsive actions have once again outstripped common sense and common decency, not to mention maritime law. The only honorable course is to return the boat to the harbor. I would advise you to turn yourself over to the authorities and throw yourself on the mercy of the court, but that would be asking more than you are willing to do. So simply return the property and walk out of the harbor with your head held high and your drug-addicted girlfriend on your arm straight to the nearest rehabilitation clinic, which surely abound in the state of California. Check yourself in and give me a call."

The sail luffs in the shifting wind. I bring the boat around and tack toward the open sea.

"Yo, nigga, don't listen yo' daddy and all that paternal, moralistic hype. Only a nigga with crack for a brain would head right back to the scene of the crime. Wha's wrong wi' you? Shit. Take my advice. Get yo' ass to Tahiti. Things ain't worked out for you in the ol' U.S. of A. Time to start over. Time to reinvent yo'self. Cage Rutledge, *el capitano*. Nothing slicker than a skipper. Imagine the bitches. *Mmm hmm.* I can see you now with a piña colada in a coconut cup, kicked back under a palm tree, fanned by topless women in grass skirts. Go for it, nigga. Show us what you got."

Two dozen surfers in black wet suits bob up and down in the water like seals where the breakers start to rise out of the ocean about two hundred yards from a stony beach at the base of a low cliff. Cyclists and skaters roll slowly along a road on the edge, against a backdrop of low sixties clapboard houses, a stand of eucalyptus, a lone palm. Emma's at the helm, smiling in the morning light, looking purified by the nautical adventure. I finish furling the mainsail, inspect the deck fore and aft, and go down for a final look at the cabin. Everything appears pretty much the way we found it. The owner will probably suss that someone's been in his boat by the empty jars of peanut butter, the near-empty gas tank. Coming up, I close the cabin door.

Emma steps back and I take the helm. The cliffs give way to piles of boulders protecting large houses with giant glass windows looking down on a sandy beach where a few kids boogie board close to shore.

"That looks perfect," I tell her.

"I want to stay with you." Her light eyes look sincere, troubled.

"What do you think Butch and Sundance would do right now?"

"Rob a bank?" Emma laughs. A new playful side.

"No. Split up and meet at the Hole in the Wall." I comb her hair back off her forehead with my fingers. "So I'll see you at, um—"

"Alisa's."

"Yeah. On Portola. Now, if I'm busted, what are you going to do?"

"Call your brother, Harper Rutledge, in the New York phone book."

"That's it. Time for you to get ready."

Emma strips down to her bra and panties and bundles her cashmere sweater, capri-cut khakis, Aussie ankle boots, and a towel in a kayaker's bag as I steer toward shore. About forty feet out, little waves rock the boat from side to side, rolling past to the break on the beach. Emma kisses my cheek and steps backward onto the stern ladder.

"Thanks for the cruise, Cage. Thanks for everything."

"Don't mention it." I hand her the bag. "Ciao for now."

"Whoa it's cold!" she shrieks.

"Go, girl!" Walking back to the helm, I watch her breaststroke toward shore, dragging the floating bag by a line around her wrist. After I'm set up as a carpenter in Santa Cruz, I'll sneak back to the *Day Tripper* and leave a hundred bucks in an envelope with a sea riddle:

Who's been eating your peanut butter?
Who's been sleeping in your bunk?
Bon voyage,

The Sailor Who Fell to Earth

Emma is reaching the shallows as I go around a point where the beach ends and bluffs begin again. On the far side is the barrier wall of the harbor. About twenty little Laser class boats are streaming through the narrow mouth like water bugs skittering about, barely touching the surface. It's nearly nine-thirty. "I reckon there's a ten o'clock race," I say nervously to myself, then in my father's voice: "Buck up, boy. You're doing the right thing." After the fleet of water bugs disperses I pass easily through the gap, so different than the dramatic midnight departure. In the sunshine, wearing bright colors and stripes, yachties are walking around the docks, climbing about the boats. A sickening ball of fear starts leaking in my gut. "Yo, crack-brain," I jive-ass myself. "I tried to tell you. Honor. *Pfff.* Just another word for stupid."

As I motor past the most seaward of the three parallel docks, everything appears to be cool. No one is looking. I can't see *Day Tripper*'s berth on the most inland dock until I come abreast of the middle one and the ball of fear explodes in my gut like an attack of diarrhea. There are two cops talking to a tall, blond, crew-cut guy wearing wraparound Oakleys, Top-Siders, and a windbreaker. He looks like the perfect candidate for SS officer training school. They don't see me. One cop is writing on a clipboard. The other is staring at the empty slip, the square of water. Gestapo is shaking his head.

"You's in trouble now, nigga. That man gonna put yo' ass in the Big House. No more Mr. Misdemeanor. You graduated now, white boy. You going to the land of Big Black Men. And they don't take to crackers, Jack. Yeah, you fixin' to reap the wages of stupidity."

"Maybe I should come about and sail right back out of here," I answer in my real voice.

The cop studying the oily water glances up toward me. At first he isn't suspicious. Then we make eye contact. I try to smile and feel my face twisting into an embarrassed confession. Without taking his eyes off me he says something. The other cop and Gestapo turn their heads in unison. Gestapo's eyes widen in disbelief, then narrow in outrage.

I cut the throttle, put it in reverse, and back into the slip with ease, as if I do it every day. Trying to appear innocent as a Boy Scout, I throw rope from the stern to Gestapo. He ties the line to a cleat on the dock and leaps on board. I extend my hand and say, "I saved your boat."

He ignores my hand. With an expression of extreme distaste he looks me up and down and I can suddenly see myself from his perspective: wild hair, unshaven face, dirty clothes. "Who the fuck are you?"

"Excuse me, sir, I may look like a wharf rat but I just brought your boat right back to your waiting arms, no?"

Gestapo smirks. One of the cops climbs on board. I see that his insignia says *Harbor Patrol*. Gestapo nods his head at me and says, "I don't know what he's on."

"Officer, I don't see why he has to malign me like this. I just brought his boat back. A couple of kids from UC took it for a joyride. They wanted to dump it in Monterey."

"Get off my boat, asshole," Gestapo says.

"Let's go." The cop grabs me by the wrist, twists it around behind my back.

"Hey, I was just trying to help," I say, shoved toward the stern. "This is the thanks that I get?"

The cop lets me go so I can jump to the dock, while the other cop waits with an amused grin and a pair of handcuffs.

"Hey, this isn't fair!" I yell as he cuffs my hands behind my back. "I'm the good guy. I'm the hero."

"You have the right to remain silent," the first cop says as they lead me along the dock and all the yachties stop coiling ropes and filling up beer coolers to watch the procession. "Anything you say can and will be used against you. You have the right to an attorney—"

"Look, man," I drown him out. "I was walking by here about midnight and I saw these two guys climb around the fence and I followed them and—"

"We'll take your statement in a minute. You have the right to an attorney—"

"I don't need an attorney. I didn't do anything."

Harper

Rainy Monday. Double bummer. Looking out the window with a tectonic hangover lingering from yesterday morning makes the gray Jersey landscape more depressing than usual. After gallons of Gatorade my head still feels like a fault line is fracturing the two hemispheres, pulling them apart, making the Great Rift Valley of my mind. The afternoon stretches ahead of me like an endless desert. I can barely focus on the screens. I'm writing code at a limp. I feel gloomy, dirty from the debauchery, and wonder once again if the emotion is produced by my body detoxing the alcohol and blow or by my conscience. I remember when I was in high school, Nick, back in Baton Rouge at Christmas from Berkeley, described the feeling after spending a night two-timing his California girl, shagging a Cajun beauty from midnight to dawn. Nick said he felt "far from God." Then he went back for another five rounds on the mat with her the next night. Just as tonight I'll get drunk and hammer the debutramp. Slaves, all of us, Cage, Nick, and me. Slaves to carnal servitude. I don't believe in God. But I do feel very far from anything infinitely pure.

My direct line flashes. The ringer has been off since a thermonuclear hangover months ago. I let the voice mail pick it up, and hit the speaker button:

"This is Harper. Please be precise. Thanks."

An automated voice that must have begun talking when my line answered comes on in midsentence: "—tional Communication Services. You have a collect call from an inmate at the Santa Cruz County jail. Do you accept the charges?"

"Yes." I moan so loud that Asgar looks up from his desk. I put my finger to my temple like a gun barrel, pull the trigger, collapse in a heap on my keyboard, and he looks away, puzzled.

"Hey, brother. Good to hear your voice. You'll never believe what's happened." Cage sounds relieved, eager, excited.

"Happy birthday, Cage." I laugh at the sadness of it. "I hoped to hear from you on Saturday."

"It's so ironic. That's when they jacked me," he says. "Pisses me off. I mean, I'm so angry."

"What'd you do?"

"I didn't do anything!" Cage sounds outraged.

"What are ya charged with?"

"Stealing a sailboat."

"Nice boat?" I put my head in my hands.

"A thirty-two-foot Erickson."

"Pretty. Why'd you steal it? Because, because, because, because, because?" Cupping my eyes, my palms feel nice and cool. "Because of the wonderful way she was?"

"I didn't steal it! I was with these junkies who stole it. I talked them into swimming to shore and I returned it to its slip."

"That sounds completely credible."

"Listen, the judge was on the verge of letting me out. But I didn't have any ID. I lost my wallet in a storm. So he set bail at six grand. Will you bail me out of here, Harper?"

"Shit, Cage. In principle, if you were telling the truth, if you had nothing to do with stealing the sailboat, then I would cough up the money. But how can I believe a word you say? It sounds exactly like something you would do."

"I haven't lied about anything. I haven't done anything wrong. Why would I take it back to the slip? I was just trying to help out."

"Did you tell them that you're bipolar?"

"Yeah. I told the judge and the public defender—"

"Good."

"I asked them for lithium but they haven't given me any."

"You got a number for your lawyer?"

"Roberto Garcia. He doesn't really look Latino."

I type the guy's number on a virtual Post-it note on my main screen. "I'll call him. I'll see what he says. Have you told Mom?"

"No."

"Call me back in an hour. Hang in there."

"I can't imagine anyone else in our family being in this situation," Cage says dolefully.

I chuckle through my nose. "The High Plains Drifter."

"That bastard." Cage laughs. "Love you, Harper."

"Love you, Cage." I click the phone off, massage my temples, the rift in my head. "*Aw fuck!*"

Asgar's head jerks in my direction. Beyond him Dooner throws me a distracted glance, keeps shouting at the traders on the other side of the partition. I reach in a drawer for a framed photograph that Mom mailed to the office so that it would actually come to reside at my desk. Thanksgiving 1986 on the porch at Cage's Bend. Everyone is still alive and well. Mom is smiling sweetly, genuinely overjoyed to have her sons together, everyone healthy and happy, counting her blessings. Dad looks happy, too. Nick has shoulder-length hair and a content expression. Cage's and my haircuts are the same—short with a floppy part, sloppy prep. I look bored, pimply, sixteen. Cage is in grad school at Vanderbilt. Smiling confidently, he looks ready to go out and conquer corporate America.

I stand up and walk to the window. Like a god, I gaze down at pedestrians flowing along the sidewalks. One out of every two hundred of them is manic-depressive. You, I point my finger at an ant-man. Fifteen million manic-depressives from sea to shining sea. Some just starting to take off, months from where others are crashing in flames. Some free-falling into the blackest depression. Some, in utter loneliness, murdering themselves. Some holding steady, clinging to stability with lithium, Zoloft, and strict routine. Back at my desk I dial the number of the public defender in Santa Cruz.

"Hello." Mama always answers phones and doorbells with the most gracious, cheerful voice you've ever heard. She's a born optimist, always sees the glass half full.

"Hey, Mama."

"Hello, honey. How are you?"

"Fine. Is Dad around?"

"He's out at a meeting."

"I thought Monday's his day off these days."

"So did I." She laughs. "Have you heard from Cage?"

"Called an hour ago from the Santa Cruz County jail. Charged with stealing a boat."

"Oh my. Oh my." Mom is silent for a second, perhaps holding her breath. "Well, at least he's safe."

"Yeah. I imagine Santa Cruz is the country club of county jails. He says he didn't take the boat, that some other drifters did, that he was just bringing it back."

"Oh, I'm sure he took it." She sounds annoyed.

"He got caught when he was returning the boat to the harbor." Mom laughs painfully. "That's . . . something."

"He's got a public defender who sounds like a bright guy. I don't see any reason to hire someone. Apparently the owner is really pissed off and some stuff is missing from the boat but with Cage's medical history he thinks the judge will reduce the charge to a misdemeanor."

"The worst thing they could do is dismiss the charges and have him crazy on the streets." Fear, anger, and depression harmonize in her tone. "This is our opportunity to get him into a place."

"He wants me to bail him out."

"You can't!" Mom almost screams. "He's likely to steal another boat, God only knows. Anything's possible when he's manic."

"Mom, I know. I know. But I guess I'll go out there. You and Dad have been dealing with this for too long."

"I'm most thankful, Harper. You're a good son. A good brother." Her voice is high and sweet, then lower, serious. "He's going to use every means under the sun to convince you to pay his bail. He's going to manipulate the brotherly bond. In the flush of feeling and sympathy you'll be mighty tempted. But—"

"Don't worry, Mama."

Lying on the bed in my boxer shorts at ten, I listen to the drunken kids going to the bowling lanes on University Place. Flipping back through my Palm Pilot, I calculate that this is the first night in two weeks that I didn't see a girl or get somewhat drunk. It was sobering to talk to Cage but mainly it's weariness. Watching *The Sopra-*

nos on HBO, I listen to the digital recorder picking up messages from Betsy, Jessica, Caitlin. Then one comes through with the automated voice from California Correctional Communications, some kind of licensed daylight robbery that charges the beleaguered friends and relatives of inmates ten times normal collect call rates, as if they didn't have enough grief. I accept.

"Hey, brother," Cage says.

"Hey."

"Will you bail me out?"

"We went through this all afternoon."

"Why not?"

"Because I don't believe you."

Cage hangs up.

A minute later the phone rings again. I let the automated voice carry through the machine, then pick up at the last moment and say, "Yes."

"Hey, Harper. I'm sorry. Sometimes the phones disconnect."

"That's okay." I sigh.

"I'm the only one who's treating you straight. The lawyer wasn't honest with you. Nobody's told you the truth. I'm the one who's telling you the truth. I didn't steal the boat. I'm paying a penalty for something I didn't do. I can't get out and work and I was honest. I was taking the boat back. I could have ditched it anywhere in the Monterey Bay. All I'm doing is cooperating with everybody. This is my time of need. I don't understand why I have to sit in jail."

"I told you that I'll come out for the hearing."

"That's in two weeks."

"Hang in there."

"Please help me get out of here, Harper. I haven't lied about anything. Please bail me out of here. I'm climbing the walls. I'm starting to get psychotic. I'm clearly different from all the inmates. None of them are educated. It's like a crazy house. I'm going crazy. I beg you. I'm afraid to go and take a shit. Harper, I'm your brother and I'm in a really crazy dangerous place and all I did was try to help someone."

"I'm sorry, brother."

"I'm sorry, brother," he says in a venomous, prissy voice. "Why not?"

"Because you're manic, Cage. You might run. You might steal another boat."

"I'm not going to go anywhere. I like Santa Cruz. I'll find a place to stay. I'm not making this shit up. If they sent bounty hunters, I could never rest. I'd always be looking over my shoulder."

"You don't know what you'd do, Cage. You're manic. You're not in control. You might mean what you say but you're so impulsive right now that your promises are no good, not even to yourself."

"I'm so lonely, man. I got here because I tried to do something good. I'm starving to death, brother. All these guys got big bags of food."

"Well, I expressed a hundred bucks to Garcia to put in your commissary. You can buy all the cigarettes and junk food that you want."

"People and promises." Cage hangs up. Twenty-dollar exchange.

I turn the phone ringer off and the volume on the answering machine down to zero.

On Friday morning the markets are up and down like a runaway roller coaster. We keep trading hundreds of thousands of shares at the exact wrong moment. When we sell, the price jumps; when we buy, the price falls. Dooner's on his feet, screaming at everyone, even Asgar and me. "Our execution quality is shit! Shit! Do you hear? What the fuck is wrong with everyone! Bunch of halfwits! I'm surrounded by midgets! We might as well be monkeys throwing darts at the Big Board."

"I'm just a monkey man. I hope you are a monkey, too!" I scream. "I'm a monkeeeeeeee!"

"Can it, you hick." Dooner glances at me with a hint of a smile. "You're as overvalued as Amazon.bomb." Then he slams down in his chair and starts pounding away on his keyboard.

My phone lights up.

"Yeah," I grunt, pissed off, though I know Dooner doesn't mean anything.

"Har-puh." Mama's voice is like molasses.

"Hey, Mama. Sorry. Markets are whipsawing. What's up?"

"I just spoke to Grandmother. Cage asked her for six thousand dollars for bail. She said she didn't have it. He said, 'Well, borrow it.'" Mom sounds on the verge of a wholesale crack-up and full of righteous anger at the same time. "He told her if she didn't send the money, he was committing suicide. He told her that he was pushed down eighteen steps today. The junk he will say. Really a new level of thoughtlessness."

"It's not Cage. It's Mr. Hyde. His shadow's running his whole psyche."

"I told her emphatically, 'Mother, under no circumstances are you to accept another call from him. He's bored and he's trying to stir everyone up.'"

"Grandmother can take care of herself. She's been through worse."

"She's codependent. She always puts everyone's needs before her own. She has high blood pressure."

"Calm down, Mama. It'll work out. You're a believer. Give it to God. You have to let it go."

"If he should take his life, that would be tragic, but it won't be because of what we have done or not done."

"That's right, Mama. Keep telling yourself that. You've done all you could. Besides he's not going to kill himself. The good Cage will come back. You'll see. But you've *got* to *let* the *worry go.* The stress is driving you crazy. Talk to Dr. Grant."

"Uuuh! What's the use of throwing away a hundred dollars? God, after the tens of thousands Cage's illness has cost. Grant can't help. It's not worth it just to vent."

"Right. Not when you can vent at me for free."

Mama half laughs. "Poor Frank. On top of all the dissension in the diocese, he has Cage and me to worry about. Promise me that if anything ever happens to me, that you will take care of Cage."

"I've promised you that, Mom."

"When I woke this morning, I thought, If I ever just don't wake up, I want you to know how much you're loved."

"I know, Mama. I love you, too. Why don't you take a swim?"
"I went at seven."

On Monday the black box is picking winners every time, out-
guessing our traders. Dooner used to say that he will never over-
ride a trader, because the box has no instinct, but lately I've seen
him overrule Ronbeck on occasion, when Dooner's own gut tells
him that box is right. Dooner seems a little sheepish about Friday's hysteria, but not enough that he wouldn't tongue-whip
everyone the moment our execution quality slipped. After a week
dry I'm focusing well on my work. Second-guessing the box, hitting a high percentage of aces. Dooner wants to plan the Hong
Kong trip the day after Cage's hearing so that I can meet up with
him, fly from San Francisco. Last night I dreamed that I loaded a
gun with nickels and dimes and quarters. I was crying. I put it to
Cage's head. I couldn't pull the trigger. My subconscious imply-
ing that Cage was emotionally nickel-and-diming me to death?
For some reason Cage wasn't able to call over the weekend and so
I feel a little distance and relief from his pain.

In the afternoon my stomach knots in dread as the automated
voice comes over the speakerphone. You don't have to pick it up.
Don't. You've bugged his public defender ten times, sent him
money, talked to the jail psychiatrist, made sure he's getting his
meds. You're gonna see him next week. You don't have to listen
to his manipulative shit. Then I picture him surrounded by guys
in blue denim, scared, lonely, guilty. I pick up the phone and
mumble, "Yes."

"Hey, Harper, you heard yet from Emma?" Cage's voice
sounds calmer than it has in a long while.

"Sorry, bro, not a word."

Cage is silent for a time, then asks, "You thought much about
Nick lately?"

"Sometimes. Other day I remembered something he told me.
What was it? . . . Why, has he visited you? Doesn't he usually visit
when you're locked up?"

"Even Nick's ghost has forsaken me."

"The rest of the family hasn't. Have you seen the psychiatrist again?"

"I was reading Deuteronomy while a guy was screaming all morning, then the shrink came in and asked me if I was hearing any voices. I said, 'Yeah, down the hall.'"

I laugh. A glimmer of the old Cage.

"They've got me rooming now with a guy who taught lit at Choate, did his dissertation on Dos Passos. He's in here for arson. He's an alcoholic in his late fifties. Says he didn't do it. I've seen him get the DTs. Shakes like a Holy Roller. The inmates call him Smokey. They call me Sailor. Time passes pretty quickly when he's telling stories. I been thinking about my plea, the jury's point of view. A drifter. No address. A history of mental illness. I'm not processing info so well right now. I don't know if I'm capable of making the right decisions. I hate to plead guilty to something I didn't do."

"Why don't you just admit that you took the boat?" I say slowly.

"I've just accepted my position," Cage says as if he didn't hear me. "It's like a burden off my shoulders because I don't have the anger anymore. After all these dark nights of the soul in the county jail, surreal dreams. In the simple language of the Holy Bible I find renewal. I'm becoming a new man in jail, born again in the Holy Spirit. Last week I thought it was cool to be the jester." He groans and laughs at the same time. "Now I just want to be cool like Robinson Crusoe until I'm out of here."

"Well, Cage . . . just . . . Garcia says if you plead guilty that they'll just put you in a dual-diagnosis program." I brace myself for a long list of reasons why he shouldn't be stuck in with a bunch of dsyfunctional addicts and madmen for three months.

Cage is silent for a few seconds, then breaks into a rap:

It's my turn now to mop the flo'.
Mo' fun to sail along the sho'.
This jail be a fucking bo'.
Later on, ya sex-addict ho'.

He rattles a mop in a bucket and hangs up.

Cage

My little brother smiles from the other side of thick Plexiglas. Walking toward the row of booths, I can read his lips: *Hey, Cage.* He looks genuinely happy to see me. My spirit flickers brighter, like a match lit in a dark room that burns for a few seconds before the gloom swallows the flame. I feel my face stretch into a smile, flooded with snapshots of him all the way back to the cradle. Trim, sunburned, longish hair in Nantucket ten years ago. Lanky, awkward six-foot crew-cut senior at Louisiana Episcopal. A freshman with bangs and a mouth full of braces. Bucktoothed with a bowl cut in a lower-school uniform. A beautiful brown toddler with long wavy hair. Closer, I see that he's turning soft above his cream button-down. Sallow skin. Cloudy eyes. His jowls are heavier than at Christmas. In the wavering reflection on the captive side of the glass, I see myself, leaner than Harper. I look fitter, stronger, faster, but appearances belie reality. My mind is flawed. I'm just as smart. I could have been a whiz-kid programmer, almost. But God gave me the defective brain. Why me?

Genetic roulette, I mouth.

He shakes his head, then raises his eyebrows. What?

I want to hug him tight just for a second, rub our family genes together. Feel the touch of someone I love, and all I can do is sit down on a plastic chair and pick up a plastic phone and put my hand to the plastic glass.

"Up close, Harper, you look like . . . shit, Harper." I laugh. "I couldn't see you so well in court. You've been partying way too much, haven't you?"

Harper grins like a kid caught with his hand in the liquor cabinet. "Kind of a shock seeing you up in the docket in a long row of orange jumpsuits. What's with the shaved head?"

"I thought I got lice in here." That's sort of true. I can't help exaggerating the conditions. Harper seems to pick up on it.

"Looks pretty nice as far as jails go from what I can see," he says. "New. Clean. Small." He stares at the side of my head. "You got a scar that looks like a cave painting of a dog."

"Where a guy hit me with a broom."

Harper smirks, wondering whether I'm lying. I'm not sure. I did get hit with a broom. Ten years ago in the place I do not name. I've never seen the scar, too far back, over my ear and usually hidden by my hair.

"The judge seemed reasonable," Harper says. "Santa Cruz seems like a cool town. Run by ex-hippies. Could be worse. You could of ended up in the San Francisco County jail. That would've been grim."

"Providence," I say, "washed me up here to recover."

"Maybe," Harper says. "The older I get, the less preposterous the idea of God seems. Happenstance, providence, whatever, you washed up in a good place. I checked out the Frontier House. It's a kinda long, low ranch on a couple of acres up in the redwoods. No fences or anything. The, uh, inmates—"

"Mental health consumers," I correct him.

"Whatever. They looked nice enough. Not too fucked up or stupid."

"Did I see you talking to those two Harbor Patrol cops in the back of the court?"

"Yeah. I asked them if they believed that you did it. They said yeah. One of them said you were lucky to have a brother like me."

I felt a twinge of envy. The good brother, the successful one, the semialcoholic womanizer. "You're a good brother, Harper. You didn't have to come out here. Thanks for putting the money in my commissary. You have no idea how good a Snickers bar can make you feel. They don't give us enough to eat. That's my main complaint about this jail. I'm hungry all the time. "

"You'll be out soon." Harper smiles. "At Frontier they said a bed would open in a few days."

"Easy for you to say."

"That's true." He looks somber.

"And you'll be gone. Hong Kong. New York. What a life." The envy wells up in me. My résumé for the last decade is a long list of little jails and nuthouses. Now it's time to start over again. The Frontier House. "The Frontier, that's where I'm stuck. The Frontier of mental illness."

"Don't look so pessimistic." Harper puts his hand on the glass. "You can build a nice life out here. You got the ocean. Redwoods. Surfing. Mountain biking. A first-class county mental health program from what I can see."

"Everyone here dropped so much acid in the sixties they have to have a good program." I make Harper laugh. Suddenly I want to cry. I clench my fists, trying to summon up the energy and drive to pull myself up, persevere, prevail. "God I'll be glad to be out of these fucking coveralls."

"I bought some khakis and sweaters and T-shirts at the Gap today," Harper says. "I left them for you at Frontier."

A cop walks along the booths, passes behind Harper, calling out something. Harper glances over his shoulder, then says, "Time's up. Hang in there, brother. I'll swing through town next week on the way back to New York. Love you."

"Love you."

I watch him pick up his blue blazer, see that he's wearing faded jeans. There's a spring to his step. He sweeps out of the room, borne on a tide of money. I put my head in my hands and watch the other visitors file out behind him. The last are a whole family of women so fat they can barely squeeze through the door frame.

The End of the World as
We Know It
1987

One Friday July morning in the hours before dawn, the streets of San Francisco were wet and empty. Fog was creeping in from the Bay, curling up the steep hillsides. The windows of the '74 Cadillac Fleetwood were open to the mist. The long, heavy four-door had been his grandfather Rutledge's last, so rarely used that it had logged only twenty thousand miles when his second wife gave it to Nick upon the old man's death and Nick christened it Pilar, after Hemingway's fishing boat and his indomitable guerrilla heroine. Six years later, Pilar was still in mint condition. Nick kept meaning to trade it in for a more eco-friendly car, but it was his sole possession that reminded him of his grandfather.

"It's the end of my world as I knew it," Nick sang loudly, personalizing the words to the song thundering from the tape deck, a game he'd played with Cage since they were boys. "*And I feel fried!*" Nick had been driving for hours, since his friend Chris, a rock-climbing partner and fellow Berkeley environmental studies grad student, had dropped him at home after dragging him out to a bar full of undergrads. The thought of lying in the bed whose sheets still smelled of Monica, in the room where the empty closet and drawers were glaring symbols of the hole in his heart, kept him roaming the dark streets, though he knew that he should turn around and go back home, if for no other reason than he shouldn't poison the atmosphere with fossil fuel that he couldn't afford to burn anyway at ten miles to the gallon. Nick's passion for ecology was his father's religious conviction translated into the secular. He could not believe in God, but he could believe in nature, and to him the last great cause was the fight to salvage what was left of the biosphere before the grand planetary ecosystem went terminal, if it wasn't already too late. "Idealism. Nihilism. Pollution. Evolution," he shouted over the song. "Dissertation. Masturbation. Fuck that!"

After drinking himself to sleep the previous Wednesday night, Nick had woken early and spent Thursday in the library working furiously. In the evening he returned to the bungalow he had shared with Monica for a little over a year and sat on the front stoop while twilight faded into night over the rooftops, trying not to think about her while every object in his field of vision pulled him back to her as if by a gravitational force—the moon to the moon they saw together climbing in Joshua Tree, the Heineken in his hand to the one he'd been drinking when they met at a party two years ago, the empty spot in the driveway to her red BMW. Look inside my head, he told her, can't you see that it's just you? But he couldn't talk to her because she was in the middle of the Pacific Ocean.

In retrospect he should have seen it coming. Perhaps he was blind because the idea was too sad to consider. Like nuclear war. There had been signs over the last couple of months. One, she no longer laughed so much at his jokes and antics. Two, she was quick to anger when he left the toilet seat up or was slow to make the bed. Three, she stopped having sex about two weeks back. But Nick was sprinting down the homestretch of his thesis, revising an article that had tentatively been accepted by *Conservation Biology*, getting his résumé out to the World Wildlife Fund, Greenpeace, the Sierra Club, and a half dozen United Nations agencies, teaching an undergraduate class. He had been working fourteen hours every day for two months, trying to finish his degree so they could spend August climbing in the Sierra before Monica had to be back at school. In the rush to the finish line Nick had been blindsided.

Four years younger than Nick, Monica Eleanor Carson was

the daughter of the vice chairman of Bank of America and a
Marin County housewife. When they met at a party, she was a
first-year law student and was charmed by the handsome
southerner passionate in a quiet way about scaling mountain
walls and defending the planet. Nick was always sweet and
sometimes funny and a gentle marathoner in bed. But in the
last months the charm wore off and she fell out of love. She
had never been sure that she wanted to follow him to Washington or Nairobi, wherever he landed a job. Certain traits of his
began to irritate her—the snippets of Yeats, Eliot, and Shakespeare that popped out of his mouth at apt moments; his dis-
approval of her parents, the number of TVs in their house, their
Republican politics, the size of their swimming pool. And Monica, with her blonde cheerleader looks and deep cleavage, had
no shortage of old boyfriends and interested suitors. Nick was
an experiment and the results came back negative.

The Monday before at breakfast, just after Nick had set a tall
glass of blended fruit and seeds in front of her and sat down
across the table, Monica had taken a sip of the smoothie, then
said softly, "I've fallen out of love with you."

Reviewing the outline of the class he had to teach in an hour
in his head, Nick was uncertain of what he'd heard and said, "I
love you, too, baby."

"See!" Monica seized the proof of his neglect, the anger to
camouflage guilt. "You hardly listen to me anymore!"

"Baby, I'm sorry I've been distracted. We'll take off for the
mountains soon."

"Forget the mountains," Monica yelled.

"We'll go wherever you want."

"It's not that, Nick." She lowered her voice. "I don't want to
go on."

Suddenly Nick saw the unthinkable. Somehow he managed
to keep his face composed, his voice steady. "You don't love
me anymore?"

"Of course I *love* you." She pronounced the word dismissively. "We had some great times. You're a sweetheart. I've just fallen out of love with you. You're not the one."

If you decide to take the heart in which I have my roots, then think that on that very day, at that very minute—a Spanish love poem began to run through Nick's head but he shut it down and willed his eyes to stay dry. Tears would be like a red flag to a bull. Monica's father had fought nightmarish battles across the frozen wasteland of Korea, his unit cut off and starving for weeks after the Chinese swept into the war to drive the Americans out of the North, and Monica's mother had been an army nurse he met while learning to walk a second time. Monica had grown up in a household that laughed at common sickness and pain. She was tough. It was one of the things that Nick loved about her. She was fearless on the end of a rope. Nick saw that she would act swiftly, decisively, take no prisoners.

She reached over the table and put her hand on his.

Nick thought she might be daring him to cry so she could walk away with less regret. "I love you, Monica. I thought I was good for you, kind of a counterbalance. This is so fast it's crazy. Why don't you give us a little time?"

"It's all I've been thinking about all summer. I'm not happy anymore."

"The flames of passion are now just ashes?"

Monica's mouth pursed in irritation.

"That was my own drivel." Nick circled the table.

"Well, that pretty much sums it up," Monica said as Nick pulled her up by the hands. "The excitement's over and I can't see us making a future together. We're just too different."

"It was fun while it lasted." Nick tried to be ironic.

"Yeah." Monica held him hard and laid her head on his shoulder. "It was a good run."

Nick pushed her back by the shoulders to look at her blonde hair and blue eyes, her clean, all-American face.

"Girls flirt with you all the time, Nick. You'll be all right," Monica said. She had lost the brooding expression she'd had for the last few days.

Nick hugged her again so she wouldn't see the rain clouds gathering in his eyes. He realized with a pang that this might be the last time he would feel her breasts pressed against his chest. Over her shoulder he said, "Let's make love right now."

"It would be like going to a funeral."

Nick's laugh was hollow. He looked in her eyes. "One last time. Like a wake."

For a second Monica had the expression of a woman staring at a dress marked down in a shop, then she said, "No, Nick. It would just spoil the good memories. It would be so awkward."

"In my experience sex at a dramatic juncture is out of this world." Nick watched her for a sign she might change her mind. He wanted to throw himself at her feet, weep and beg, to rip off her clothes, carry her to the bed, and ravish her for hours. His voice was thick. "What are you going to do?"

Monica angled her eyes to the smoothie melting in her glass. "I'm flying to Hawaii to get on my parents' boat."

"When?"

"Today."

"What?" Nick shouted, pulling away. "You drop this on me like a bomb and disappear?"

"I booked the ticket last week and I was sort of hoping that I'd change my mind."

"This is so cold." Nick stood still with a dazed expression.

"You've got to be cruel to be kind," Monica quipped.

Nick felt as if he were falling through space, waving his arms with nothing to catch onto. Outside on the street a car honked. Nick staggered a few feet back and collapsed onto a sofa.

"There's Chris."

"I'm not going anywhere," Nick said.

"Please go." Monica crossed the room and grabbed Nick's satchel by his desk. It was green Italian leather, a birthday present she'd given him to replace his threadbare rucksack. Nick always packed it before he went to bed. Monica carried it to the sofa and sat down beside him. "Chris is out there."

"I just had open-heart surgery. How can I teach?"

The car honked three short bursts, then a long wail.

"Nick, dammit, pull yourself together. You know how I hate scenes," Monica said. "We'll talk when you get back, okay?"

Nick returned immediately after class but she was already gone. He read a note on the kitchen table:

Dear Honey Bear,

I decided it's better for us to talk about this when I get back in a couple of weeks. I'll call you from the sat phone on the boat. I do love you, you know. We're just not made for each other. We could still go climbing sometime.

Love,
Monica

"Fuck you," Nick said, and the tears he'd been holding back gushed out in a great swell that left him bent over, grasping the table as if he could be washed away.

Through that week when the sun set, memories arrived like un-invited guests invading the living room of his mind to reminisce of the glory days over cocktails, impersonating her cheerful California accent. *Nick*, what if we had a girl and she had your dark skin and dark eyes and my blonde hair? Your full lips but the shape of my mouth? Your long legs and my long torso? Wouldn't she be *so* gorgeous? Nick wanted to escape but he was trapped. Some of the visitors prodded him toward honesty: Come on, boy, admit that much of her appeal was the family money. You could pursue your do-gooder career knowing that you would always drive BMWs and spend Easter in Venice. "I love her!" Nick yelled to himself on Thursday night, spilling his gin and tonic in his lap. "She's the only girlfriend I ever had that I didn't cheat on!" At nine o'clock, when it was eleven in Nashville and Cage would be back from the library, he turned down the Talking Heads on the stereo and picked up the phone, dialed with unsteady fingers.

"Nick?" Cage answered.

"Yep."

"I knew it was you. I just tried to call. Had the stereo up?"

"Yep."

"Heard from her yet?"

"Nope."

"I kinda admire her coldness. She decided it wasn't going to work and the best thing was a clean break and she followed through. It's better for you, too. You've just got to get over her and move on. There's plenty of fish in the sea. You never had any problem landing a looker."

"I don' wan' anyone else," Nick slurred. "She's purfec'."

"Perfect? Two weeks ago you were complaining that she had never heard of Dostoyevsky."

"She's beautiful."

"She's hot. No doubt about that. But, man, there're a million girls out there that look like her."

"I'll never find someone like her."

"Come on, Nick. We go through this night after night. She wasn't perfect. She was hard-hearted." Cage just blurted it out: "And she was unfaithful."

"What the fuck are you talking about?"

Cage was silent. He hadn't really meant to tell him and wondered if it was meanness from an impulse to kick him while he was down or if truth had its own momentum. Since Monica left, Cage hadn't been able to decide whether to finally fess up. If Nick knew that Monica had seduced him, which didn't take much effort on her part, he had to admit, then maybe the anger would help Nick move on. Or Nick might hate him for a long time. Cage could lie, say that Monica had confided in him about someone else, but the truth would out when she got back from Hawaii.

"Who'd she fuck?" Nick sounded a little less drunk.

"Brother, I've felt horrible about this since I was out over spring break. Remember that night when you stayed late studying and Monica and I ended up shooting tequila?" Cage heard the sound of glass shattering from the other end of the line.

"We started playing truth or dare and she dared me to kiss her and I did and . . . We were both drunker than Cooter Brown." In the quiet that followed Cage waited, picturing the outrage and hurt on his brother's face.

"Was it good?" Nick whispered coldly.

Fantastic, Cage thought. "It didn't really work. I don't remember."

"You brotherfucker! You'll pay for this," Nick yelled, and hung up.

Cage called him back and let the phone ring twenty times. He got no answer every ten minutes for the next hour and then called Chris and asked him to go around and check on Nick. Around eleven when Chris walked through the open front door into a wall of sound, the Police playing "Bring On the Night" on Monica's Bose system, Nick was at his desk. In a diary entry titled *Heard It through the Phoneline*, he had written only, *I should beat Cage with a baseball bat. He should have told me when it happened.* He stood up and left the pen between the pages with the top off. His face was dry and he did not appear to be obviously drunk. He told Chris, "Next time I see Cage I'm going to kill him." Then he laughed and asked, "Isn't *Homo sapiens* absurd?"

On Saturday morning at ten, a few minutes after a dean at Berkeley, who the day before had called his parents numerous times unsuccessfully, calls the number on his Decks Unlimited business card which was in Nick's wallet, Cage will go to the Nashville airport without calling anyone in the family. Chris will meet him at the San Francisco airport that evening. They will have a few drinks at the bar where Chris took Nick, will even run into some of the same girls. For several hours before falling asleep Cage will read Nick's diary. The phone will wake him on Sunday morning. It will be Monica calling from the Pacific. When they hang up, he will call Memphis before remembering that his parents are still on a spiritual retreat, then he and Chris will drive out on the bridge to look for the skid marks and glass. When Cage sees what he guesses is the site, a bumper sticker

from Louisiana about a bug squashed on the windshield of life
will come to mind. They will go home in silence and start packing up Nick's little house. That night he will call Memphis again
and his father will answer. Monday morning he will go with
Chris to the morgue and identify the body by a scar on the shin
where Nick had once walked into a horseshoe stake in the dark
and will arrange for the mangled corpse to be cremated and
then spend the afternoon by himself locating the wreck of Pilar
in a junkyard and an hour sitting in the backseat of the crum-
pled cabin. Tuesday he will spend most of the day trying to find
the patrolman writing the accident report, with no luck. Dreading Monica's arrival, knowing that seeing her would be painful
and weird and the extreme emotions of the situation might
even lead to an obscene animal consolation, Cage will leave
Nick's place on Wednesday morning after the UPS and Salvation Army vans come for the boxes, riding with Chris by the funeral home to pick up Nick's ashes and then to the airport. On
the plane ride back he will begin to reconstruct the last five
days of Nick's life, and through a long talk on the phone with
Monica the next day he will fill in some gaps. A few weeks later
he will receive the police and coroner's reports. Down through
the years he will ponder what passed through Nick's head in his
last moments of consciousness. He will never believe that Nick
could have had time to see his life flash by even at the speed
of light.

Cruising in Pilar through the last hour of night, Nick was heading south on the 101 in Marin after a pointless surveillance run
past the Carsons' house in Ross just to make sure there was
nobody home. He had planned to drive up Mount Tam to watch
the sun rise but the sugar levels in his bloodstream were low,
the alcohol edging into the legal zone, and he was suddenly
hungry and very tired. The highway ran through a tunnel, then
curved around the mountainside, and the Golden Gate rose out
of the dark cloud that cloaked the city across the Bay. The
lamps of the bridge cast diffuse yellow light through the fog.
Outside, the bright mist rushed past like the interior of a comet

and visibility stretched a hundred yards. Inside, green light glowed from the dash. Nick switched off the R.E.M. tape and listened to the wind through the windows. "It will hurt for a while but I'm over the worst part," he repeated aloud what he'd told Chris several times in the bar. Acclerating up to seventy or eighty, Nick passed a Coca-Cola truck, moving from the middle lane into the lane bordered against the oncoming traffic by reflecting plastic wands which were set for the morning rush hour, dividing three lanes into the city and two coming out. When Nick was about a hundred feet beyond the cola truck, an '86 Corolla driven by Reginald T. Johnson, forty-three, a car salesman on amphetamine whose blood alcohol level was three times the legal limit, veered across the barrier of plastic wands. The impact could have killed Nick instantly, from a brain injury against the roof of the car or by ripping out his aorta from the heart, which floats free in the chest. Or perhaps Nick glimpsed Johnson, his murderer, who was likely already dead strapped in his seat belt, as he flew through the windshield. He may have been conscious flying through the spray of glass over the Toyota and fifty feet farther through the air, a sensation akin to free-falling off a rock face that he had grown not to fear.

Harper

All the leaves are gone. The weak reds and washed oranges that the trees managed after the long, dry summer came and went in a couple of weeks. When I'm bored with making money for Hong Kong Pacific, when the adrenaline is dry and the shouts of Dooner and the traders grate my ears like the cries of loud drunks in a sports bar, when I wish I was in a kayak or on a ski slope, anywhere but our new office on Madison Avenue, even with the view of Central Park, I play with my latest toy, a Canon digital camera with an array of 35mm lenses, and record the progress of autumn in the middle of Manhattan. As soon as I hit the shutter an image appears on my computer. Framing the screen in a chronological sequence, the rich green trees first pale and yellow, then blush briefly and finally brown.

The light by my second line, which receives calls kicked from my home, blinks. I brace myself for Caitlin and start thinking of excuses—Sorry, some clients came in from Bangkok and my cell went dead—trying to repress an image of dancing naked with a big-breasted coat-check girl whose name I can't recall.

I pick up the phone. "Howdy."

"Is this Harper?" asks a strange girl's voice.

"Yeah." Who is she? Someone I've forgotten? I get a creepy feeling from a dream I had last night. A girl I did not know who insisted that I'd slept with her called to tell me that the state health authorities were requiring her to call everyone whom she might have infected with HIV.

"Hey, um, my name's Emma."

"Emma?" Christ, my dream's coming true.

"You're Cage's brother?"

"Yeah," I say with a rush of relief, thinking she's another girl whom Cage owes money coming out of the woodwork.

"Is he okay?"

"He's having a hard time. Where did you know him?"

"San Francisco. Santa Cruz. I egged him into stealing a sail-boat."

"So you really exist." I remember her name now. "You were on the boat. You sort of broke his heart. Just disappeared."

"Yeah. It was hella uncool. I capped him, totally. I was really fucked up. I'm back in school in Santa Cruz now." She has a sad, weary laugh. "I think about him whenever I look out at the bay."

"He dropped you on the beach so you wouldn't get busted."

"Cage was stand-up. I saw the cops driving him away. I should have visited him or called you. I should have done something. I was worried they'd catch me, too . . ." She's quiet for a moment. "He's a really nice guy. I'm sorry. Did he have to go to jail?"

"The court put him in a rehab program for a few months and he got out and was working as a carpenter—"

"Cage is in Santa Cruz?" Emma sounds excited.

"Well." I always hate explaining this. "Did you know he's bi-polar?"

"Yeah. He made a big deal about carrying around a bottle of lithium but he would only take it when he felt really good."

"That's logical." I laugh. "When you met him, he was manic, tons of fun, high as a satellite."

"No shit. He wouldn't sleep for days at a time."

"Right." I watch the clouds moving across the sky over Harlem, wonder if she's as pretty as Cage said. "What goes up must come down. About a month ago he hurt his back and he couldn't work. That's what triggered it. Lying on his bed all day . . . imagine . . . staring up at the ceiling, thinking how he's almost forty years old and his life's been a long series of fuckups, how all his peers have families and houses and new SUVs and va-cations, and he's out there trying to start over, but he can't 'cause his back hurts, so thoughts keep swirling around and around his head until they carry him down the drain into a black hole of de-pression."

"That's hella sad." Her voice sounds bummed, then rises. "Where is he? I'll go visit him."

"He's two thousand miles from you." Talking about Cage makes me tired. "Got to where he was afraid to leave his room. He's at my grandmother's. Holed up. Paranoid. Terrified of the world."

"Back in the spring he wasn't afraid of anything," she says with disbelief. "Nothing. Nobody. He was fucking fearless and he had so much energy, so much"—she sucks in air through her teeth, finding the words—"life force."

"Gone for now," I whisper, then try to sound cheerful. "He'll bounce back."

"I wish there was something I could do," she says softly.

"I wish there was something to do."

"Cage really helped me, you know," she says earnestly and with a bit of awe. "He got me to stop shooting up."

"That's a major accomplishment." I didn't mean to sound sarcastic.

"You don't know."

"Hey, I—"

"Your brother is a great listener. He's got a deep soul. He cares about people. And he loves you. He talked about you a lot. He really respects you."

"Harper, you're holding us up!" Dooner shouts from across the room. "Quit talking to your bitches!" On the screen the black box is asking permission to buy ten thousand shares of Lamar Advertising. I glance over at Dooner, who yells, "Don't look at me, junior, it's in your basket!"

"Sorry, uh"—I can't remember her name for a second—"Emma. I gotta go. Give Cage a call. It would mean a lot for him to hear from you. You got a pen?" Giving her Grandmother's number in Thebes, I call up the LAMR curve on the screen, watch the line starting to climb. "You're welcome, Emma. Take care of yourself." I hang up, make the trade, and think how so much of my life takes place on telephones—dumping women I'd just as soon never see again, getting dumped by women who never want to see me again, talking to old college friends whom

I'll probably never see again. The last words I ever heard from Nick were over the telephone. He said, Try not to upset Mama. The odds are, the last words I hear from my Nanny, Mom, Dad, Cage, my cousins, everybody, will be over the telephone.

Cage

No insect noise, no birdsong, no sound of traffic from the road or the lake. On my hands and knees I advance along a row of damp, chocolate-colored soil, freshly turned, pushing corn seeds an inch deep with one finger, then brushing dirt to fill the holes. Even my own movements are silent. Maybe a side effect of this antipsychotic is temporary deafness. Ink-black clouds race across the sky over the lake toward Cage's Bend on a mute wind. Midway along the row, my finger touches something hard and cold. I sweep the dirt away and find a wedge of dark stone. Looking at the chipped edges, I realize that it's a tomahawk blade. I slip it in my pocket and continue down the row. Reaching the edge of the plowed field, I rise, then look back thirty yards along the row. At the far end something is sticking out of the first hole, wiggling. I squint, straining to see. Hole by hole, thin black shoots sprout out of the ground, coming closer. I want to move but my legs are frozen. Between my feet, where I planted the last seed, black shoots push up through the brown earth. The sprouts look like human hair. I raise my head slowly, looking along the row to the end, where the shoots have grown into cabbages of hair flapping in the wind. Scalps.

On the back steps Grandmother stands, waving, calling soundlessly. She points at the sky and gestures for me to come inside. As I look up, a shadow suddenly covers the garden and the first drops begin to land on my forehead. My legs won't move. I grab my right thigh with two hands and try to lift it. The rain showers heavier, splattering my khakis with pink spots. The rain is not water. It's red, warm. Blood. I scream and hear nothing. Looking up, I see Grandmother closing the last storm shutters on the back porch. My clothes and hair are drenched with blood. It fills my eyes faster than I can wipe them with my sleeve. My legs begin to move. Blinded by the blood, I stumble across the field, trip and fall over one of the scalps, which breaks loose and rolls over, revealing the face of a Cherokee warrior a few inches away between my hands. The lids blink open and solid black eyes peer into mine. Something forces my head down. The Cherokee's mouth, full and feminine, parts slightly, sensuously. His tongue traces his lips, then reaches out and licks blood off my own. Clawing my fingernails in the dirt, I twist away, drag myself across the field toward the lawn and the house. As I pass, each of the scalps pops out of the ground, pushed up by the heads of men, women, and children, young and old, all Cherokee, all watching me, grinning, leering lasciviously. I crawl out of the blood-soaked field onto the dry lawn and am able to stand and walk to the steps of the house. Pausing on the back porch, I force myself to turn and look back. The scalps are gone. I feel the heavy blade of the tomahawk in my pocket. I walk around the old brick house and up the steps to the front veranda and stare out at the four oaks towering a hundred feet overhead and see myself high in the top of a tree, impaled on a limb.

I run from the vision through the French doors. Opening them, I can hear again. My grandmother calls from her sitting room in a high, sweet voice, "Cage, be sure to wash the blood off your feet. Don't track it on the carpet. Do you hear me, Cage?"

Something puts its hands on my shoulders, tries to pull me backward, calling my name, impersonating my grandmother like a siren. "Cage." The hands jerk at my shoulders. "Cage."

I grit my eyes shut and thrash wildly, trying to jerk loose of the hands. When I open them, I find myself stretched out on a leather easy chair.

"Cage, do you hear me?" Grandmother smiles kindly. "It's just a dream."

I run my hands down my face and look at them. No blood.

"Just a dream. You're okay."

"Just a dream," I say. "My voice works."

"Yes, honey. You're fine. You were talking in your sleep."

"What did I say?"

"The sins of the fathers." Nanny pats me on the shoulder. "Odd, you sounded just like your grandfather while you were sleep-talking." She backs away a few steps and lowers herself into a wingback chair. "What were you dreaming?"

"It's too terrible, Nanny."

"Morgan had nightmares, too." Nanny looks up at his photograph over the fireplace. "Oh, the news has started already."

I hit the remote and Tom Brokaw's face appears on the screen saying, "Suggestions that Governor Bush used cocaine in his youth and his inability to answer these allegations directly have contributed to his decline in the latest poll." Brokaw is looking at me. He occupies a position toward the top of the hierarchy of the Order. He smiles and his eyes tell me, Your days are numbered. You can't hide at your grandmother's house forever, a grown man, almost forty years old, too weak to work, to give anything back. You take and take and take while the rest of the world is building something useful. You are a weakling, a poor excuse for a man. Look at you, cringing in your grandmother's house. You're a parasite. You're a termite eating away at the foundation of this house, at the foundations of society. Quickly I stand and leave the room. Maybe he'll forget about me. Maybe it will buy me more time before they send someone to get me.

I'm met by the collective gaze of the portraits of the five Morgan Elijah Cages all staring at me. The first has long flowing hair like Custer's and wears a blue army uniform with gold buttons. The second has a gray Confederate uniform. The last, Poppy, has short hair and the leather jacket and cap of a World War II bomber pilot. They all have dark, cold eyes which follow me down the hall as they whisper, You are the firstborn of the last generation, the last male to carry our name. We were the pillars of Thebes. We were respected by our peers and the town. We contributed to the community. You are an affront to our legacy. You have drifted, accursed outcast, across our great nation, a wandering jester, a joke. You don't deserve our name. I run up the hallway, trying to escape their whispers. You are not a man. You have no guts. No grit. No resolve. I leap up the stairs two steps at a time. You are weaker than a woman. Yellower than a Injun. Feckless as a nigger. A traveling circus freak.

The sound of a car crunching on the gravel carries from the driveway. They're coming. It's finally time. The ghosts know. I pause on the landing and stare out the window, watch the mail truck circle in front of the house, then pull away. The ghosts laugh. How dare you call yourself Cage? You should change your name to Coward. You cowering worm. You don't deserve to wipe the dirt off the postman's boots. He holds a job. He gets up and works. You just lie around your grandmother's house, eating her food, dirtying her sheets. You're a burden. Dead weight. Dross. A buffoon. A mockery of man. I put my hands over my ears and dash up the last flight of stairs, trip on the last step, and land in a heap at the top.

I feel my ancestors laughing. You can't run. Wherever you run, you're still stuck with yourself. Why run like a deserter? It's too late to start over again. I stand up and put my hands on my ears. I'm crying now. Accused by my own ancestors. A deserter has only one destiny. There is but a single noble course of action. To remove the burden from your family and eliminate their despair. You must stare down your fear, look deep within yourself for the courage that we bequeathed you in our blood, which flows through your veins. Our blood demands honor. Our blood demands your blood.

A calmness stills my heart as I walk down the hallway toward Poppy's old study. The floor creaks beneath the long, narrow Turkish carpet. The voices of my ancestors lose their stridence, continue in comforting tones. Only through an irrevocable act of ultimate courage can you redeem yourself. Only then will our blood claim your blood.

The voices cease when I enter the study. On the walls of knotted cypress are hunting and horse racing prints, fading photographs of the Tennessee Senate in the teens and twenties. I don't look for the fourth Morgan Elijah Cage among the fifty little oval portraits, don't want to see the contempt in his eyes. I go to the gun case and remove Poppy's gun, an over-and-under Browning twelve-gauge, and see him carrying it, open at the stock, angled over the crook of his elbow, smiling down at me when I barely reached his chest. I'll join you, Poppy, in the fields of forever. You and Nick. We'll be together, like the sunny days when we were boys. I stick my hand under the desk and pat around until I find the deer slug that I found and hid after Nanny threw out all the boxes of shells. I snap the barrels open, slide the shell in the top, click the barrel shut. The singleness of purpose blunts the gnawing shame that has haunted me for weeks, forever really, as even when I'm feeling good it lurks there in the back of my mind. I will attain absolution with an act of courage. I'll no longer be a source of worry and anguish for my parents, a financial and emotional drain. They will mourn me for a time and then move on, as they did after Nick's death. Easier than with Nick, for he died with so much promise and they were proud of him. Whereas I represent only disappointment and shame.

Sitting in Poppy's swivel chair, I write on a piece of his stationery on the leather surface of his desk:

Dearest Nanny,

I'm sorry that my messy life ended up one last mess for you to clean up. But this is the best way. I can't bear to be a burden any longer. My dark world holds no joy, no light, no peace, no help for pain. I have let us all down, those born and those not born. It is only fitting that I should take my life with honor before they come for me and take with me the congruence of black-sheep blood that spoils our lineage. Know that I love you and all the good ones in our family.

Cage

I set the butt of the gun on the floor and the barrel in my mouth and lean forward, grasping at the trigger, but the barrel is too long, so I lay the gun on the desk and search the shallow center drawer for a length of string, which I tie to the trigger. Just a few feet outside the window, high in an oak, a pileated woodpecker hammers the bark. Poppy's favorite bird, his spirit come to guide me. I raise the barrel to my lips with my left hand. The cold barrel tastes of oil. My right begins to shake as I take the string. Yes, the ghosts whisper. An honorable death will redeem you. My hand shakes worse than Tom Hanks's on the bridge at the end of *Saving Private Ryan*. My eyes blink rapidly, squeezing out tears, then I focus at the corner of the desk, a photo of Nick and me, four and five, wearing matching sailor suits. Sorry, Nick, I say. Sorry for what I did. I'm coming to see you. Jerking the string with my trembling hand, I hear his voice saying, Don't listen to them, then the roar of the gun.

My left eardrum explodes and a ringing fills my head. I stare at the little boys in sailor suits, unsure if I consciously pushed the barrel away at the last instant or inadvertently from the violent trembling. The odor of burned powder fills the study. I can't hear any ghosts, just the reverberation of the shot between my ears. Suddenly I imagine Nanny downstairs, terrified that I've just killed myself. She could never bear the sound of a shotgun. I set the gun on the desk and dash down the hall, yelling, "I'm okay, Nanny! I'm okay!"

Downstairs, when I come into her sitting room, Nanny's on the floor, trying to pick up the phone. She looks up and says, "Oh, thank God."

"I'm sorry, Nanny." I get down on my knees and hug her, help her into an easy chair, and put the phone on the table. "I just thought . . ." I can't finish the sentence.

"Oh, thank God." Her eyes are wet. "Oh, you poor, poor boy. My heart's thumping in my ears. My fingers were shaking too hard to dial 911."

"I'm sorry, Nanny. I could have given you a heart attack."

"Curse the damn illness that's haunted every generation of this family!" Nanny makes a little fist like my mother does when she's angry. "You promised me, Cage. Oh, you poor boy, you poor, poor boy. Oh, thank the Lord you are alive."

"It went in a *Reader's Digest* book of condensed novels," I say.

Nanny squints, shakes her head. "Beg your pardon?"

"The slug"—I laugh miserably—"lodged in a volume of condensed novels on Poppy's bookshelf. *Reader's Digest.*"

Nanny takes a deep breath. "Let's go into the kitchen and make some tea." She lifts the remote to turn off the TV just as Tom Brokaw says, "From all of us at NBC News, good night."

Harper

Though I'm sitting behind the bulkhead on the aisle, I'm the first on the plane because I have a Northwest Elite card, since I average about forty thousand miles a year. I watch the business cabin fill up and then the coming line of convict class led by a three-hundred-pound Jabba the Hutt in a cowboy hat whose belly is compressed by the seats on either side. *Please don't sit here, no, no,* I pray. His double chin rotates from side to side like a spectator at a tennis match, checking out the seat numbers. I have to lean away as he passes to avoid getting slimed. Then there is a tall black guy in a tight black T-shirt. *Roll on by, muscleman.* His eyes are cold, look right through me. An anxious sixtyish woman with white eyebrows and jet-black hair creeps tentatively along. *You can do it, granny, one foot in front of the other, just a few more rows.* Behind a Hasid with a thick beard and ringlets dangling from under his fedora, a bleached blonde with a leathery weasel face, and a pimply boy with superwide bell bottoms, my eyes land on a girl in her late twenties with short, spiky red hair. Those in line beyond her are walking statistics, four more of the fifty million American hogs. Sweet Jesus, let her be the one. She's clutching some magazines and pulling a little wheeled suitcase. She slows down beside me. *Yes.* Looks at her boarding card, then at the empty seat opposite. *No.* She glances over my head, then down at me, and smiles slightly.

"Beg your pardon," she drawls.

Thanks be to God. Standing up, speculating on her breasts swelling beneath a cream mohair pullover—extra-medium, close together, never easy to guess the diameter of her nipples, probably large given her full lips—I say, "Let me help you with your bag."

"Thanks." She's very pretty when she smiles, not in a conventional Betsy Sloan TV-face sense, but an unusual beauty. Her face is wide, her chin squarish, her nose large and Roman. She's about five-six, slender. As she squeezes by, I check out her round butt in a pair of brown corduroy jeans.

She settles by the window as I put her bag overhead. I study her profile for a second, the clean line of her nose, wondering what a red bush looks like. Of the hundred-odd girls I've slept with, I've never lucked into one. God, boy, you're single-minded. Your imagination is trapped in your glands. She holds a copy of *Modern Photography* with long, slender ringless fingers.

After a few minutes I ask, "Are you a photographer?"

She looks at me with calm greenish eyes. "I come up to New York a couple of times a year to see the exhibitions. I'm a kind of, um—"

"Exhibitionist?"

"Uh, no." Her full-blown smile transforms her face into something extraordinary. "An amateur."

"I'm a sort of amateur collector. I've got an Eggleston and a couple of Huger Footes and a Herb Ritts." I don't say that I bought the photographs to get into the pants of a Danish beauty who worked for a gallery in SoHo.

"Really?" She raises her eyebrows. "Eggleston and Foote—do you live in Memphis?"

"No, but my parents do."

"I didn't think you did. Your hair's too long." She looks up at my hair. Her eyes are laughing. "You've got nice hair. What's your name?"

"Thanks. Harper Rutledge."

She examines my face. "Is your father Bishop Rutledge?"

"Yeah." I smile. The strength of my father's charm and position has broken the ice with two Memphis belles on my belt.

"Really!" She pats my arm as if she's known me for years. "We go to the cathedral. The first time your father preached, I thought he was God. I mean, I was fifteen."

I always thought he was a fool, a handsome well-meaning fool who couldn't make it in the world of commerce. "He's kinda like a rock star in Memphis, among his generation, I mean. Up on that pulpit. Our generation looked to musicians for meaning. His looked to preachers." I'm not sure which is more ridiculous, I think, watching her.

She leans her head to one side.

"Rock and roll stole his thunder. I didn't catch your name."

She holds out her hand like a man, makes her face stern and her voice deep. "Isabella Ballou."

"Sounds like a Tennessee Williams character." I take her hand. "Unusual but beautiful. Like you."

Isabella grips my hand hard, then turns my palm over. "You live in New York."

"Yes."

"You juggle girlfriends." She traces my life line. "You've got five in the air at this moment."

Close. Three. "No."

"You're a Peter Pan. You're a player."

"A player?"

"Don't play dumb. I never met a preacher's son who wasn't a very naughty boy."

"Repudiating everything our fathers stand for?"

"Yeah. Shameless." She laughs. "What's up with that?"

"Easy target." I shrug. "Compelled to show our peers that we're not God-squad sissies?"

The plane startles her, backing away from the gate, and she lets go of my hand. "God I hate to fly. Take off, anyway. And land."

For a second I think she's still acting but the mischievous glint is gone from her eyes.

"We're going to be fine," I say gently.

She stares at the seat back in front of her.

"Isabelle?"

"Isabell*a*." She doesn't glance at me.

"But your seat belt—"

Her hands tremble as she fastens the buckle. Maybe she lost someone in a plane crash. As we accelerate down the runway, she looks like she's in pain. Her hands clench the armrest so tightly that her fingers turn red. I reach over and pry her hand off gently. She glances at me questioningly. Her fingers intertwine around mine and she nearly crushes my hand.

"It's okay," I whisper as we lift off the ground, looking past her, out the window where the rushing runway turns suddenly to brown water. While the plane angles up at an impossibly steep incline over the dreary landscape, the g-force pulls our bodies back into our seats. Out the portal the dark towers of Manhattan rise through a sickly yellow haze. Still climbing over New Jersey, the plane creaks and groans, bouncing up and down like a truck going fast on a bad road. Isabella starts to crush my hand again. I wonder how to distract her.

"Ride 'em, cowboy!" I laugh as the plane heaves up and down. "It's fun. Like an amusement park ride."

Isabella turns her head an inch, glares at me with one eye, and whispers fiercely, "Listen to the plane."

"It's just a little turbulence, maybe from the warm smog hitting a colder part of the troposphere."

Isabella's one eye looks uncertain and her hand relaxes a bit.

"Listen, these planes can take a lot more g's than this tad of rough air. These big jets can pull out of five-hundred-mile-an-hour nosedives."

The image makes her grimace and squeeze harder.

"I'm on my way to Nashville to see my brother, who just tried to shoot himself."

She finally rips her gaze from the flotation sticker on the seat back. "That's awful." She lets out a low shriek as a big bump lifts us out of our seats. "Why?"

"Deep, black depression. His psyche is punishing him for his fuckups. He's manic-depressive. He's a really sweet, smart guy."

Isabella shakes her head sympathetically, drawls, "Haunted by demons?"

"Call it that, I guess. Or cursed by bad brain chemistry."

"I'll bet he'll be glad to see— Aaah!" The plane yaws to one side, throwing her shoulder over the armrest into me. "I remember a guy in college. He was really cute. Very charismatic. He was so much fun to be around," Isabella says rapidly as if we were in a hurry. "Sometimes he was extremely spooky. He hung himself in his parents' basement Christmas of senior year. Hard to get your head around."

Suddenly the sky is calm and the captain's voice apologizes and promises a smooth flight on to Memphis. Isabella puts her hand in her lap. "Thanks for your kindness. Players are often very considerate gentlemen."

"I'm not—" I start to protest.

"A gentleman?" Her laugh sounds wise and sarcastic. "You know how R.E.M. defines a gentleman?"

"No?"

"Gentlemen don't get caught." She starts humming the song.

"I don't know how you can call me a player."

She hums louder.

"When you're such a flirt."

She raises her eyebrows. "Me? Flirt?"

"You flirt."

"You Peter Pan." Isabella laughs. "Me unavailable."

"Married?"

Smiling, she shakes her head like a little girl.

"Boyfriend."

She nods rapidly.

"Occupation?"

"Doctor."

"What kind?"

"He's an intern in anesthesiology."

"So I don't stand a chance?"

"Not a chance."

"I could take you places you've never been."

"Not anywhere I want to go."

"I'm not talking metaphorically. Do you want to live the rest of your life in Memphis?"

"Not particularly."

"So I have a chance?"

She shakes her head slowly, then stops smiling. "That's terrible about your brother. I think I remember seeing him in church. Cute, really cute, brownish hair and blue eyes. Kinda stands out in a crowd? Bright smile?"

"That's Cage."

Cage

"Hello, brother." Someone who looks like Harper dressed in blue jeans and a green sweater and an old leather bomber jacket comes in the room and flicks on the light. He stands beside my bed and looks down where I've been lying on the cover since lunch, staring at the fishbowl light on the ceiling, waiting for them to come.

"Get up, brother." His grin looks like a death mask. He pats my leg, then moves to the window and opens the blind. "Get up and give me a hug."

"Is it really you, Harper?" I want to believe I have a brother.

"Of course it's me, Cage. There are no body doubles running around trying to trick you. It's me, the one and only Harper. Your brother who loves you." He leans down and grabs my arms just below the shoulders. I want to believe that it's Harper, not an impersonator trying to get me to reveal my secrets. As he pulls, I slide my shoes to the floor and stand up. My whole body is weak and cramped. He lets go and I sag, a puny specimen.

"Let's go to the garden." Harper's smile is fake. "It's a beautiful day."

"No."

"Come on. Let's go walk in the sunshine."

"No."

"Why not?" Harper asks.

"I wouldn't be comfortable."

"You'd feel better than you do in here."

"I don't want to see anyone."

"You won't see anyone you know. No one here knows you."

"I wouldn't be comfortable."

Harper scratches his head.

"Is it really you, Harper?"

"No, it's the motherfucking Grim Reaper. Who else could I be?"

"I wasn't sure because your face looks so fat."

"Thanks a lot." Harper laughs and wraps me in a big hug, squeezes me like an empty sponge. "Yeah, I drink too much and don't exercise enough."

"Remember what happened to Uncle Ned?" says the part of me that can still talk, the part that sees doom where it lies. "He was successful in computers. Like you. He never worked out. Like you. His heart wore out in his sixties. Young really. Think about it. You're a big guy like him. It could happen to you."

Harper leans back and looks in my eyes, and I peer into his, trying to figure out if it is really him. "You're all right, Cage." He grabs a Kleenex off the dresser top and wipes off my face.

"This shit makes you drool." My laugh sounds like a horrible squeal. "After you drool all day for a week you can't be bothered."

"What do they have you on?" Harper tries to stifle a grimace.

"Call me half-wit Hal. Look how my hands shake." I raise my right hand out in front of my chest and it trembles like an old man's. "Haldol. I wonder what it really is?"

"It's what they say it is. Haldol. No one's tricking you." Harper clasps my hands between his and looks at me steadily. "You won't be on it forever. It's going to help you through the delusions."

"I want to believe you, I try to believe you." I feel drool dribbling out of the corner of my mouth and raise my hand to wipe it off but I don't really have the energy. "But after you're gone I'll be back alone in my head. And it's a dark place, brother. I've done terrible things."

"Cage, on the scale of human evil you hardly register. Everyone has sinned against his neighbor." Harper shakes my shoulders. "Every single person you know and admire. You're not different, not worse."

"They haven't stolen things."

Harper's silent for a second. "Well, most of them probably shoplifted candy when they were kids. You're a kind person. You've always helped everyone you could. Everyone who knows you thinks you're a kind, smart person, battling a lifelong disease. You have to forgive yourself for whatever you did while you were being run by the disease. It's like you were under the spell of a bad computer program."

"Terrible things," I mutter.

"Nothing so terrible. You never murdered anyone," Harper says, but the look in his eyes says, *I know you killed Nick.*

I slump back down on the bed and groan, squeezing my eyes shut. Fratricide soaks my dreams with blood. Opening my eyes, I see Harper leaning over me, reaching to pat my shoulder. Suddenly my mouth blurts out, "Even as Sodom and Gomorrah giving themselves over to fornication and strange flesh are set forth for an example, suffering the vengeance of the eternal fire."

Harper laughs like a guy in a bar. "You're referring to me? I admit I've been stuck in a rut, banging my head against the wall."

"Find one woman, be true to her, procreate a new, pure life," I hear myself telling Harper. "It's the only thing that matters, the only thing that's sacred."

Harper smiles sardonically. One of the damned.

"Harper," my voice says, "you remember in Baton Rouge when Mrs. Mosby was dying of cancer behind us?"

"You could hear her moaning across the fence." Harper stands up. "Mom used to make us take her dinner and flowers and clean up around her yard. I hated it. I hated going into her room. It stank."

"You said she'd be better off dead. Truth from the mouths of babes. You were only about eight." The cold rational side of my psyche speaks while the rest of my mind can't keep my body from listing or stop the drool trickling down my face.

"When I was in the room alone with her, she told me she wanted to die." Harper relaxes back in the vinyl seat. "She said the doctors were taking her house and she would have nothing left to leave her children."

"You agreed with her. You came back and got into an argument with Dad at dinner about euthanasia." I manage to wipe the drool on my sleeve because I want him to take me seriously. "You were right, weren't you?"

"Yeah. People who are terminally ill, racked with pain, deserve a way out. I'm all for Dr. what's-his-name, Dr. Death?"

"Kevorkian." I smile for the first time in weeks. "Well, what's the difference between Mrs. Mosby and me? All I've done is consume family resources. My illness is permanent. I'm a nut. Nothing but a nut. I'm racked with pain. *Racked*. I'm nothing but pain and darkness."

"But it's not the same, Cage." Harper kneels by the bed, takes my hand. "You don't have cancer. You've got an illness that you've never learned to manage. You did at times for a year or two but you let it go. You're paying for the manic ride through California. You're paying for that high. But you'll come out of the darkness. You always do. And if you don't let yourself go so high, then you won't ever fall this low. You won't be stuck in this depression. You won't always want to die. You'll get your spirit back. You always had a strong lust for life, more than most people. You'll put your life back together."

As Harper's on his knees pleading, a shallow pond of drool collects in the corner of my mouth and slides down to the cleft of my chin. I tell him, "Your life has been a steady progression of achievements, a strong continuum." The saliva starts to spill into the air. "My life's not like Lincoln Logs or an Erector set." The string stretches toward the floor. "It's like broken panes of glass on top of panes of glass, a heap of shattered glass. I'd be better off dead."

"That's not true." Harper leaps up. "You can't let yourself believe that."

"Look at my life. A heap of shattered glass."

Harper wipes off my face with a Kleenex. "You can build a nice life, Cage. You've got skills." He dabs drool off the floor. "You're a good carpenter. Jesus was a carpenter. So was Harrison Ford."

"I'm a fraud. I can't keep up with a good crew. I can't handle the pressure."

"Yes, you can. You built some fine homes in Memphis. You're smart." Harper throws the ball of tissue in a basket by the bed. "You did well in college, grad school."

"My brain has been damaged by drugs."

"No, it hasn't. You're having a perfectly intelligent conversation right now. Your problem is self-esteem. You've got to get your self-esteem back."

"Look around you, Harper. You're in a mental hospital. Your brother is a nut. I'm not fit for the world. They're going to lock me away in a dark place. They're going to let me starve or put me down. I'm a misfit. I'm a career criminal."

"You're not a criminal. You've done some stupid crazy shit while you were manic, suffering from the disease. No one's going to take you anywhere, brother. When these awful drugs clear your mind of delusion, they'll let you out. In a couple of months you'll be your charming old self, happy-go-lucky Cage."

His voice sounds strange. Can he be my brother? "Is it really you, Harper?"

"Yes, Cage." He hugs me tight. "I know it's rough but you've got to hang in there."

"The family'll be sad for a while and then they'll get over it. They'll be better off not saddled with a nut."

"Cage, everybody would be crushed. Mama. Dad. Nanny. Me. All your friends from Baton Rouge and Sewanee. We already lost Nick. Everybody would be sad for years."

"Everybody dies."

"Yeah, but the idea is to go in a nap in your eighties, not when you're young and strong and so many people love you. We would carry that sadness around for years."

"The rest might. You'd get over it. That's why I asked you to come." My voice is steady. "You've understood since you were eight. I want your permission to kill myself."

Harper tries to hug me.

I push him away. "I don't see why everyone doesn't commit suicide. Life is like an all-night party with rivers of blow and naked playmates, but to get into the party you have to pass through a filthy hole, slathering yourself with excrement, and buy a ticket by prostituting yourself, and at the end of the night you have to squeeze back out through the fetid crack into nothingness."

"That doesn't sound like you, the theist of our generation. Maybe Papa *is* right." Harper looks unconvinced. "Maybe there is some sort of afterlife beyond human imagination."

"If there is, I'll be in the seventh circle stewing in a vat of boiling blood. That's what my dreams tell me." I turn slowly and reach for my notebook on the pillow and hand it to Harper.

He looks at the cover. "This is from your last depression, when you were pulling out of it."

"I was too scared to work, so Mom dropped me off at the library every day, made me spend the day there. Read the last page."

"Whoever no longer wishes to live shall state his reasons to the Senate, and after having received permission shall abandon life. If your existence is hateful to you, die; if you are overwhelmed by fate, drink the hemlock. If you are bowed with grief, abandon life. Let the unhappy man recount his misfortune, let the magistrate supply the remedy, and his wretchedness will come to an end." Harper stops and looks at me gravely. "Cage—"

"I know you don't have any hemlock. I'm not asking for your help. I just want your permission." Only death excites me now, gives me the energy to focus and speak. "The Romans thought it was an honorable way to die. A courageous choice. A way to redeem yourself."

In the chair Harper crosses his legs, runs his hand through his hair.

"You want to leave? Leave. Just give me permission."

"Let's take a walk in the garden."

"I'm too tired." I flop back on the bed.

"Cage, you're too depressed to see the light on the horizon. You have your best years in front of you. You have to be optimistic. You—"

"Stop bullshitting me, Harper. My past is a train wreck and my future's a disaster waiting to happen. Everyone'd be better off if I were—"

"Alive, well, and happy."

"Impossible. Inconceivable. Preposterous. Absurd. Go away, Harper. Go to your job, your girls, your money. Enjoy the party while it lasts."

Harper

Isabella Ballou is sipping something clear on ice at the bar, sitting up straight on a high stool. In blue jeans, low riding boots, and a sage turtleneck sweater, she looks like she came from the stables. This is a waste of time and energy. She knows what I'm holding and she's not in the market. No chance for a trade. *But he loved women* should be my epitaph if I died tomorrow. I worship women. I wake up from the doldrums, forget the underground fountain of eternal despair in the presence of a beguiling face and soft eyes. I'll touch my cheek to hers and kiss the air, both sides, a habit picked up in Europe that plays dramatically in the provinces. Sometimes it backfires, but it's a good test of temperament and besides I have nothing to lose. This is practice. I try to amp up the lumens in my eyes and smile widely like Cage at the height of his charm on Nantucket ten years ago, my age now, radiate that spark, that warmth and kindness, the light in his eyes that promised high altitudes of excitement. I call out, "Hey, Isabella."

She turns and checks me out like a cad, letting her eyes travel from mine down to my loafers and back up again. Her face hard as a hanging judge, she holds up five fingers with one hand and makes a fist with the other.

Ha, ha, I mouth, coming closer.

She seems plainer than I remember, then she smiles and it's almost like looking at a different person, a take-your-breath-away beauty. "I'll bet you held up cards in the yard of your frat house as defenseless, self-conscious girls walked to class."

"Actually, no." I laugh. It's the truth. "I felt sorry for them."

She sticks out her hand, which I grasp, bending forward for her cheek.

"What do you take me for?" she says, leaning away in her chair. "Euro-trash? You're in Memphis now, sonny." Isabella's laugh sounds almost like a boy's. Her spunky tomboyishness appeals to me. This is a girl who brooks no bullshit. I'll bet she is a wildcat in the sack. "I got a bunch of girls to rate the boys. The guys were primitive. Hostile. Couldn't handle it as well as the girls." She takes a slug and swirls the drink around in her glass.

"Where'd you go to school?" I ask, trying to catch the bartender's eye.

"UVA." She sets down her drink.

"Must have gotten a lot of bad sunburns," I say as she looks down the bar and raises her hand.

She sort of laughs and yells, "Tater!"

"No, I'm impressed. Virginia's hard to get into, especially out of state."

"Aren't you beyond all that?" She holds my eyes for a second, then says to Tater, a shaggy-haired kid who looks thrilled to be talking to her, "The usual. And this homely specimen will have a . . ."

"Stoli on the rocks." Normally I would order grapefruit juice, too, but it sounds weak in front of Isabella.

"So you're wondering why I came?" she says.

"To humiliate me?" I ask, climbing into the stool beside her.

"You can take it." She laughs dismissively.

"To fill me with impossible longing?" A festive mood radiates from her, and after three dry days I'm thirsty, and though I know this will end abruptly in a half hour, I'm able to exist completely in the moment as long as she's next to me at this bar. Then I'll drive back to Chickasaw Gardens, a forties fantasy of mixed-breed architectural styles under a canopy of old oaks and magnolias, to my parents' white-brick colonial where I'll try to sound upbeat through a quick, gloomy dinner before Dad and I go to bed early while Mom lingers late with a pile of magazines in front of the TV only to be up at five-thirty to share fifteen minutes over coffee, cornflakes, and bananas, before I catch the 7:05 Northwest flight three hours northeast to La Guardia to resume my pointless debauched lifestyle. I take the drink as soon as Tater sets it on the shiny redwood, knock back a mouthful, try to not let my lips twist at the first bite of the vodka.

"You're the last man I want to lead on." Isabella smiles conspiratorially, like both our private selves know that I really want to sleep with her but our public selves won't mention it.

"You're the prettiest girl I ever met on a plane."

"You're too smooth." Isabella raises her glass. "To Peter Pans."

"And to the girls who keep their dreams alive." We knock glasses and she takes a tiny sip.

"How's your brother?" she asks quietly.

I swallow about half my drink in one controlled gulp.

"I'm sorry." She touches my sleeve, squeezes my forearm, and pulls her hand away quickly with less intimacy than we shared through the turbulent afternoon three days ago. "I mean, I know it's a situation that no one else can appreciate. I don't believe you can really put yourself in someone else's shoes as much as you try, but I know it must have been horrible. And I hope Cage gets better."

"Thanks. It's tough seeing him, and if it's tough just to see, imagine what it's like to *be* him. Like you said, you can't. He, like, set out a Socratic argument on why he should kill himself." I finish off my drink, wave the empty glass at Tater. "It was hard to refute. At one point I wanted to say, Just go on and do it! Not really, but it's so frustrating trying to break through, to get him to conceive that he could be happy again."

"The world is scary." Isabella runs her hand through her shock of red hair. "The world is so fucked up sometimes you think the correct response is psychosis."

"Like the sane people are crazy and the crazy sane?"

"Yeah." Isabella shifts in her chair and starts to sit like a cowboy, with her legs open and her boot heels chocked on the low rung of the chair. "It takes a certain amount of self-delusion to get up every day and smile."

"Exactly," I say. "And in the bottomless pit of depression, even with his mind reeling from antipsychotics and his own paranoia, Cage can be incredibly lucid."

Tater delivers another drink, nods confidently at me, and grins at Isabella, who smiles at him for a second, then swings her gaze on me.

"So." I take a sip. "If you can't muster the mind-set that lets you ignore that one in three of us is going to get cancer, that most everyone you know is going to die painfully—that is, if we don't all barbecue under the greenhouse or get nuked or—"

"Shot in high school by an angry fourteen-year-old," Isabella throws in.

I roll a piece of ice around my mouth. "And if you can't ignore the millions starving while you climb into your two-ton SUV to head off to work as a small cog of the big juggernaut, if you see the world clearly in all its horror—"

"And if your own life is a mess, then . . ." Isabella raises her eyebrows. "Well, what does he do now? How does he get his smile back, that self-delusion that lets you whistle while you work?"

"I don't know how Cage gets his smile back. It just sort of happens. Eventually he goes back out in the world and one day he's Mr. Happy." The vodka is warming the back of my head. I feel good for the first time in days. Of course I feel bad about Cage but this has been going on for so long. "Then, a year later, if he doesn't keep a close watch on the covert chemical war in his brain, if he doesn't send in enough replacements at the right time for the lithium troops fighting the rising tide of manic barbarians, he'll turn into Mr. Happy on a runaway freight train and eventually, in a futile attempt to keep the train from derailing, he'll become Mr. Hyde."

"I've been thinking about him." Isabella rests her hand on my sleeve. "I remember seeing him and your mom singing in church. They both had good voices. Your mother can really belt out a hymn." She laughs. "Your mother is so nice."

"She's sweet. She puts on that perfect southern belle graciousness at church or the flower festival, but at home . . . her stress level is linked to Cage's well-being. When he's manic, she's jumpy and stressed-out; when he's depressed, so is she."

"But you wouldn't know it if you ran into her on the street. That's the perfect southern lady."

I look down at her hand on my sleeve. "Why did you come?"

"Isn't it obvious? You're a nice guy. Your brother's having a hard time."

"Is that all?" I say, emboldened by the vodka.

"That's not enough?" She crosses her legs.

"Plenty, but I . . . I don't know."

"Come on." She shoves my shoulder with one hand.

"There's something really special about you. A wild streak. And a very kind intelligence." I pause, thinking how vodka makes it much easier to say these things. "And you're beautiful."

"*Pshaw!*" Isabella shoves my shoulder again. "The things you Peter Pans will say."

"I'm serious."

"Well, that's sweet of you. But you know I've got a boyfriend."

"Do you love him?"

"Yes." Her eyes register uncertainty or annoyance, something hard to read.

"Will you tell him that you had drinks with me?"

"Of course. Why would he care? Maybe you came here tonight with ulterior motives but I didn't. Not everyone's got a one-track mind. Most guys do, it's true. And just because you're secretive." She mimics me, " 'Will you tell him?' I told him about meeting you on the plane, about Cage."

"You're just a good Episcopalian."

Isabella laughs. "And you're a bad one."

I nod. "Do you want another?"

"No thanks. I've got to meet some girlfriends." She waves at Tater, then draws a check sign in the air.

"Well, thanks for coming. I had fun." I drain the rest of the vodka from the ice. "I needed a drink."

Isabella laughs. "Or three."

I put a couple of twenties on the bar and stand up.

"You always a big tipper?" Isabella slides off her chair.

"Ever since I could afford it. I was a really bad waiter in a restaurant on Nantucket about ten years ago. It taught me respect for the foot soldiers of the food service industry."

Isabella laughs.

"Thanks a lot," Tater says to our backs as we start for the door.

I raise a fist over my head and walk on without turning around and realize I'm already drunk. Outside, we pause. "Where are you parked?"

She tilts her head over her right shoulder and says, "Behind Midtown Yoga. You?"

"Right there." I nod at the Avis Firebird on the street. "Thanks for coming. Good luck. Maybe I'll see you in Memphis the next time I'm in town."

Laughing, Isabella raises her hand. "Yeah. We can go hear your father preach."

Her grip is strong. I lean in and kiss her cheek on one side, American style.

"I'll pray for Cage."

"Thanks."

"And that you'll become an honest man."

"I'm honest."

Isabella smiles skeptically and nods. She pulls her hand free. "Bye."

"Bye."

Margaret

At one end of the Virginia-walnut Georgian table that's seen the last hundred Thanksgivings at Cage's Bend, Frank blesses the dinner, then while we are still holding hands, at the opposite end Mother says, "Let's go around the table and each of us name something that we are particularly thankful for this year."

"That's a wonderful idea." I smile at Mother, then look at Cage staring into space with his forehead pinched. I am thankful that he did not shoot himself. Harper sighs and lets go of my hand. For a long time he has been uncomfortable with public affection. "Mother, why don't you start?"

"Yeah, Nanny, you're the matriarch," Harper says, and takes a big swallow of wine.

"Well, there are so many people who don't have anything." Mother's voice always reminds me of a down duvet. "Three thousand homeless on the streets of Nashville. So many people who are down at the missions, people with jobs who can't afford a place to live. We should be thankful for our homes and a family that loves us."

"You couldn't have phrased it more eloquently, Mary Lee," Franklin says, "or more to the point. People forget too quickly how much they have. And forget those who don't have anything."

"Most of the homeless are mentally ill." Cage speaks very slowly, looking at everyone in turn. "I am thankful that you all brought me back here, that I have someplace to go. It's kinda surreal being here."

"This will always be your home," Mother says.

"You have a family that loves you, Cage." I squeeze his hand. "I'm grateful to have you all in my life, a mother over ninety who can still cook a delicious holiday meal, a husband who has cherished me for forty-one years, two handsome, bright sons who have made me proud. And Nick, whose spirit is with us."

Harper clears his throat loudly and pours more wine in his glass.

Franklin says, "Harper, is there a particular motive behind your disruption?"

"No, sir," Harper says with a sardonic smile.

"He's just hungover. Irritable." Cage's voice is hollow. "New York is a party town."

Smiling like a naughty child, Harper shrugs his shoulders and eyebrows.

"This year," Frank says, "I give thanks to God that he delivered Cage safely home to us through his perilous journey and pray every day that Cage will get stronger and stronger."

Cage smiles sweetly at his father and for a second love eclipses the pain in his eyes, then he says, "So do I. Back to being the designated patient, the focus of everyone's anxiety."

"Hapuh?" Mother asks from the end of the table. "We haven't heard from you."

"I'm thankful for the women in the family." Harper raises his fork and is about to stab a slice of turkey when Mother says, "That's very gracious, Hapuh, might you kindly tell us why?"

"I love women," Harper says. "And our family has beautiful, sensitive, caring, strong women. To my mind the women in our family tower over the men. In fact, in society as a whole, women tower over men. Wars, crime, everything that's wrong with the world is mostly men's fault."

Mother, Franklin, and I laugh. Cage is staring again into space, probably taking the blame for all the men. I say, "Well, your father—"

"Dad's great. He rarely lost his temper with us. He was always ready to listen," Harper says. "But he was an industrial dad like all the rest of them. He wasn't around all that much. It's a societal thing, not particular to him."

"Your father is a wonderful man," Mother says. "Why—"

"He never taught any of us how to throw a baseball, how to bat. By the time I arrived, when he wasn't working, he was in his office studying for his doctorate," Harper says matter-of-factly. "He—"

"His father was *never* around." Cage looks at Harper with haunted eyes. "Dad took us backpacking every chance he got. He gave us the mountains."

Frank listens calmly, his face neutral like he's counseling a couple. Mother stares at Harper and says, "Your father worked hard and provided—"

"I'm not complaining, Nanny. You asked and I want to toast the women in our clan." Harper raises his wineglass.

"To the Cage women." Frank laughs. "God bless them."

Cage is the last to lift his glass. With his voice wavering he says, "The paradigm, Nanny, is your grandmother. I thought about her in—when things were tough. I thought about her being eighteen, alone on their farm at the end of the war. Her own mother dead, her father still gone, no one left but her." Cage's voice becomes steadier. "I imagined her waking at first light to see Yankee soldiers rounding up the cattle and tying the mules together and her running out into the field and calling her mare and climbing up on it bareback and refusing to come down, sitting straight and tall all day long while the soldiers ransacked the house, just sitting there until the soldiers moved on. She must have been something."

"Why she wasn't shot or raped is a mystery," Mother says. "She was a little slip of a girl."

"Her slaves had run off?" Harper asks. "That's why she was alone?"

"They didn't have slaves," Mother says. "Not in the mountains of East Tennessee. They were too poor."

"She passed on the expression 'to take hold,'" I say. "I remember my grandmother—her daughter—telling me. When times were rough, you just have to take hold."

"She never let go, once she took hold," Cage says.

But how do you take hold of your son's illness? A boy with such promise, now a man who can't bring himself to walk to the front gate. I see the sadness in Frank's eyes and know that he is thinking the same thing. What do we do now? Why has God wasted such a bright mind? When and how will it end? If we cannot somehow provide for him after we die, will he end up an old crazy man on the streets? Harper wouldn't necessarily take care of him, not if Cage repeatedly stole from him in his manic episodes and wrecked everything he touched. Harper might be forced to cut him off. Tough love. Looking at Cage now, it is impossible to conceive that he could lie, manipulate, and steal. Just as impossible to imagine that he could hold down a job and manage independence.

"To Great-Great-Grandmother Madeline." Harper raises his glass. "And all her female descendants."

Frank reaches over and taps his glass against mine, saying, "And to Mars, who carries those tenacious genes." He leans back and smiles. "She's the power behind the throne. Only the secret is out. In half the churches in the diocese they don't even call me the bishop anymore. They refer to me as the husband of the bishop's wife."

Mother and Frank laugh genuinely as Cage looks on like a smiling ghost and Harper has an amused, slightly superior look. When he smiles now, Frank's eyes are simply slits, little crescents. Frank turns the glass in his hand by the stem and takes a sip.

Harper says, "The ultimate in henpecked."

Laughing, Frank almost coughs up wine, then clears his throat. "That's your mother. Domineering. Controlling."

"I am not!" I protest, my eyes wide in disbelief. It's true that when the boys were young and misbehaved, I always won the arguments over what was just punishment. I put my foot down because Frank, taking a self-serving position, always wanted to let them off too easy. Of course our biggest quarrels were over money. Frank always insisted that we tithe, even when it was so hard just to pay bills. That's one contention I never won. It infuriated me that he would not ask the vestries for bigger raises, that I had to run the household finances like a draconian efficiency expert. But that's all long ago.

"They call Margaret the bishop's wife because she's so active," Mother says. "You boys ought to admire her. She's a wonderful woman. She works so hard."

"We know that, Nanny," Cage says.

"Nanny, I admire you both." Harper smiles. "I just toasted you."

"After we moved to Memphis I became more involved in the church as a way of helping Frank," I say. "Perhaps at first it was to fill up the hole from Nick's death."

Mother looks at me with a sad, sweet smile, then says, "Well, the food's getting cold."

"It looks delicious, Mary Lee," Frank says. "I don't know how you do it."

I lean over and give Frank a kiss, thinking how neither of us has raised a voice in anger at the other for years, how we've grown with each other. If I could assemble anyone who ever lived around this big table, it would be Carl Jung, Louisa May Alcott, C. S. Lewis, Emily Dickinson, who'd be too shy to come, Walker Percy, and Franklin Rutledge. I wouldn't get to say a word! I whisper to Frank, "I'm most thankful for you."

Harper

In the back of a cab from the Village to Chelsea I wait for Betsy to complain about why I canceled the trip to Cozumel on the weekend. I'll apologize fifty times, remind her that I'm eating the tickets and hotel, suggest that she take someone else. Maybe I should tell her that I've gone off sex, that I think I've had sex with too many women. Dooner told me today, "You're always down on yourself when you're getting too much pussy." As the taxi slows to the curb outside Bungalow Eight, I see about twenty people waiting in the cold and tell Betsy, "Forget it. I'm not standing around freezing my ass to be blackballed by those punks corrupted absolutely by their tiny bit of power."

"Gripe, complain, whine." Betsy climbs out onto the sidewalk. "Like Oscar the Grouch. Once upon a time you were a lot of fun."

"Reminds me of the velvet ropes they sometimes use for altar railings." I pay the driver. "We come humbly beseeching to enter the kingdom of your bar."

"Ronnie!" Betsy yells, pushing through the crowd and dragging me by the arm.

"Betsy, darling!" the smaller of the two doormen squeals, unhooking the rope. "You look divine. Love the shoes."

"Ronnie, this is my ex-boyfriend, Harper."

I give her a quizzical look.

Clutching a clipboard to his chest, Ronnie winks at me. "Pass him my way." He turns to the big Latino bouncer in a long leather jacket and says, "Elisabeth Sloan is royalty. Don't you ever forget."

The muscleman nods seriously and opens the heavy metal door.

"See you, sweetie." Betsy kisses Ronnie, then tugs me. "Come on, grumpy."

A bass beat pulsates through a dark corridor. I push open the next door into a dim pond of noise, hip-hop and the roar of young New Yorkers making themselves heard over the music. What's Isabella Ballou doing right now? Thursday night in Memphis is show-and-tell at Incognito, a black gay bar, where she is occasionally one of the few white clientele watching big black men impersonate Tina Turner and Diana Ross. A heroin-thin hostess comes up and talks to Betsy, touching her lightly on the shoulder. Betsy turns back to me and shouts something about a table upstairs. I smile and nod. The girl then leads us away from the stairs to two seats at the bar, says something to Betsy, and walks off.

"Two greyhounds," I shout at the bartender, then to Betsy, "Perfect place for quiet conversation."

"What?" Betsy raises her eyebrows, then she smiles and yells, "Maybe this was a bad idea." When the bartender delivers the drinks, Betsy throws down a hundred before I can reach my wallet, then she holds up two fingers. The barman smiles and turns away and Betsy shouts, "Immediate resupply!"

Drinking with Betsy is very much like drinking with a guy, only she drinks faster and holds her liquor better than most traders I know. After knocking back half the first drink I decide that it's not so bad to be in a noisy club with my buxom friend. I rub her neck and put my lips to her ear. "You are a great American. And a beautiful woman."

"I want to explain something to you," Betsy shouts.

Here it comes. Cupping my hand to my ear, I lean toward her face.

"I feel like when we first got together. It was exciting. But something has happened between us. You're ambivalent about seeing me. It breaks my heart—I've had more fun with you. I feel so comfortable around you." Betsy drains her first drink, sets it down.

Shaking my head slightly, I'm confused. Did she think we were in a monogamous relationship? I had assumed that she was fucking other guys on occasion, but was I leading her on, letting her think that we were a unit?

When I don't say anything, Betsy takes a sip from a full glass. "I can't make all the effort. I want to be courted. What woman doesn't? There are so many men out there and I don't want to be with one who makes me feel bad about myself."

"I make you feel bad about yourself?"

"*Duh.* You can't even tell." Betsy narrows her eyes. "Is that all you can say?"

"Do you have any blow?"

Betsy's eyes widen into an insane glare.

"I was just joking, Bat Girl." I put my arm around her shoulders. "I'm sorry, really. I love you. I think you're great. Look—"

"You don't love anyone but yourself."

"That could be true." I take a gulp from the backup grey-hound. "You're better off with one of the high rollers who're always chasing you with limos and roses. I'm a lost boy."

"Hey, Harper."

I turn and see Caitlin with a couple of girls I vaguely recognize and my stomach falls and I try to smile. The first night we met, after I got her number, lit on blow like a lightning bug, I called Cait about two a.m. and told her that it was love at first sight and I couldn't sleep until I came over and ravished her until dawn, which I did that night and many more, but lately I've been dodging her calls. "Hey, Caitlin."

"Get back early from Hong Kong?" she shouts.

Betsy is craning around me with a who-the-fuck-are-you? face.

"Caitlin, may I present Betsy. Betsy, Caitlin."

"I've seen you on TV," Caitlin says.

Betsy smiles benignly.

"Is that why you wear so much makeup?" Caitlin asks.

"What?" Betsy looks fierce, the old attack forward on the champion lacrosse team ready to slam into a defender.

Caitlin ignores her. "So you never went to Hong Kong?"

"Hong Kong?" Betsy shouts.

"So you were just blowing me off." Caitlin drops her sarcastic expression, suddenly looks hurt.

I puff my cheeks like a blowfish. "No, no. I—"

The bartender shouts something at Caitlin and her friends.

Someone taps me on the shoulder and I spin around and nearly fall off the barstool at the sight of Camille, a young lawyer from Baton Rouge, a very close friend and rare lover. She's seen me evolve from Cub Scout to playboy, and when she's between boyfriends, we sometimes get roaring drunk and practice the *Kama Sutra*. As it happens, she just dumped a guy at Goldman a few days ago.

"Harper. I thought it was you, surrounded by beautiful women."

"Hey, Camille." I stand up long enough to kiss her on the cheek. "This is Betsy. And Caitlin." Betsy and Caitlin's mutual hostility is suspended for a moment by mutual suspicion of

Camille's open, disarming smile. Caitlin's friends look on impassively like animals grazing in a field.

"I've known Harper since kindergarten," Camille shouts. "He was an ancient third-grader."

"Camille had the curliest hair I'd ever seen," I yell. "I can still picture her back then."

"So you straighten your hair?" Caitlin shouts.

Camille doesn't hear or ignores her. "I used to think Harper's daddy was God. He was so handsome and so kind."

"How could God sire such a devil for a son?" Betsy asks.

Camille yells, "A difficult theological question."

"He deserves the Inquisition," Betsy shouts.

Caitlin looks like she's trying to think of something to say. She turns to grab her drink. I slap a couple of twenties down on the bar, spin back around on the chair, and ask Camille, "What are you drinking?"

"I'm at a table with some friends. You think I cruise these places by myself? See you tomorrow night. Pick me up?" She kisses me hard on my lips, then smiles at Betsy and Caitlin. "Nice meeting y'all!"

As Camille turns away, Caitlin pours a tall glass of tomato juice in my crotch and walks off. I'm too tired and ashamed to feel any anger. I say softly, "So long, Cait."

Betsy and the bartender are laughing. I ask him for a towel and he hands me a bunch of napkins. Betsy shouts, "The chicks came home to roost."

"I imagine you have a few"—I'm tempted to say cocks—"roosters out there."

Betsy forces a smirk into her anchorwoman look of deadly seriousness. "I thought we had something more."

Are you crazy or kidding? I almost ask.

Betsy suddenly looks very sad.

"I love you, Betsy." I hug her and say, hoarse from shouting, "I'm there if you need me. I'm there if you're blue. But it's not love with a capital *L*. It's not the union of souls, caring more about the other than yourself. We're just two people who are very

fond of each other, who both love sex. That's why we're so comfortable together. That's it."

Betsy pulls loose and looks at me with tears in her eyes, then
glances away. The bartender sets two more greyhounds on the
counter and says they're on him. Betsy picks hers up and turns
the glass in her hand. I drape my arm around her shoulder and
she shrugs it off. I tell her, "My mama used to say, 'All good games
end in tears.' "

Cage

The ceiling is white, blank, big as a cinema screen waiting for
light to throw images upon it in a pantomime of life. Lying on my
back in the middle of the old king-size bed where my mother was
born, I can almost project the picture of Nanny, half my age,
bringing her into the world, or fast-forward some twenty years to
the scene of Mama arriving here from the hospital in Thebes
with me, a child who smiled long before most, as if my happiness
which began prematurely would spend itself prematurely and
plunge the family into more sadness than anyone had ever
dreamed, bearing the legacy of violence which the Cages brought
to Tennessee, a curse of blood which would reach forward
through time and seven generations to haunt the innocent soul of
the firstborn and the last to carry the family name. Will the curse
die with me, die with the name? I will not procreate, not I, a half
man, hobbled back from the West to hide in the home of an old
woman, nor will Harper, a serial lover whose mildly unhappy
childhood left him with no desire to perpetuate the absence of the
fathers. Is it evolution taking its course, the weeding out of bad
genes? Was I simply hastening the natural process when I loaded

the shotgun next door in Granddad's study? The screen of the ceiling replays the scene—the twin black caves of the barrels enclosed by my trembling hand—the end of one act in a lifelong play of flops, theater of the absurd, for even then I failed to achieve the goal.

"Cage!" Nanny sounds like some rare tropical bird. "Coffee's on!"

"Coming!" I pull on yesterday's khakis and plaid wool shirt, then go into the bathroom. "Hello, Mr. Bipolar. How are you today?" the face in the mirror says. "Got any big plans? Going to the office? Just going to cower and skulk?" I don't answer. I brush my teeth, throw some water on my face, and walk down the wide staircase, then pass through the dining room into the thin winter light spilling through the kitchen windows.

Nanny, small and pear-shaped in a blue winter jogging suit, is breaking eggs on the side of a big iron skillet. Nanny's lived through the First World War, the Great Depression, the Second World War, the cold war, an alcoholic husband, the deaths of her grandparents, parents, husband, one grandchild, and nearly all her contemporaries, and now, a ninety-something in the new world order, she is as peaceful and content as any Buddhist monk. She believes in Jesus, forgiveness. She is not afraid to die. Appalled by the relentless cascade of violence and crime on the news, she mourns the days when you never locked the doors, has no illusions about the human capacity for weakness, addiction, excess, pure incomprehensible evil, and she always sounds like a sweet, cheerful child. Turning at my footsteps, she smiles and says, "Good morning. It's a beautiful day. They predicted rain but I don't think it's going to rain."

"Morning, Nanny." I come into the circle of brighter light around the stove. "Let me do that."

"No, no, I'm almost finished." Her hands, gnarled like old roots, stir the skillet rapidly with a spatula that I seem to remember from my childhood. "Pour us some juice, please."

In the breakfast room, set through double lattice doors off the kitchen in the back corner of the house, filling the juice glasses from a carton of Tropicana, I see a crow fly through the mist and land on a bare branch close to the window. Nanny glides to the table in slow motion with her slippers never leaving the floor, carrying the skillet. She peers through a dead stranger's transplanted corneas out the window at the crow and says, "Good morning, Sam."

Caw, caw, caw, Sam calls.

"Here, Nanny," I say, taking the skillet.

"Thank you, son." Nanny sits down by her bowl of Grape-Nuts and a slice of grapefruit.

"Granddad would have liked Sam." I carry the skillet back to the sink. "I remember how he put suet out for the woodpeckers."

"Morgan loved wildlife. One cold fall Sunday he found a little hummingbird just lying on the back steps, alive but half frozen. I went off to church and he took it up to your room, where the sun was streaming in through the windows, and revived it with a mixture of sugar water and whiskey from an eyedropper. When I got back, it was flying around in the bright light. The day had warmed up and Morgan opened the window and out it flew. We hoped that it would catch up with its kin migrating south. Morgan was a kind, gentle man."

Women always forget what they don't want to remember, and remember what they don't want to forget. In the end the dream is the truth. I wonder, "Did you have many suitors?"

She seems to stare over my shoulder back into time. "Oh, yes, I had many beaus."

"Why'd you pick Granddaddy?"

"I liked him the best."

"When did Granddad resurrect the hummingbird?"

"Oh, it was long after the girls were gone." Nanny brings her gaze to my face and smiles. "Probably in the sixties. You know, Cage, time means so little to me anymore. Time flies by so fast now. I'm so lucky. Most old people sit around with nothing to do. I don't have time to catch my breath. There is always a chore around the house or at my desk. It seems like Christmas was yesterday and tomorrow will be Easter."

After breakfast, as I am scraping the bits of egg and toast on top of last night's collard greens and chicken bones into a plastic bucket, Nanny asks with a slightly tentative note in her cheerful voice, "Do you want to feed Sam this morning?"

I laugh loudly at my pitiful condition. "You mean since yesterday was the first time in three months I was able to make it all the way out the door and down the steps and across the yard?"

"It's good to hear you laugh again. I missed that sound. You had the most wonderful laugh as a little boy. You were the most merry little elf, more than all my grandsons." Nanny sets her hands on the table and slowly pushes herself up.

I set the plates in the sink and pick up the bucket. "Wish me luck."

"I'll come as far as the back steps." Nanny takes down Nick's old Kappa Sig windbreaker off the hook by the door to the back porch. "I want to see the February gold." I slide the two chains off the heavy wooden door, then unlock the glass storm door and hold it open for Nanny to step into the shadows of the back porch, where the screen walls are shuttered for the winter.

"Oh, how beautiful, how gorgeous, my, my." Nanny shades her eyes with one hand, looking at the golden field of daffodils stretching back a hundred yards toward the wide black lake and then the gray wooded hills at the bottom of the blue sky. "Like a golden cashmere blanket. You know they've been here forever. I think as long as the Cages. I planted some in the thirties, but they were here long before."

I smile and walk through the yard. Coming around the corner of the house, the crow sees me and dives off its perch, calling, *Caw, caw, caw!* It lands on a sycamore, screams and flies again, circles me twice, and touches down on the top of a cedar that resembles a tall green flame. At the edge of the lawn the strands of old barbed wire are barely visible, running through young cedars and dogwood along the property line. Screaming, the crow dive-bombs within an inch of my hand on the bucket handle. I pour the scraps at the bottom of a fence post, where a few bones remain from yesterday. Hidden by the wall of bristly cedars, something bounds through the woods, crashing through the thick bush. Startled, I clench the bucket and restrain the urge to run. Breathe in. Breathe out the paranoia. It's just deer. Shivering in the cold, I jog across the yard, back up the steps, and into the house.

"Did you chain the door?" Nanny asks from her heavy electric reclining chair by a big, ugly gas heater set in the fireplace of her sitting room.

"Yes, ma'am, but even if I hadn't, I think we're pretty safe at dawn way out here in the country."

"Cage, there have been *invasions*. Not a mile away, some young men just burst into a home and robbed the family on a Sunday morning," Nanny says urgently as if to a stubborn child. "With so many people on drugs these days, nowhere is safe. *You must always lock the doors.*"

"Yes, ma'am."

Nanny nods and looks back at CNN, where Senator John McCain says, "Remember all the establishment is against us. This is an insurgency campaign. I'm just like Luke Skywalker trying to get out of the Death Star. They're all coming at me from everywhere."

"Nanny, would you like for me to drive you into town?"

She smiles and her eyes light up as if she's just witnessed a miracle. "Why, Cage. What a wonderful surprise."

"Yeah. I feel like Forrest Gump today," I say. "Brave enough to face Wal-Mart." Every citizen of Thebes, every pedestrian, every shopper and uniformed employee, will be watching me, judging me, aware of what a freak I am, but I will breathe through the terror, dispel the delusions like bad breath, and walk on down the aisle.

Nanny laughs delightedly as the recliner back rises with an electric whir. "Oh boy, I won't have to wait till Thursday to pick up a new humidifier."

Harper

I wake up around five about to wet my bed from the gallon of water that I drank to dilute the coming hangover. There is a dream vivid in my head. My great-grandmother Madora was behind the wheel of a Mercedes convertible. I was overjoyed to see her because she's been dead for so many years. I jumped in and hugged her, saying, I'm so happy to see you. And I started crying. I noticed in her handbag a book that said *Hannibal* on the spine, saw it twice, once up close, like a camera zoom.

She said, You can't know someone in death.

No? I asked.

She shook her head and said, But I'll be your little friend.

I got the sense that she would always be there to comfort me. In the backseat was my grandfather Rutledge, stooped over, like when he was dying of cancer, but with black hair that I'd only seen in old photographs. When I leaned over the seat, he sat up straight and said, I'm growing now. Madora waved as they drove off, leaving me in a Baton Rouge bar called South Downs, where the dream turned suddenly to black-and-white. The bar was full of high school friends, and Nick's friend Rowan Patrick was there with President Clinton. I joined a greeting line and spoke to Clinton in the flash of many cameras. Caitlin and Betsy and five other girls I slept with surrounded me in plastic raincoats and I knew they were vampires and I left and was suddenly back in Technicolor in my father's two-story paneled office and I went to his desk and saw two signed and rubber-stamped letters. I picked up an embossed stamp and impressed the letters, feeling I was doing something wrong, then I walked out a big arched window onto the balcony with the view of the Mississippi and the two humps of the bridge outlined in twinkling lights and Isabella Ballou was there in a fifties Sunday dress. She looked up at me and smiled and said, I thought you would never come.

The lights of the bridge changed into the lights of all the cities of earth far below. Isabella and I were in a gigantic Concorde, which I understood to be a sort of staging area for death. We had just died. The flight attendants wore futuristic plastic uniforms and little caps like the ones in Kubrick's *2001*. I asked one, So there is no consciousness after death? That's right, she said pleasantly, adjusting my seat belt. But you have nothing to fear.

An old man originally from Atlanta who went to seminary at Sewanee before studying Jungian analysis in Switzerland, Dr. Pearce has a kind, bearded face and a fondness for western string ties. He never takes his eyes off me as I read my dreams from my Palm. This is my favorite hour of the week. It's better than the grind of work and the mindless pursuit of excitement in nightclubs and always feels somehow cleansing. It is my confession. Dr. Pearce pulls the unlit pipe out of his mouth and asks, "So what do you make of it?"

"I woke up almost as if I was supposed to remember this one." I yawn and stretch out on the leather easy chair. "Madora, my great-grandmother, was this very dignified, upright figure, so it's interesting that she was driving the car. And Grandfather Rutledge was the opposite. He was handsome and charming and a philanderer who abandoned his family in the Depression. I think my father became a priest as a reaction to his father's behavior. I think old Grandpa Rutledge is my shadow. He said he's growing, which is sort of alarming. Then Clinton is clearly another image of my shadow—a celebrity sex addict."

"Like your recurring Elvis impersonator."

"Yep. And all the pretty girls—vampires, sirens calling out to seduce me, who would drink my blood and trap me in the night world. Then I'm not sure about my father's office—the rubber stamp and the embossed stamp." I pause, picturing the stamps, struggling for associations.

"Are you carrying on the work of your father?" Dr. Pearce suggests. "Are you seeking his authentic approval, not simply his rubber-stamped approval?"

"Definitely only his rubber-stamped approval—his approval of my income," I say. "He would be disgusted, literally nauseated, if he knew what a sexual glutton I am."

"Whom do you think your great-grandmother represents, assuming that she is symbolic of a component of your psyche? She drives up in an expensive sports car to 'comfort' you?"

"Anima? My undeveloped femininity?"

"*Great*-grandmother," Dr. Pearce says slowly. "The *great* mother. And Hannibal? The dream zoomed in on that word."

"Hannibal the Cannibal, the serial killer who eats his victims," I say quickly.

"The Great Mother, your little friend, will eat you alive." Dr. Pearce looks hard at me, waiting several seconds for me to say something, goes on, "Then, passing through your father's workplace, you are delivered to the lovely, chaste Miss Ballou and a peaceful vision of the night." Dr. Pearce rises, heading with his empty cup for the espresso machine.

"As if by following my father's ethical code I will attain a girl that I can love and a sense of peace?"

Dr. Pearce turns back to me and nods almost imperceptibly.

"My unconscious is giving me moral advice?"

"In so many words."

"But then we die. Twice I asked people—"

"Women, you asked women."

"—if there is some form of life after death. Do you think my unconscious is telling me that there is not?"

"No, I think these are just expressions of your fear of death. Perhaps the death in the dream is a symbolic death." The steamed coffee hisses through the tube into his cup. Dr. Pearce clears his throat. "The death of your old self, the death of your shadow, that you will have to survive if you are going to change your life."

"You can kill off your shadow?"

Dr. Pearce laughs gently. "Most guys and gals never change. Some do through serious psychotherapeutic experience or near-death experience. Is this part of your psyche going to die and go away? No. You're going to have to live with the son of a bitch for the rest of your life. The Elvis impersonator is pretty well entrenched and it's going to take a while to be sure that he doesn't get out. It's going to be a slow, hard-fought battle."

Suddenly I twig Madora's words, *You can't know someone in death.* You can't know someone while you're a creature of the night.

Cage

The early shrubs flower in March. The snow-on-the-mountain bushes pile up against the house like high drifts left after a winter storm. Around the columns supporting the porte cochere roof over the drive are yellow forsythia and white lilies. Along the five-foot-high stone foundation of the front porch are pink and blue hyacinths. At the edge of the front lawn, a shaggy row of burning bush—reddish pink and orange japonica—flickers in the wind like a wall of fire. Beyond, on the field of tall grass that rolls a quarter mile to the road, the tall oaks and elms are bare skeletons, and under their lowest branches dogwoods and redbuds tremble white and red. In the clear sky a V-shaped line of geese heads north. The murmur of a ceaseless stream of cars swooshing along the road reaches the front porch. Cage's Bend is my Walden Pond. Thoreau's cabin was only a stone's throw from Concord and my little sanctuary is hemmed in by Nashville sprawl.

There's a low diesel rumble from the gate, hidden behind a stand of cedars, and a minute later a tractor comes slowly up the drive. I go down the steps and along the walk to the flaming row of burning bush, nervous about meeting John Henry Clay, who is from a long line of farmers, the owner of the last big farm on the road, though he's retired now and only keeps some cattle while his descendants wait for him to die so they can sell the property for millions. I used to duck-hunt on his ponds when I was twelve, thirteen. I haven't seen him in years but he must have heard that I'm a nut. The old man's weathered face looks severe as he rolls to a stop at the end of the walk. Nanny comes out on the porch and waves just as he cuts the throttle down to idle.

"Morning, Mr. Clay," I say. "Thanks for coming."

"Morning there, Cage." He climbs down and takes off his faded Ford cap and waves it by the bill. "Morning, Mary Lee."

"Good morning, John Henry," Nanny calls from the porch. "Isn't it a beautiful day? So much rain over the winter, bound to be a beautiful spring."

"Yes, ma'am," John Henry yells. "Everything is going to blossom like wildfire."

"I can't wait!" Nanny calls with delight.

John Henry laughs and says, "She sure is a sweet lady, your granny."

"Yes, sir." Looking at my feet, I wonder if he knows that years ago I got her to sell ten grand in stock, a huge hit for her, to keep Korean loan sharks in Nashville from killing me. I look back at John Henry's craggy face. "Yes, sir, she sure is."

"You go on in, Mary Lee. It's too cold for a ninety-year-old lady to be standing politely on the porch."

Nanny laughs. "What about an eighty-three-year-old man out driving a tractor in this wind?"

"Cage is going to till his own field. I'll be in directly for coffee."

Nanny waves and goes inside and immediately locks the winter storm door.

"So, son, you going to try your hand at farming?"

"More of a garden, really." I look past him at Nanny now locking the glass French doors. "I worked on some organic farms out in California."

"I hear out West they're crazy about *organic farming.*" He stretches out the term sarcastically. "Hell, all it is is going back to the forties before we had good fertilizer and pesticides. I don't know why they got such a fancy name. Might as well just call it primitive."

"How 'bout *natural*?" I force my eyes to stay on his face.

"Cage, son, you can call it whatever you want. It's going to be you toting buckets of cow shit around, not me." John Henry laughs and claps me on the shoulder.

I try to smile. "I've got it staked out behind the house, down near the lake."

"Then let's get at it." John Henry climbs back on the tractor.

At a slow jog I lead him past the house, past the ruins of the formal garden of tall hedges and a dry wishing pool, past the boarded cabin and the low foundation stones of three others to a flat stretch of crabgrass before the land slopes another hundred yards to the lake.

"Reckon you got about an acre and a half," John Henry says from the tractor seat. "This is where the Cages always kept their kitchen garden."

"When I was a little boy."

John Henry nods. "Started long before that. About the time they built the new house, I imagine. The turn of the last century."

"They were organic farmers."

John Henry laughs and climbs down from the tractor, with the engine still idling. "Cage, you ever driven a tractor?"

"Yes, sir, in the summers at Rugby when I was a teenager."

"That's a mighty pretty place up there on the plateau," John Henry says, squinting, then he smiles. "Well, I'm happy to let you borry it. I ain't got much use for it anymore. Hardly use it at all."

"Yes, sir."

"Climb on up. You got your work cut out if you want to have it planted out by Easter."

The old metal seat is worn silver except at the rust-brown edges. I sit astride the thrumming transmission and go through the pedals and handles and John Henry nods and says, "You still know your way around. Bring it back when you're finished."

"How are you getting home, Mr. Clay?"

"Call me John Henry. I'll take the old path. If I'm lucky, I'll see a pileated woodpecker." He turns abruptly and walks toward the back porch.

I lower the disks behind the tractor and commence to till the old garden for the first time in thirty years, ripping out the grass along the boundary between the stakes with the satisfying feeling of immediately seeing the results of the work, of finally being back at work after so many months. A few cedar waxwings dart over the field. Sam flies over and sits on a bare oak branch, watching from a distance. A plane circles over the lake, passing almost directly overhead. Is it looking at me? Strange synchronicity of flying objects—the waxwings, the crow, the plane, which is now coming from the lake back over Cage's Bend. Listen to the sound of your breath coming in through your nose. Exhale. Tell yourself it's just a plane. After plowing the perimeter I till the first row again, then tear up the grass in parallel rows, laying out the garden in my head, the seedbeds for corn, beans, peas, cabbage, carrots, potatoes, tomatoes, celery, garlic, eggplant, and even asparagus, a four-year commitment. One corner will be for a variety of lettuces, another for cut flowers—statice, purple cornflower, stock, nasturtiums. On the end by the lonesome faucet sticking up out of the open field, from a kit with a hooped metal frame and plastic, I'll build a little greenhouse to start seeds. The wind drops and the sun feels warm on my face.

Sowing seeds, preparing the way for life to come, is like stepping forward in time. And then, in only a few revolutions of the world, before the oaks and elms are even showing leaves, the first shoots appear in the long straight rows raised between the furrows. My mind burrows beneath the soil like a mole, imagining the exploded seeds, the white net of little roots spreading deeper. The voice of a towhee darting over the garden is like a fine silver wire singing of the peace of wild creatures who cannot burden themselves with the forethought of grief or sins gone old unforgiven, and I see that to be at home in this world I must like a thrush travel beyond words, outside of regret and fear of the future.

*   *   *

At dawn, past tall cedars standing like guardians, I walk across the dewy grass into the rows of black mulch, careful not to break spiderwebs shimmering like sails between poles where tomato vines are starting to twine skyward. I stand looking at the first bunches of lettuce, half mature, thinking how my body will one day nourish the soil, how farmers embrace death yearly in the darkness of winter and come back with the lengthening light. My life stands in this place, rooted like the garden.

Harper

"April is the cruelest month, mixing soil with cow shit."

"What?" It hurts to open my eyes. I squint at Cage standing over me.

"Come on, get up," he says, "you overpaid Wall Street face man. You self-centered last-born narcissist. You vodka-swilling, coke-snorting, pussy-chasing sensualist."

"FYI, I haven't done any blow for a while." I clear phlegm from my throat. "Not to mention my dry workweeks."

"That's only because I call you every night to check." Cage laughs. "I still think you should go to meetings."

I don't want to go into this now. "What time is it?"

"Nanny done made breakfast and cleaned up and wrote cards to sick folks from church," Cage says in exaggerated redneck. "I done weeded the carrots and moved the drip tape from one side of the garden to the other. Now it's time for the morning run."

Swinging my feet to the floor, I think how far he's come since Christmas when he was obsessed with a doomsday Y2K scenario. Not until the world was still turning on New Year's Day would he believe that 1 January 2000 was an arbitrary, man-made date of

no cosmic significance. "I'm glad you're through the bad delusions." I give him a big bear hug. "They are just too fucking much
to deal with."

"Tell me about it." Cage breaks loose and hands me some old
sweats and trainers. "Dem ol' delusion blues."

"You on an antipsychotic?"

"Nope. Nothing but lithium." He looks slightly annoyed, points
to the desk. "Quaff that OJ. This weekend is your boot camp."

I guzzle the juice, wipe my mouth, and say, "I was thinking I
might drive down to Memphis early tomorrow morning so I can
hear Dad preach."

"You can't bamboozle a bullshitter. You been dropping down
to Memphis on weekends to catch a glimpse of that Ballou chicky.
That's the only reason."

"What if it's love?" I slide my legs into the sweats.

"I'll be surprised." Cage shakes his head. "You just want what
you can't have."

After the first mile on a path worn by his feet up and down rolling
pasture, Cage is way out ahead. My lungs wheeze painfully and
my legs feel weak as noodles. Cage turns around, running backward, yells, "John Henry Clay walks faster than you run." I'm
huffing too hard to reply. Cage smiles and spins back around on
one foot, streaks over the top of the next hill. Gardening every
day, jogging every day, grocery shopping twice a week, dropping
Nanny at church on Sundays: Simple routine and simple accom-
plishments pump Cage's spirit back to life, lightening the spirits of
four others—Nanny, Mama, Dad, and me, though Mama still
frets about his future, whether he'll be able to hold a steady
course, how he'll provide for himself when they are gone. Give
those worries to God, Mama. He'll do it, I tell her once a week.
Cresting the top of the hill, I think that families are put here to
help each other through this thing, life, whatever it is. I need him
as much as he needs me. Maybe Cage is my redeemer. Or maybe
I'm beyond redemption.

*   *   *

Old Hickory Lake. The name commemorates a mass murderer, Andrew "Old Hickory" Jackson, running buddy of Cage's namesake. I must have been nine years old the last time I was out here, skimming across the murky surface in Poppy's flat-bottomed metal fishing boat. From the front I watch the bow rushing over the brown glass and omelets of white scum, listening to the whine of the antique outboard. In the stern, his hand behind him on the throttle, Cage stares past me into the middle distance, his face twisted, perhaps absorbing the sting of a flashback, maybe an image of his birthday cruise a year ago today. In the middle of the lake, a mile from our dock, Cage cuts the engine off and the boat glides forward in the abrupt silence.

"What you thinking about?" I ask his profile.

Cage glances at me, then stares back at the lake. "Nick, gentle Nick. You and I were both kinda angry but he was a happy camper."

"Come on, Cage. It wasn't your fault. You've got to forgive yourself."

"No." Cage turns back to me. His eyes are red like he'd cried without shedding a tear. "It's not that easy. You got to keep forgiving yourself. Again and all over again."

I watch a ski boat across the lake, the rooster tail wake. "Nick was just as bad as us. How come we were so different from Mom and Dad?"

"It's only natural to rebel against your parents." Cage studies his palm. "We were just like our friends. Everybody thought that as long as you got good grades and won races, then you were entitled to party down."

"Yeah," I nod. "Our parents represent Depression Man, raised in austerity, while we are Consumer Man, spoiled by abundance. Nobody thought drugs and sex were self-destructive. It was just recreation. Consumer choices."

"After you were talking about your shadow on the phone the other day," Cage says, "I thought how we were Dad's worst nightmares made manifest."

I laugh loudly from a sharp pang of shame.

"It's like everything Dad repressed successfully," Cage goes on, "came out in us. Maybe you're not struggling with your shadow but Dad's."

"Whoa." I'm impressed. "Wonder what Dr. Pearce will say about that?"

"Theories are like assholes." Cage shrugs. "Everybody's got one."

Cage

Since before I was born, Dr. Hardeman's office has been in a red-brick Federal three-story on the square in Thebes. With a Civil War statue of Morgan's Raiders in the middle of the lawn, the square looks at first glance much as it did in the twenties, though the town hall, the post office, and the big stores moved out to suburbia in the direction of Nashville in the eighties, leaving the square behind like a postcard of a simpler time. Some of the glass fronts are boarded, some are dollar stores and cheap suit shops that cater to the blacks who've colonized the neighborhoods within walking distance. Only one of the three original banks remains, and Park's Drugs, which had a long counter where Poppy took Nick and me to listen to farmers and Rotarians talk about fishing and UT football, is now a discount pharmacy with no soda bar. When Dr. Hardeman retires or dies, the last tie to the past will be cut and few white men will venture into the old center of Thebes.

After parallel-parking the Subaru wagon Mom and Dad bought me, I walk to the glass door and hesitate. What if I'm positive? After all, I slept with a junkie in San Francisco and any number of sluts on my manic rocket rides. Should I spare my family more pain and hardship and kill myself? Wouldn't it be my luck to claw out of depression just to learn that I have a terminal illness? I open the glass door and climb up a flight of stairs to Dr. Hardeman's second-floor waiting room. There are a few black women with children and a couple of older white folks. The receptionist smiles and calls out, "Hello, Cage."

"Morning, Mrs. Leonard." I set two bags of vegetables on the counter. "Carrots and potatoes from an organic farm down in Alabama, one for you and one for the doc."

"You are too sweet," she gasps. "Why, thank you."

As I cross the room to an empty chair, the others' eyes follow me reproachfully, and I remind myself that it's not real, only chemicals in my mind.

Dr. Hardeman comes into the waiting room. "Hello there, Cage."

"Morning." I stand up, studying his craggy old face for signs of the death sentence.

"The farm must be coming along. I see you brought me some more produce." Dr. Hardeman gives me his meaty hand.

"Actually it came from—"

The old doctor clasps me by the shoulder. "The test came back fine. You got nothing to worry about."

I feel a rush of relief, the tension evaporating all at once. "Thank God."

"A young buck can't be too careful this day and age." From his perspective Dr. Hardeman sees me as someone half my age. "Now, get on out of here. I've got real patients waiting."

"What about the bill?"

"We took it out in trade." He pushes me toward the door. "Give Mary Lee my regards."

Across the back of the stall a banner reads *Naked Lunch Organics*. On the table are piles of lettuce and celery, bundles of herbs, and there are baskets of potatoes, carrots, and fennel on the ground. I wonder if I'm delusional when beautiful housewives smile at me. Harper might long for a whole life to devote to each, some particular way to make love only to her. I'd settle for just one. Now that my system has excreted the last traces of antipsychotics, my mojo has come out of long hibernation. But it's hard to believe that any women other than fellow lunatics would want to have anything to do with me. If they heard what I was up to the last decade, no one would blame them for stepping back a few feet to keep a safe distance. The family insists I was an easy, funny conversationalist but I don't remember what it was like to be me at twenty, and now whenever I meet someone new, I feel awkward and tongue-tied.

A businesswoman in a navy linen suit who looks like she ain't the type to suffer fools gladly pauses at the stall. She is in her mid- or late thirties and her black hair has a striking widow's peak and a white stripe that runs back from the center of her forehead. She has a handsome face with a long sharp nose, hazel eyes. She picks up a bundle of basil, several heads of lettuce, then looks over my shoulder at the banner and says, "I never read that, but the movie sucked."

"I read it fifteen years ago. Only thing I can remember is being grossed out."

She laughs and takes one of the recycled paper bags hanging from a nail and starts filling it from the baskets, glances up, and says, "So did you grow all this?"

"Only the lettuce. The Naked Lunch farm's way down in Alabama. Comes up on the bus. The real harvesting up here won't start till later in the season."

"What's the name of your farm?" She puts some potatoes on the scales.

"I'm still pondering that." Sliding the weights along the bar, I don't mention some that have crossed my mind—Recovery Farm, Manure Madness. "I was thinking about Oedipal Organics since it's out in Thebes."

The woman laughs and asks, "You come into Nashville every Saturday?"

"*Sí, señorita*. I'm the Naked Lunch rep now. Impressed?" I almost say, I must be the least successful of Vanderbilt's Owen School of Management, class of '88. She looks like she might have gone there. It's only a matter of time until I run into an old classmate. I'm not sure if I'll be embarrassed.

"Yeah, I am." She pulls a wallet out of her handbag. "I think there's a future in organic farming and it's socially responsible."

"Tastes better, too," I say, totaling her bill. "Seven dollars, if you please."

After she puts the change in her purse she sticks her hand out and smiles. "My name's Rachel."

"Rutledge," I say, clapping the dirt off my hands. "Cage Rutledge."

Rachel laughs and says, "See you next week, Cage."

Harper

"I can't put my finger . . ." Isabella's voice trails off and her eyes stray over my shoulder at the giant palm leaves painted on the wall. It fascinates me how different she appears from different angles or with different expressions and how people who meet her at the same time can have entirely different impressions of her. At drinks before the movie, Dooner told me that she was plain looking and Ronbeck whispered she was a stunner. The longer I know her, the more beautiful she appears. Her green eyes lock on mine as she finds her thought. "At first I thought it was a reaction against the smart-ass hit men in *Pulp Fiction*. Forest Whitaker's samurai was Jarmusch's answer to the Bible-quoting Sammy Jackson. But it fell apart in the last half hour. The comic murders made me stop caring. If anything, I wanted Whitaker to die so the thing would come to an end."

"Too many cartoons," I say. "I got tired of the cartoons."

"That was sort of heavy-handed." Isabella seems slightly less self-assured than she did the last couple of times I saw her at the cathedral.

"But I liked Travolta and Jackson. I liked *Pulp Fiction*."

"Little boys like to play with guns." Isabella laughs. "It's a guy thing."

"So what brings you to New York so suddenly? I was totally surprised when you called. It was chaos, the markets were closing, I thought you were joking. I thought you were really in Memphis."

"Did you break a date to see me?"

I pause, deciding to be honest. "Yeah, I did."

"Was she angry?" Isabella watches me closely.

"Nah, not at all. Camille said, 'Isabella Ballou, the girl of your dreams? Go. Go.' "

"Who's Camille?" Isabella smiles at the corners of her mouth.

"An old friend from Baton Rouge. Girl I've known since I was eight. A lawyer."

"Do you sleep together?" Isabella laughs slyly.

I take a long, slow sip from my drink. "I don't see how that's your business."

The waiter brings the appetizers. When he leaves, Isabella raises her eyebrows. "I'm just trying to understand you."

"Actually we've slept together off and on over a few years in New York when she's between boyfriends." I wonder if telling her this is somehow a mistake.

"A sport and a pastime." Isabella tries to name it. "How can a woman be so intimate, open herself up, when there's no emotion to go with it?"

"There's deep affection. Out of boredom, maybe. Or biological need."

"That's not enough for me." She takes a tiny sip of Scotch, then picks up a slice of seared beef with her chopsticks.

"Maybe you're just repressed by your Christianity."

"No, it's a different attitude. I can't say, 'Well, should we go to a movie or jump in the sack?' to a guy I've known since I was a kid no matter how cute he is or how much I like him. I've had casual sex. Just never felt right."

"You didn't answer my question. What are you doing all of a sudden in New York?"

"First things first. How's Cage?" Her forehead arches in concern.

"He's great. The garden's growing. He sounds cheerful whenever I call."

"That's *so good*." Isabella looks genuinely thrilled and she is as beautiful as anyone alive. "I'm so happy for him."

"He calls or e-mails every day to check on *me*, make sure that I'm keeping my new year's resolution to stay dry on work nights." I wait for her to respond but she just gives me a blank look. "So what brings you to New York out of the blue?"

Isabella takes a bite of a spring roll, looks away.

"You've been coy about it all evening."

"I . . . ," Isabella says to her plate. "I found out John was cheating on me. He's been fucking a nurse, maybe several." She looks up. "Stop smiling."

"I'm sorry. Just the idea of you single makes me happy."

"Well, try to put yourself in my shoes, Harper. Jesus." Her eyes flash like lightning on an empty plain.

I've never seen her angry before. She looks positively sexy. "Sorry. I was just expressing myself honestly. I—"

"Something new for you?"

"I know you must be in a lot of pain."

She laughs loud enough to turn heads, then whispers, "*You*. You know because you've made women feel this way. That's what *you* know. What *he* feels like."

"I've been betrayed before. I've been heartbroken."

"So you've been getting back at women ever since?" Squinting, her mouth pinched, Isabella is not pretty.

"I think she just opened a door for me," I say softly. "I'm sorry, Isabella. I'm sorry you feel like shit. I'm sorry your dreams came tumbling down." I hesitate, then suggest, "Maybe you can work it out."

"No. It's over." She looks defeated and small. "I can't trust him. He's not who he pretended to be. Men don't change."

"Maybe some can." I consider telling her how I've felt like I've been bumping my head against a wall for so long, about my dreams, how my unconscious has been urging me away from promiscuity, but I don't want to go on about me. The waiter arrives with plates of Vietnamese noodles and squid. Isabella barely sees him, smiles wearily, then leans against the table, resting her arms on the cloth. Her knuckles look like little broken spines.

"It's as painful as anything." I reach across and cup one of her fists. It's cold and limp. "Losing someone you love is like a death."

"That's what they all say." She pulls her hand away and takes her chopsticks, picks at a bowl of steamed rice, then sets the sticks across her plate. "You know, I'm suddenly very tired. I'm really sorry—"

"Then let's go." I watch her take a large drink of water.

"I'll catch a cab. You finish your dinner."

"You want me to drop you at Gramercy Park?"

"It's out of your way." She shakes her head.

"Do you want to do something tomorrow? The Met? The MoMA? The Museum of Natural History?"

"Let's go there." Isabella looks like she could cry, stammers, "I liked Dooner." Suddenly the threatening squall is gone. She laughs. "I had fun tonight, Harper." She stands up. "Thanks for dinner and the movie."

"I always love seeing you." I rise from my seat. "You're the real reason I visit my parents." I curve my arm around her waist and walk her toward the door. "My mother loves you for that."

Isabella laughs. To the hostess I say, "Be right back."

"Sure, Harper."

"She's pretty," Isabella says, going out the door. "Have you ever fucked her?"

"No." I laugh.

"But you thought about it."

"Not recently." I fight back a grin. "Look, it rained while we were in there."

A cab is coming up Lafayette, the tires sizzling on the wet pavement. I wave my hand and whistle.

"I'll call you in the morning," she says. "Thanks. You cheered me up a bit."

"I rekindled your belief in the goodness of men?"

"No, in the adorableness of some rakes." She kisses me hard
on the lips and jumps in the cab.

Isabella stares at the typical all-female family of elephants frozen
in midstep on the fake African plain, the old matriarch trailed by
daughters and grandchildren, the young males cast out in adolescence to wander alone or in temporary boys' clubs. As I explain
the social system, Isabella bites her lower lip, and her vulnerabil-
ity and defiance almost make me faint. I lose my train of thought.
Isabella glances at me, waiting for me to finish, then suddenly fo-
cuses in on my eyes as if she sees something new there. Neither of
us speaks for a moment.

"No hypocrisy in the elephant world," Isabella says.

"No secrecy. They mate right out in the open."

"No casual sex." Isabella smiles. "They only mate to procreate."

"No romantic love," I counter. "Strong blood ties but no pair
bonding."

"Like you." Isabella laughs. "How'd ya know all this?"

"I was a nut about Africa as a kid. Read all kinds of books. One
story I'll never forget. In the sixties in Uganda rangers culled a
bunch of elephants from a big herd. Back then they thought there
were too many. They put the ears and feet in a shed to be sold
later for handbags and ashtrays."

Isabella looks hurt, then turns back to the stuffed animals.

"That night a group from the herd broke into the shed and carried off all the ears and feet. They definitely have a knowledge of
death and a sense of mourning."

"Jesus," Isabella whispers, still staring at the enormous tusked
females.

"Let's go to Africa," I say.

"What?" Isabella laughs.

"Let's go on safari."

"You say this to all the girls."

"I've never said this to anyone. Let's go. Let's leave tonight."

"That would probably seduce me." Isabella pushes me on the

shoulder. "I better not. Besides I've got nineteen kids waiting for me Monday morning in Memphis."

"Get a substitute teacher. They were great. You just had to do homework."

Laughing, Isabella checks her watch. "I've got to take off for yoga. You sure you don't want to come?"

"I don't have any clothes."

"You like to throw money around." Isabella grabs me by the wrist. "Buy some there."

Surrounded by women in tights and flimsy T-shirts sticking their asses up in the air, or sitting with their legs spread wide open, or bending over at the waist and grabbing their ankles, it's not easy for me to enter a blank, meditative state of mind. I try not to let Isabella see me gaping at anyone else and watch her as our heads hang in the downward-facing dog position. She isn't wearing a bra and even upside down her breasts look high and firm. The instructor calls us to the front of our mats and Isabella and the others all leap to a squat, then unfold to a standing position while I walk my legs to the front and try to catch up. Concentrating on the sound of their own breathing, the others don't seem to notice whenever I stumble or nearly fall over. In the forward lunge I can feel my old ripped hamstring. Halfway through the hour I'm sweating and breathing heavily. On my hands and feet, staring up at the ceiling, arching my back high, I collapse suddenly onto the mat, worried for a moment that I've dislocated a vertebra. Isabella whispers for me to sit up and touch my toes to stretch my spine in the opposite direction. I skip the headstand and the handstand, taking refuge in child's pose, lying on my stomach with my arms flat in front of me and my legs cocked at the knees like a frog. At the end, with the class sitting in lotus position, the instructor plays some sort of Indian accordion and everybody sings a simple yoga song, though Isabella doesn't open her eyes or her mouth until they are finished.

"I could do without the happy clappy bit at the beginning and the end," she says as we walk toward the changing rooms.

"I hurt in about a hundred places," I say.

"You did well for the first time." She wipes my face with her towel.

"I must have been a yogi in a previous life."

"Somehow"—Isabella bangs me on the head with a rolled mat—"I doubt it."

Reddish brown against her creamy white breasts, Isabella's areolas are unusually large, two inches in diameter. I trace the edge so slowly it takes minutes to complete the circumference. She makes a soft whimpering sound. I taste Scotch in her mouth, then glide my lips to her other breast. I think of a lesbian who told me that I move my hands like a girl, my fingers like feathers. I slip my hand down her pants. She's dripping wet. No, she moans weakly without tensing up. I let it linger, cupping her gently, then slide my hand out and run my fingers through her short hair, stare into her green eyes. I've never seen her drunk. It took three and a half double Dewar's with a splash of soda. Around the middle of the third, she changed from funny to sad. At the beginning of the fourth I dove on the bed beside her and kissed her. I'm fairly certain that I would not even be in her room at the Gramercy Park Hotel if she were sober. She places her hand on the back of my head and pulls my mouth onto hers. I kiss her softly and she bites my lip hard enough to make me yell.

"Why are men such bastards?" She glares up at me.

"We just are."

"Why can't we do without you like elephants?"

" 'Cause you need us to make you whole."

"Then why do you make us feel broken?"

"Because we're fucked up." I think that I taste blood.

Isabella reaches up and touches my lip. "I'm sorry."

"You don't look sorry."

She laughs. "I'm just angry."

"Well, don't take it out on me."

"Why not? You're just like him."

"No. I'm worse."

"It's time for you to go." She pushes me hard by the shoulders and I roll over on my back.

"Just let me lie here quietly for a while."

I place my head on her belly and snuggle up close and listen to her breathing slow down.

"My dreams tell me that chasing pussy is destroying my psyche."

"What?" she whispers above my head. "How?"

Staring with one eye over the curve of her breast, I tell her the dream about my great-grandmother with the zoom shot of the *Hannibal* book in her purse and Dr. Pearce's interpretations. "Remembering my dreams, examining my dreams—it's the first time that I've considered the possibility of a spiritual side to life. The first time I've thought that humans might be more than animals."

Isabella raises up on one elbow, letting my head roll to the bedspread, and looks down at me with a skeptical expression.

"I haven't loved anyone in a long time," I say with vodka-fueled fervency. "But I think that I'm falling in love with you."

Isabella lifts a finger to her lips and shakes her head.

I want to kiss her. "I'm wrestling with my *shadow*. He shows up in my dreams as an Elvis impersonator or Bill Clinton. And I am falling in love with you—your irresistible, sassy spirit. And falling in love with you is making it easier to struggle with my shadow."

Isabella laughs. "Yeah, and Clinton told Hillary that he was working very hard on himself, very hard. He had become more aware of his past and what was causing his behavior."

"So I'm not the only one," I say lamely.

Isabella sits up and crosses her legs, then strokes my hair. "Well, since we are being so straightforward . . ." She suddenly looks much less drunk. "One, it's way too soon for me to leap right into another relationship. Two, you've slept with too many girls. I won't start sleeping with you until you haven't slept with anyone for three months. If then."

I laugh. "Until August?"

"Make it September first, after the long, hot summer." She smiles. "You probably haven't gone three days in ten years."

"I've gone longer than that," I say, thinking, Catch me if you can.

Isabella clasps my chin between her thumb and forefinger. "I'll know. Women can always tell. The only time we're duped is when we're not suspicious. Obviously that won't be the case."

"I'll do it," I say, wondering if I can.

Isabella laughs, then lowers her lips softly on mine. "You can crash here but our underwear is staying on."

Cage

The west face of the gorge cuts the sun off half the river. Rachel, steering in the stern, keeps us in the light. In the shadows Harper and Isabella paddle steadily, trying to catch up. Looking up at the tall walls of limestone and the canopy of old trees along the edge that escaped the ax a hundred years back, it's possible to imagine what the land was like in the time of the Cherokees. I rest my paddle across my thighs and turn around. "What do you think of Isabella?"

"I like her." Rachel looks past me, watching for rocks. "She's down-to-earth. She's warm. There's a nice light in her eyes."

"A good egg." I think how the ocean of the divorced makes it possible for even a fuckup like myself to run with someone kind and attractive like Rachel. Over the bow of the canoe I recognize the bend in the river that flows into the Ladies' Pool. "Just around the corner is a big rapid, no way around it. I suggest we plow right through and hope for the best."

"Lay on, Macduff." Rachel smiles and glances over at Harper and Isabella, who are angling for the sunshine. They vanish behind a high boulder as we swing around the bend into the noise of white water. Switching sides back and forth, I lean out over the front of the canoe, knifing the water to pull us away from the rocks, with Rachel mirroring my strokes. The canoe rises and falls and a wave swamps us and we somehow stay upright. A big stone looms directly ahead with water curling back off it like a fountain. Jabbing it with my paddle, I push us away and suddenly we are in the wide, slow pool with the enormous weeping willow that still shades the beach where the utopian Englishwomen bathed for a few summers in the 1880s. Letting the canoe drift sideways, we watch upstream. Isabella kneels in the bow, laughing as the waves splash over her. Harper leans backward over the stern with his hands almost in the water, using the paddle for a rudder. Sailing over a shelf with half the canoe in thin air, they dive sideways back into the stream. The canoe capsizes and they disappear.

"They should have been wearing helmets," I say too low for Rachel to hear. Harper comes up first and wipes the water from his eyes, twisting his head for Isabella, who pops up on the other side of the last big rock. Rachel and I move to intercept the canoe and a paddle, as Harper, arching his back, looking frantically behind him, and Isabella are swept along the sides of the boulder and dropped next to each other in the swimming hole. Harper laughs and tries to kiss her. Isabella splashes him with a chop. I grab the empty canoe and we guide it to the sandy beach.

"Does anyone want to go for a walk? There's a beautiful full moon," Mom says as Harper passes dirty plates to me at the sink.

"I'd like to stretch my legs," Rachel says.

"Last night there was the most magnificent orange harvest moon," Isabella says.

As Rachel follows Isabella and Mom out the screen door, Dad picks up his glass of wine. "Think I'll get back to my book."

"What are you reading, Papa?" Harper asks. "The sermons of Cotton Mather?"

"*A Perfect Storm.*"

"I like the bit about the woman," Harper says, "who dreams that her husband is dying right about the time that his ship goes down."

"The human mystery," Dad intones in a *Twilight Zone* voice on his way out of the kitchen.

"The bishop is not the kind of guy to sit around and chew the fat," Harper says.

"Sometimes he does. Dinner parties with his old friends." I never liked the way Harper pokes fun at Dad. "So have you slept with her yet?"

Harper hesitates. "No."

"Mom and Dad were virgins when they got married."

"A long, long time ago." Harper takes a cloth and starts drying a glass from the drainer. "In a galaxy far, far away."

"Yeah, but it's good for you to be a born-again virgin. Have you gotten naked with her?"

"Half clothed and sweaty. That's it."

"Isabella's one of those southern girls who believe blow jobs are more intimate than intercourse?"

"In a word—yes." Harper puts the glass in a cabinet, picks a plate from the drainer.

"Given anybody else the high hard one?" Grilling Harper gives me a déjà vu of some long-forgotten conversation with Nick.

"No." Harper appears to be telling the truth.

"Come on."

"Okay. Once. Truly. Right in the beginning 'bout a week after she left New York. I was drunk off my ass of course and I'd done some blow. The next day I woke up completely miserable. I decided that I don't want to have secrets. I don't want to have to hide things. I don't want to have to weave a web of lies. I've come to think of this as a period of purification. Papa would say absolution. That was the last time I did blow. Instead I do yoga."

"You're in love?"

"Yeah." Harper laughs. "This must be love."

"Mama adores her."

Harper imitates Mom's soft drawl: "Isabella is a many-layered sensitive woman with more depth than anyone you've gone out with. I feel a real bond with her. I don't know why—maybe we're old souls."

"As they say out in Californication"—I try to sound peaced-out like someone from Santa Cruz—"Isabella's way bitching."

"So is Rachel." Harper gives me a little congratulatory clap on the back. "She's a bit too earth mama for me, but you always liked her type."

"You should meet her weekday persona when she's selling commercial real estate in Nashville. Tough as nails, dressed to kill."

"Many-layered." Harper laughs.

I set the last dish in the drainer and without a word we walk outside together.

Low over the horizon of mountaintops, streaked red like a blood orange, the moon resembles a setting sun. We follow the murmur of voices across the yard to a fence by an open field. Isabella sits on the top rail while Mom stands and leans forward against the fence. Rachel is a vertical shadow out in the field, petting a cow. Over the sound of crickets and bullfrogs, they don't hear us approaching from the side.

"When Nick and Cage graduated from college, I thought they would settle down quickly, the way our generation did. I just never expected anything different," Mom says mournfully. "Then Nick died and Cage had his breakdown and Harper came along with a new girlfriend every month for the last, I don't know, six years. I've been so sad, plagued by the thought that we will never have grandchildren . . . Isabella, may I be frank?"

"Sure, Margaret."

"What is wrong with my son?"

Isabella shifts on the rail. Harper and I stop dead.

"I mean Harper of course," Mom says. "There's a name for Cage's condition."

"They've got a name for Harper's, too." Isabella clears her throat. "Sex addiction."

You can see the silhouette of Mom's head flinch. I grin at Harper, whose mouth is hanging slightly open.

"But that's too strong." Isabella touches Mom's shoulder. "Harper is a *player*. That's the word. Most of the single men I know are players. Or they want to be. It's easier for the handsome ones. I ought to know."

"Your last boyfriend," Mom says.

"Another Casanova," Isabella says. "Harper's trying. He hasn't gone out with another woman for two months."

"He loves you. I can tell. It's a pleasure to see you together."

"I love him. I felt something the moment I saw him on the airplane." Isabella laughs. "Though that might just have been his nice hair."

Harper whispers in my ear, "She's never said that to me. She only says, 'I loke you.' Loke—somewhere between like and love."

"In the end that's all a mother wants." Mom sighs and pats Isabella on the thigh. "When I met Frank, I knew I didn't ever want to be apart from him. I'd been in love a few times, but never like that. I never wanted the life of a clergy wife—moving from city to city, entertaining people, being *a wife*, but I didn't want to live any other way but with him. And we're still in love forty-one years later."

"I'd like that. I just don't know if I can trust him."

"Make an honest man of him." Mom laughs. "Isabella, you're so—forgive me for using a therapy term—self-actualized. You are strong within yourself. You know where you're going."

Out in the field Rachel starts walking back toward the fence.

"Where is that?" Harper asks.

Mom turns toward us, and Isabella swings her legs over the fence, drops to the ground, and says, "It's not polite to spy, gentlemen."

"Hey," Harper says. "We just came out to marvel at the moon."

Rising higher in the sky, the moon is shrinking, turning a pale orange.

Margaret

After dinner, as thirty men and women file up onto the stage to form a choir, I'm light-headed with pride, sitting at the head table across from Frank and between my two handsome sons. Cage so resembles his father at forty with his blue eyes and his sandy hair graying at the temples, which he graciously cut for the party. He sees me gazing at his profile and smiles. Oh, how my heart soars to see the brightness back in his eyes. Dear Jesus, please help him stay this way. And thanks again for introducing Harper to Isabella. Dear Lord, please give him the strength not to step out on her. When the pianist starts playing a rousing hymn, over three hundred friends from across the South packed at round tables in the parish hall quiet down and the choir begins:

Leaving Memphis for Thebes soon,
Old Hickory Lake beneath the moon.
Now there's time for you to sail!
To hike the Ap-pa-lachian trail!

Frank's nearly blushing at the effort that all these people have made to honor him. We kept the show a surprise. The writers spent months talking to parishioners from several states, digging up little facts, such as that he'd built a sailboat when he was a bachelor priest which he gave to the Boy Scouts when we moved the first time and will build another when we move to Cage's Bend. After the song Harper leans across me to whisper, "Cage, guess we know where your sailing obsession originated."

Cage's smile is easy. "Dad took me out in that Lightning. When we left it behind, I was pissed."

"You were only two." I laugh. It's remarkable how we can

make light of his illness when he's well and how simple some things appear in retrospect. I've kept one secret about our retirement from everyone, including Frank. Going over the finances with our adviser, I decided that we can afford to build a pool amongst the overgrown hedges of the old formal garden. After tithing to the church and living frugally all these years, surely I deserve one grand indulgence. Cage has already added a new bathroom upstairs in the big house and he's begun the renovation of the cabin in back for himself. We'll be like one of those Old World country families, three generations living together with a chicken coop and a vegetable garden. I read that manic-depressives have a better recovery rate in the third world because all the members of the extended family are close by and supportive. Surely that's the healthiest way to live. Harper says his anger stemmed from the absence of his father with no grandfather nearby to take up the slack. The nuclear family has much to answer for.

At the podium near the choir, Frank's oldest friend, King Shelby, is saying, "Named to Catholic High's hall of fame and later a distinguished alumnus, Frank once worked as a paperboy but they didn't know about one unique accomplishment—memorizing the love sonnets of Elizabeth Barrett Browning to recite to girls on dates." Laughter fills the parish hall.

"Jesus, like fathers, like sons," Harper says. "That's exactly what Nick and Cage used to do. Always struck me as goofy."

"You're such a romantic," Isabella says.

Harper rolls his eyes at the corny lyrics and he has the usual sarcastic hint of a smile that he always wore in church, but he listens intently to the narration and the comic chorus as they speak of Frank's years in the army, working his way through UT delivering laundry, hitchhiking to Montana in the summers to fight fires.

Jump out, jump out the airplane right near burning trees,
Don't land in bushes with flames up to your knees!

"Your dad is so much cooler than you," Isabella tells Harper. The choir sings of Frank's struggle to choose between seminary and forestry, how his grandfather, old Bishop Rutledge, encouraged him to become a priest, but they leave out the real catalyst, which was the death of his best friend in a hunting accident. Shelby goes on, "From seminary, Frank became the deacon-in-training here at the cathedral and lived nearby in a house where he worked with the youth. Hundreds of teenagers came to the Friday night dances. Frank's job was to check the boys' john, peering into toilet tanks for bottles of whiskey." As everyone laughs, Harper whispers to Isabella loud enough for me to hear clearly, "He never searched our rooms for pot. He and Mom didn't have a clue what we were up to."

"That's what's called the generation gap," I tell them, smiling.

"You and Dad were basically two generations behind," Cage says. "You were more like your parents than our friends' parents. It's like you missed the sixties."

"It's true, boys. There's a great gulf between the way we look at the world."

"In Atlanta, where he served as chaplain at Georgia Tech," King goes on, "which was beginning integration, Frank was famous for his reply to the legendary racist politician Lester Maddox, whose chicken restaurant he would visit with black students. Maddox once asked, 'Well, Father, I guess you want all dark meat.' Frank replied, 'No. We want it mixed!'"

"The Rutledges spent the sixties in East Tennessee in the foothills of the Appalachian Mountains. The young rector was scaling peaks every chance he got. His two sons remember camping in the mountains from the time they could toddle. Since those were the days before Pampers, Frank boiled their diapers on a camp stove."

His *three* sons remember. The old loss echoes through my body like the bell in an empty church and I feel like crying. Nick loved the mountains so much he was on the path that Frank chose not to take. As the choir sings about miles on the trail to the tune of "Bottles of Beer on the Wall," Frank turns from the far side of the table and holds my eyes. His are moist. He's never been afraid to show his emotions. Cage sees us and pats my shoulder, says, "Nick's here tonight."

"Yeah. Maybe it's like that movie where Whoopi Goldberg was a medium talking to everyone's family ghosts who were hanging around all the time," Harper says, putting his arm around my back. Onstage, King is saying, "It was in Baton Rouge that Dr. Rutledge committed the worst sin of his life. Margaret forbade bacon and eggs. One morning after she left, Frank threw six strips of contraband bacon and five eggs in a skillet, when he looked out and saw Mars pulling in the driveway. In a panic the future bishop of Tennessee grabbed the skillet and dumped everything down the disposal."

The crowd howls, then the chorus sings about Frank's secret love affair with fried chicken and fudge sundaes. Harper calls across the table, "Gee, Dad, I never knew you were such an addict. No wonder you run every day."

Frank laughs. "I'm sorry you found out this way, son."

Isabella calls out, "Ask Harper what his worst sin is!"

The rest of our table, the Wolffs from Baton Rouge, the Addingtons from Atlanta, and the McCutcheons from Roanoke, laugh at the exchange. Louis Addington says loudly, "That's best kept in the privacy of a confessional." Cage's deep laughter pours into the emptiness that the memory of camping with Nickfish left behind. King continues, "Under Bishop Rutledge the diocese donated land to three black Baptist churches, and Episcopalians put together a federally funded housing program for the elderly. Our program of vocational training for the homeless has been so successful that it was featured on NBC national news."

The chorus sings, "All this from a man who would rather sleep in a tent, good Lord."

"One parishioner in Baton Rouge says, 'Frank is the most godly man I've ever known, the personification of a modern, saintly man. He gives of himself with great generosity. At the end of the day you are the pastor to a group of living, sinning, stiff-necked sons of guns that you've got to keep in the tent. His ability to do that, despite the frustrations that come with the corporate responsibility of managing a diocese, stem from his deep prayer life, which is like him sticking his fingers into an electric circuit that allows him to recharge his batteries.' "

To the tune of the French children's song "Frère Jacques" the chorus catalogs his virtues. Frank is blushing again. Cage makes the whole table laugh by remarking, "The music at this party makes me wish Dad was a black bishop!" Then, to the tune of "La Cucaracha," the choir sings of Frank's dream, his first goal after retiring: "Kilimanjaro! Kilimanjaro! Grab your ice ax and let's go!"

"You know," Harper whispers to me, "probably only ten people would come to my retirement party if they had to travel very far." He's lost his skeptical smile. It may be wishful thinking, but I think I see a new look of admiration in his eyes for his father. Perhaps he can see now that Frank's life was important to many people, that leading a community of faith is a challenging, high calling. So often children fail to appreciate the greatness of their parents.

"And now it's time for a few words from the person we are really honoring tonight." King looks past Frank at me and says, "Ladies and gentlemen, I present the first lady of our diocese." Everyone claps as I make my way up on the stage. I give King a kiss and a hug. He looks down at Frank and says, "Oh, and I almost forgot the husband of the bishop's wife. Frank, please join us." King guides me to the microphone.

"I'm very proud of Frank Rutledge, 'fiercely partisan,' in one friend's phrase." The laughter is loud enough to make me pause. "In my generation women stayed home to raise children and transferred their own ambition to their men. As a clergy wife I devoted myself to making it possible for my husband to serve the church as best he could. Tonight I know that I have succeeded." There's more laughter and clapping. "So I'll just keep skipping and hopping and dancing around thankful for my world and all of you who people it, and for the privilege of being along for the ride with Frank Rutledge." On my tiptoes I kiss Frank on the lips.

King says, "Unlike her husband, Margaret believes in succint speeches."

"Clearing out my office the other day, I looked at a photograph

of your new bishop and myself on the steps outside the cathedral
just after his consecration," Frank says. "We were both smiling.
The difference, I thought, is that I know why I am smiling." The
hall fills with laughter. "Indeed, Margaret and I shared a joint
ministry. She was always beside me, telling me how I could do a
better job."

Suddenly I feel like laughing and I can't stop and have to cover
my mouth.

"Every Sunday lunch I endured a ruthless critique of my sermons. She would have made an excellent prosecutor." There's
more laughter, then Frank continues, "I have great feelings of
nostalgia for all the friends that I may never see again, but mostly
I have profound feelings of joy and gratitude. There are so many
of you to whom I must pay tribute. I shall start with my old pal,
King Shelby, who . . ."

Searching the dimmed light of the hall beyond the stage, I single out tables with couples from the seven cities where we lived
over the last forty-two years, friends who would go to the well
and back for us. I recollect others who are not here. No small
number divorced. There were scandals, even among the Episcopal priests. Harper's own godfather was caught having an affair
with a man and left his wife and the church. Over time Frank
and I grew more understanding of others, less judgmental of
those whose behavior was so different from our own. I watch as
they unveil the oil portrait of Frank smiling but dignified in his
white collar, purple shirt, and seersucker jacket, hear everyone
laugh as Frank says, "A portrait always struck me as a tombstone.
Now I'll be hanging up there on the wall in that graveyard of old
dead bishops."

2001

Harper

Isabella slumps naked on a wingback chair with her legs draped open. Her eyes are closed. Her lips are curved in the trace of a smile between pleasure and pain and her breathing is ragged. Her jaw tightens for a few seconds and she moans, curling her fingernails into her palms. In a low voice I speak slowly, "Imagine you are floating in a warm pool filled with the golden light of sunset. Smell the lavender fragrance in the humid air. Look at the water rippling around you. See the light glittering on the surface in spiral patterns. As I count back from ten, you will fall deeper and deeper along the spirals of light beneath the surface of the water." Isabella's jaw relaxes.

"Ten. The water laps over your head as you sink ever so slowly."

Her fingers uncurl and she turns her palms out.

"Nine. You see the light above you on the top of the water, shifting and sliding."

Her breathing slows and steadies.

By the time I reach one, she's floating just above the bottom of her imaginary pool, hypnotized. I warm shea butter between my palms and massage it gently over her swollen breasts, which are about five times bigger than they used to be. Keeping her in the deep meditative state of semiconsciousness without fear and anxiety requires me to keep talking about the quality of light, the sensation of the water against her skin, recycling over and over her own store of soothing images which she dug up in a hypnotic trance with the therapist who taught us. In the six weeks that I practiced hypnotizing her almost every evening after work, made her do it even when she was tired or queasy, Isabella told me more than once that she knew from the first moment we met that I was actually good, though it was almost impossible to see. Since the big surprise of her pregnancy and our shotgun wedding, I have felt better than I ever remember. I don't feel like a cad anymore. I feel like a decent guy.

A contraction racks her body, drawing her mouth tight and coiling her fingers into fists. She does not moan. Jotting the time on a notebook, I say, "You are relaxed, riding a wave in a warm bed of seaweed, cradling our baby, riding the wave closer to shore. Look up at the moon."

Isabella tilts her head back and opens her eyes, which look distant, and stares unfocused at the ceiling.

"Now follow the moonlight down to the water."

She moves her chin slowly down until her blank gaze reaches her feet.

"Watch the light playing on the water, puddles of white against the darkness."

As the contraction seems to stop, I make another note. "Now you are floating between the waves. The sea is calm. You are tired, your eyelids heavy. As you wait for the next wave, just close your eyes and take a little nap."

Isabella shuts her eyes and her breathing becomes more shallow. Asleep, her head falls to the side.

This is real. It's finally happening, I think with a rush like a line of good blow or more like I was eight again on Christmas Eve. I stand up and stretch my arms toward the ceiling, then touch my toes and throw my legs back, moving through a yoga sequence. After months of classes three times a week, when I stand now my spine is straight, as if I'm dangling like a skeleton from a wire attached to the top of the skull. I'm not crooked anymore. Isabella has a theory that there is a connection between the straightness of your spine and your moral health. She made an honest man out of me. I don't have to tell lies anymore. I watch the second hand sweep around my watch. After six minutes her cheek twitches and I kiss her forehead and whisper in her ear, "A wave is coming. When you open your eyes, you will feel refreshed and relaxed, calm but full of energy. *Open your eyes.*"

They open and brush past my face without seeing me to fix on the ceiling.

"The moon is hanging peacefully in the sky, big and round as your belly and as serene as you feel."

She moans as all at once the uterine muscles wrench upward, peeling the mouth of her womb wider.

"Float on the wave. Let the sound of your breath surround you, the sound of the wind across the water."

I talk and talk from four in the morning till nine, sometimes making her sleep between the contractions, sometimes walking her around the bedroom, which we have covered with sheets of plastic to protect the sisal carpet. When her waters break and the waves have been hitting every three minutes for two hours, we decide it's time to go to the hospital.

"You're ten centimeters dilated." Dr. Duva kneels with her hand inside Isabella, who's sitting with her legs spread wide on a birthing stool, a half-doughnut of an ancient Egyptian design. "I can't believe you were eight when you got here. Most women come screaming into the hospital at three. I love women like you. I hate that whole epidural thing."

Isabella smiles wearily and just manages to nod.

As the doctor stands up, I whisper to Isabella, putting her to sleep.

"Can you knock yourself out like that?" Dr. Duva asks. "Looks like you could use it."

Yawning, I shake my head and take in her oval face and thick curly hair and large athletic build. Her big hands remind me of a Russian basketball player who used to toss me around like a Raggedy Andy doll, and out of old habit I start to imagine the good doctor beneath her white lab coat, wonder if that is the stirring of my shadow, the Elvis impersonator waking in his coffin. The doctor says softly, "I gotta say that this hypno-birthing thing makes the man do more than just pacing the room."

"Now she's in the transition stage?" I whisper, thinking I would like to hypnotize her and tell her to take off all her clothes and deliver the baby buck naked.

"Yes, the contract—"

"We don't use that word because of the painful connotations," I say softly. "Call them waves."

"Now the nature of the waves changes," Dr. Duva says, nodding. "Instead of pulling up to open the womb, they push out to expel the baby." She leans over and studies Isabella's face, which lies against the shawl around her naked shoulders as she squats on the stool, napping. I study the fabric of the doctor's baggy surgical pants stretching over her powerful haunches with a wistful feeling like a retired explorer gazing at a map of exotic lands he will never experience in the flesh.

"Pretty amazing," Dr. Duva says. "How did you hear about it?"

It takes a second to understand, then I say, "My brother's into hypnotherapy. He found a woman in Westport on the Web and gave us the first session. He kept bugging me until we went. We thought it was all New Age bullshit until she showed us a video of tranced-out women in labor and the babies sliding out like seal puppies. For centuries women have been conditioned to expect overwhelming pain. It's a matter of reprogramming through visualization. Like professional athletes—"

"*Aaah . . .*" Isabella throws her head back and stands up in a half-squat like a sumo wrestler.

"You and the baby are surrounded by ferns," I start, "soft ferns of all—"

"Shut up, Harper," Isabella barks. "I'm about to have it." She has a fierce light in her eyes, sweat glistening on her face. The muscles in her arms and legs are sharp and taut. "*Aaaah.*"

Dr. Duva kneels in front and I kneel behind Isabella.

Isabella collapses onto the stool and looks up at me like it's the best high of her life.

"Wait until your body tells you to push," Dr. Duva says. "You'll get a strong spontaneous urge to push. Just go with it."

"*Aaaah.*" Each time the waves hit, Isabella comes off the stool into a cocked squat and screams like a warrior running into battle, then whispers, "Come on, come on, come on, contraction."

Panting, back on the stool, she gasps, "Okay, cool, cool, cool." Then a few seconds later she is back on her feet. "*Huh. Huh. Huh.*"

Leaning around her side, I see what appears to be a hairy turd protruding out an inch between her legs.

"Why is it going back in?" Isabella moans, falling back on the stool.

"That's what it does." I stroke her back lightly in a circle with my fingertips. "Out two inches and back in one."

"*Oooooo,*" she moans very low, leaping to her feet. "It's not coming."

"Yes, it is," Dr. Duva says calmly. "Push now. Show your man!"

"Oh, please come out," Isabella pleads quietly.

I glance over her shoulder and can see only a puddle of blood on the floor.

"*Uuh huh, uuh huh, uuuh.*" Isabella sounds like she's taking a huge dump.

"Here he is," Dr. Duva says. "He's gorgeous."

I come around to see her cradling a tiny boy, smeared with a blue-white wax, with a head of bright red hair. His eyes are closed and for a second my stomach drops, thinking he's stillborn, then the doctor spanks his bottom and his eyes open and seem to lock on mine, though I know that he cannot see me.

Something overpowering, an emotion purer than any I have ever felt, surges through me and I realize that this is the true definition of love at first sight, that I would throw myself in front of a train to save the little guy, that I could never fuck Dr. Duva or any other woman because I would never want to hurt *him*. I kiss Isabella, tell her, "You are a giant, a god," as she pulls the baby to her breast. Already it's not about her, it's not about me, it's all about him. Looking at his miniature face, I am not alone. Like coming around a corner to the edge of a bottomless cliff, the new vista of the years ahead, the prospect of guiding my son into the world, is suddenly unsettling, and I see that every parent does the best he can. We all start off groping in the dark.

Cage

"*The masters' mile! All milers forty and over!*" The starter shouts through a megaphone, "*Last call for the masters' mile.*" Several forty- and fifty-something guys whom I'd pegged for middle-distance runners jog toward the starter. They're hard to tell apart, with their clipped hair and stoic expressions, wearing minishorts and sleeveless T-shirts on their slender frames, with their glaring tendons and veins like rope. Self-conscious, hanging at the back of the six as they present the numbers pinned on their chests to a man in a baseball cap who writes on a clipboard, I look down at my cutoff sweats and paint-speckled T-shirt and tell Rachel, "I feel like the Stranger."

"Sloppy is good on you. Long hair is cool. They are not cool." Rachel smiles happily. "You're undercover." She looks around the high school stadium where there are more competitors warming up on the field inside the track than spectators dotting the empty stands. "Very esoteric. Not like big ten-K runs or marathons."

"A subculture within a subculture." I grab my foot behind my back.

"Nervous?" Rachel asks.

"*Mmm hnn.*" I nod. "First time on a starting line in a long time. I keep telling myself all that time since wasn't a waste."

Rachel shakes her head impatiently. "What do you remember most about the last time?"

"I knew I was going to win. The race. In life. The world was at my feet."

"Look down at your feet. It's still there."

I show my number to the man in the cap and take the position in the seventh lane. I smile at Rachel, who seems to be the only girlfriend in the vicinity. "The stranger in the outside lane."

"You're going to run 'em all in the ground." Rachel stamps my cheek with a lipstick kiss and backs away.

Two guys lift their legs high like prancing horses, one bends over, touching his toes, another stretches one leg behind him as if on starting blocks, while the one in the inside lane jiggles one foot a few inches off the ground, then the other, as if shaking shit from his shoes. Balding, inscrutable, he resembles the Russian president, Vladimir Putin.

"Hi," I say to the guy next to me, probably the oldest. He has a thin gray mustache. "What sort of time do you run?"

Surprised to have his little personal ritual interrupted, he drops his thigh from his chest. "I'll be lucky to keep it under six minutes." He has a strong country accent. "The man in the first lane, he's the one who sets the pace."

"How fast?" I shake a little tension out of my arms.

He's opening his mouth when the starter says, "Runners on your mark."

You're going to win. You're going to push through the pain. I look along the red rubbery track to the white lane lines merging at the curve.

"Set."

I raise my hands to the line.

"*Go!*"

Angling across the track to the inside lane, I find myself out front and slow down, letting the favorite pass me as we enter the curve. Following his red shorts and T-shirt, I gradually pull away from the sound of the other ten soles slapping the track. In Baton Rouge people used to ask me, Why do you run? I'd say, To get back to my primitive self. On the plains of Africa early man spent his days chasing prey on foot. Twenty-five years later, I've got a real reason: To keep from going crazy. To structure my life. To burn up the anxiety and regret which pop up each day like weeds that will never go away, no matter how many times you pull them because it's impossible to rip out the roots. If I miss a day of running—no matter how many hours of hard work in the garden or how much organic produce I've delivered to restaurants and stores around Nashville—I feel slightly nervous, off-kilter. Dr. Price has me on a minimum dosage of lithium, since none of the next-generation mood stabilizers work for me and the drug that works in concert to make a successful therapeutic combo is running. Maybe a daily dose of endorphins keeps me from slipping into depression, while the lithium keeps a lid on the mania. In the fourteen months that I've been running daily I've felt more comfortable with myself than since I was a star student and athlete in high school, in those twenty-two years that seemed so long while they were happening but now feel like a bad dream.

Hanging behind the favorite isn't so hard. Gliding smoothly along in his ultralight clothes and racing flats with my breathing like a mosquito in his ear, he wonders if I'll take him or fall away. I've got no clue myself as I haven't raced a mile on a track in so many years. After building a foundation of eight-to-twelve-mile days for ten months, I started training for the mile by alternating distance days with speed work, killer quarter-mile and half-mile intervals until I can hardly walk—and then a light jog on the seventh day, all on the fields and roads around Cage's Bend.

"Sixty-three!" the starter yells Putin's split, then mine, "Sixty-four!"

"Go, Cage!" Rachel yells.

If he maintains the pace, he'll run a 4:12 mile, two seconds faster than my best time in high school, ten seconds short of the masters' world record. Clearly I'm pushing him beyond the envelope, which means I'm also in danger of burning up. Surprised that it's not that painful, I cut back and fall three strides behind him. Midway around the curve, he's fallen back to me and I ease up again, deciding it's safer to conserve energy than take the lead. A light headwind is blowing up the back straight. I draft off him, staying right on his heels. The burning starts suddenly in my calves and the bottom of my lungs. For a few strides I think wildly that I've gone out way too fast and I'm about to crash, then I scold myself, Remember the way you ate the pain? In the curve I find my old racing stride, the extra quarter inch that came only in competition, and on the straight I feel the forgotten sensation of floating like an antelope.

"You're strong!" Rachel shouts. "Stick on him!"

Without thinking I respond by pulling alongside Putin.

"Two fifteen," the starter yells our half as we pass him simultaneously. Seven seconds slower that lap. At this rate we'd log a 4:40 mile, the masters' standard of excellence. This is probably about his normal pace. His stride is smooth, his breathing controlled, his face emotionless. Forty yards later, still shoulder-to-shoulder at the end of the straight, Putin glances over at me.

"I have a dream!" I try to sound like Martin Luther King.

Looking slightly alarmed, he speeds up and I stay with him.

"I want to be the first man over forty to break the four-minute barrier!"

He smiles, thinking I'm joking. Or crazy.

In the curve I drop behind him to draft down the back straight. The fire has filled my lungs with smoke. I try to switch off the pain by concentrating on the pounding of my heart and the billowing of my lungs. I turn up the volume until I am inside the sound, striding long down a roaring wind tunnel. I lean into the next curve as if gravity will slingshot me out onto the straight. I can't hear Putin through my private windstorm. The flames jump to my shoulders and neck.

Rachel waves her cell phone and yells something. I only catch the word "uncle." You're a monkey's uncle? Man from U.N.C.L.E.?

"Three twenty-five!" the starter calls. "Last lap!" I feel the momentary jolt of relief starting the last quarter mile that used to come with the shot of the timer's little pistol.

"Go, Cage!" Rachel yells.

I nod my eyes at her and lean to the inside and strangely hear myself mutter, "Hang in my wind shadow, Nick."

Putin accelerates as I pull in front, keeping me wide through the endless curve. When we hit the straight, I slip behind him out of the headwind and he slows. He's hurting, wounded. I'm the hyena. I can take him. I am dizzy. From hunger. From the long pursuit. Again I have the strange feeling that Nick is right behind me. Looking back, I see the other runners in a cluster a half a lap behind. I focus back into the roaring tunnel, down the long straight, nearly clipping his right shoe with each stride. The magnitude of agony invading my body all at once is off the scale of training pain . . . yet paltry next to the psychic suffering of my past. As I go into the last curve, my exhalations sound like howls. *Kick, Cage. Kick! You can take him,* Nick yells. *Start your kick now!* I step outside and pull even with Putin, who looks straight ahead, his skin tight against his skull. Shortening my stride, raising my knees higher, I lean forward and sprint past him, moved by the perspective beyond the physical pain down the hundred strides of the final straight, kicking with perfect form. I figure I'm too old for the rebel yell, realize that there is no tape across the line. Rachel has her hands high over her head.

The timer says, "Four thirty-two. Hats off to you, partner."

"My champion!" Rachel yells, then speaks into her phone and cuts it off.

Momentum carries me a few yards and I hear Putin's time called six seconds slower as I stumble onto the field and roll onto my back.

"You crushed 'em," Rachel says. "Are you okay?"

Too stunned to speak, I'm a fish in dry air, opening and closing my mouth pointlessly.

"You'll never guess what." She kneels by my shoulder.

I raise my eyebrows.

"Hey, buddy, way to go." Putin hangs his head over mine, squatting with his forearms on his thighs. "That was a helluva kick. I was dreading that last straight, just holding on for dear life, and you went blazing past like John Walker. 'Member him?"

"Long hair and a black uniform?" Rachel says.

"Yeah, New Zealand runner. Gold metal in '76. Held the mile record at 3:49 from August '75 to July '79."

"That's his hero." Rachel squeezes my shoulder.

I smile and nod. They are suffocating me. I'm going to die. The pain I shoved aside on the last straight has come back angry in the form of a heart attack. I'm going to die looking up at a clear, balmy spring sky and the face of the woman I love and a sweating, drooling, obsessed master miler. Smiling at Rachel, I try to compose some poignant dying words and remember Thoreau's last: Moose. Indian.

"My name's Ronny Renfro." Putin extends his hand over my sternum.

I cough, spreading my fingers over my pounding heart, then remind myself, Grace under pressure, and raise my hand to his. "Good race."

"What do you do, Ronny?" Rachel is trying to figure him out.

"I'm a lawyer with the IRS. Did you run in college?"

"I's 'posed to but I's depressed," I splutter earnestly, waiting for my life to flash in front of my eyes, wondering what images will compose the final cut out of all my sins and all the time with those who loved me, everybody who wanted to save me, which moments will count. Or maybe there will be no last montage and my movie will freeze on Ronny Renfro's Putin face and cut to black.

"Did you?" Rachel asks him.

"Yes, ma'am, East Tennessee State." Ronny smiles at me. "Have you been running steady all these years?"

"No." Rachel replies for me. "Not the last twenty-odd years."

"I thought he was crazy out there." Ronny laughs madly. "I have a dream!" He looks up at the sky, leaving only his chin against the clouds, then back down at me with an apostolic gleam. "You might do it! You haven't worn out your legs! You might be the one!"

Rachel leans away from him, frowning.

"Y'all Jehovah's Witnesses or something?" Ronny says. "Look, Walker ended his career with crippling Achilles tendinosis trying to run a subfour after he turned forty. Of course he had already run over a hundred subfours over the years. But *this* guy." He pauses and smiles at me conspiratorially. "The runner in him has been dormant, preserving his cartilage, tendons, and skeletal muscles, for two decades! He can withstand the quantity and intensity of the speed work necessary to run a subfour."

That kind of speed work might make me manic. I have to escape. I roll onto my stomach and crawl away from Renfro for a second until I realize how ridiculous I must look, so I stand up and shake his hand. "Hey. My name's Cage."

"You got something." Ronny smiles bashfully.

"You don't know." I sway on my legs, dizzy. "We got to do that again. That chesslike competition and the aggression of rivalry. Be like high school."

"Or the middle ages," Ronny jokes, smiling and nodding his head. "You need a coach and a training companion to push you through intervals. I'm just the man."

Rachel takes my arm before I stumble backward.

Elbow at his waist, Ronny points his finger like a gun. "You don't have to kill yourself again. You could work out the splits. Get the timing perfect."

I see that Ronny Renfro is a scientist of the mile and try to smile. Rachel hands me a bottle of my homemade herbal electrolyte drink.

"I have a dream." Ronny laughs, backing away. "I'll get my card from my car."

I put my arm over Rachel's shoulders and we start to move slowly toward the center of the field. The wind has dropped and it's suddenly humid and sticky. I nuzzle my face into the curve of her neck and sigh. These are the small ecstasies, all that are granted to mortals. The shots of the final cut. The instants that make you concede the possibility of happiness. Just these little moments. "Are you happy?"

"Very happy." Rachel squeezes her arm hard around my waist. "What a funny guy. Intense. He's like a hillbilly version of Putin."

"That's what I thought." I guzzle down half the bottle, wipe my mouth with the back of my hand, then ask, "Guess what?"

"Oh!" Rachel cries with delight.

Then I understand. "Harper and Isabella."

"A boy. A little redhead."

I let out a weak whoop of joy, then cough.

"Isabella's great. Harper said the hypno-bullshit was bulletproof. Isabella was so tranced out the kid was born asleep." Rachel chatters on, a childless woman excited by the idea of a baby. "They still can't agree on a name. Harper wants Morgan."

"A new life. I hope they pick Nicholas," I say. "A little redheaded Nick would be nice."

Rachel gives my waist another hard squeeze. "I told Harper your time. He wants to send the whole family to the European masters. I told him your plan to run a subfour." Rachel laughs. "He said that sounds manic."

On the track a handful of gray-haired men leap over hurdles. A couple of cheers drift across the still air. I stop walking and gaze at Rachel, take in her calm hazel eyes, the exquisite sharpness of her nose, the white stripe that runs from her widow's peak through her raven hair, the fullness of her body beneath a loose cotton dress. Tilting my head back, I drain the last dark green rivulets from the bottle and watch a lone cloud, driven by a strong high-altitude wind, scudding quickly across the empty sky.

Much love & gratitude to:

Saskia
for happiness and some damn good editorial advice.

Cleopatra Mary
for lighting a fire under me.

My Father
for his strength and steadiness.

My Brothers
for being there, mostly, when I needed them.

My Grandmother, Margarette Barnette Dorris Hughes,
the paradigm of a Southern gentlewoman.

The Dream Team—Larry Kirshbaum, Jamie Raab
& Lynn Nesbit—for their infinite patience.

My Readers—Scott Noland, Sheba Phombeah, Beth O'Donnell,
Bret Ellis, Jeff Hobbs, Claire Taylor, Mary Hall—for their light
down the dark passage.

George & Betty Johnson, Allen & Joanie Penniman and
Sean & Jennifer Reilly, whose support of the African Rainforest
Conservancy kept the wolves from my door.

Paul Wender, MD
Technical Advisor

George Plimpton,
for sixteen years of generosity and counsel.